SCALES & SCOUNDRELS

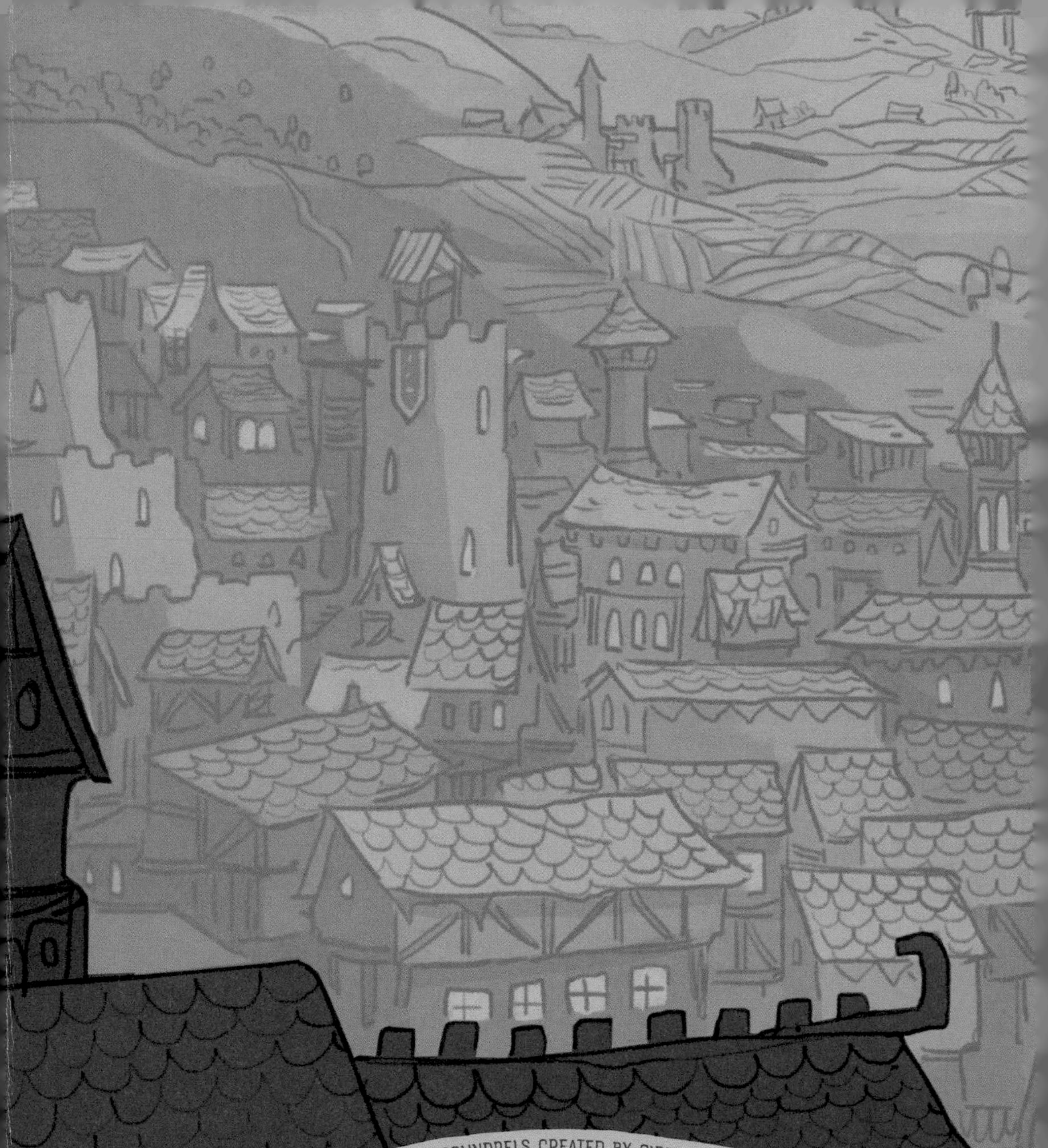

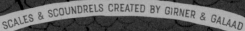

SCALES & SCOUNDRELS CREATED BY GIRNER & GALAAD

COLLECTION DESIGN BY
JEFF POWELL

PRODUCTION BY
ERIKA SCHNATZ

IMAGE COMICS, INC.

ROBERT KIRKMAN – CHIEF OPERATING OFFICER
ERIK LARSEN – CHIEF FINANCIAL OFFICER
TODD MCFARLANE – PRESIDENT
MARC SILVESTRI – CHIEF EXECUTIVE OFFICER
JIM VALENTINO – VICE PRESIDENT
ERIC STEPHENSON – PUBLISHER
COREY HART – DIRECTOR OF SALES
JEFF BOISON – DIRECTOR OF PUBLISHING PLANNING & BOOK TRADE SALES
CHRIS ROSS – DIRECTOR OF DIGITAL SALES
JEFF STANG – DIRECTOR OF SPECIALTY SALES
KAT SALAZAR – DIRECTOR OF PR & MARKETING
DREW GILL – ART DIRECTOR
HEATHER DOORNINK – PRODUCTION DIRECTOR
BRANWYN BIGGLESTONE – CONTROLLER

IMAGECOMICS.COM

SCALES & SCOUNDRELS, VOL. 1: INTO THE DRAGON'S MAW. FIRST PRINTING. FEBRUARY 2018. PUBLISHED BY IMAGE COMICS, INC. OFFICE OF PUBLICATION: 2701 NW VAUGHN ST. SUITE 780, PORTLAND, OR 97210. PRINTED IN THE USA. FOR INFORMATION REGARDING THE CPSIA ON THIS PRINTED MATERIAL CALL: 203-595-3636 AND PROVIDE REFERENCE #RICH-773934. FOR INTERNATIONAL RIGHTS, CONTACT: FOREIGNLICENSING@IMAGECOMICS.COM. ISBN: 978-1-5343-0482-6.

GIRNER
GALAAD
POWELL

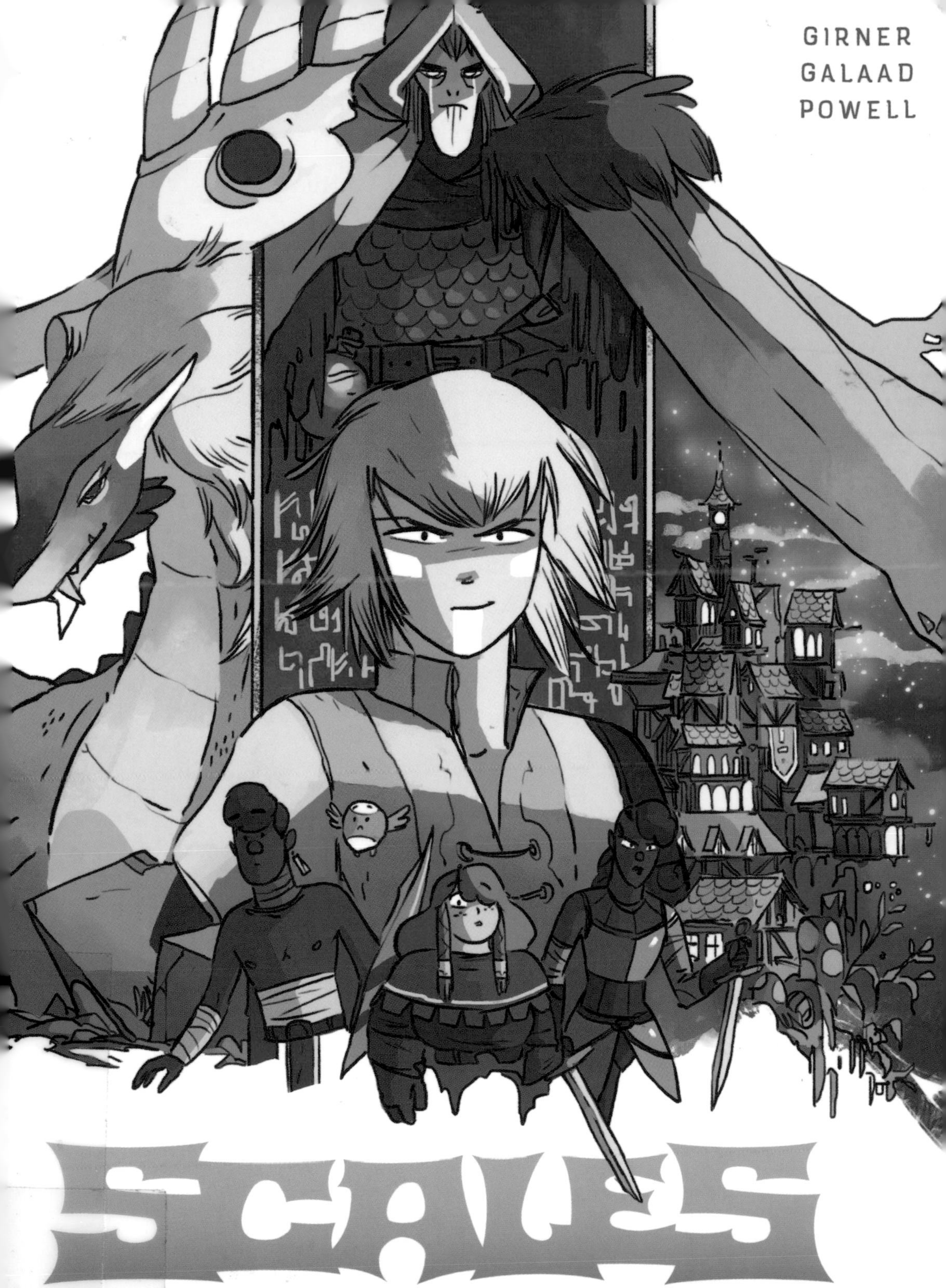

SCALES & SCOUNDRELS™

VOLUME 1: INTO THE DRAGON'S MAW

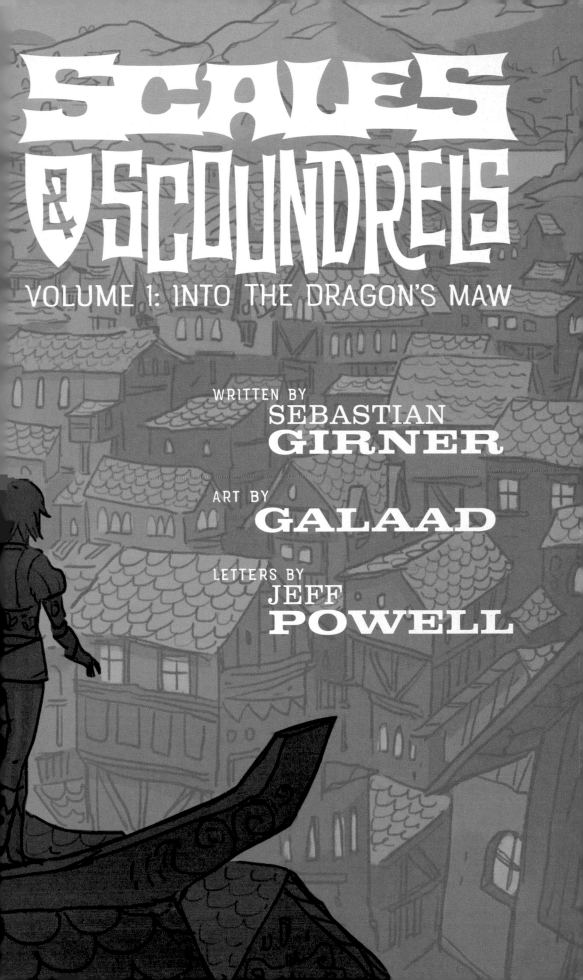

SCALES & SCOUNDRELS

VOLUME 1: INTO THE DRAGON'S MAW

WRITTEN BY
SEBASTIAN GIRNER

ART BY
GALAAD

LETTERS BY
JEFF **POWELL**

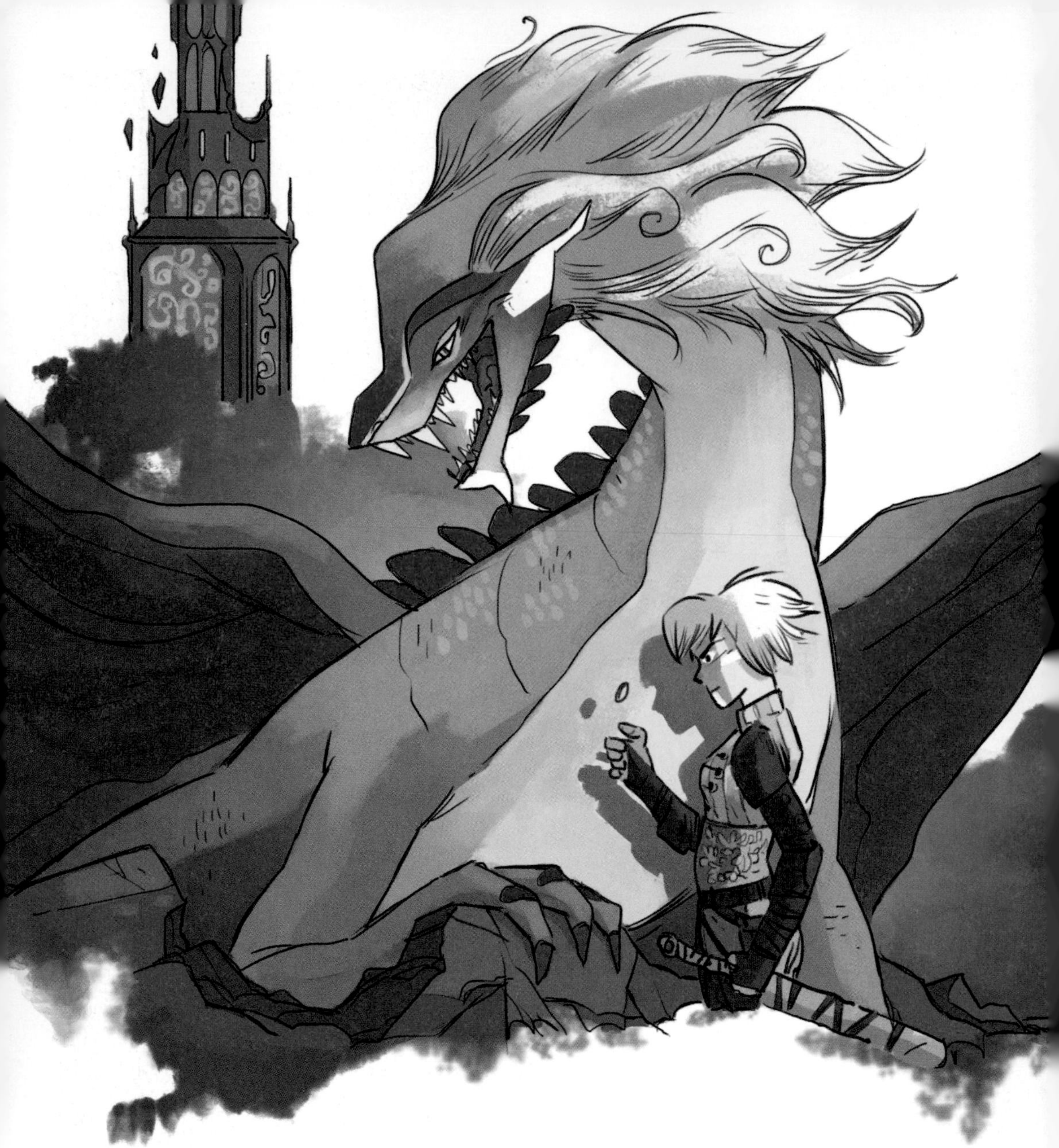

1

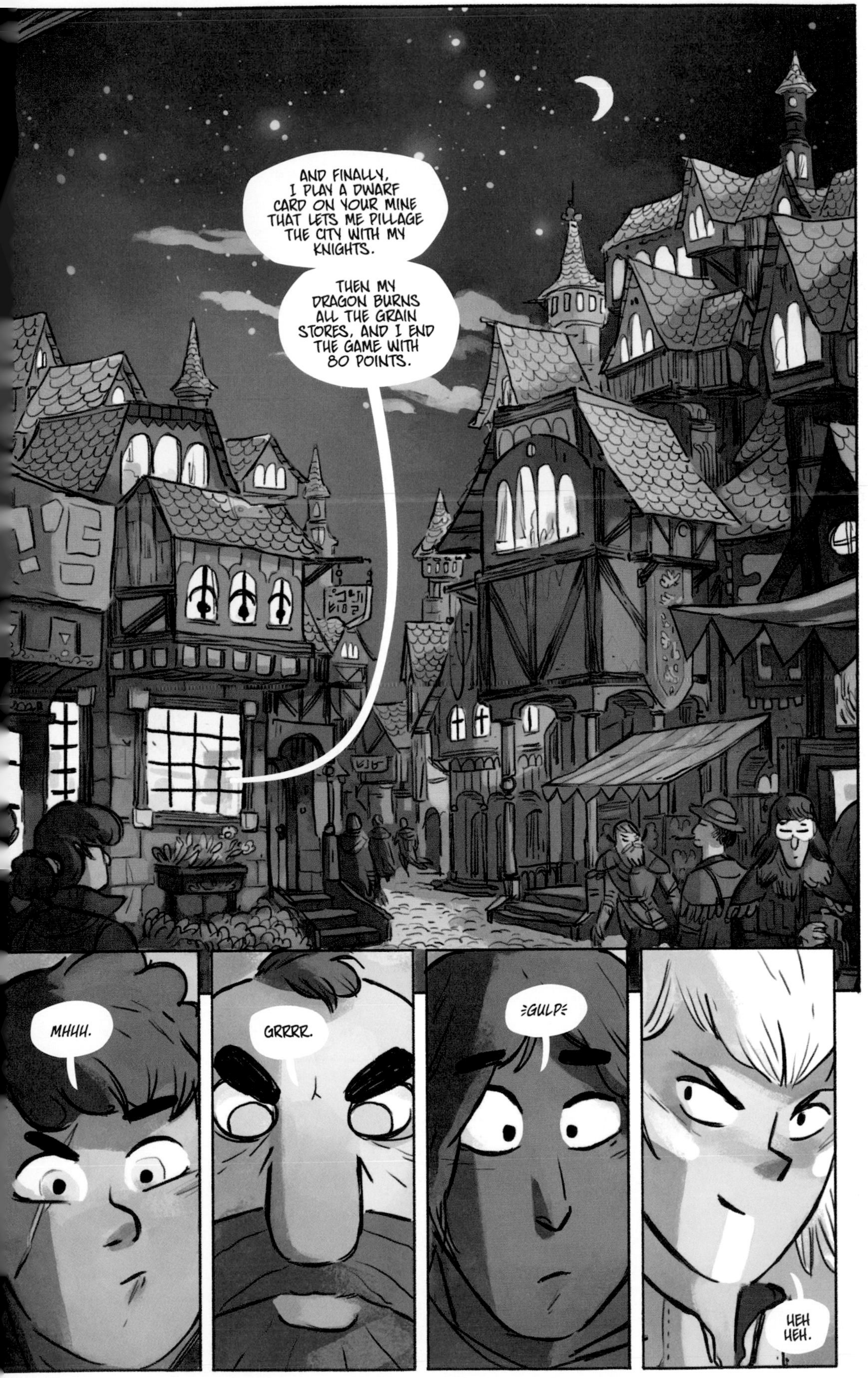
AND FINALLY, I PLAY A DWARF CARD ON YOUR MINE THAT LETS ME PILLAGE THE CITY WITH MY KNIGHTS.
THEN MY DRAGON BURNS ALL THE GRAIN STORES, AND I END THE GAME WITH 80 POINTS.
MHUH.
GRRRR.
GULP
HEH HEH.

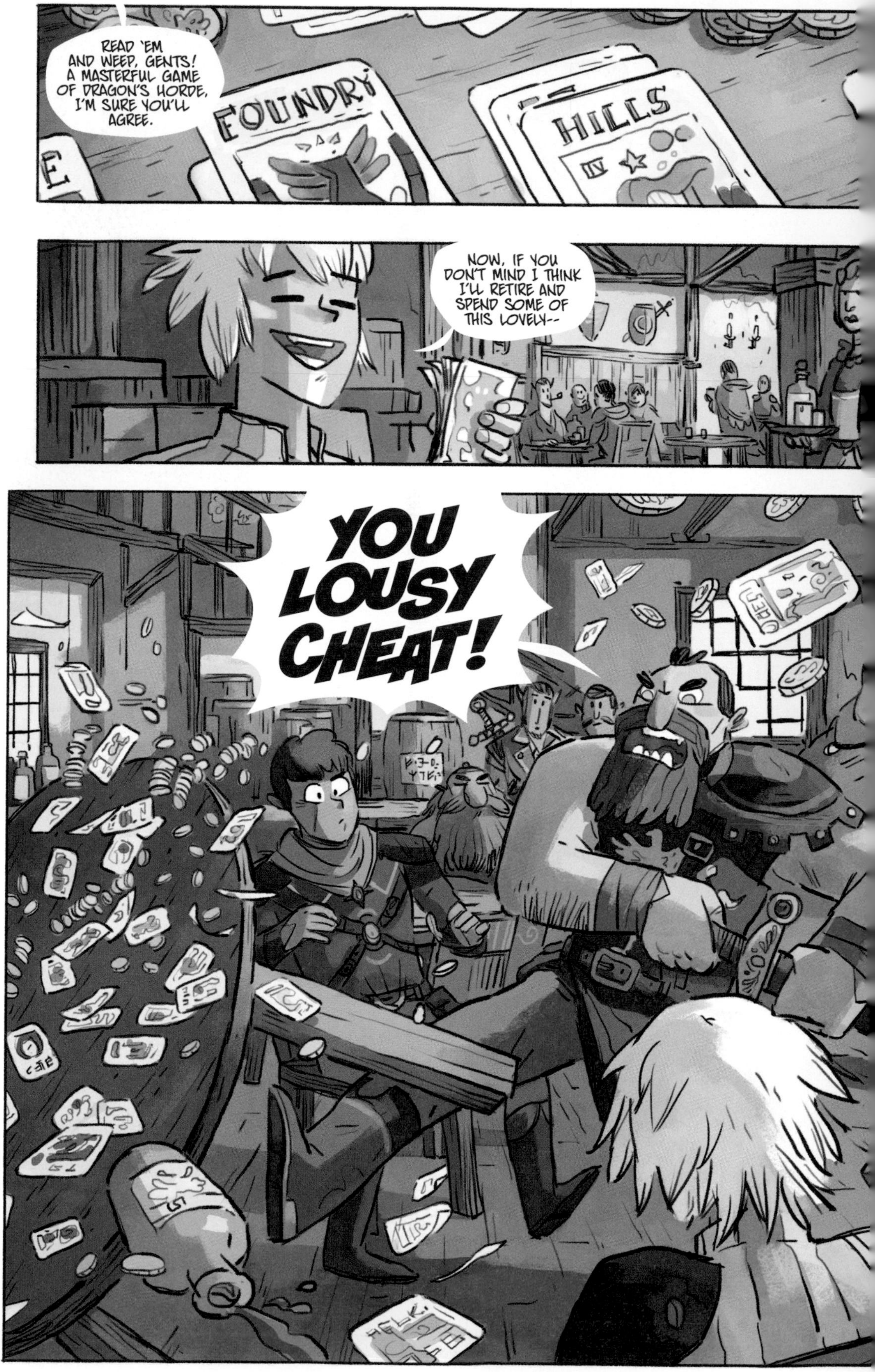
READ 'EM AND WEEP, GENTS! A MASTERFUL GAME OF DRAGON'S HORDE, I'M SURE YOU'LL AGREE.
FOUNDRY
HILLS
NOW, IF YOU DON'T MIND I THINK I'LL RETIRE AND SPEND SOME OF THIS LOVELY--
YOU LOUSY CHEAT!

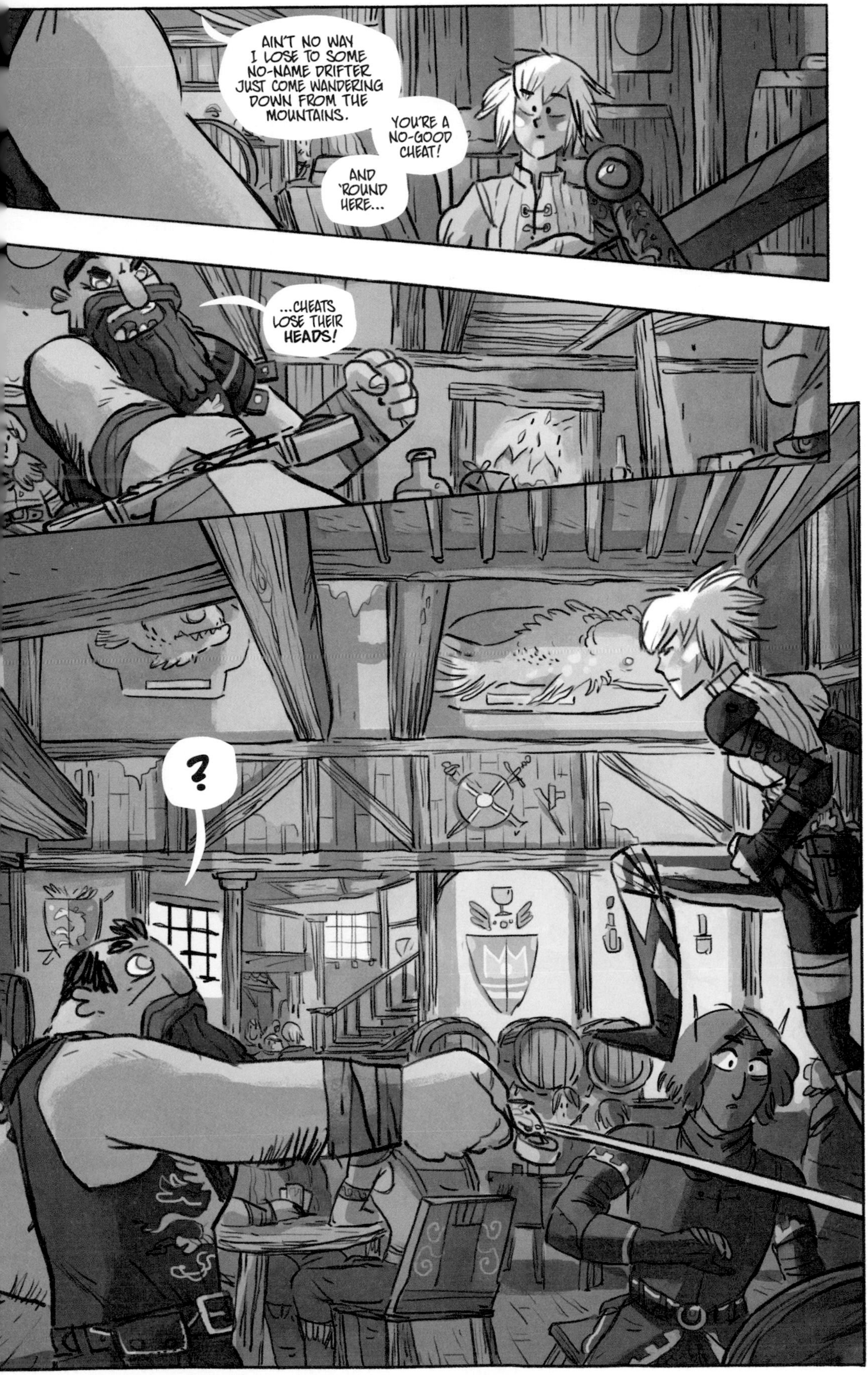
AIN'T NO WAY I LOSE TO SOME NO-NAME DRIFTER JUST COME WANDERING DOWN FROM THE MOUNTAINS.
YOU'RE A NO-GOOD CHEAT!
AND 'ROUND HERE...
...CHEATS LOSE THEIR HEADS!
?

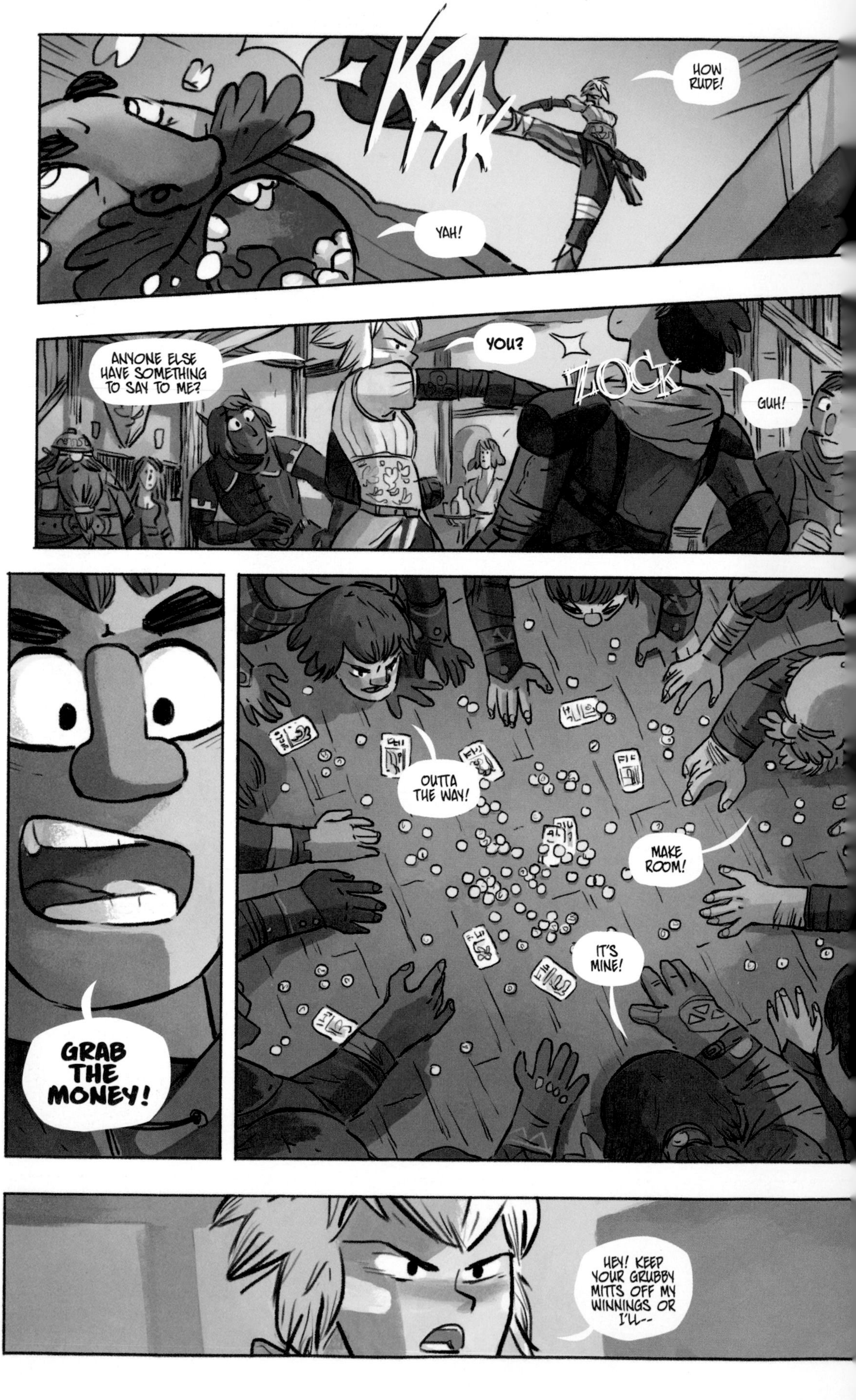
KRAK
HOW RUDE!
YAH!
ANYONE ELSE HAVE SOMETHING TO SAY TO ME?
YOU?
ZOCK
GUH!
GRAB THE MONEY!
OUTTA THE WAY!
MAKE ROOM!
IT'S MINE!
HEY! KEEP YOUR GRUBBY MITTS OFF MY WINNINGS OR I'LL--

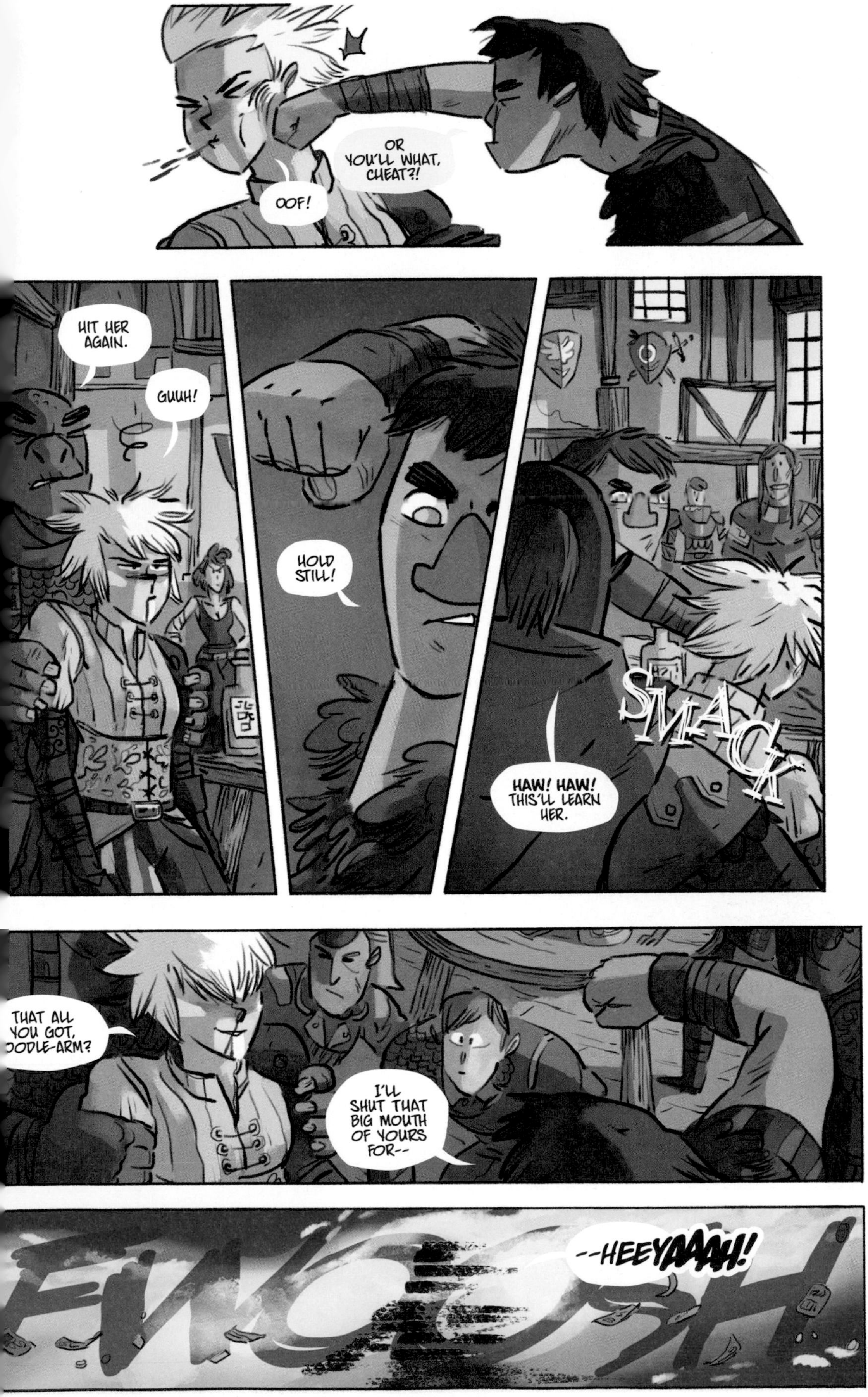
OR YOU'LL WHAT, CHEAT?!
OOF!
HIT HER AGAIN.
GUUH!
HOLD STILL!
SMACK
HAW! HAW! THIS'LL LEARN HER.
THAT ALL YOU GOT, ODLE-ARM?
I'LL SHUT THAT BIG MOUTH OF YOURS FOR--
--HEEYAAAH!
FWOOSH

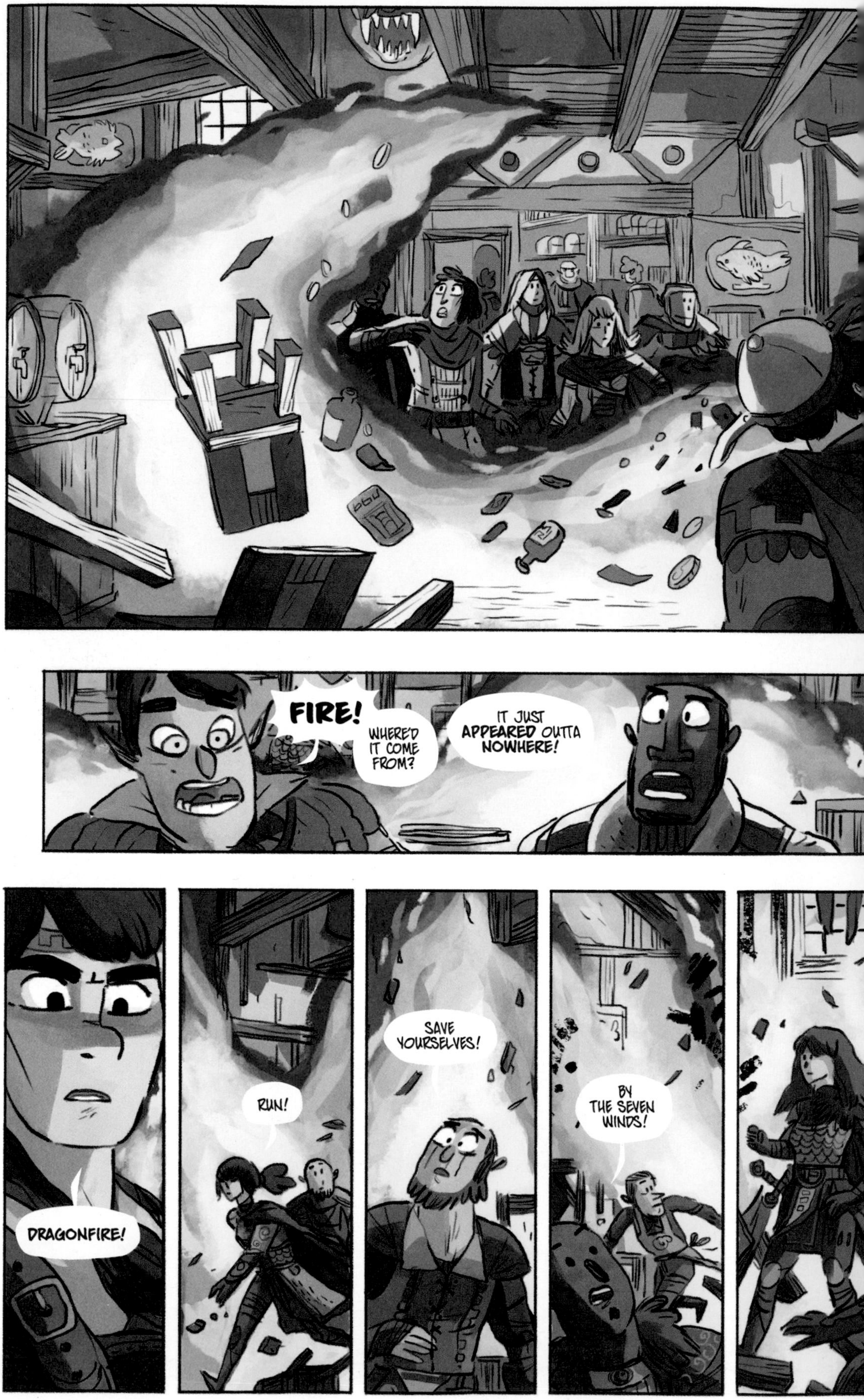
FIRE!
WHERE'D IT COME FROM?
IT JUST APPEARED OUTTA NOWHERE!
DRAGONFIRE!
RUN!
SAVE YOURSELVES!
BY THE SEVEN WINDS!

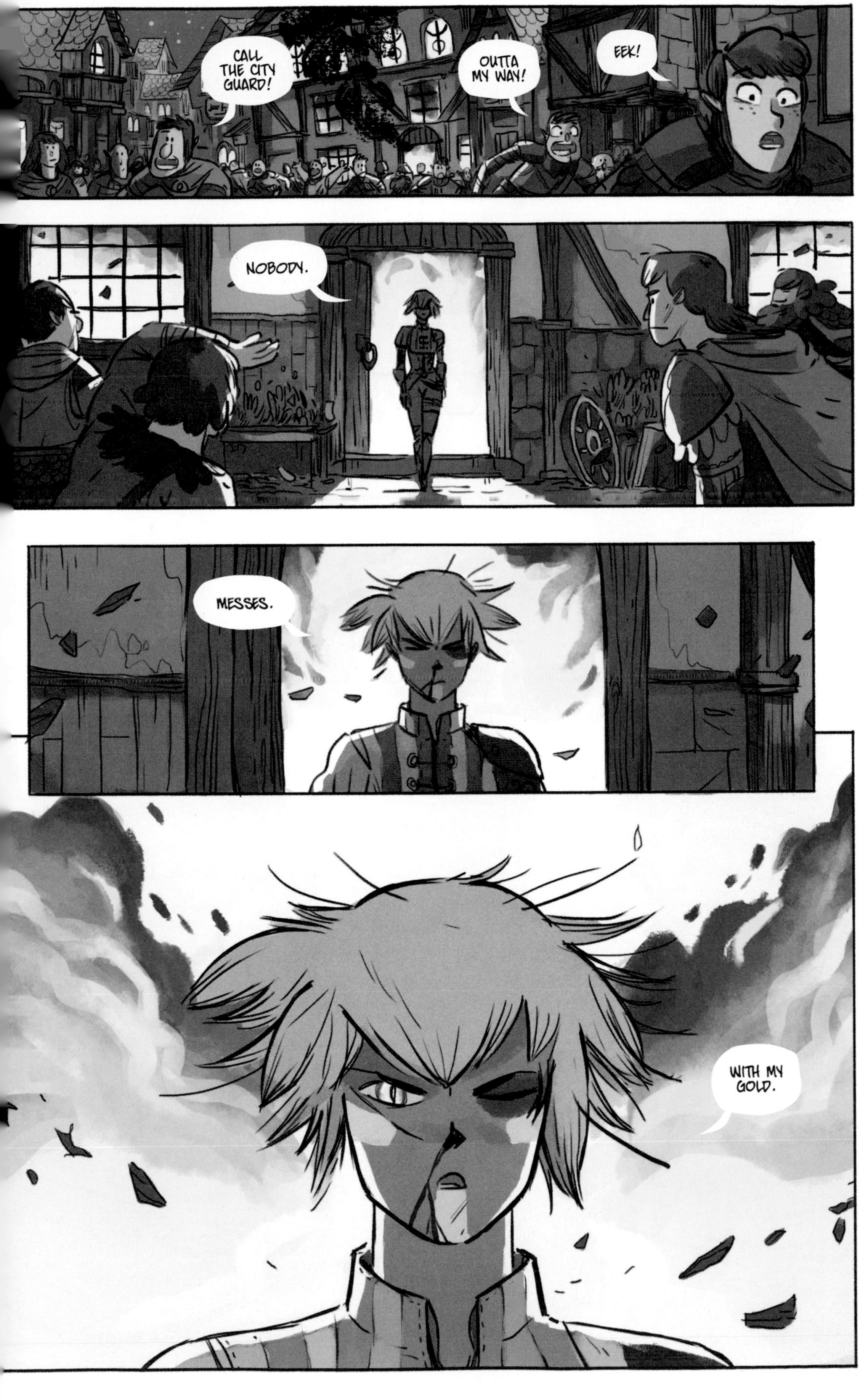
CALL THE CITY GUARD!
OUTTA MY WAY!
EEK!
NOBODY.
MESSES.
WITH MY GOLD.

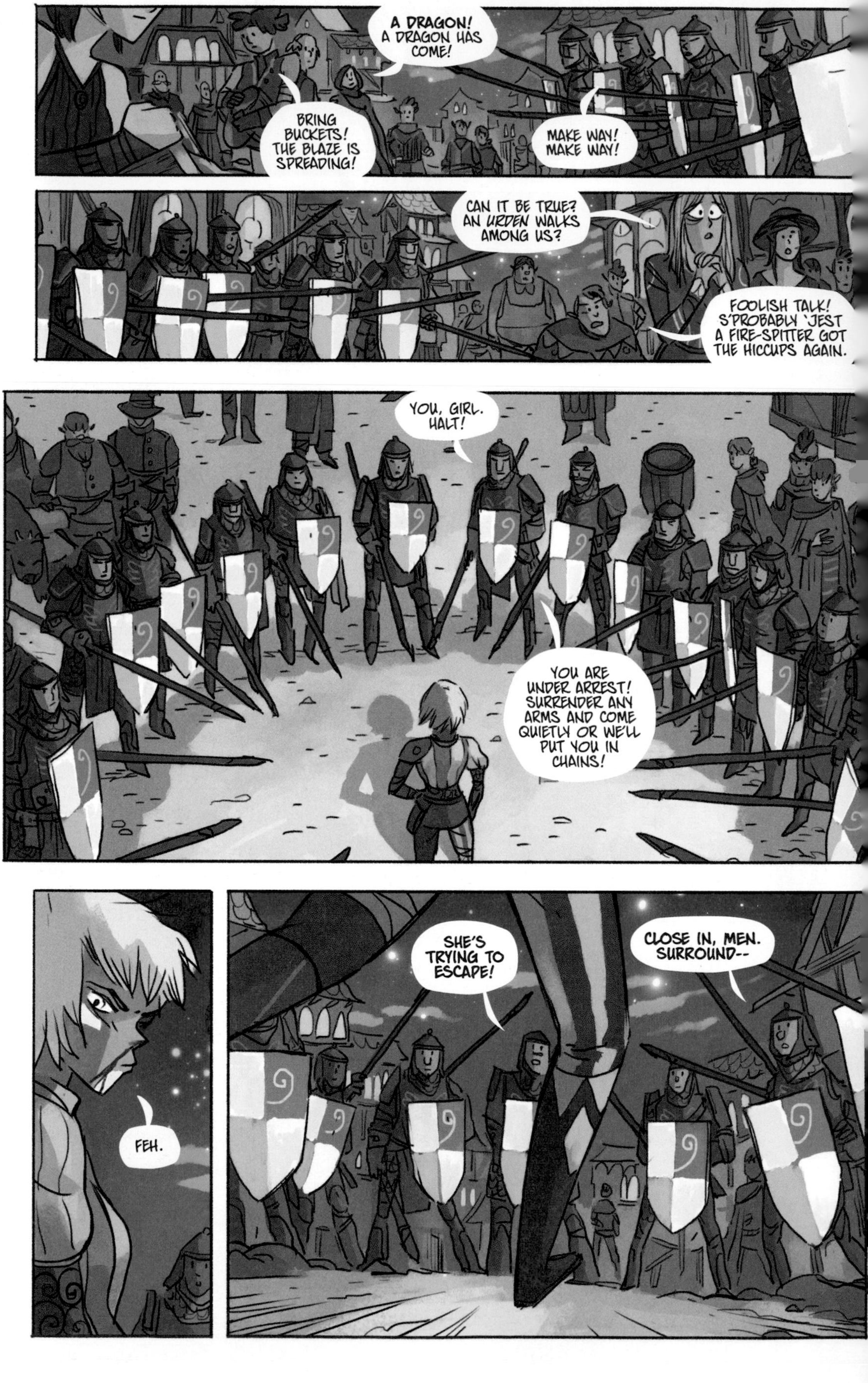
A DRAGON! A DRAGON HAS COME!
BRING BUCKETS! THE BLAZE IS SPREADING!
MAKE WAY! MAKE WAY!
CAN IT BE TRUE? AN URDEN WALKS AMONG US?
FOOLISH TALK! S'PROBABLY 'JEST A FIRE-SPITTER GOT THE HICCUPS AGAIN.
YOU, GIRL. HALT!
YOU ARE UNDER ARREST! SURRENDER ANY ARMS AND COME QUIETLY OR WE'LL PUT YOU IN CHAINS!
FEH.
SHE'S TRYING TO ESCAPE!
CLOSE IN, MEN. SURROUND--

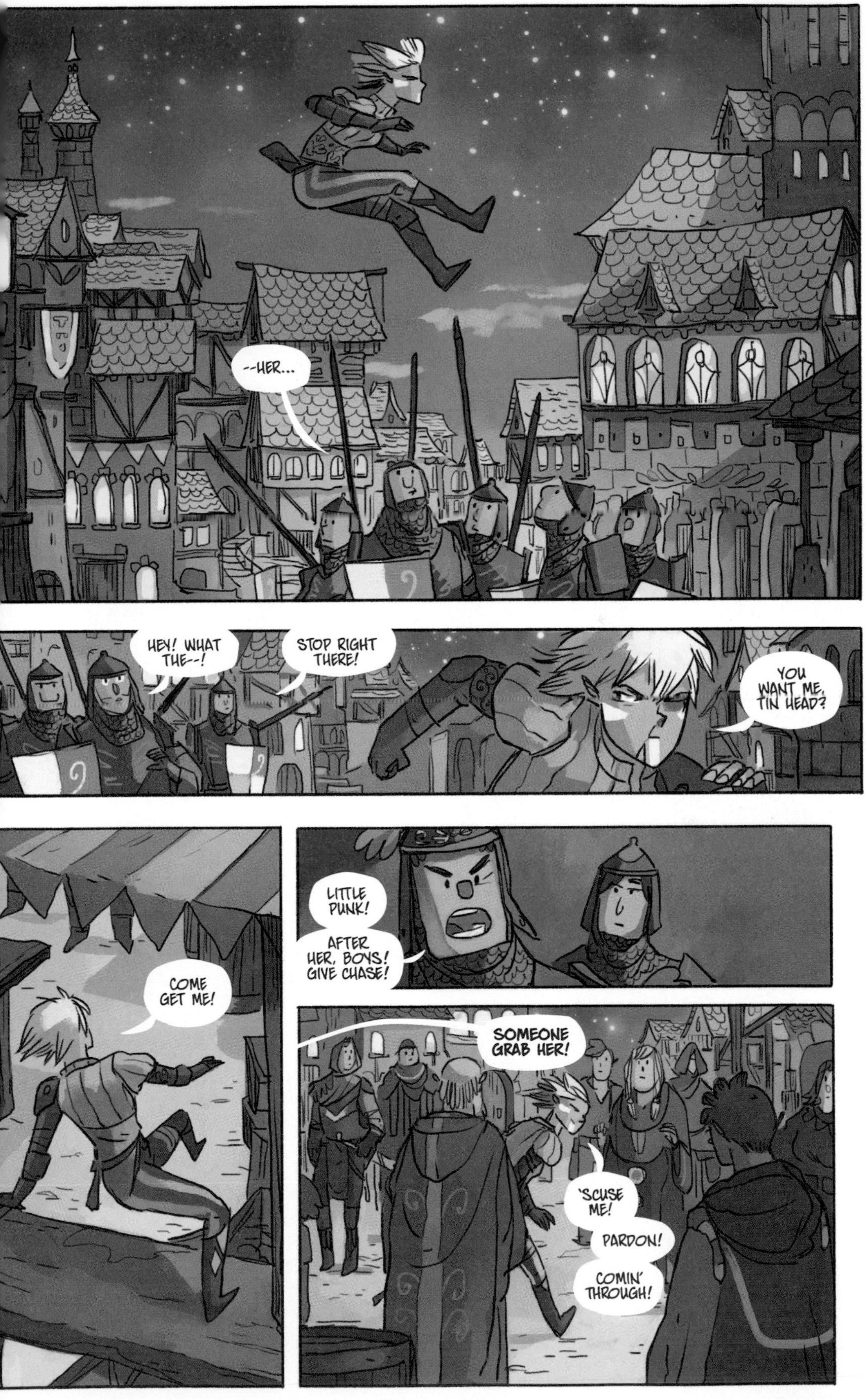
--HER...
HEY! WHAT THE--!
STOP RIGHT THERE!
YOU WANT ME, TIN HEAD?
COME GET ME!
LITTLE PUNK!
AFTER HER, BOYS! GIVE CHASE!
SOMEONE GRAB HER!
'SCUSE ME!
PARDON!
COMIN' THROUGH!

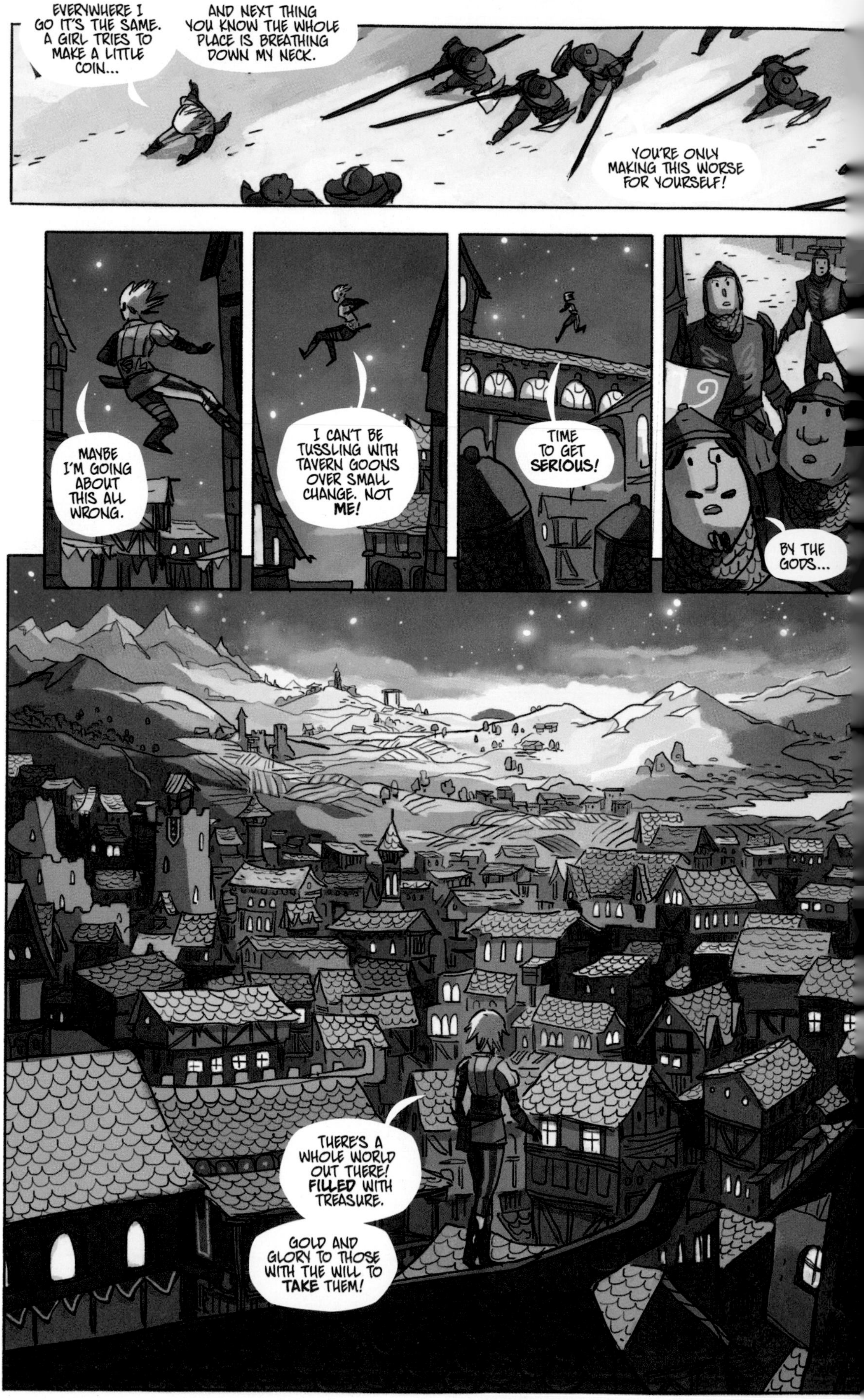
EVERYWHERE I GO IT'S THE SAME. A GIRL TRIES TO MAKE A LITTLE COIN...
AND NEXT THING YOU KNOW THE WHOLE PLACE IS BREATHING DOWN MY NECK.
YOU'RE ONLY MAKING THIS WORSE FOR YOURSELF!
MAYBE I'M GOING ABOUT THIS ALL WRONG.
I CAN'T BE TUSSLING WITH TAVERN GOONS OVER SMALL CHANGE. NOT ME!
TIME TO GET SERIOUS!
BY THE GODS...
THERE'S A WHOLE WORLD OUT THERE! FILLED WITH TREASURE.
GOLD AND GLORY TO THOSE WITH THE WILL TO TAKE THEM!

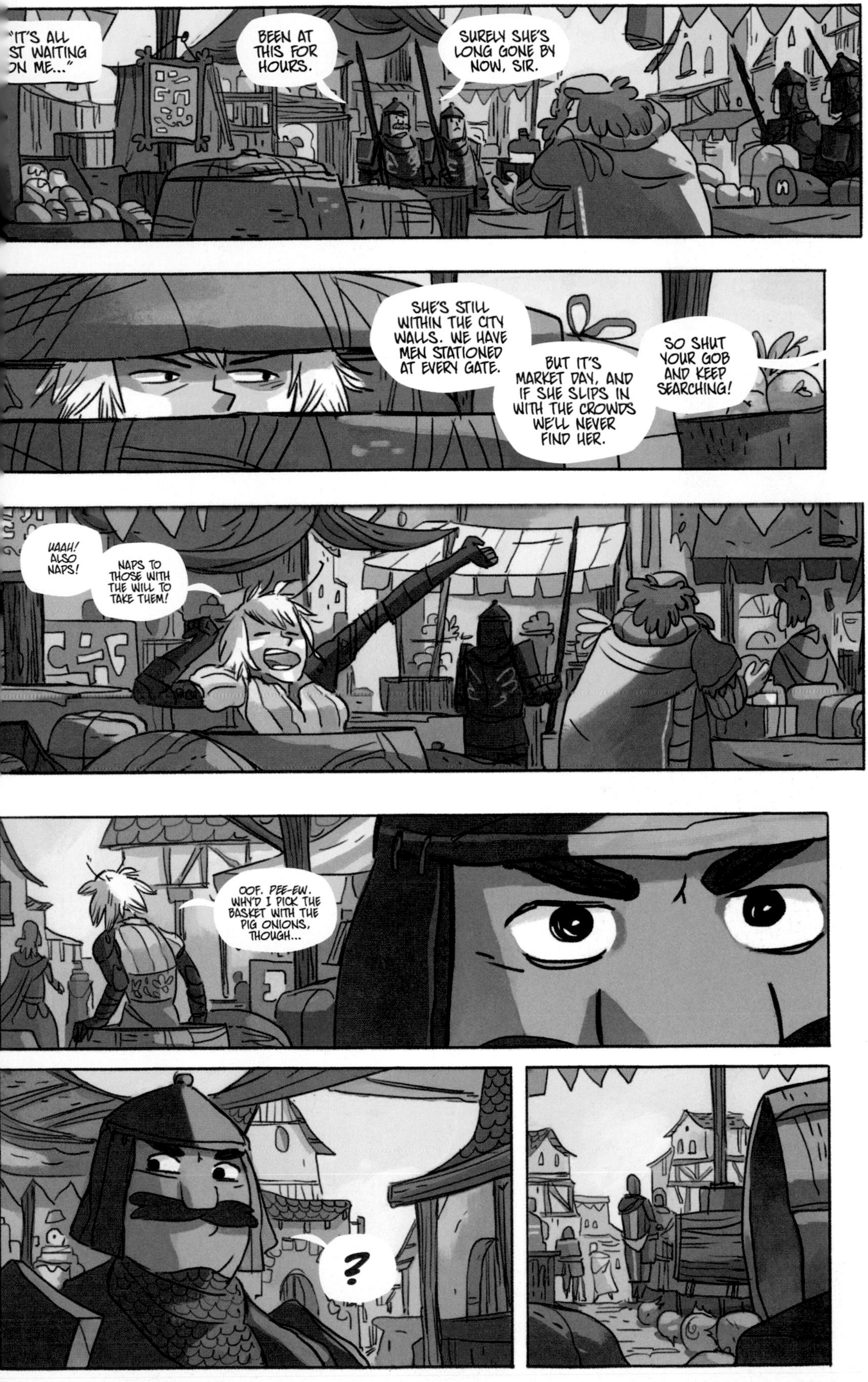

"IT'S ALL
ST WAITING
ON ME..."
BEEN AT THIS FOR HOURS.
SURELY SHE'S LONG GONE BY NOW, SIR.
SHE'S STILL WITHIN THE CITY WALLS. WE HAVE MEN STATIONED AT EVERY GATE.
BUT IT'S MARKET DAY, AND IF SHE SLIPS IN WITH THE CROWDS WE'LL NEVER FIND HER.
SO SHUT YOUR GOB AND KEEP SEARCHING!
UAAH! ALSO NAPS!
NAPS TO THOSE WITH THE WILL TO TAKE THEM!
OOF. PEE-EW. WHY'D I PICK THE BASKET WITH THE PIG ONIONS, THOUGH...
?

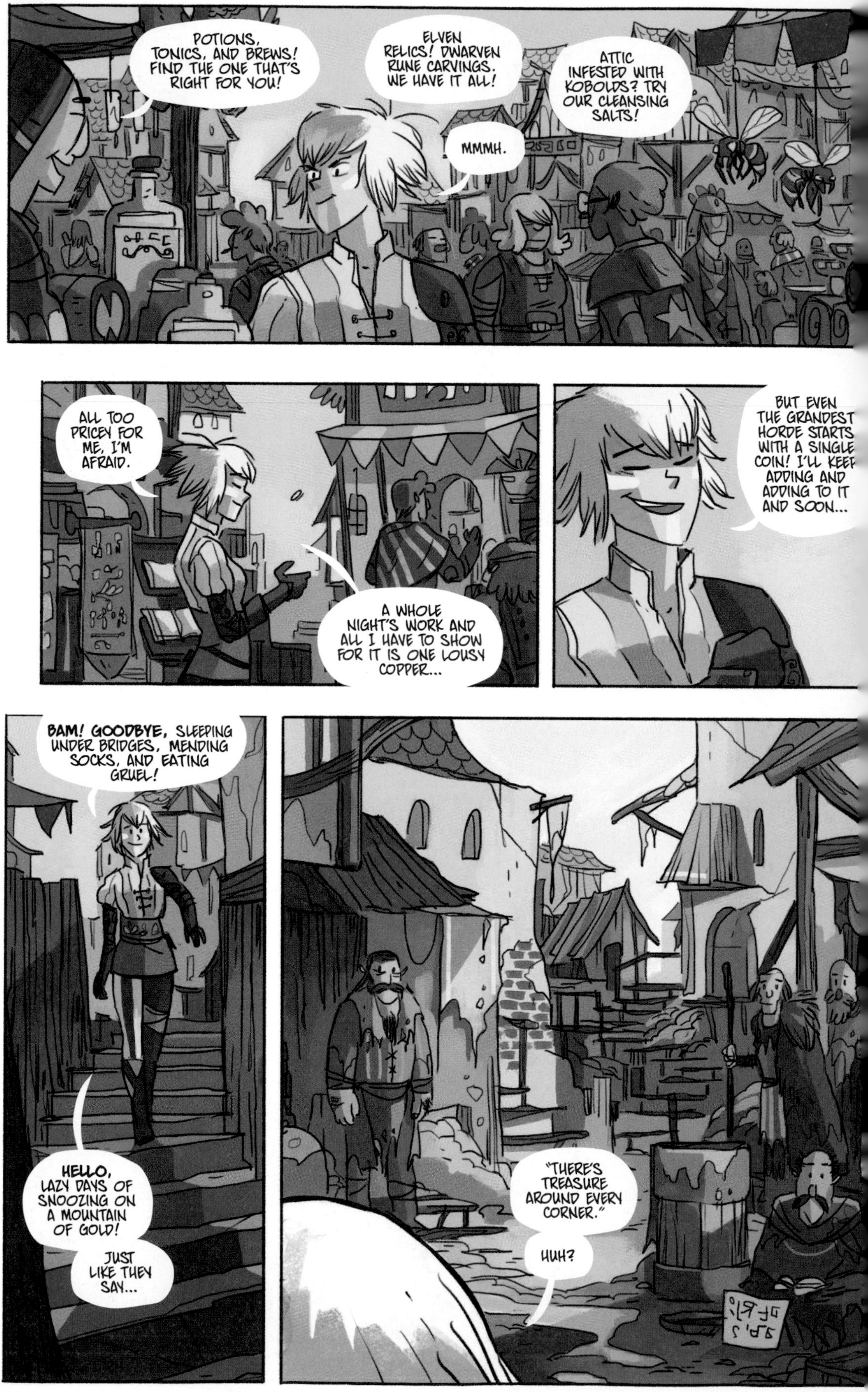
POTIONS, TONICS, AND BREWS! FIND THE ONE THAT'S RIGHT FOR YOU!
ELVEN RELICS! DWARVEN RUNE CARVINGS. WE HAVE IT ALL!
ATTIC INFESTED WITH KOBOLDS? TRY OUR CLEANSING SALTS!
MMMH.
ALL TOO PRICEY FOR ME, I'M AFRAID.
A WHOLE NIGHT'S WORK AND ALL I HAVE TO SHOW FOR IT IS ONE LOUSY COPPER...
BUT EVEN THE GRANDEST HORDE STARTS WITH A SINGLE COIN! I'LL KEEP ADDING AND ADDING TO IT AND SOON...
BAM! GOODBYE, SLEEPING UNDER BRIDGES, MENDING SOCKS, AND EATING GRUEL!
HELLO, LAZY DAYS OF SNOOZING ON A MOUNTAIN OF GOLD!
JUST LIKE THEY SAY...
"THERE'S TREASURE AROUND EVERY CORNER."
HUH?

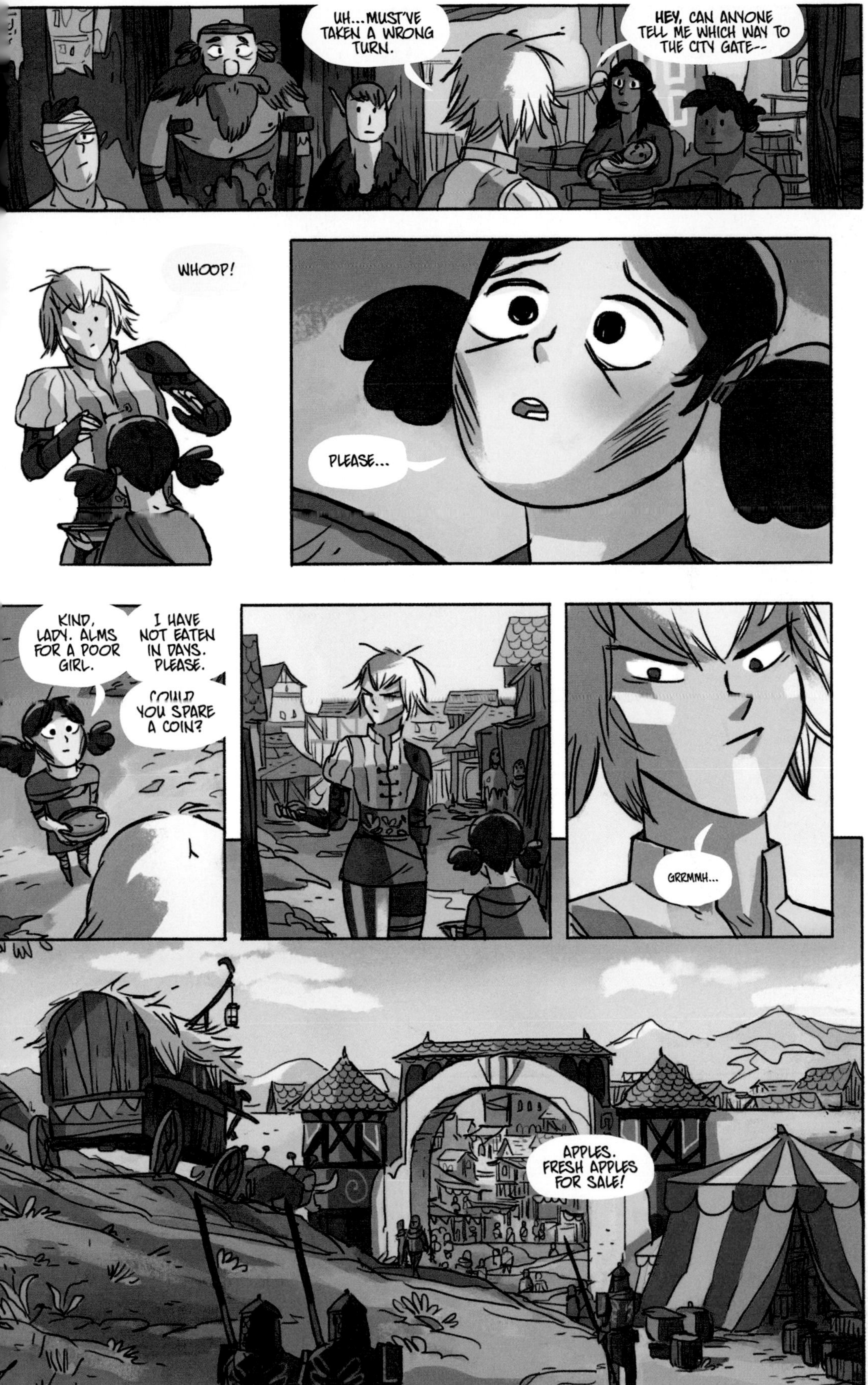
UH...MUST'VE TAKEN A WRONG TURN.
HEY, CAN ANYONE TELL ME WHICH WAY TO THE CITY GATE--
WHOOP!
PLEASE...
KIND, LADY. ALMS FOR A POOR GIRL.
I HAVE NOT EATEN IN DAYS. PLEASE.
COULD YOU SPARE A COIN?
GRRMMH...
APPLES. FRESH APPLES FOR SALE!

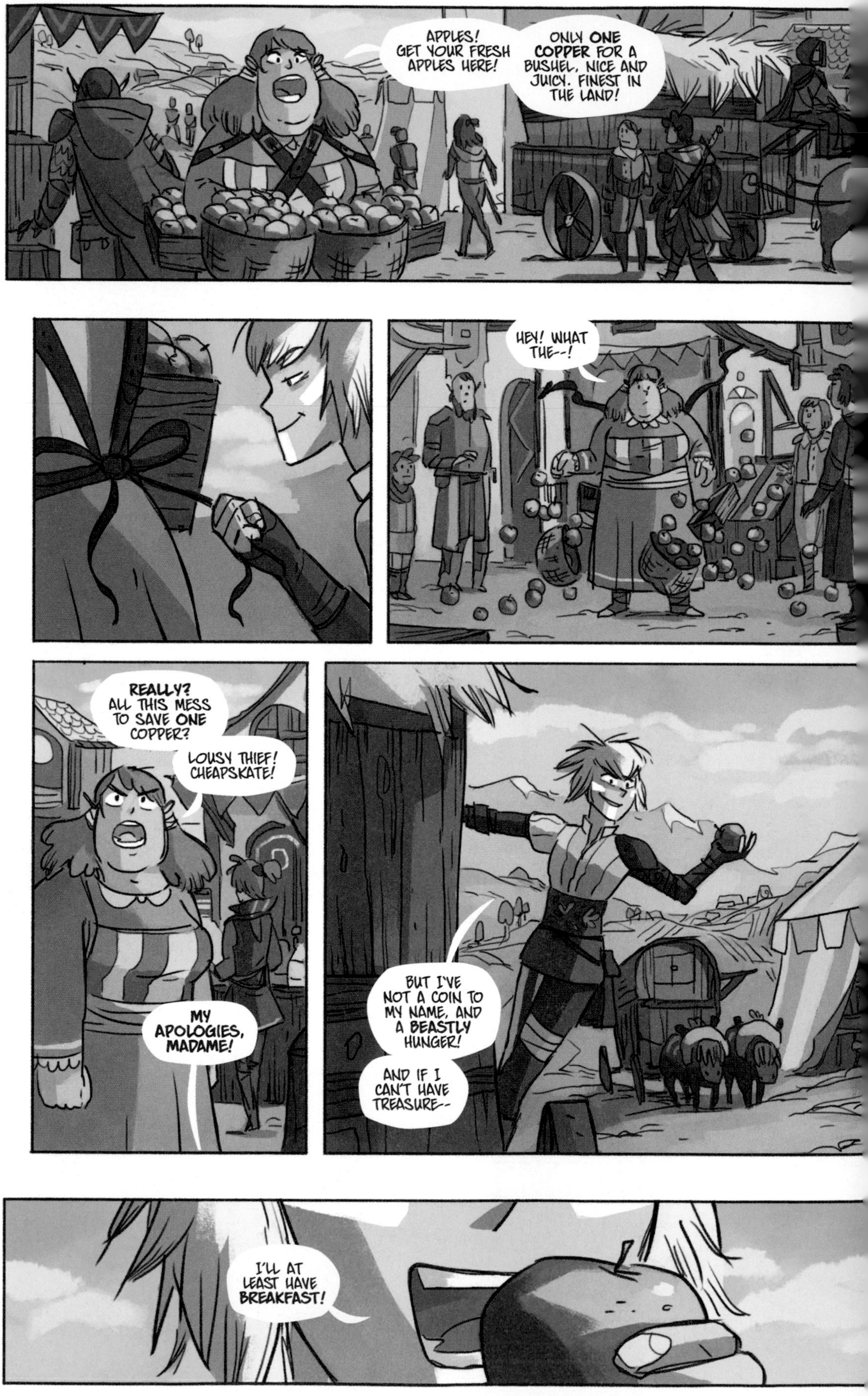

APPLES! GET YOUR FRESH APPLES HERE!
ONLY ONE COPPER FOR A BUSHEL, NICE AND JUICY. FINEST IN THE LAND!
HEY! WHAT THE--!
REALLY? ALL THIS MESS TO SAVE ONE COPPER?
LOUSY THIEF! CHEAPSKATE!
MY APOLOGIES, MADAME!
BUT I'VE NOT A COIN TO MY NAME, AND A BEASTLY HUNGER!
AND IF I CAN'T HAVE TREASURE--
I'LL AT LEAST HAVE BREAKFAST!

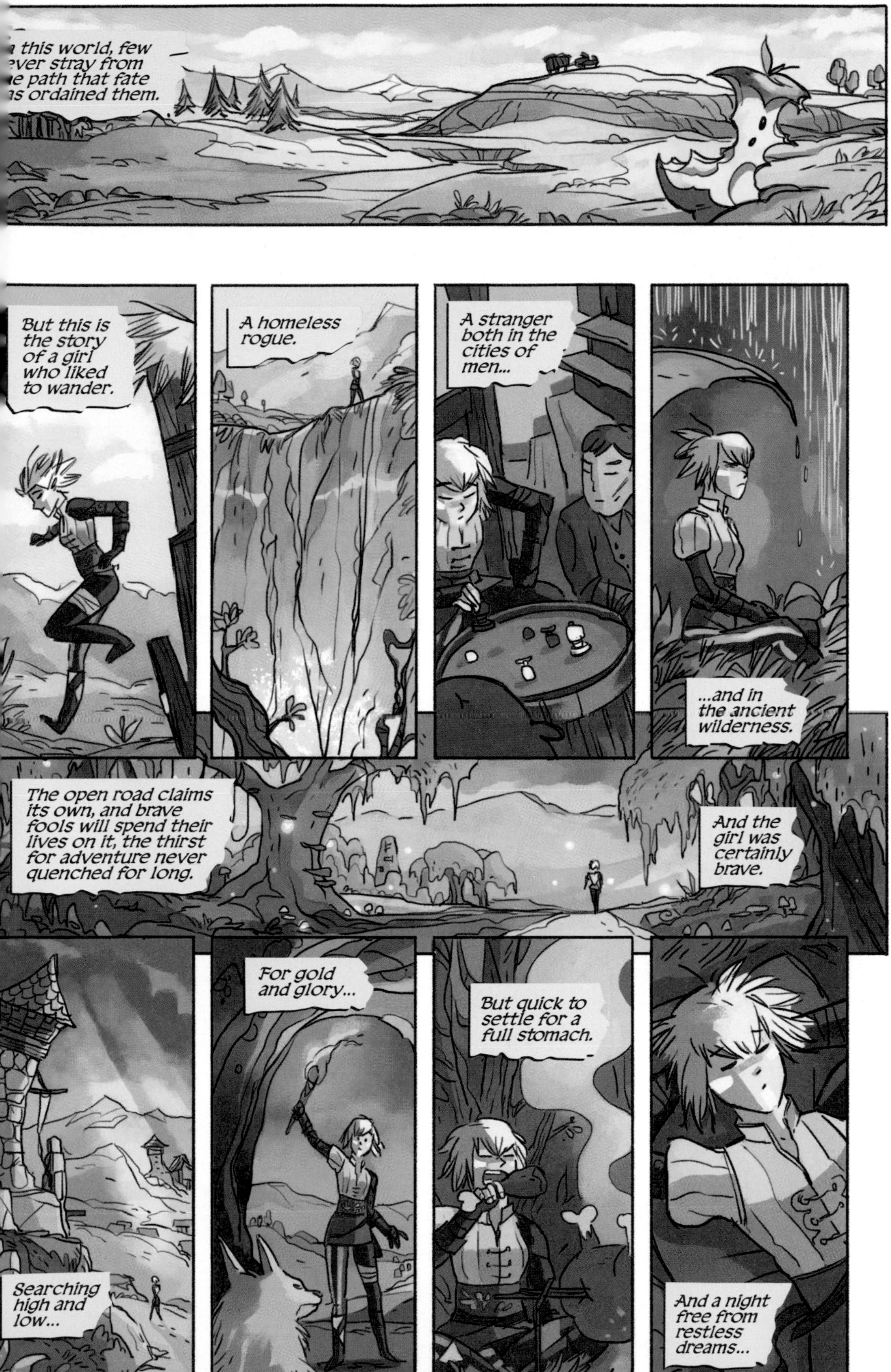

n this world, few ever stray from e path that fate as ordained them.
But this is the story of a girl who liked to wander.
A homeless rogue.
A stranger both in the cities of men...
...and in the ancient wilderness.
The open road claims its own, and brave fools will spend their lives on it, the thirst for adventure never quenched for long.
And the girl was certainly brave.
Searching high and low...
For gold and glory...
But quick to settle for a full stomach.
And a night free from restless dreams...

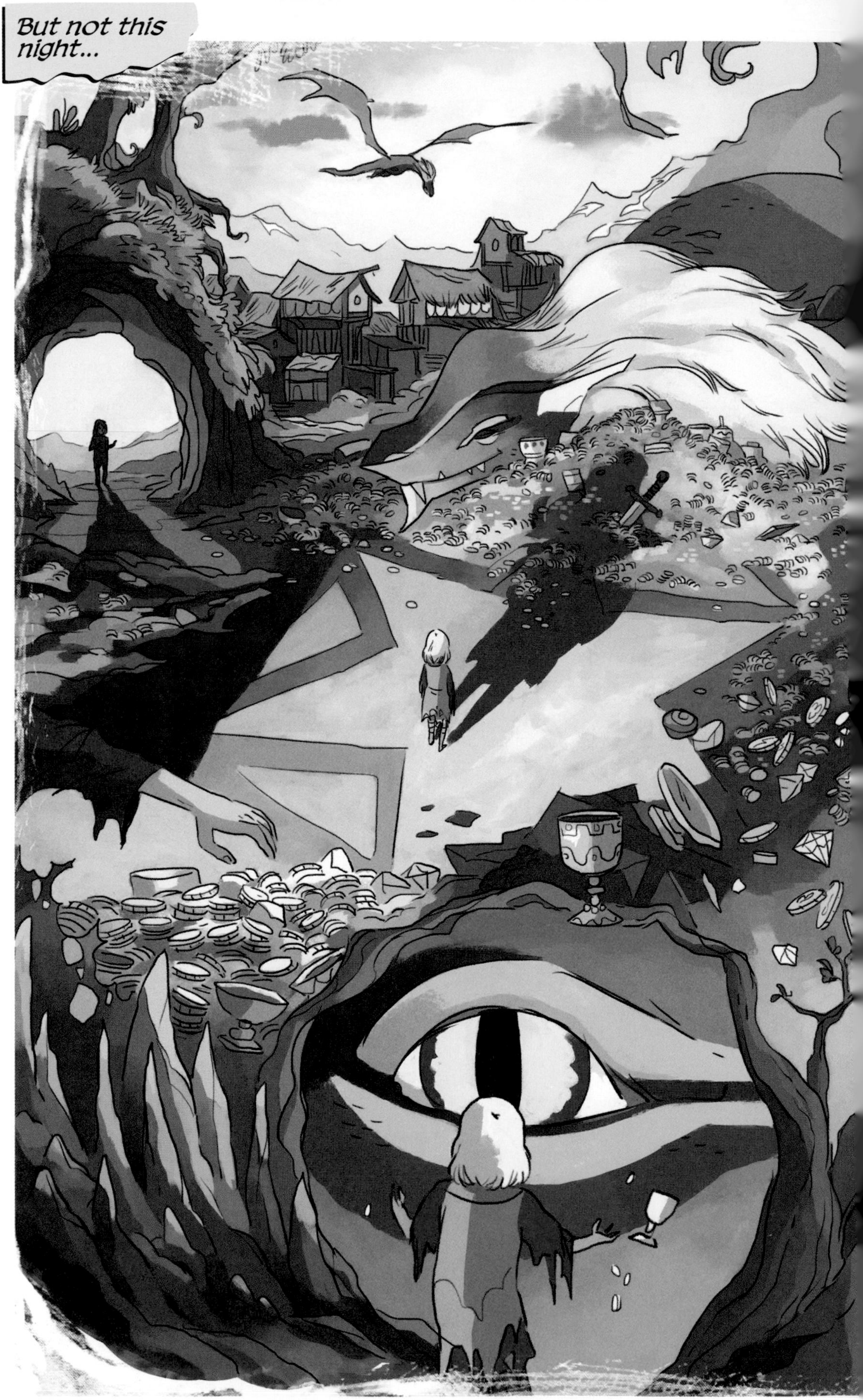
But not this night...

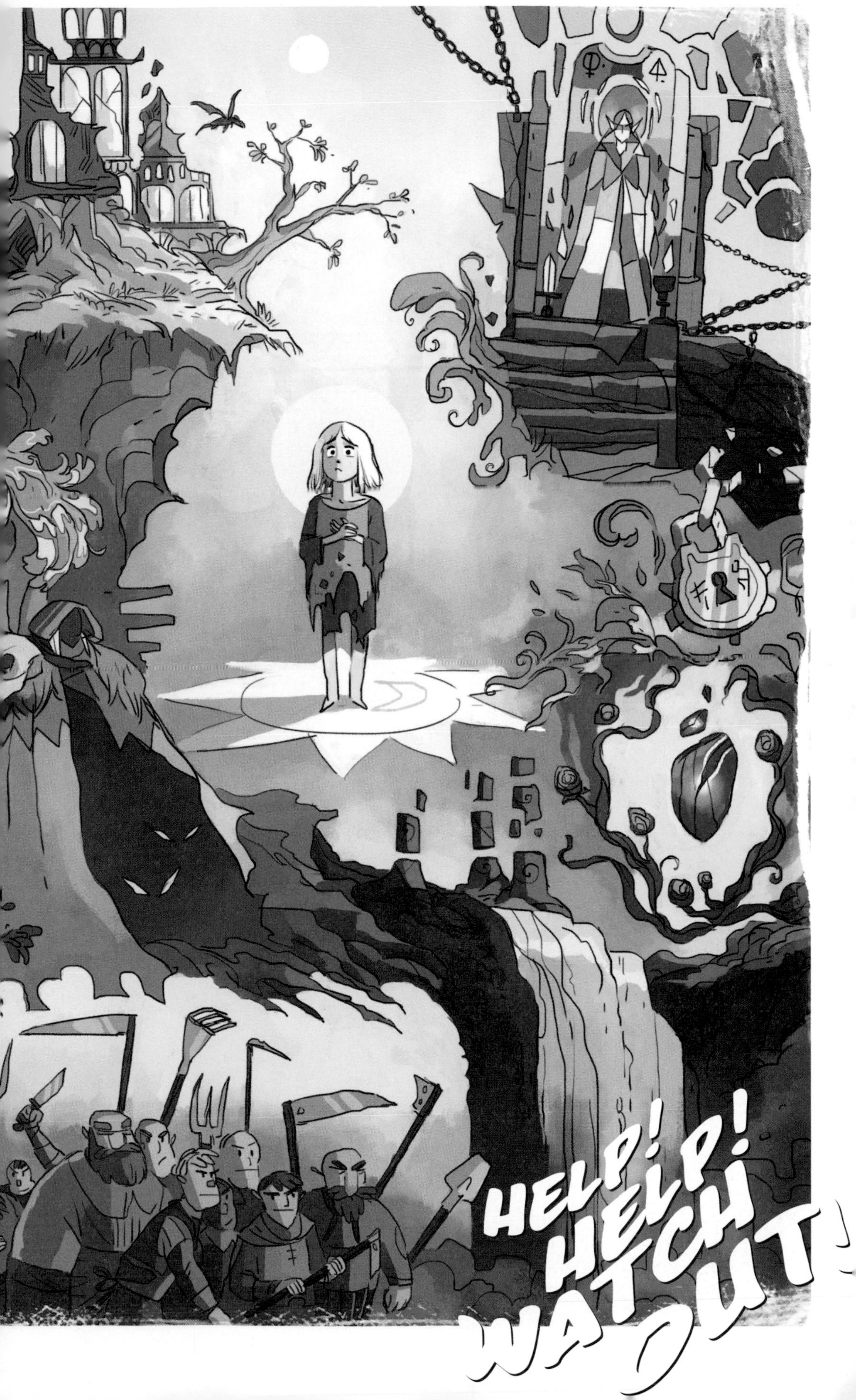
HELP!
HELP!
WATCH
OUT!

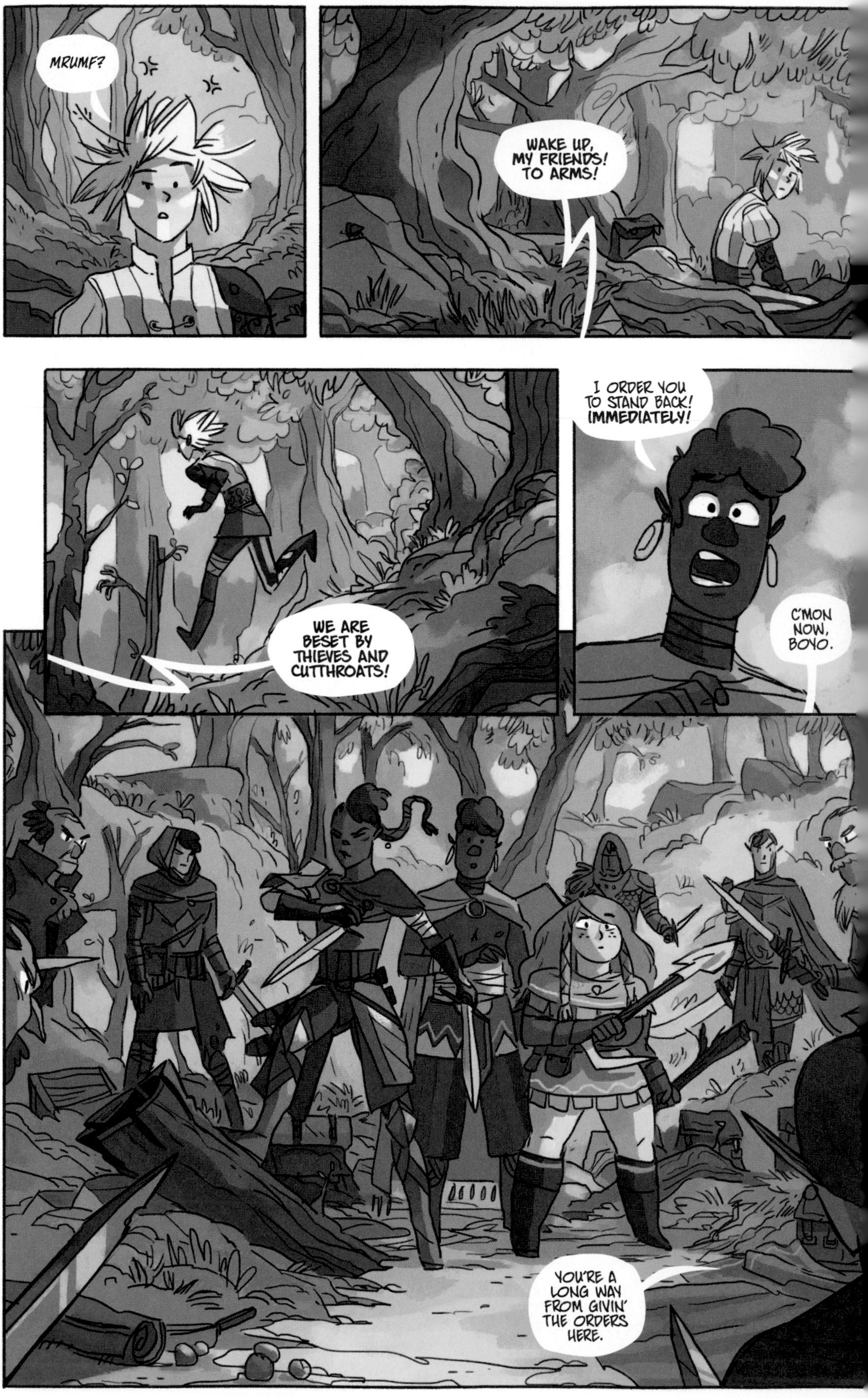
MRUMF?
WAKE UP, MY FRIENDS! TO ARMS!
WE ARE BESET BY THIEVES AND CUTTHROATS!
I ORDER YOU TO STAND BACK! IMMEDIATELY!
C'MON NOW, BOYO.
YOU'RE A LONG WAY FROM GIVIN' THE ORDERS HERE.

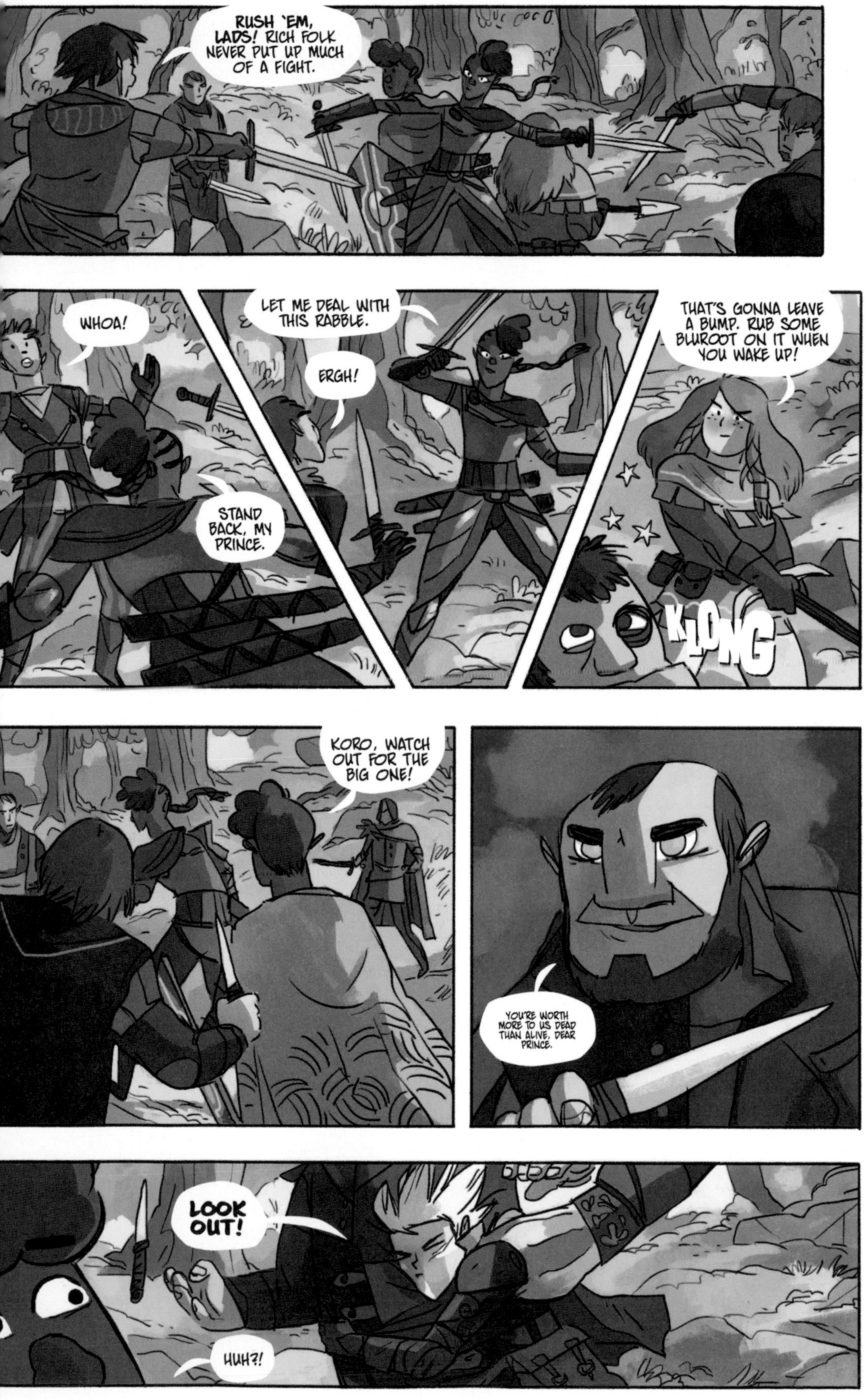
RUSH 'EM, LADS! RICH FOLK NEVER PUT UP MUCH OF A FIGHT.
WHOA!
STAND BACK, MY PRINCE.
LET ME DEAL WITH THIS RABBLE.
ERGH!
THAT'S GONNA LEAVE A BUMP. RUB SOME BLUROOT ON IT WHEN YOU WAKE UP!
KLONG
KORO, WATCH OUT FOR THE BIG ONE!
YOU'RE WORTH MORE TO US DEAD THAN ALIVE, DEAR PRINCE.
LOOK OUT!
HUH?!

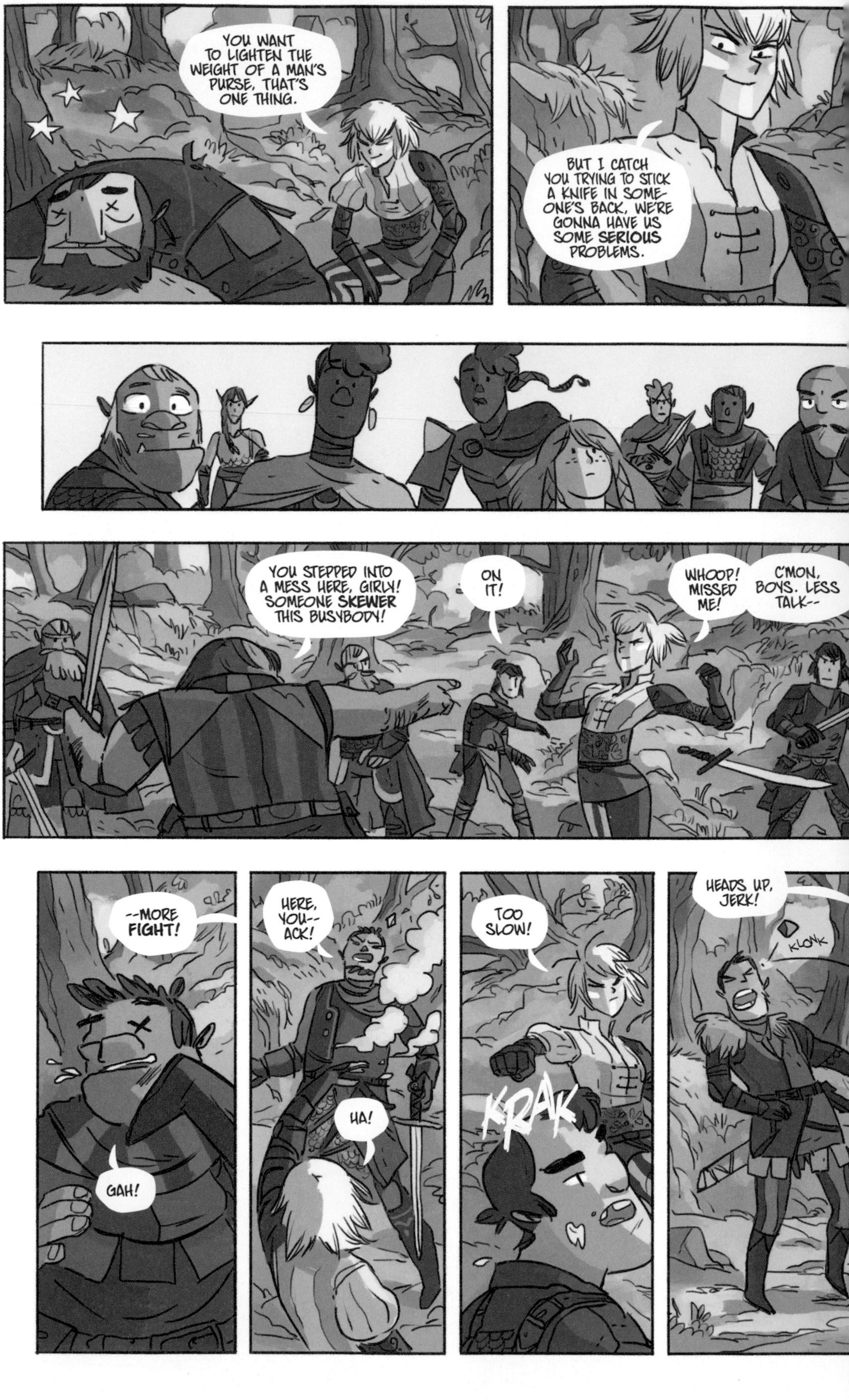
YOU WANT TO LIGHTEN THE WEIGHT OF A MAN'S PURSE, THAT'S ONE THING.
BUT I CATCH YOU TRYING TO STICK A KNIFE IN SOME-ONE'S BACK, WE'RE GONNA HAVE US SOME SERIOUS PROBLEMS.
YOU STEPPED INTO A MESS HERE, GIRLY! SOMEONE SKEWER THIS BUSYBODY!
ON IT!
WHOOP! MISSED ME!
C'MON, BOYS. LESS TALK--
--MORE FIGHT!
GAH!
HERE, YOU--ACK!
HA!
TOO SLOW!
KRAK
HEADS UP, JERK!
KLONK

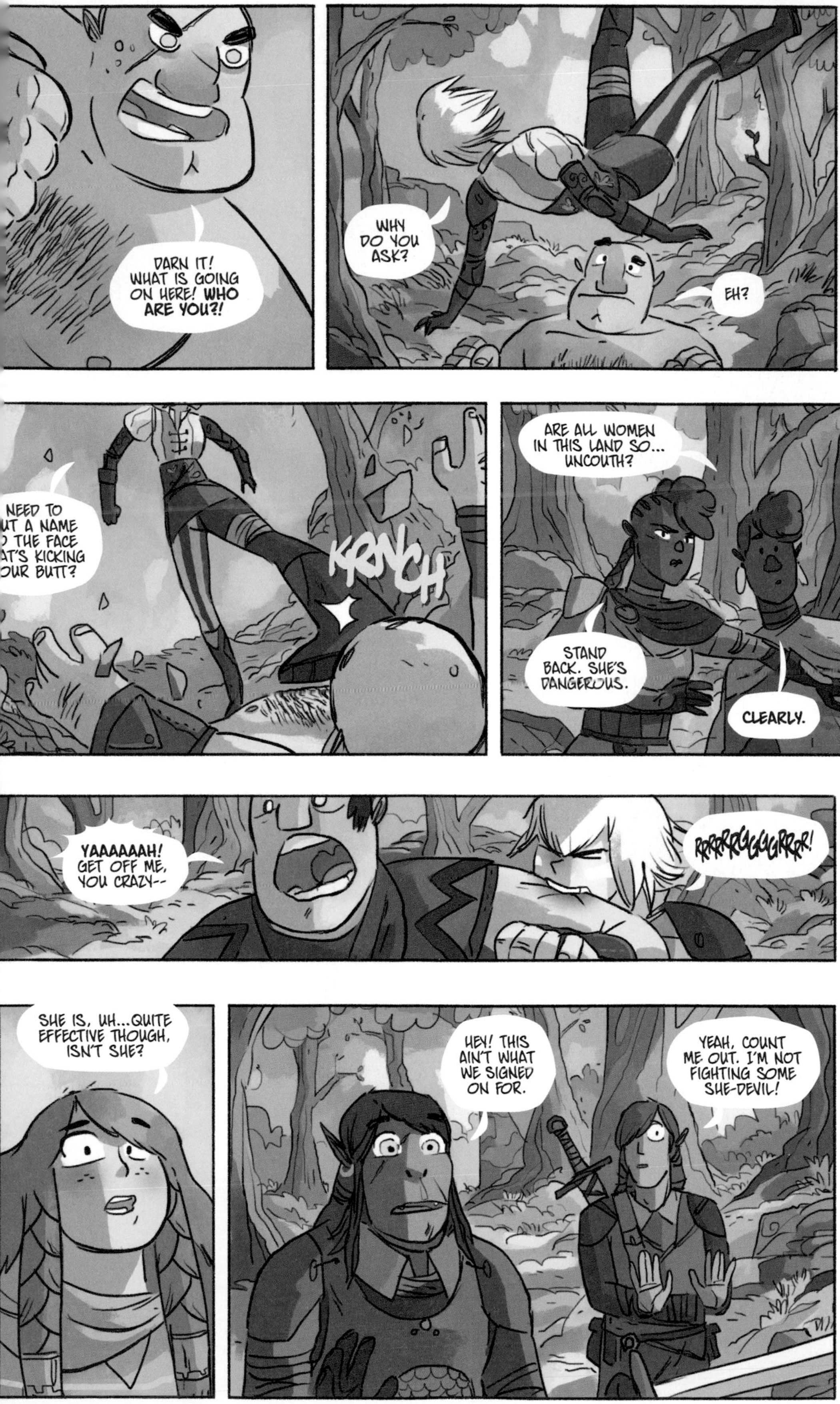
DARN IT! WHAT IS GOING ON HERE! WHO ARE YOU?!
WHY DO YOU ASK?
EH?
NEED TO UT A NAME O THE FACE AT'S KICKING OUR BUTT?
KRNCH
ARE ALL WOMEN IN THIS LAND SO... UNCOUTH?
STAND BACK. SHE'S DANGEROUS.
CLEARLY.
YAAAAAAH! GET OFF ME, YOU CRAZY--
RRRRRGGGGRRRR!
SHE IS, UH...QUITE EFFECTIVE THOUGH, ISN'T SHE?
HEY! THIS AIN'T WHAT WE SIGNED ON FOR.
YEAH, COUNT ME OUT. I'M NOT FIGHTING SOME SHE-DEVIL!

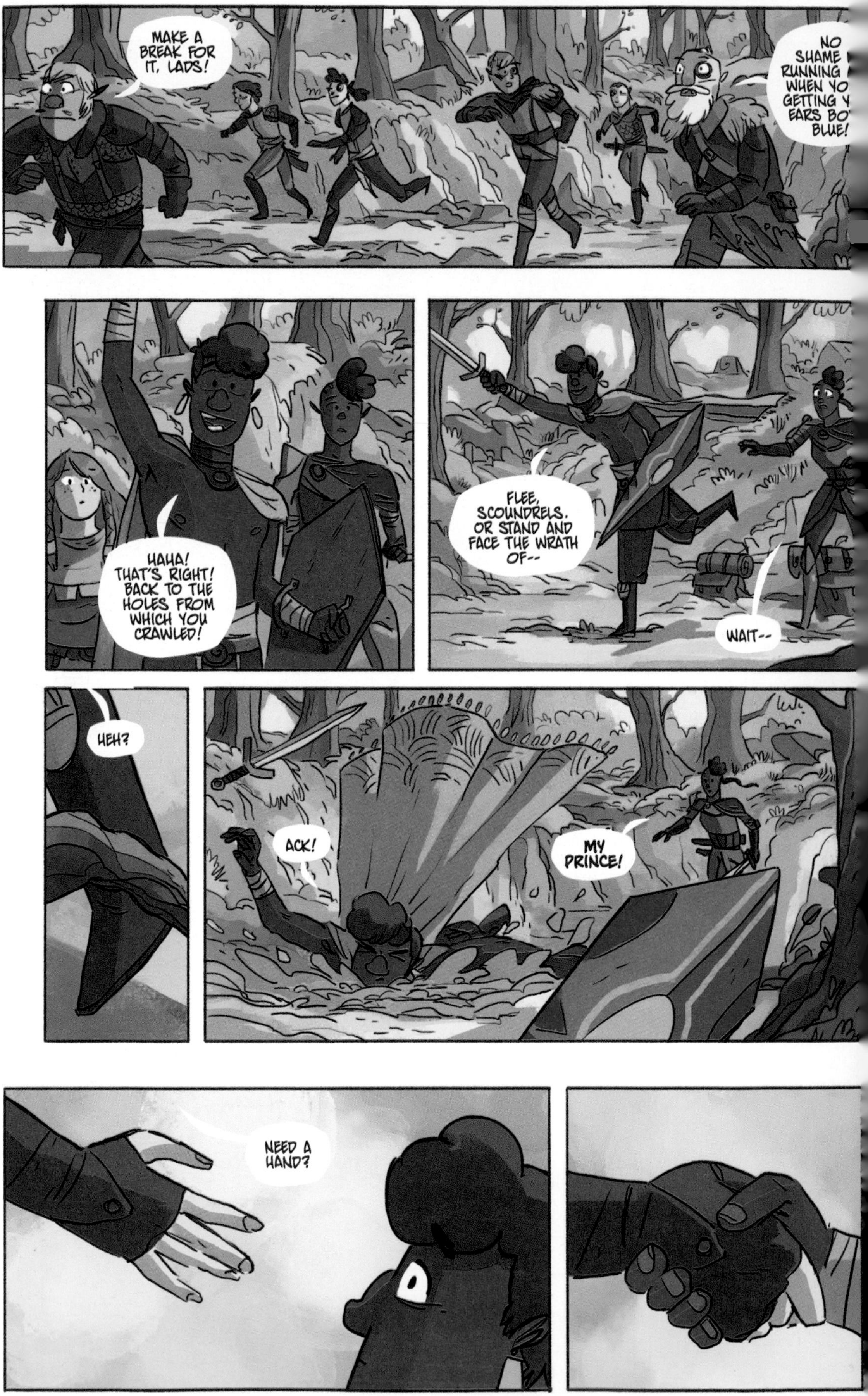
MAKE A BREAK FOR IT, LADS!
NO SHAME RUNNING WHEN YO GETTING Y EARS BO BLUE!
HAHA! THAT'S RIGHT! BACK TO THE HOLES FROM WHICH YOU CRAWLED!
FLEE, SCOUNDRELS. OR STAND AND FACE THE WRATH OF--
WAIT--
HEH?
ACK!
MY PRINCE!
NEED A HAND?

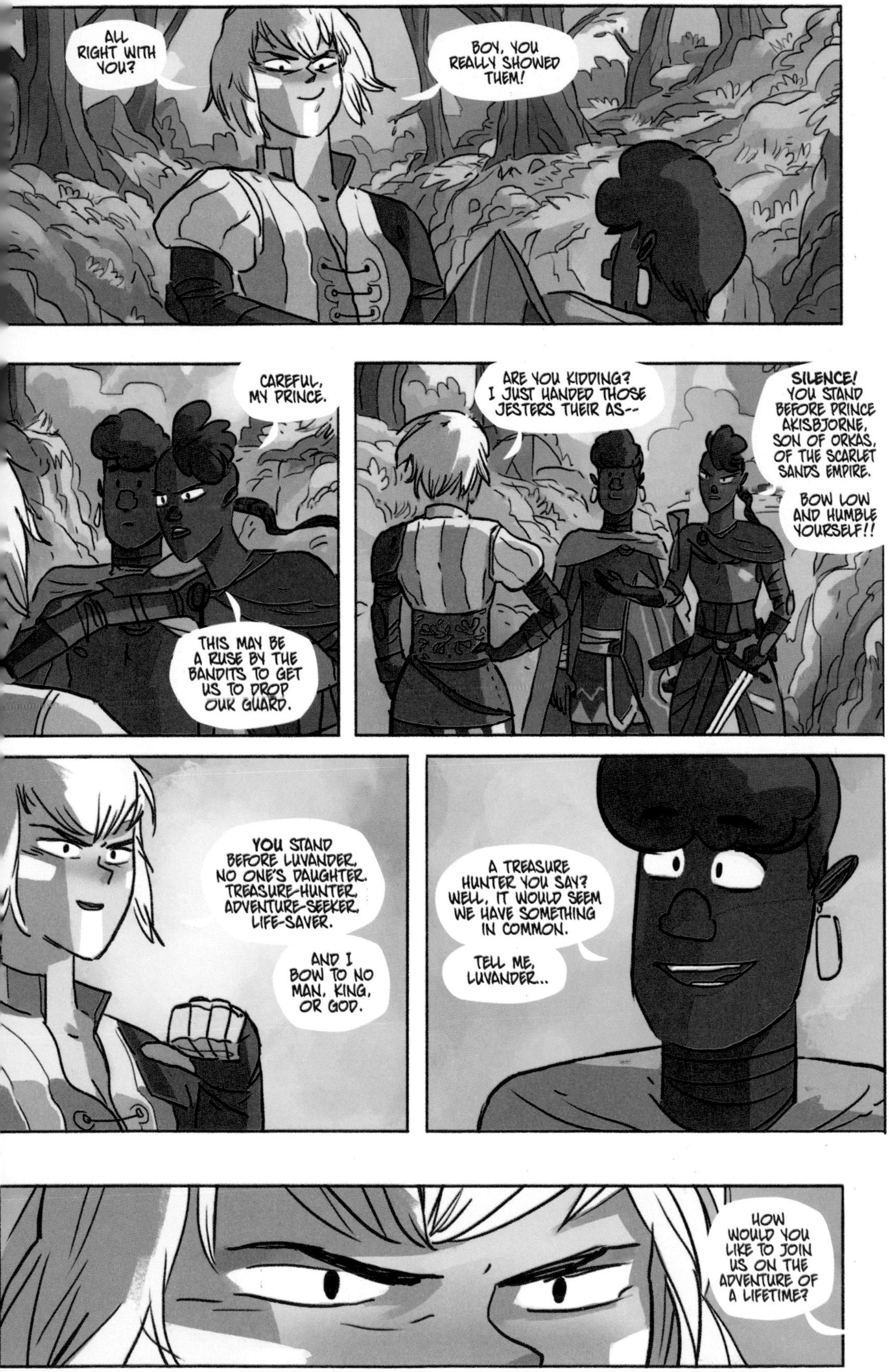
ALL RIGHT WITH YOU?
BOY, YOU REALLY SHOWED THEM!
CAREFUL, MY PRINCE.
THIS MAY BE A RUSE BY THE BANDITS TO GET US TO DROP OUR GUARD.
ARE YOU KIDDING? I JUST HANDED THOSE JESTERS THEIR AS--
SILENCE! YOU STAND BEFORE PRINCE AKISBJORNE, SON OF ORKAS, OF THE SCARLET SANDS EMPIRE.
BOW LOW AND HUMBLE YOURSELF!!
YOU STAND BEFORE LUVANDER, NO ONE'S DAUGHTER. TREASURE-HUNTER, ADVENTURE-SEEKER, LIFE-SAVER.
AND I BOW TO NO MAN, KING, OR GOD.
A TREASURE HUNTER YOU SAY? WELL, IT WOULD SEEM WE HAVE SOMETHING IN COMMON.
TELL ME, LUVANDER...
HOW WOULD YOU LIKE TO JOIN US ON THE ADVENTURE OF A LIFETIME?

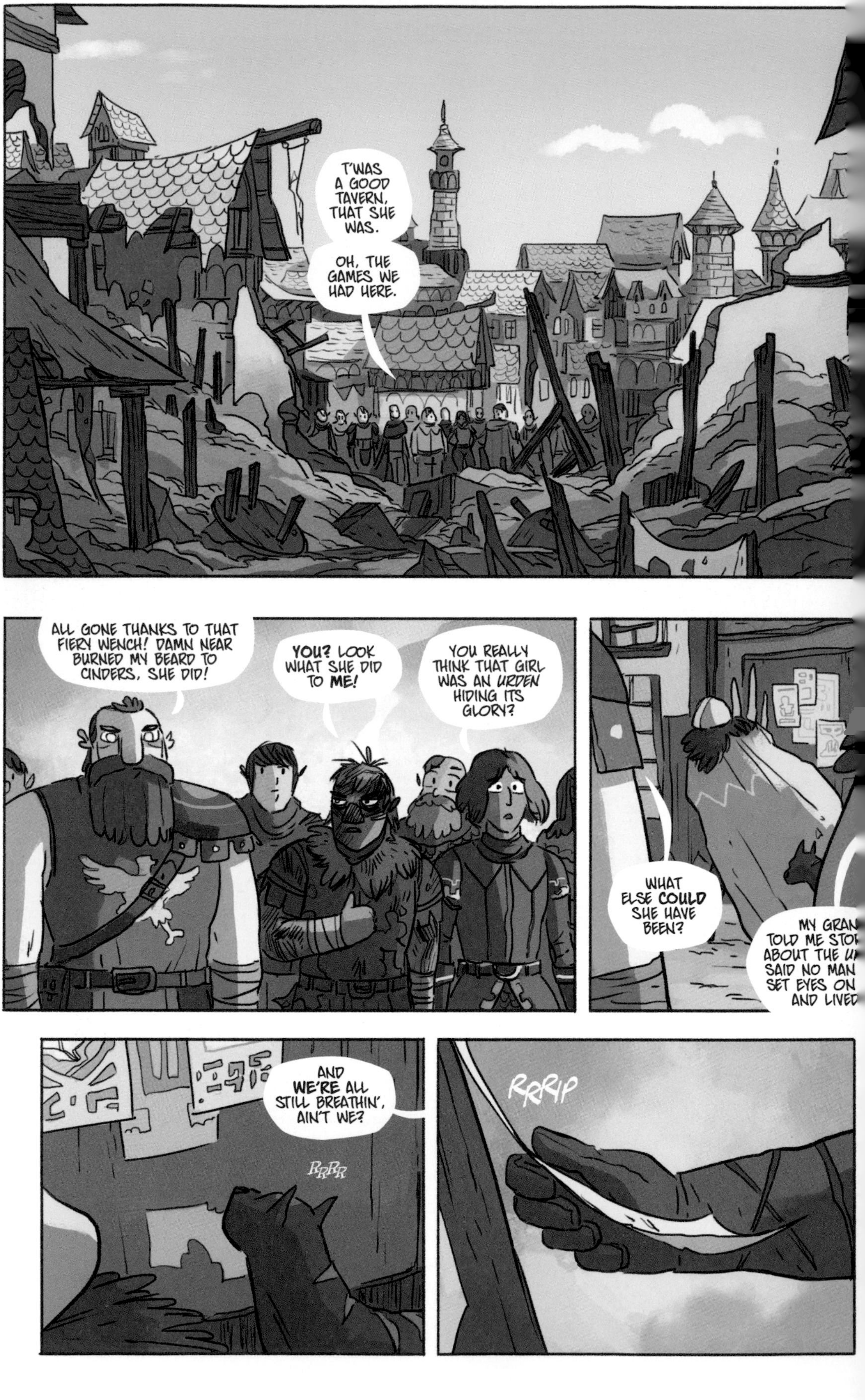
T'WAS A GOOD TAVERN, THAT SHE WAS.
OH, THE GAMES WE HAD HERE.
ALL GONE THANKS TO THAT FIERY WENCH! DAMN NEAR BURNED MY BEARD TO CINDERS, SHE DID!
YOU? LOOK WHAT SHE DID TO ME!
YOU REALLY THINK THAT GIRL WAS AN URDEN HIDING ITS GLORY?
WHAT ELSE COULD SHE HAVE BEEN?
AND WE'RE ALL STILL BREATHIN', AIN'T WE?
RRRR
RRRIP

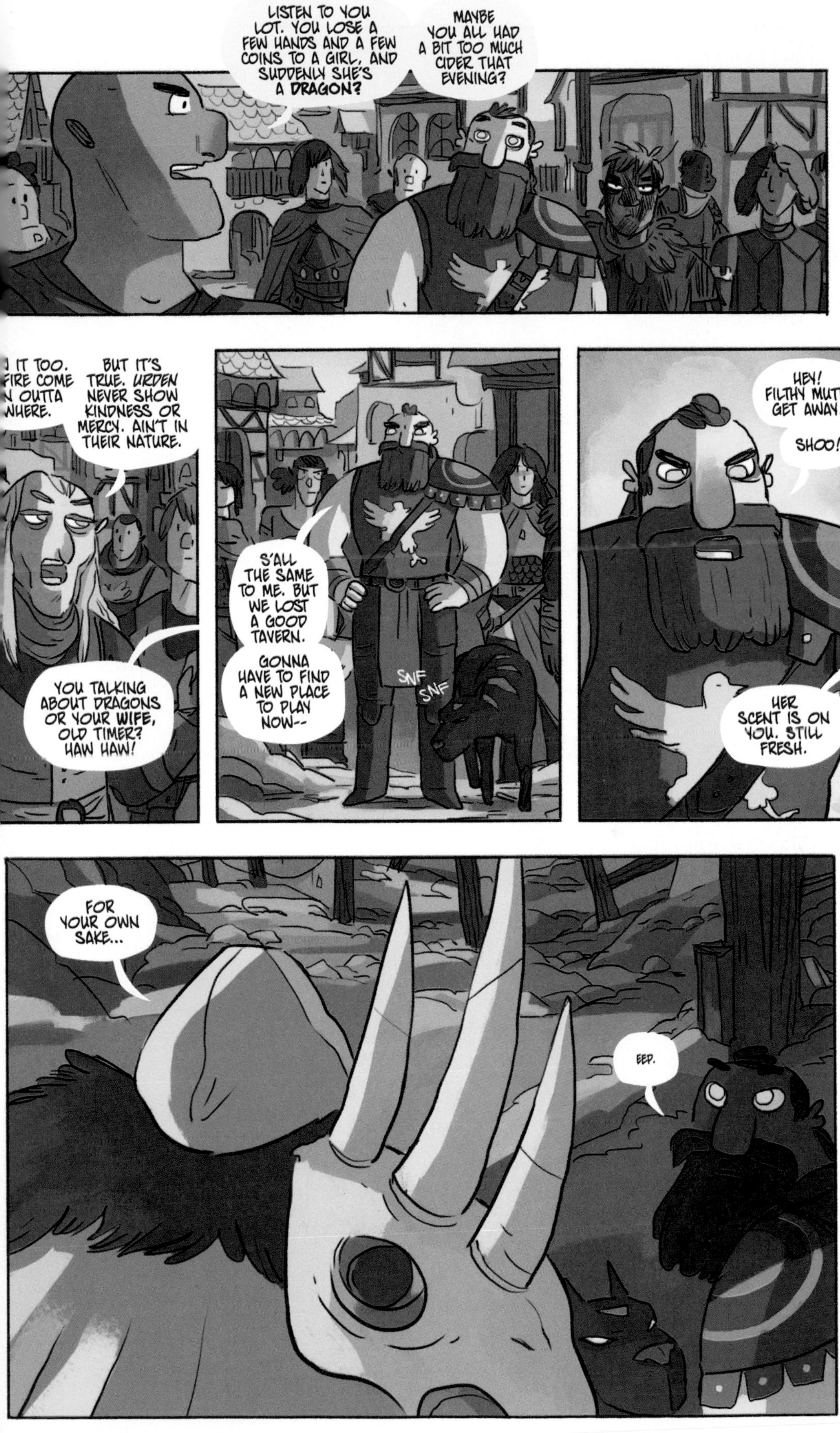
LISTEN TO YOU LOT. YOU LOSE A FEW HANDS AND A FEW COINS TO A GIRL, AND SUDDENLY SHE'S A **DRAGON**?
MAYBE YOU ALL HAD A BIT TOO MUCH CIDER THAT EVENING?
IT TOO. FIRE COME OUTTA
BUT IT'S TRUE. *URDEN* NEVER SHOW KINDNESS OR MERCY. AIN'T IN THEIR NATURE.
YOU TALKING ABOUT DRAGONS OR YOUR **WIFE**, OLD TIMER? HAW HAW!
S'ALL THE SAME TO ME. BUT WE LOST A GOOD TAVERN.
GONNA HAVE TO FIND A NEW PLACE TO PLAY NOW--
SNF
SNF
HEY! FILTHY MUTT, GET AWAY.
SHOO!
HER SCENT IS ON YOU. STILL FRESH.
FOR YOUR OWN SAKE...
EEP.

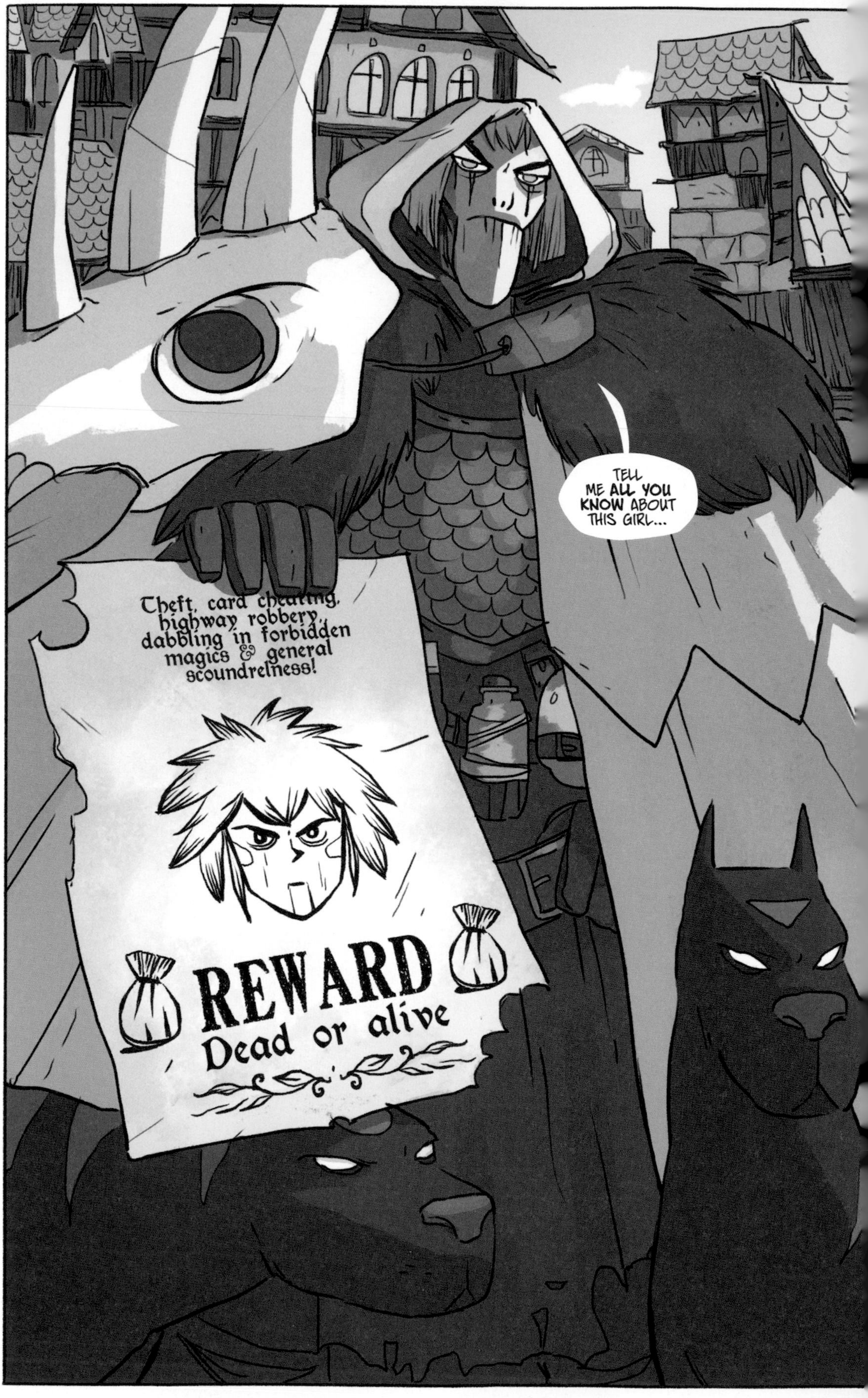
TELL ME ALL YOU KNOW ABOUT THIS GIRL...
Theft, card cheating, highway robbery, dabbling in forbidden magics & general scoundrelness!
REWARD
Dead or alive

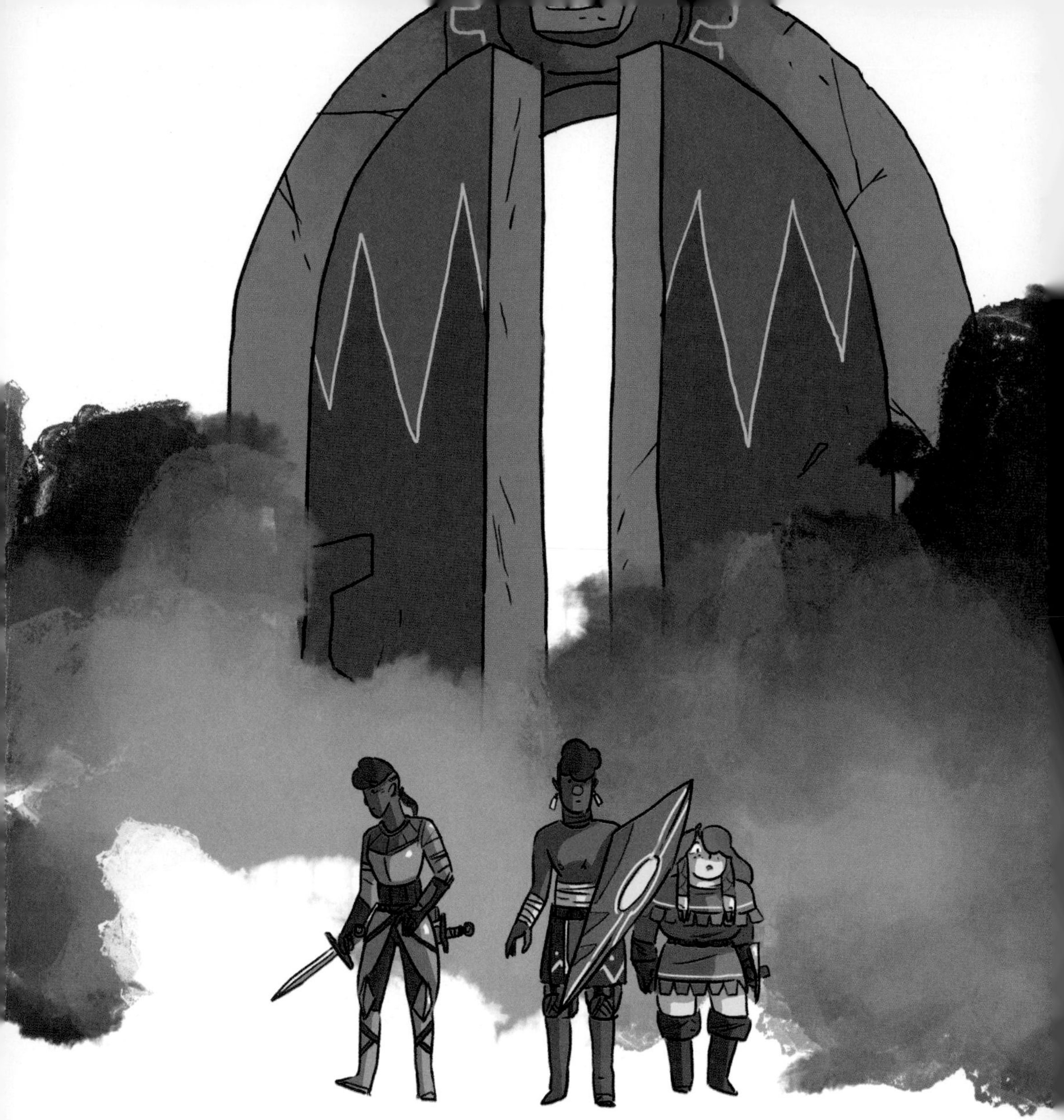

2

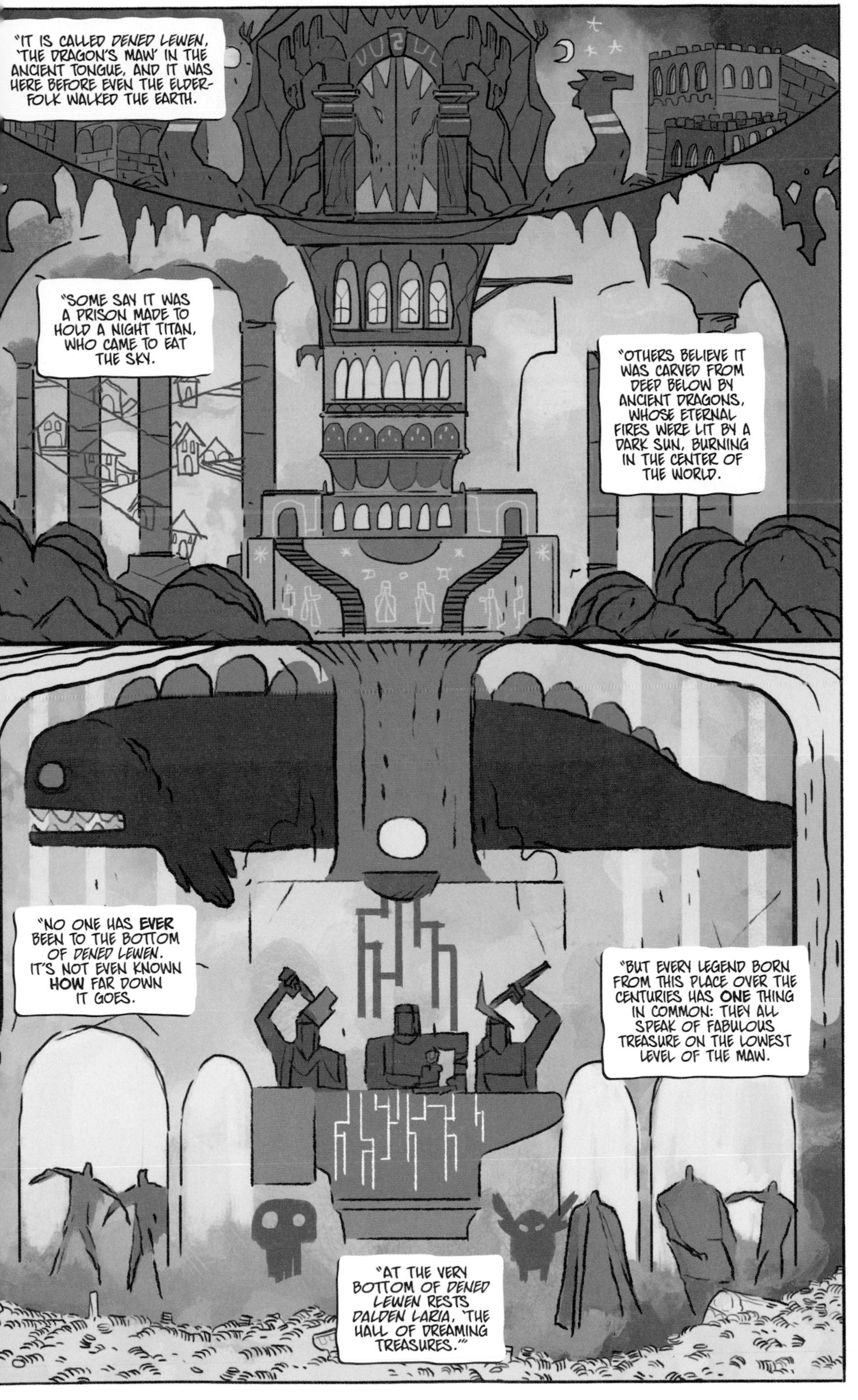
"IT IS CALLED *DENED LEWEN*, 'THE DRAGON'S MAW' IN THE ANCIENT TONGUE, AND IT WAS HERE BEFORE EVEN THE ELDER-FOLK WALKED THE EARTH.
"SOME SAY IT WAS A PRISON MADE TO HOLD A NIGHT TITAN, WHO CAME TO EAT THE SKY.
"OTHERS BELIEVE IT WAS CARVED FROM DEEP BELOW BY ANCIENT DRAGONS, WHOSE ETERNAL FIRES WERE LIT BY A DARK SUN, BURNING IN THE CENTER OF THE WORLD.
"NO ONE HAS **EVER** BEEN TO THE BOTTOM OF *DENED LEWEN*. IT'S NOT EVEN KNOWN **HOW** FAR DOWN IT GOES.
"BUT EVERY LEGEND BORN FROM THIS PLACE OVER THE CENTURIES HAS **ONE** THING IN COMMON: THEY ALL SPEAK OF FABULOUS TREASURE ON THE LOWEST LEVEL OF THE MAW.
"AT THE VERY BOTTOM OF *DENED LEWEN* RESTS *DALDEN LARIA*, 'THE HALL OF DREAMING TREASURES.'"

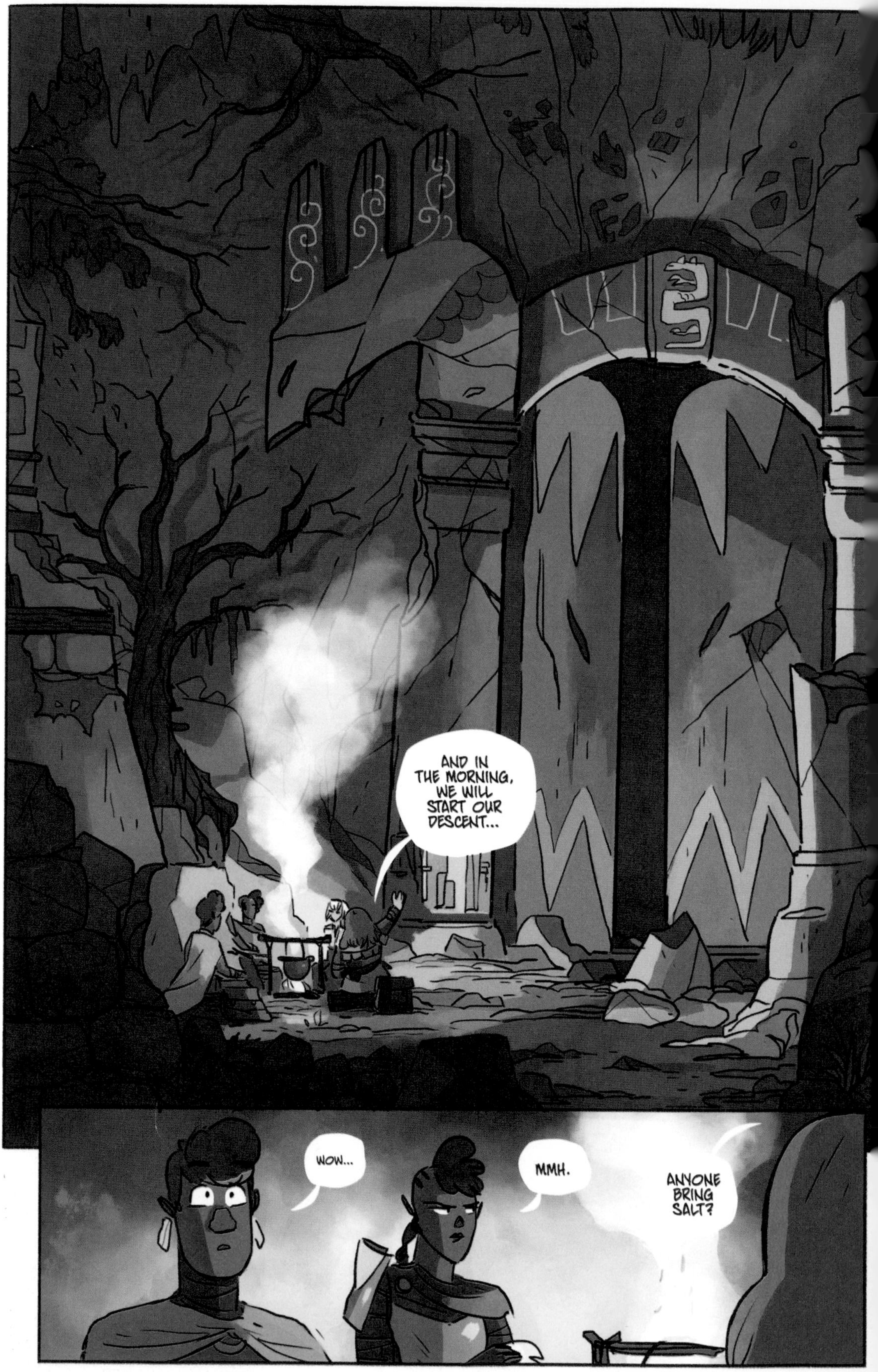
AND IN THE MORNING, WE WILL START OUR DESCENT...
WOW...
MMH.
ANYONE BRING SALT?

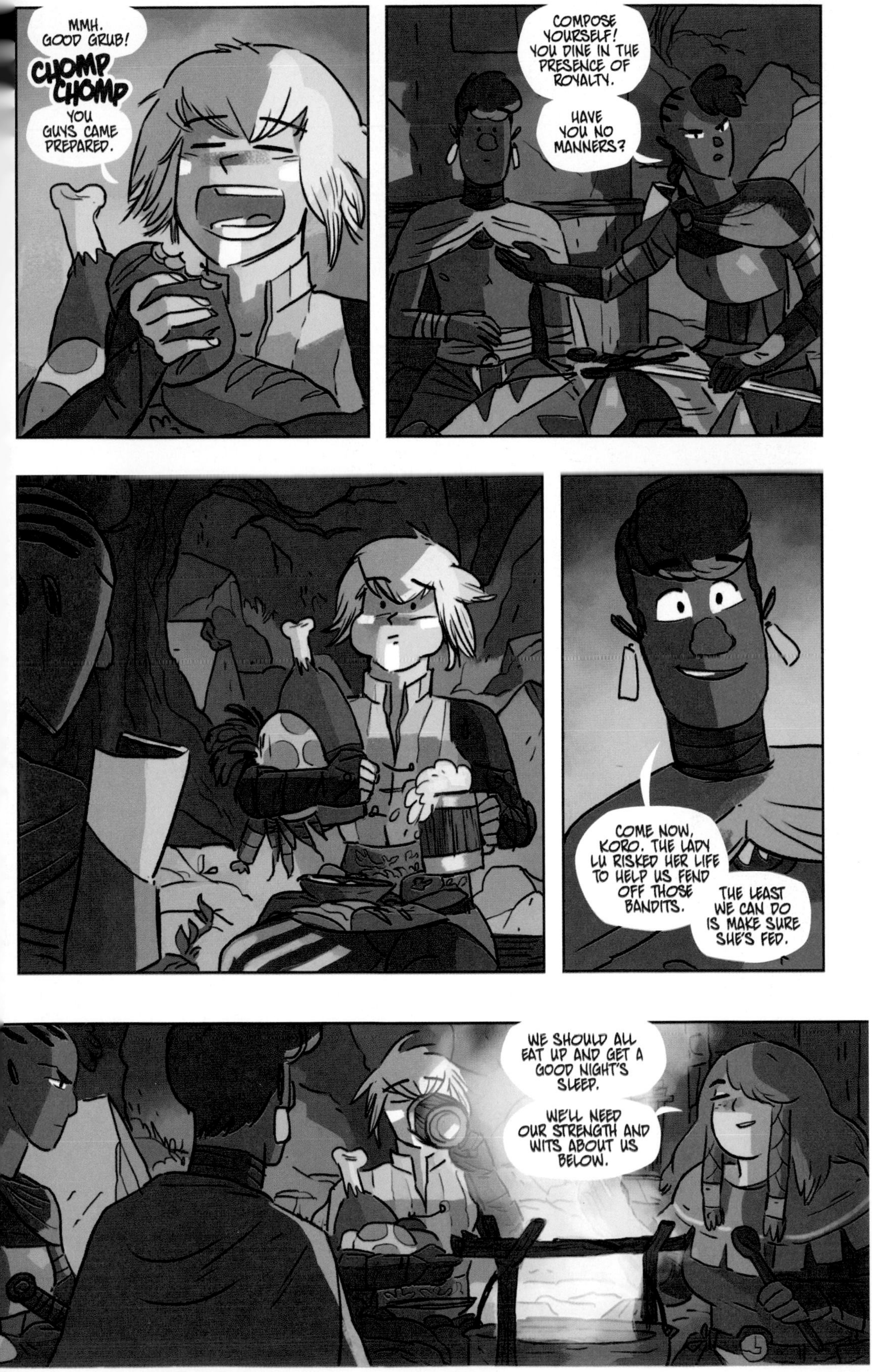
MMH. GOOD GRUB!
CHOMP CHOMP
YOU GUYS CAME PREPARED.
COMPOSE YOURSELF! YOU DINE IN THE PRESENCE OF ROYALTY.
HAVE YOU NO MANNERS?
COME NOW, KORO. THE LADY LU RISKED HER LIFE TO HELP US FEND OFF THOSE BANDITS.
THE LEAST WE CAN DO IS MAKE SURE SHE'S FED.
WE SHOULD ALL EAT UP AND GET A GOOD NIGHT'S SLEEP.
WE'LL NEED OUR STRENGTH AND WITS ABOUT US BELOW.

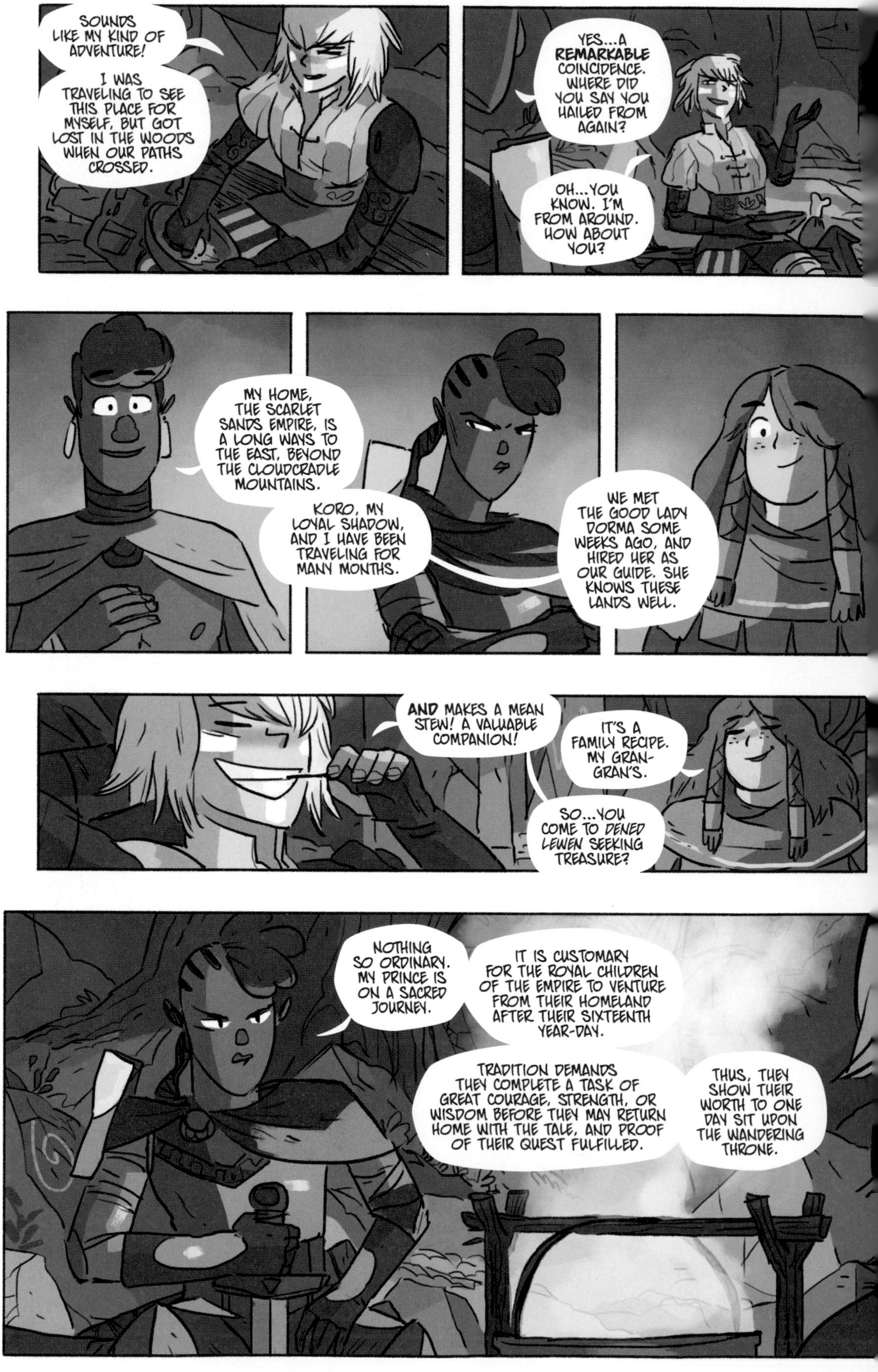

SOUNDS LIKE MY KIND OF ADVENTURE!
I WAS TRAVELING TO SEE THIS PLACE FOR MYSELF, BUT GOT LOST IN THE WOODS WHEN OUR PATHS CROSSED.
YES...A **REMARKABLE** COINCIDENCE. WHERE DID YOU SAY YOU HAILED FROM AGAIN?
OH...YOU KNOW. I'M FROM AROUND. HOW ABOUT YOU?
MY HOME, THE SCARLET SANDS EMPIRE, IS A LONG WAYS TO THE EAST, BEYOND THE CLOUDCRADLE MOUNTAINS.
KORO, MY LOYAL SHADOW, AND I HAVE BEEN TRAVELING FOR MANY MONTHS.
WE MET THE GOOD LADY DORMA SOME WEEKS AGO, AND HIRED HER AS OUR GUIDE. SHE KNOWS THESE LANDS WELL.
AND MAKES A MEAN STEW! A VALUABLE COMPANION!
IT'S A FAMILY RECIPE. MY GRAN-GRAN'S.
SO...YOU COME TO DENED LEWEN SEEKING TREASURE?
NOTHING SO ORDINARY. MY PRINCE IS ON A SACRED JOURNEY.
IT IS CUSTOMARY FOR THE ROYAL CHILDREN OF THE EMPIRE TO VENTURE FROM THEIR HOMELAND AFTER THEIR SIXTEENTH YEAR-DAY.
TRADITION DEMANDS THEY COMPLETE A TASK OF GREAT COURAGE, STRENGTH, OR WISDOM BEFORE THEY MAY RETURN HOME WITH THE TALE, AND PROOF OF THEIR QUEST FULFILLED.
THUS, THEY SHOW THEIR WORTH TO ONE DAY SIT UPON THE WANDERING THRONE.

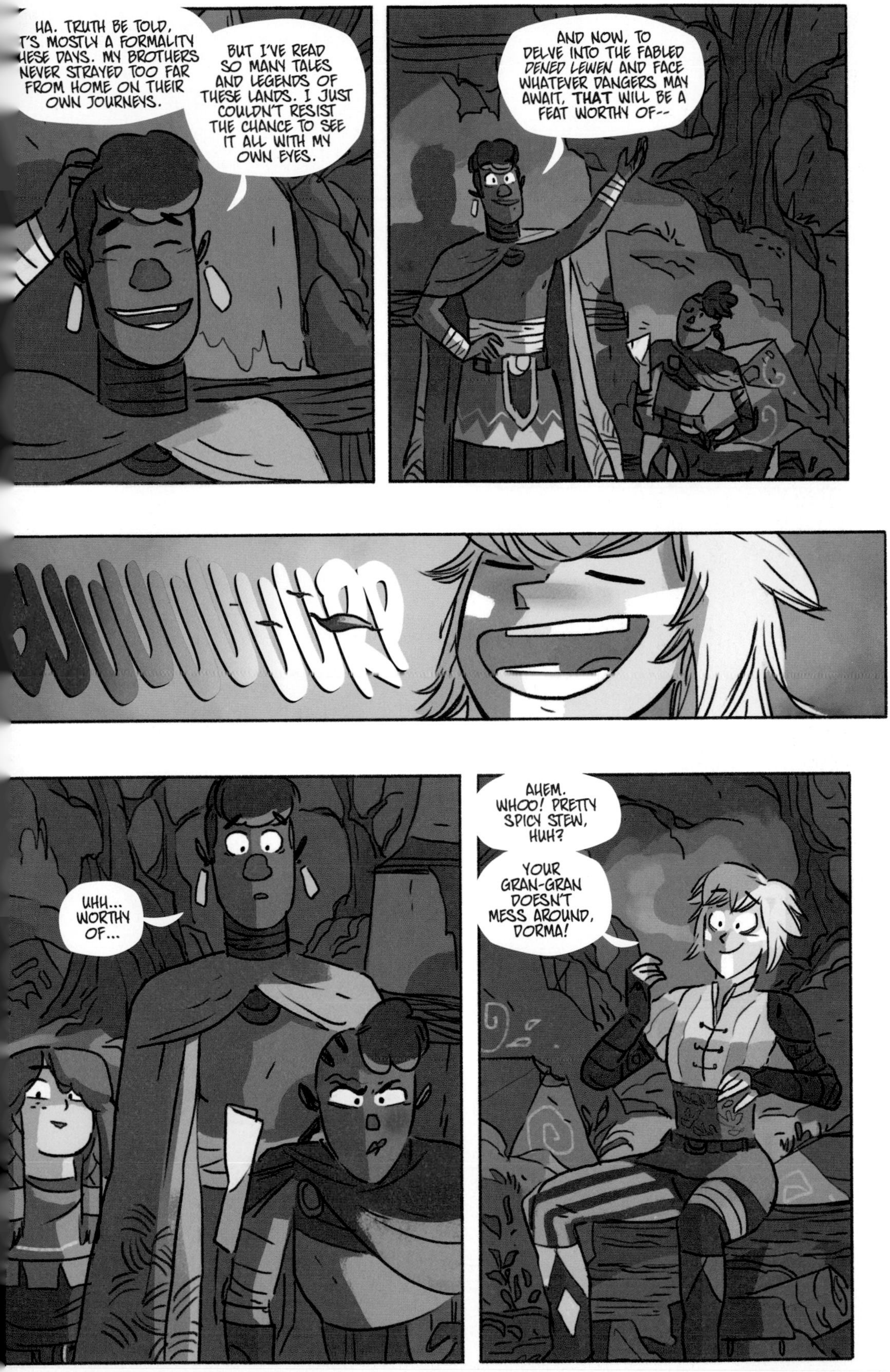
HA. TRUTH BE TOLD, IT'S MOSTLY A FORMALITY THESE DAYS. MY BROTHERS NEVER STRAYED TOO FAR FROM HOME ON THEIR OWN JOURNEYS.
BUT I'VE READ SO MANY TALES AND LEGENDS OF THESE LANDS. I JUST COULDN'T RESIST THE CHANCE TO SEE IT ALL WITH MY OWN EYES.
AND NOW, TO DELVE INTO THE FABLED DENED LEWEN AND FACE WHATEVER DANGERS MAY AWAIT, THAT WILL BE A FEAT WORTHY OF--
SHUUUUUURP
UHH... WORTHY OF...
AHEM. WHOO! PRETTY SPICY STEW, HUH?
YOUR GRAN-GRAN DOESN'T MESS AROUND, DORMA!

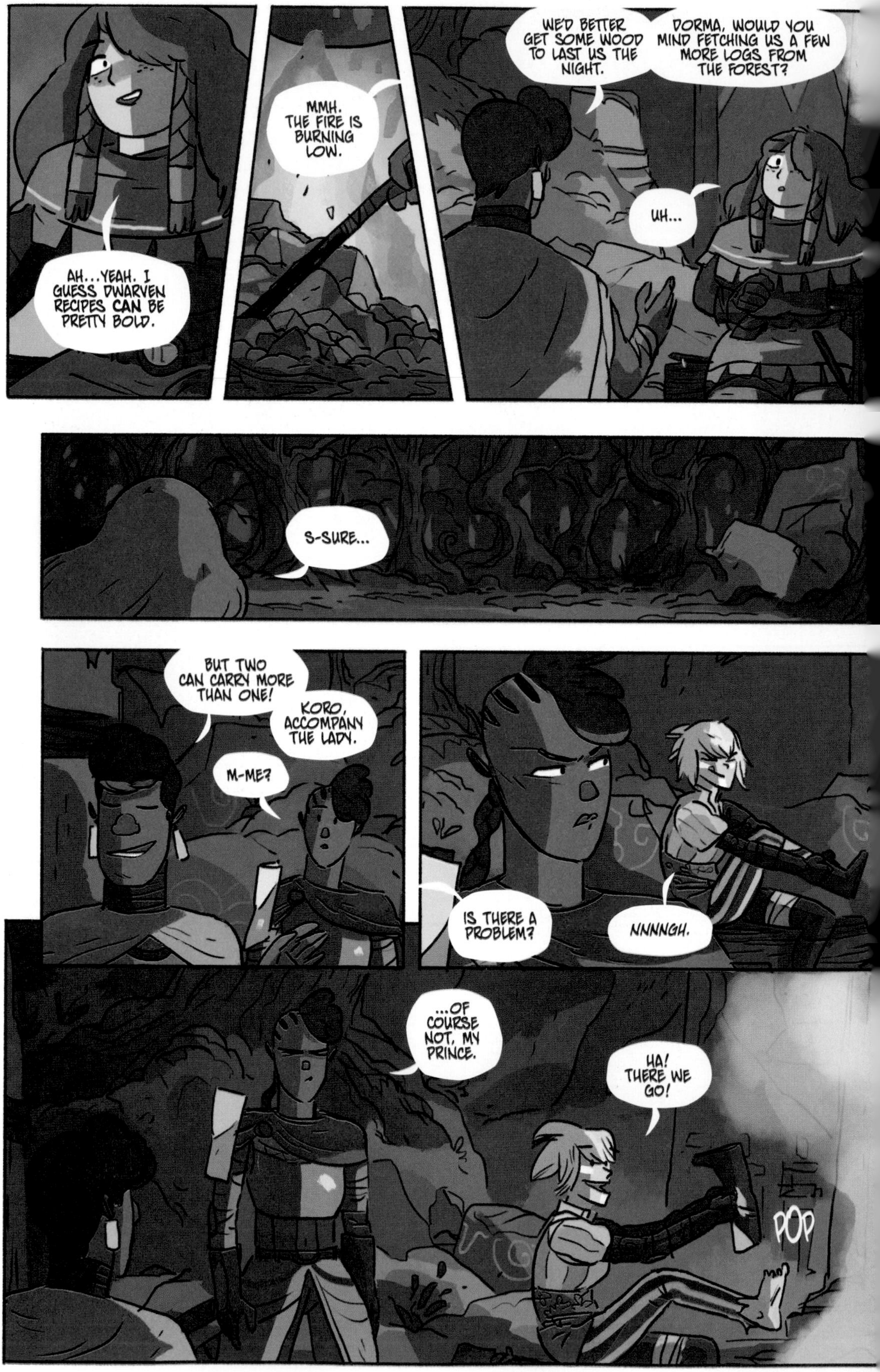

AH...YEAH. I GUESS DWARVEN RECIPES CAN BE PRETTY BOLD.
MMH. THE FIRE IS BURNING LOW.
WE'D BETTER GET SOME WOOD TO LAST US THE NIGHT.
DORMA, WOULD YOU MIND FETCHING US A FEW MORE LOGS FROM THE FOREST?
UH...
S-SURE...
BUT TWO CAN CARRY MORE THAN ONE!
KORO, ACCOMPANY THE LADY.
M-ME?
IS THERE A PROBLEM?
NNNNGH.
...OF COURSE NOT, MY PRINCE.
HA! THERE WE GO!
POP

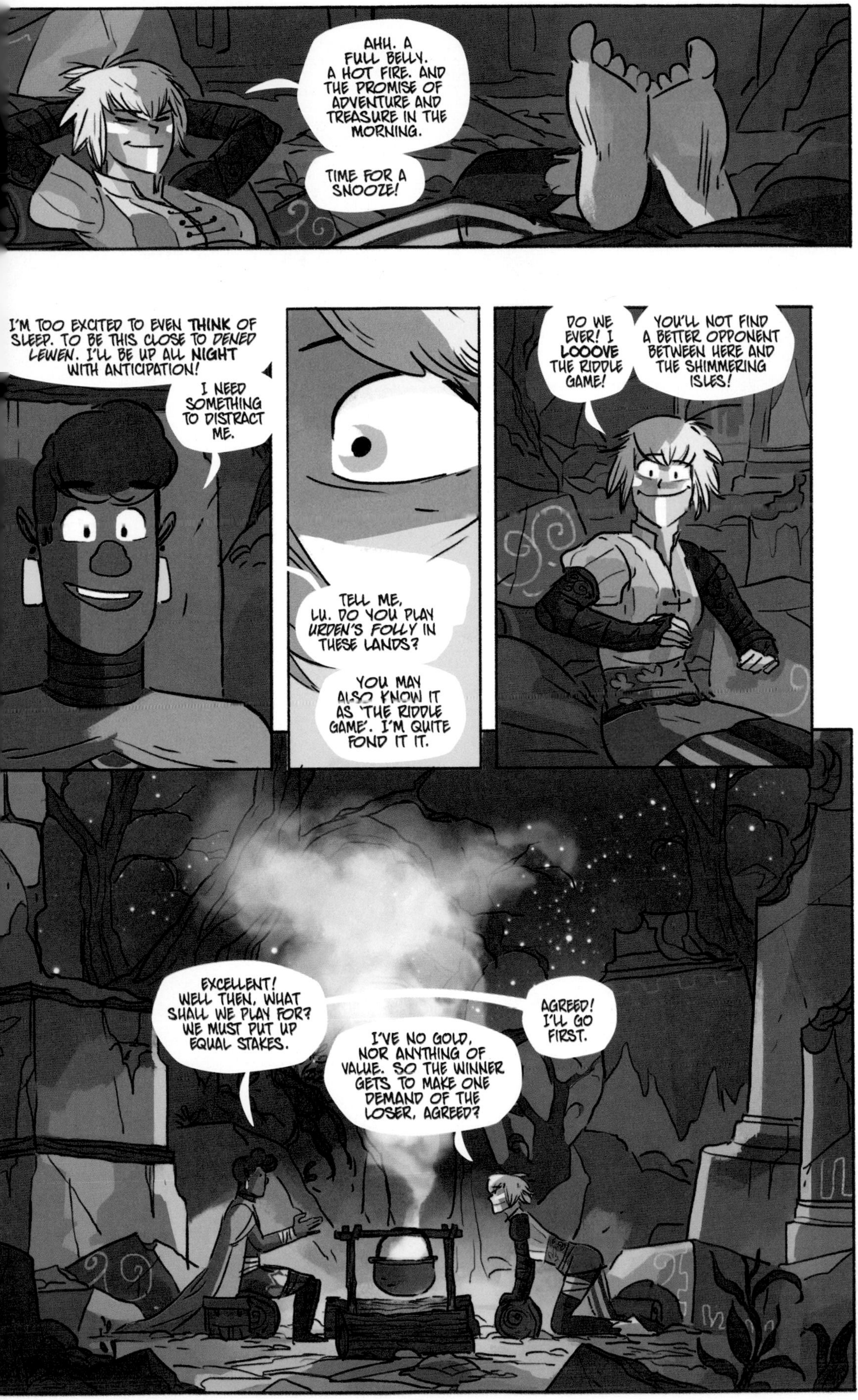
AHH. A FULL BELLY. A HOT FIRE. AND THE PROMISE OF ADVENTURE AND TREASURE IN THE MORNING.
TIME FOR A SNOOZE!
I'M TOO EXCITED TO EVEN THINK OF SLEEP. TO BE THIS CLOSE TO DENED LEWEN. I'LL BE UP ALL NIGHT WITH ANTICIPATION!
I NEED SOMETHING TO DISTRACT ME.
TELL ME, LU. DO YOU PLAY URDEN'S FOLLY IN THESE LANDS?
YOU MAY ALSO KNOW IT AS 'THE RIDDLE GAME'. I'M QUITE FOND IT IT.
DO WE EVER! I LOOOVE THE RIDDLE GAME!
YOU'LL NOT FIND A BETTER OPPONENT BETWEEN HERE AND THE SHIMMERING ISLES!
EXCELLENT! WELL THEN, WHAT SHALL WE PLAY FOR? WE MUST PUT UP EQUAL STAKES.
I'VE NO GOLD, NOR ANYTHING OF VALUE. SO THE WINNER GETS TO MAKE ONE DEMAND OF THE LOSER, AGREED?
AGREED! I'LL GO FIRST.

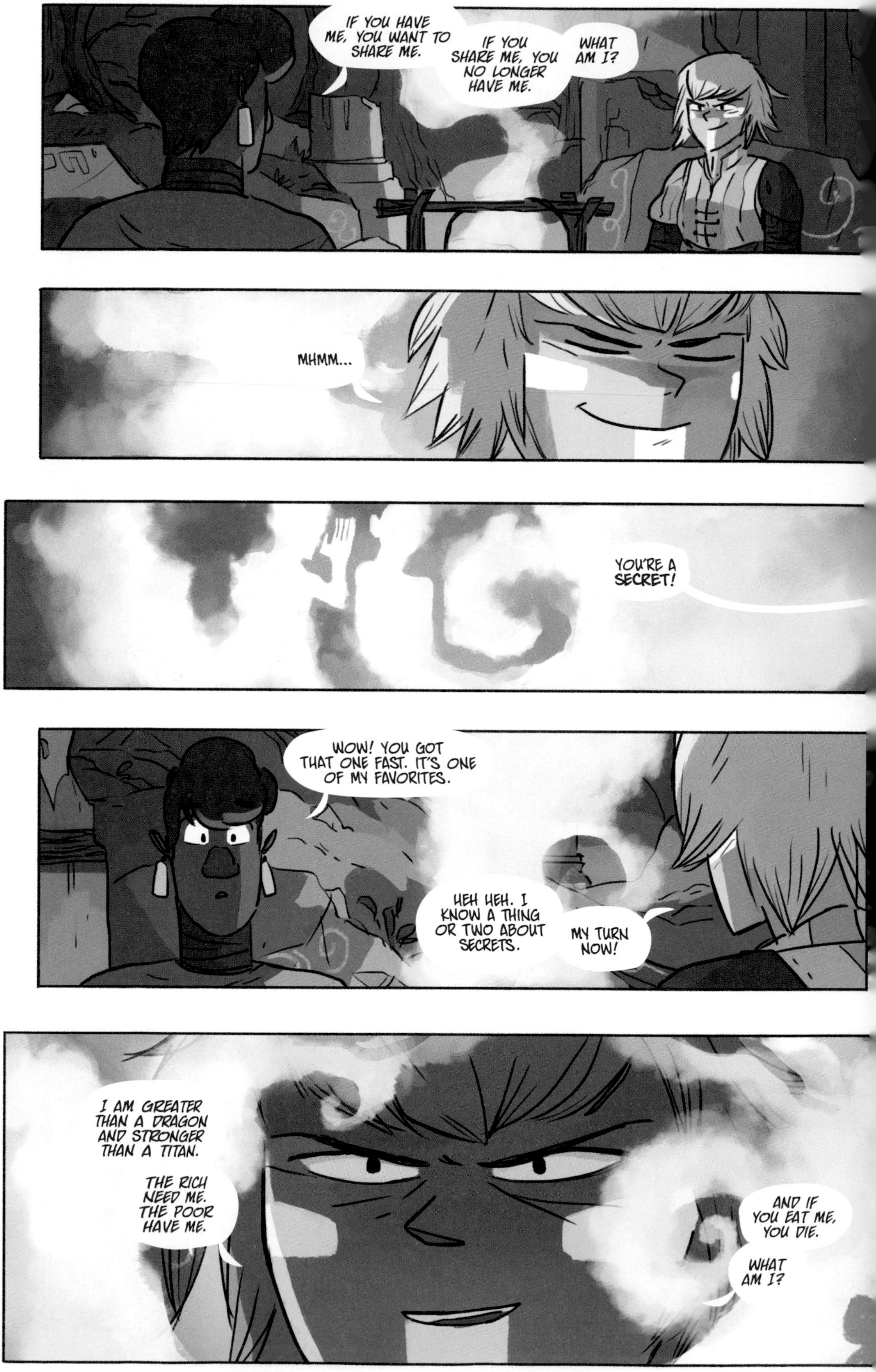
IF YOU HAVE ME, YOU WANT TO SHARE ME.
IF YOU SHARE ME, YOU NO LONGER HAVE ME.
WHAT AM I?
MHMM...
YOU'RE A SECRET!
WOW! YOU GOT THAT ONE FAST. IT'S ONE OF MY FAVORITES.
HEH HEH. I KNOW A THING OR TWO ABOUT SECRETS.
MY TURN NOW!
I AM GREATER THAN A DRAGON AND STRONGER THAN A TITAN.
THE RICH NEED ME. THE POOR HAVE ME.
AND IF YOU EAT ME, YOU DIE.
WHAT AM I?

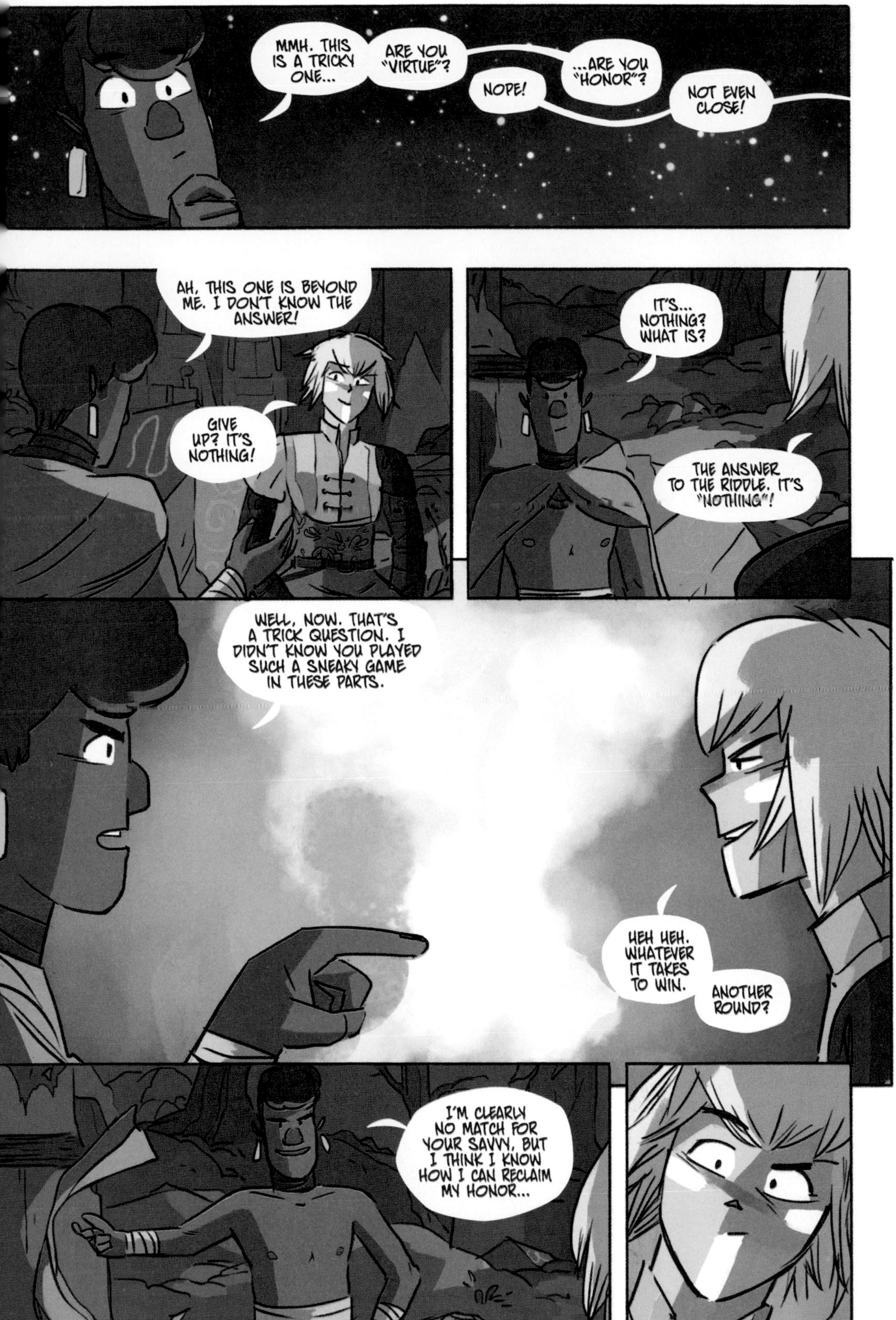
MMH. THIS IS A TRICKY ONE...
ARE YOU "VIRTUE"?
NOPE!
...ARE YOU "HONOR"?
NOT EVEN CLOSE!
AH, THIS ONE IS BEYOND ME. I DON'T KNOW THE ANSWER!
GIVE UP? IT'S NOTHING!
IT'S... NOTHING? WHAT IS?
THE ANSWER TO THE RIDDLE. IT'S "NOTHING"!
WELL, NOW. THAT'S A TRICK QUESTION. I DIDN'T KNOW YOU PLAYED SUCH A SNEAKY GAME IN THESE PARTS.
HEH HEH. WHATEVER IT TAKES TO WIN.
ANOTHER ROUND?
I'M CLEARLY NO MATCH FOR YOUR SAVVY, BUT I THINK I KNOW HOW I CAN RECLAIM MY HONOR...

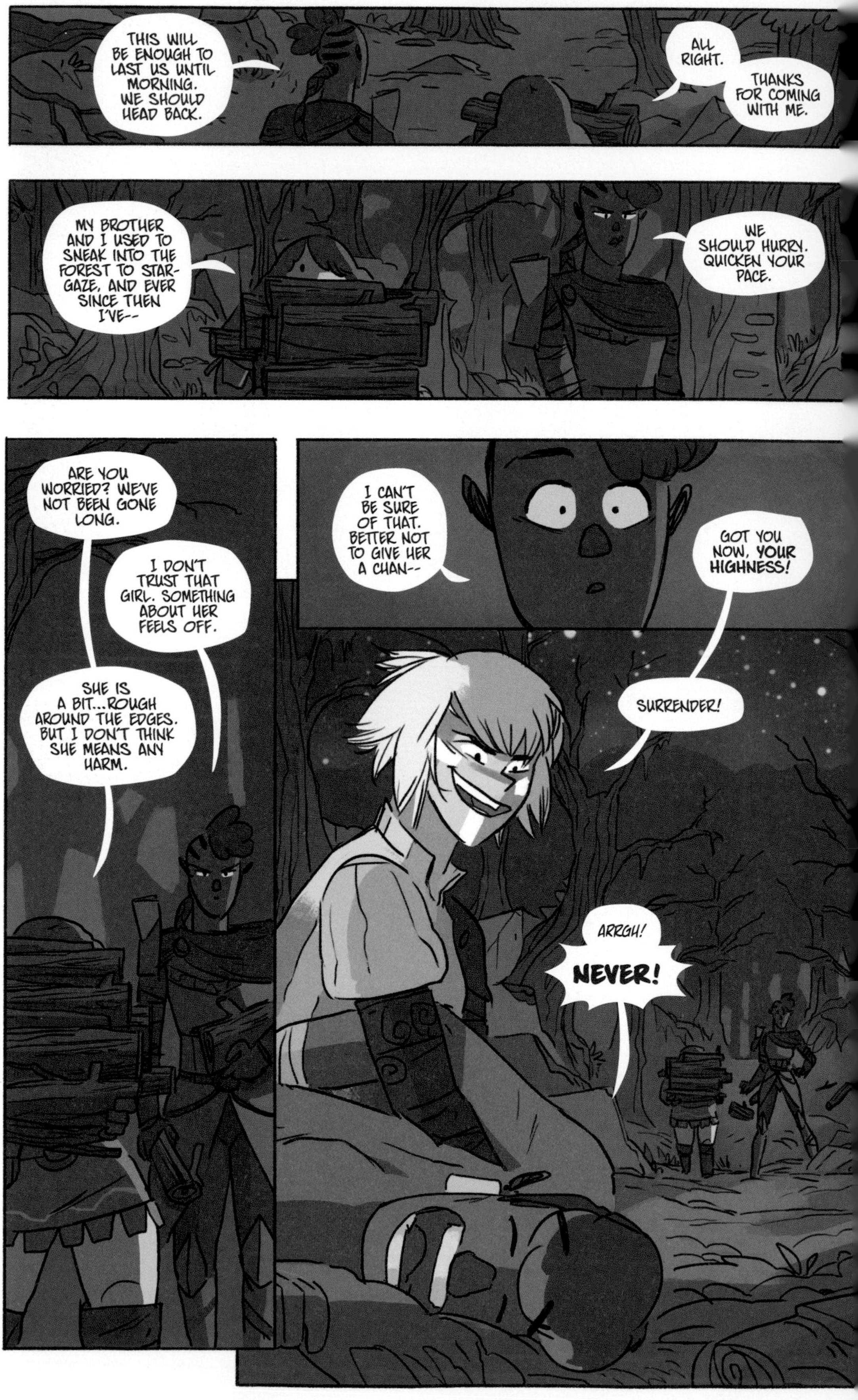
THIS WILL BE ENOUGH TO LAST US UNTIL MORNING. WE SHOULD HEAD BACK.
ALL RIGHT.
THANKS FOR COMING WITH ME.
MY BROTHER AND I USED TO SNEAK INTO THE FOREST TO STAR-GAZE, AND EVER SINCE THEN I'VE--
WE SHOULD HURRY. QUICKEN YOUR PACE.
ARE YOU WORRIED? WE'VE NOT BEEN GONE LONG.
I DON'T TRUST THAT GIRL. SOMETHING ABOUT HER FEELS OFF.
SHE IS A BIT...ROUGH AROUND THE EDGES. BUT I DON'T THINK SHE MEANS ANY HARM.
I CAN'T BE SURE OF THAT. BETTER NOT TO GIVE HER A CHAN--
GOT YOU NOW, YOUR HIGHNESS!
SURRENDER!
ARRGH!
NEVER!

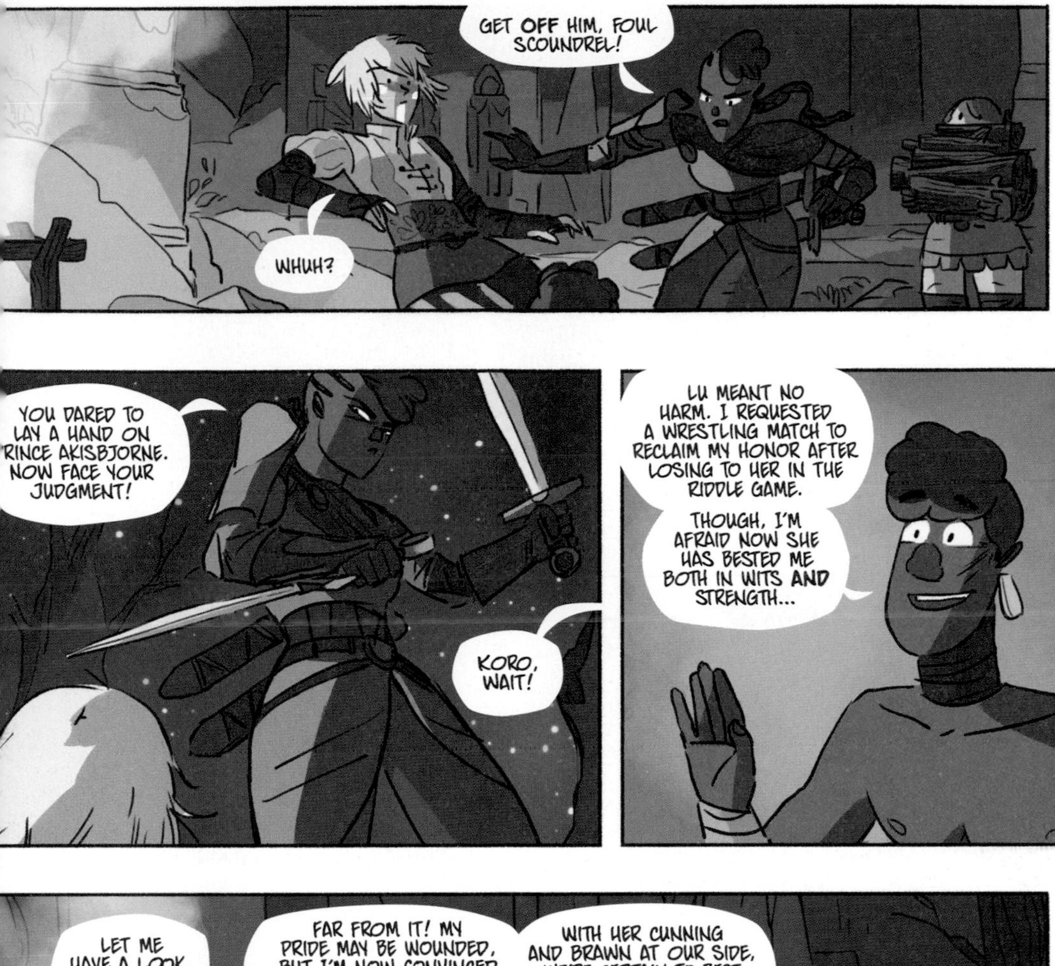
GET OFF HIM, FOUL SCOUNDREL!
WHUH?
YOU DARED TO LAY A HAND ON RINCE AKISBJORNE. NOW FACE YOUR JUDGMENT!
KORO, WAIT!
LU MEANT NO HARM. I REQUESTED A WRESTLING MATCH TO RECLAIM MY HONOR AFTER LOSING TO HER IN THE RIDDLE GAME.
THOUGH, I'M AFRAID NOW SHE HAS BESTED ME BOTH IN WITS AND STRENGTH...
LET ME HAVE A LOOK. ARE YOU HURT?
FAR FROM IT! MY PRIDE MAY BE WOUNDED, BUT I'M NOW CONVINCED THAT FATE HAD US CROSS PATHS WITH LU.
WITH HER CUNNING AND BRAWN AT OUR SIDE, WE'RE CERTAIN TO BEST ANY DANGER THAT MAY LURK BELOW.
I'M SO BRIMMING WITH CONFIDENCE, I DARESAY WE MAY EVEN SLAY A DRAGON!
UH... WHAT'S THIS NOW?

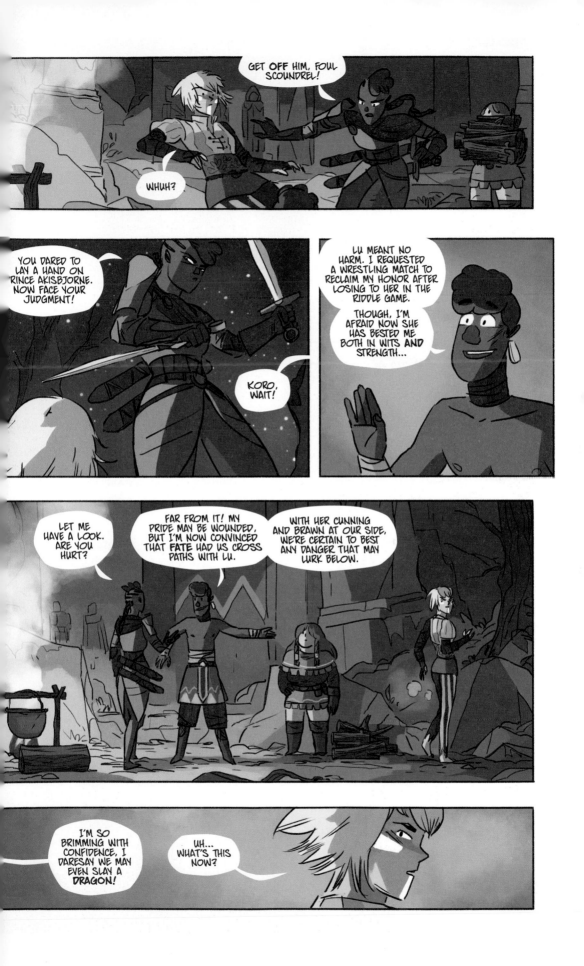

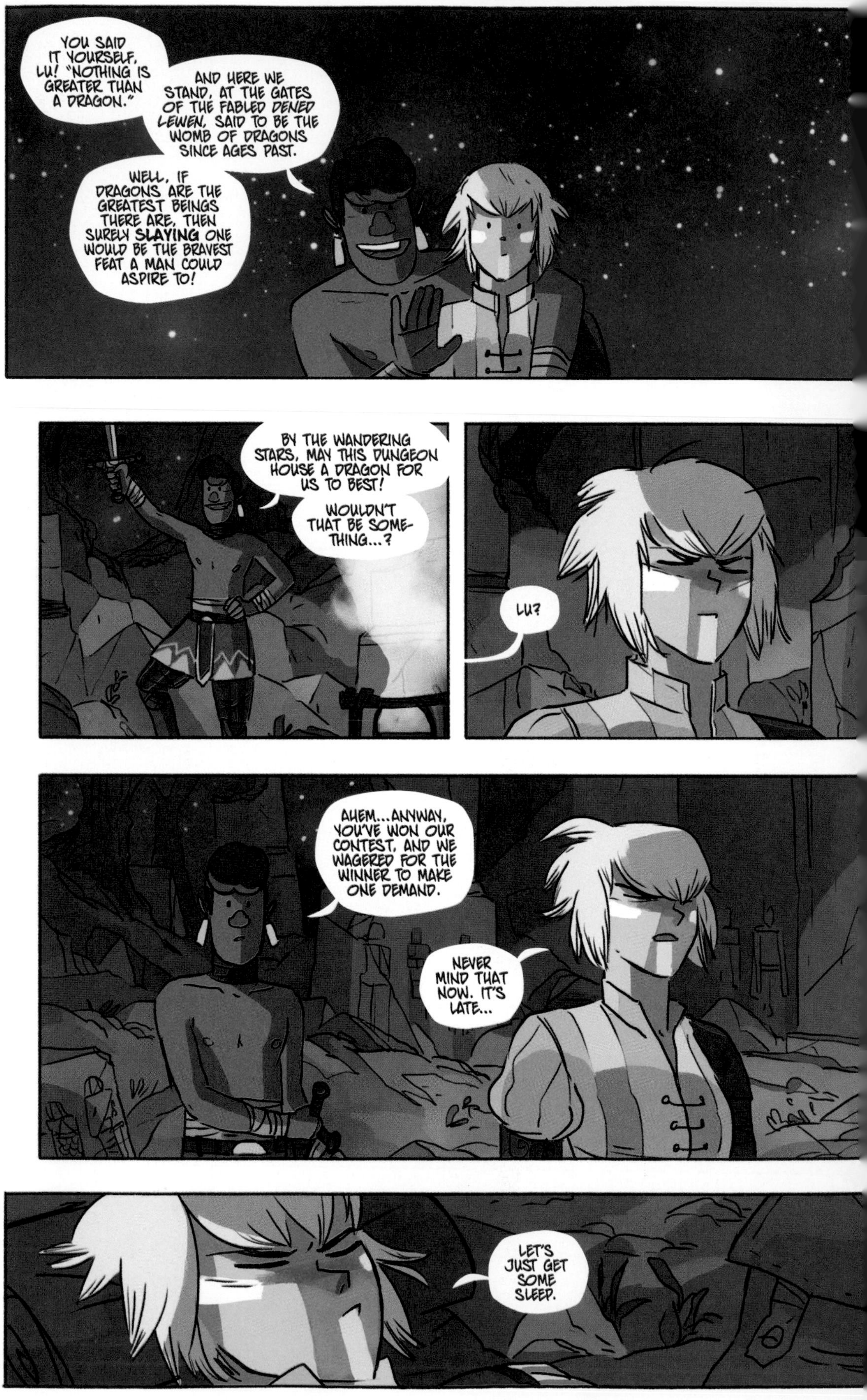
YOU SAID IT YOURSELF, LU! "NOTHING IS GREATER THAN A DRAGON."
AND HERE WE STAND, AT THE GATES OF THE FABLED DENED LEWEN, SAID TO BE THE WOMB OF DRAGONS SINCE AGES PAST.
WELL, IF DRAGONS ARE THE GREATEST BEINGS THERE ARE, THEN SURELY SLAYING ONE WOULD BE THE BRAVEST FEAT A MAN COULD ASPIRE TO!
BY THE WANDERING STARS, MAY THIS DUNGEON HOUSE A DRAGON FOR US TO BEST!
WOULDN'T THAT BE SOME-THING...?
LU?
AHEM...ANYWAY, YOU'VE WON OUR CONTEST, AND WE WAGERED FOR THE WINNER TO MAKE ONE DEMAND.
NEVER MIND THAT NOW. IT'S LATE...
LET'S JUST GET SOME SLEEP.

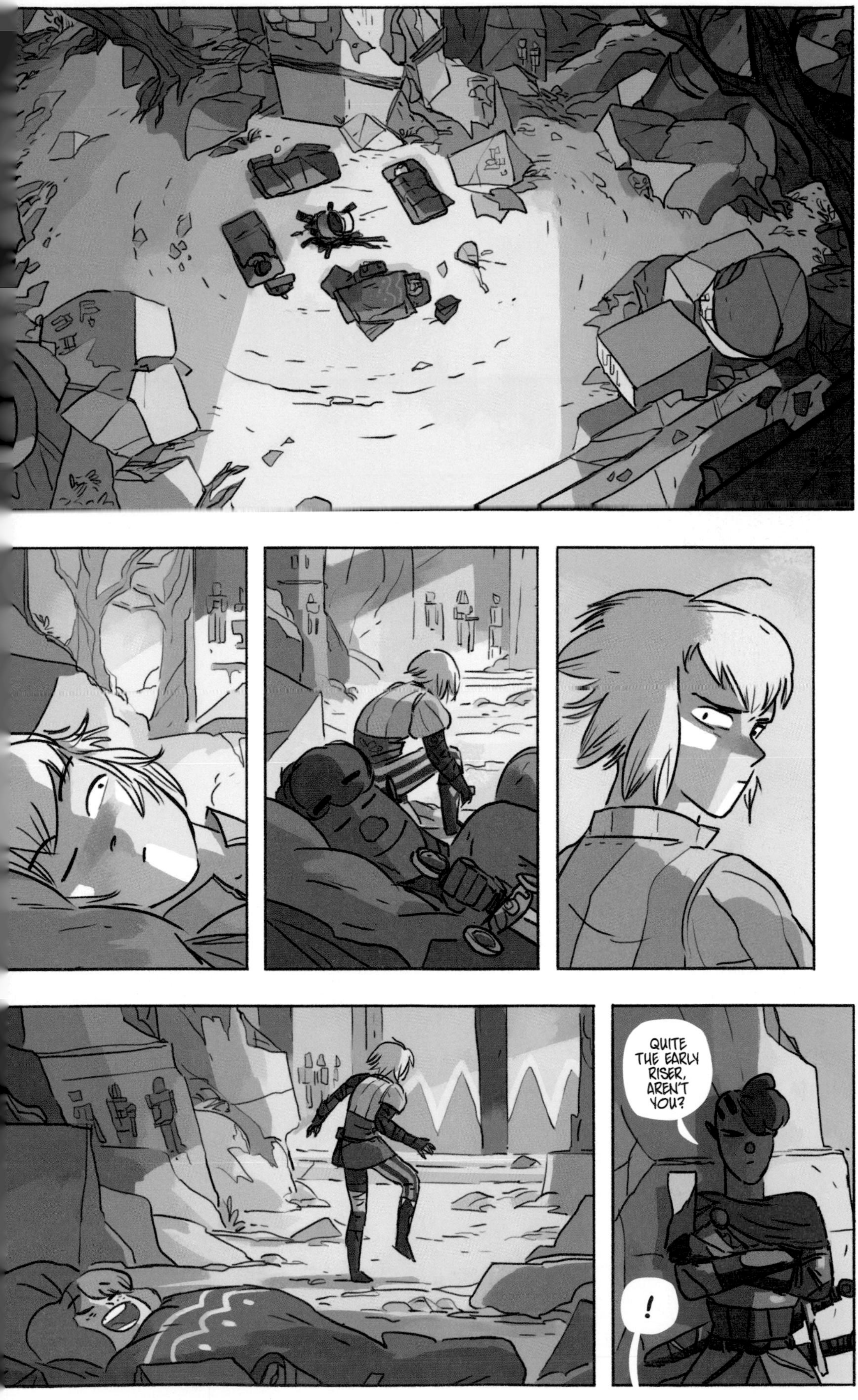
QUITE THE EARLY RISER, AREN'T YOU?
!

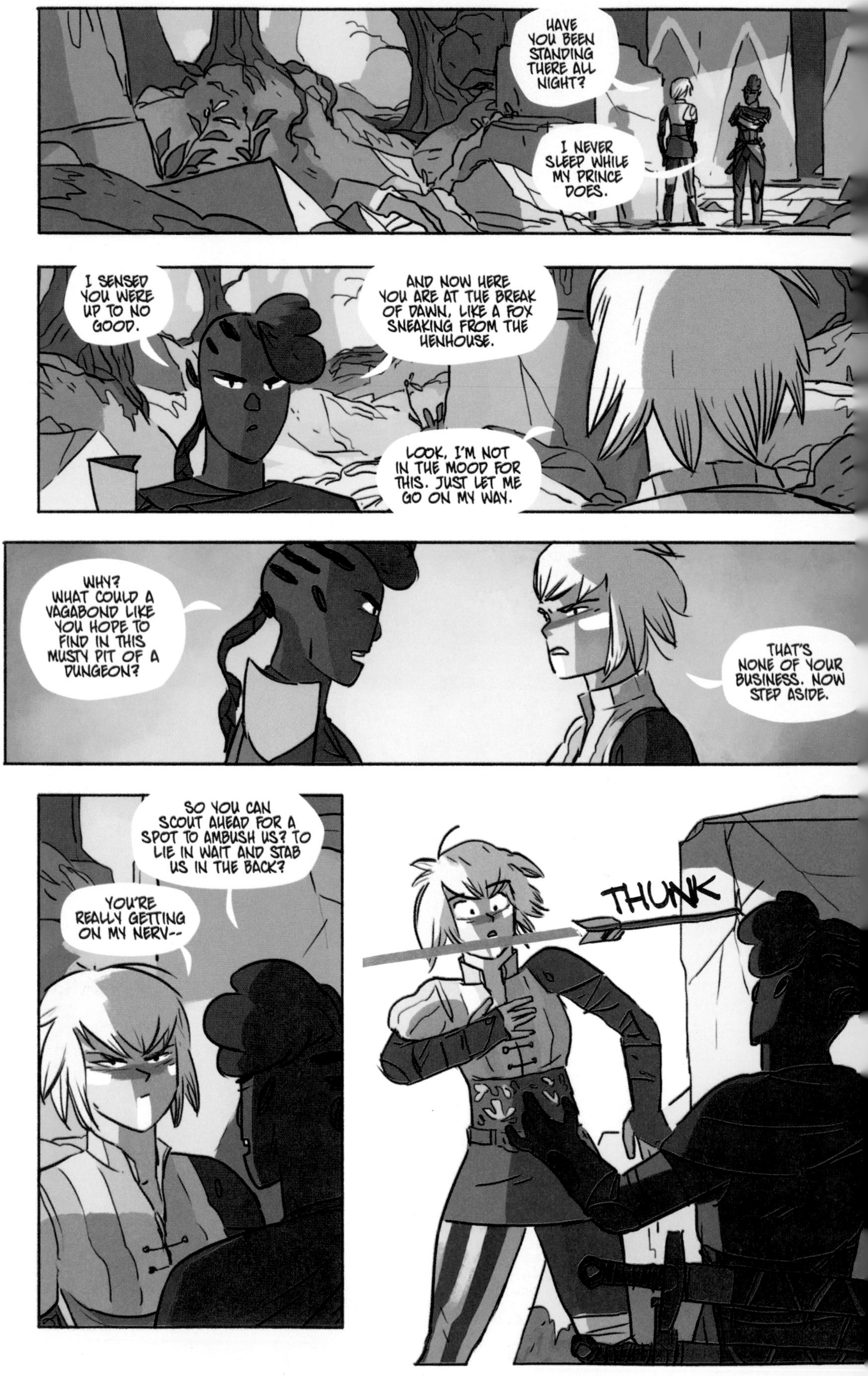
HAVE YOU BEEN STANDING THERE ALL NIGHT?
I NEVER SLEEP WHILE MY PRINCE DOES.
I SENSED YOU WERE UP TO NO GOOD.
AND NOW HERE YOU ARE AT THE BREAK OF DAWN, LIKE A FOX SNEAKING FROM THE HENHOUSE.
LOOK, I'M NOT IN THE MOOD FOR THIS. JUST LET ME GO ON MY WAY.
WHY? WHAT COULD A VAGABOND LIKE YOU HOPE TO FIND IN THIS MUSTY PIT OF A DUNGEON?
THAT'S NONE OF YOUR BUSINESS. NOW STEP ASIDE.
SO YOU CAN SCOUT AHEAD FOR A SPOT TO AMBUSH US? TO LIE IN WAIT AND STAB US IN THE BACK?
YOU'RE REALLY GETTING ON MY NERV--
THUNK

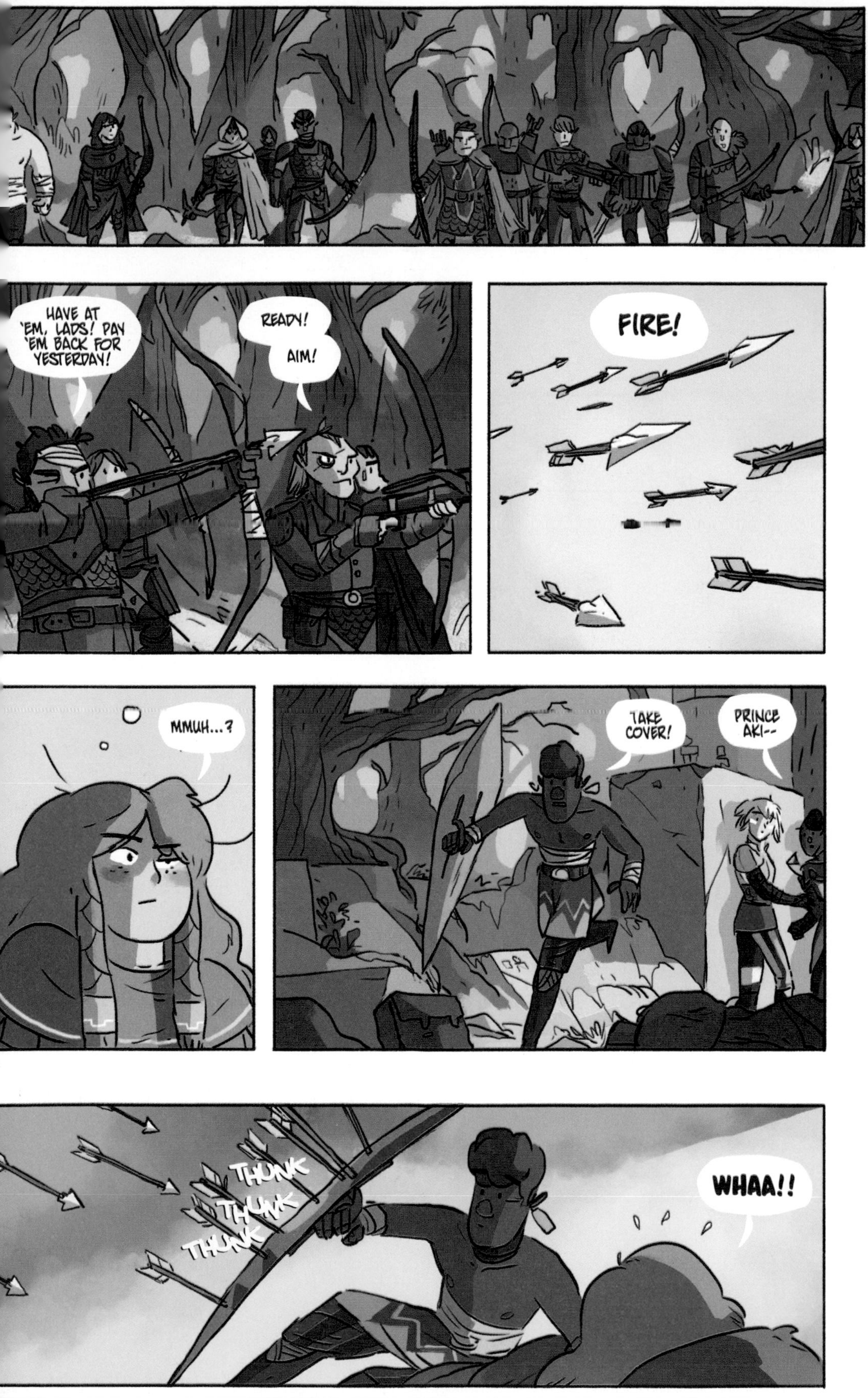
HAVE AT 'EM, LADS! PAY 'EM BACK FOR YESTERDAY!
READY!
AIM!
FIRE!
MMUH...?
TAKE COVER!
PRINCE AKI--
THUNK
THUNK
THUNK
WHAA!!

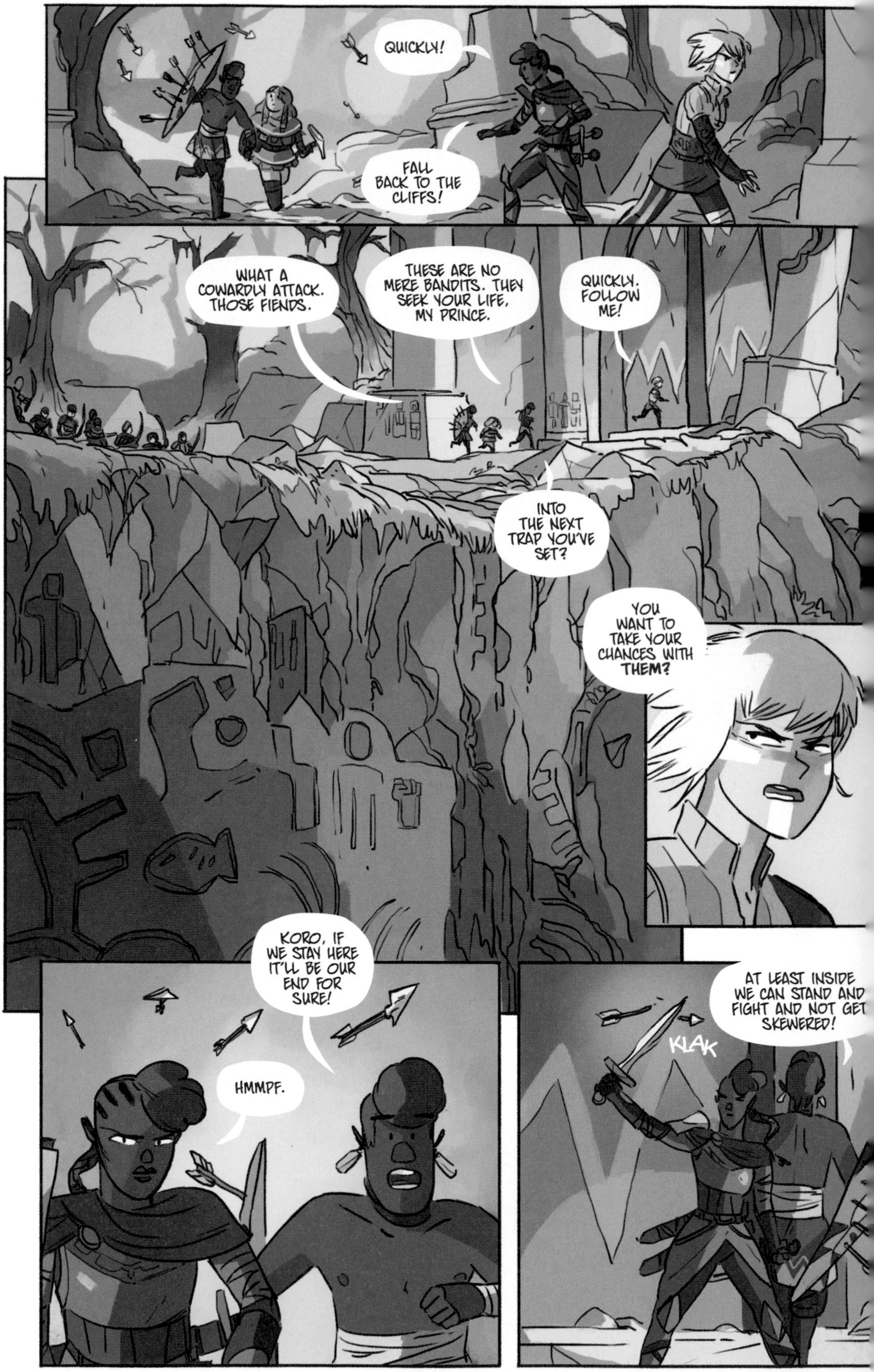
QUICKLY!
FALL BACK TO THE CLIFFS!
WHAT A COWARDLY ATTACK. THOSE FIENDS.
THESE ARE NO MERE BANDITS. THEY SEEK YOUR LIFE, MY PRINCE.
QUICKLY. FOLLOW ME!
INTO THE NEXT TRAP YOU'VE SET?
YOU WANT TO TAKE YOUR CHANCES WITH THEM?
KORO, IF WE STAY HERE IT'LL BE OUR END FOR SURE!
HMMPF.
KLAK
AT LEAST INSIDE WE CAN STAND AND FIGHT AND NOT GET SKEWERED!

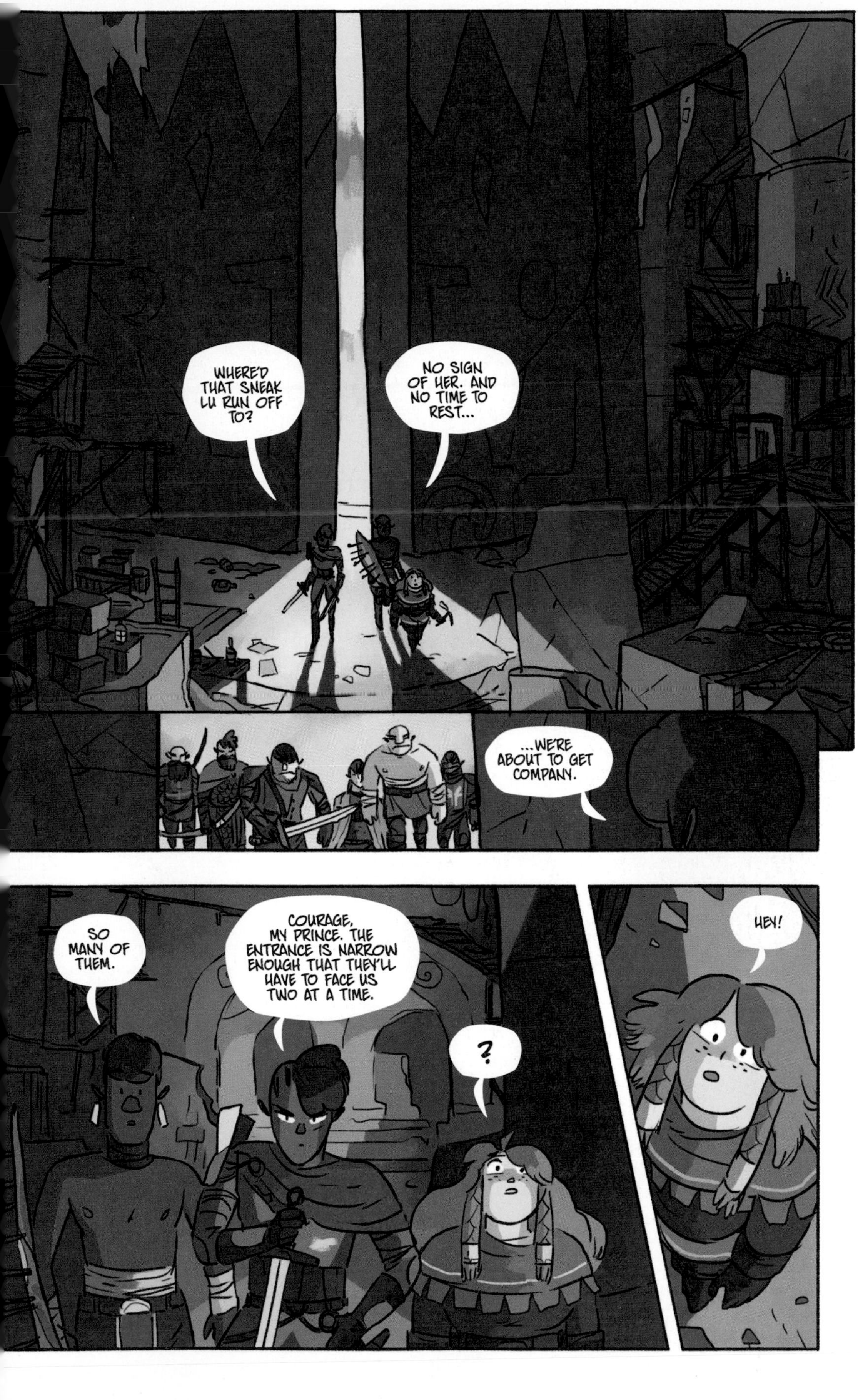
WHERE'D THAT SNEAK LU RUN OFF TO?
NO SIGN OF HER. AND NO TIME TO REST...
...WE'RE ABOUT TO GET COMPANY.
SO MANY OF THEM.
COURAGE, MY PRINCE. THE ENTRANCE IS NARROW ENOUGH THAT THEY'LL HAVE TO FACE US TWO AT A TIME.
?
HEY!

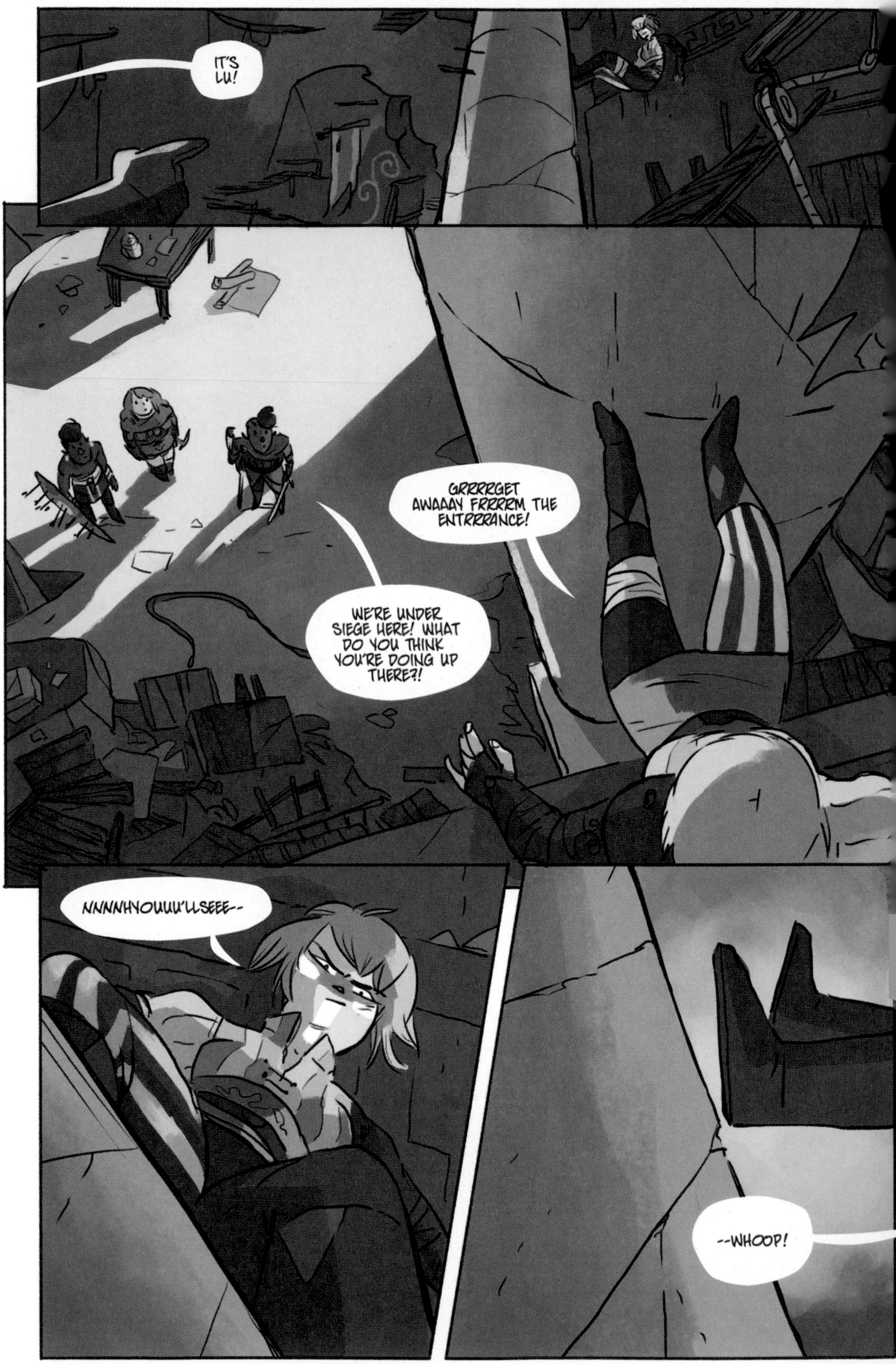
IT'S LU!
GRRRRGET AWAAAY FRRRRM THE ENTRRRANCE!
WE'RE UNDER SIEGE HERE! WHAT DO YOU THINK YOU'RE DOING UP THERE?!
NNNNHYOUUU'LLSEEE--
--WHOOP!

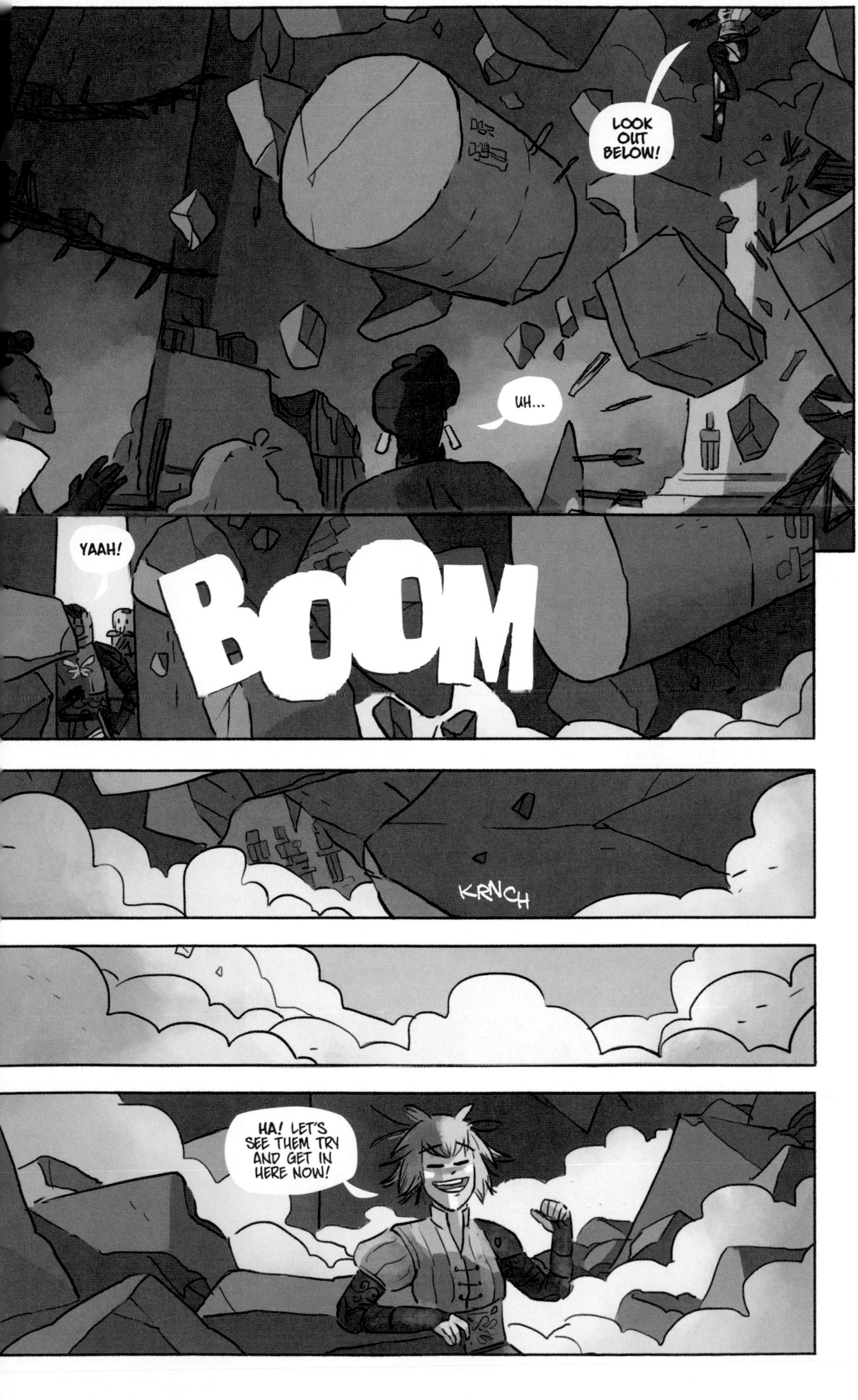
LOOK OUT BELOW!
UH...
YAAH!
BOOM
KRNCH
HA! LET'S SEE THEM TRY AND GET IN HERE NOW!

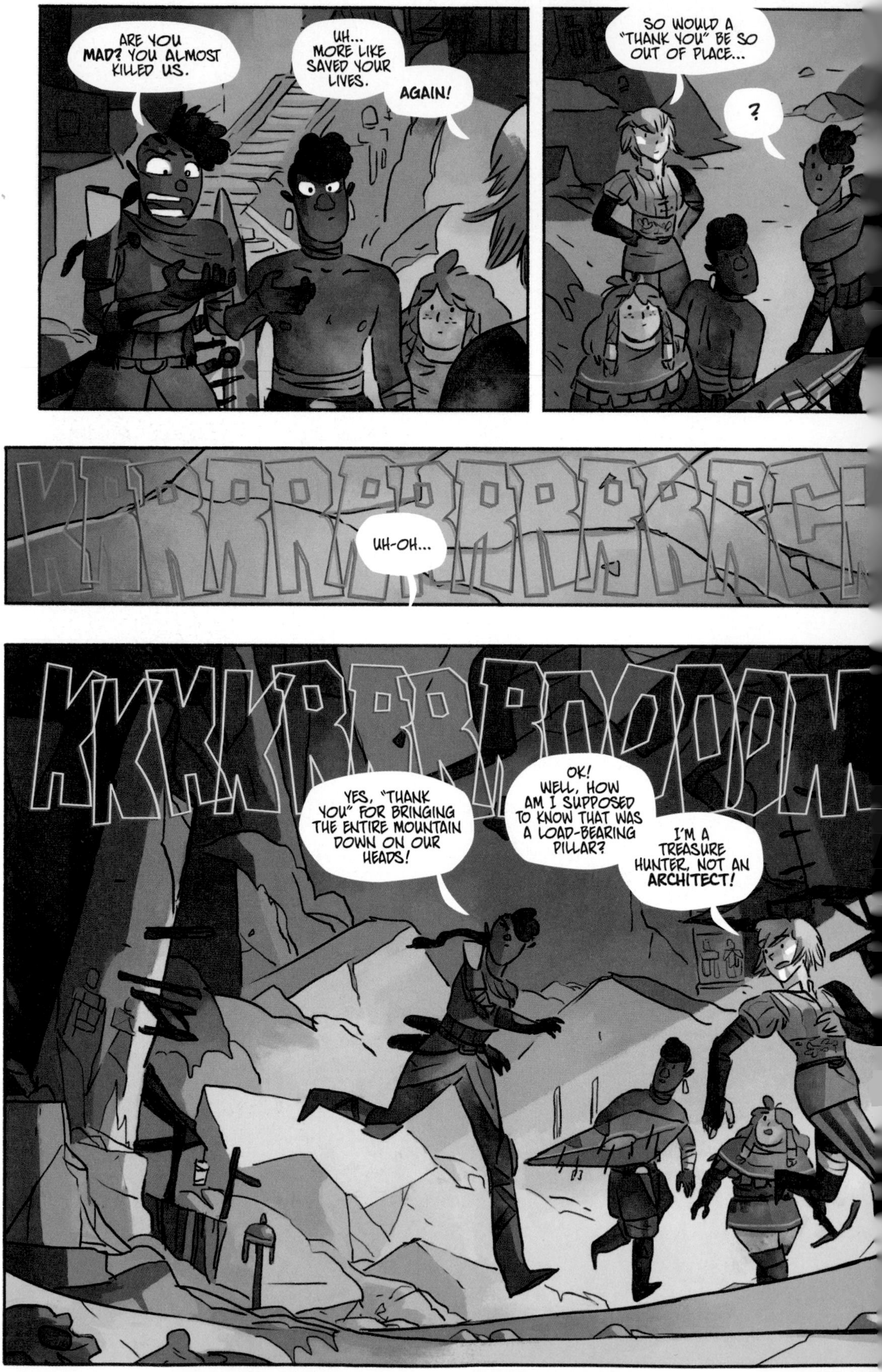
ARE YOU MAD? YOU ALMOST KILLED US.
UH... MORE LIKE SAVED YOUR LIVES.
AGAIN!
SO WOULD A "THANK YOU" BE SO OUT OF PLACE...
?
UH-OH...
YES, "THANK YOU" FOR BRINGING THE ENTIRE MOUNTAIN DOWN ON OUR HEADS!
OK! WELL, HOW AM I SUPPOSED TO KNOW THAT WAS A LOAD-BEARING PILLAR?
I'M A TREASURE HUNTER, NOT AN ARCHITECT!

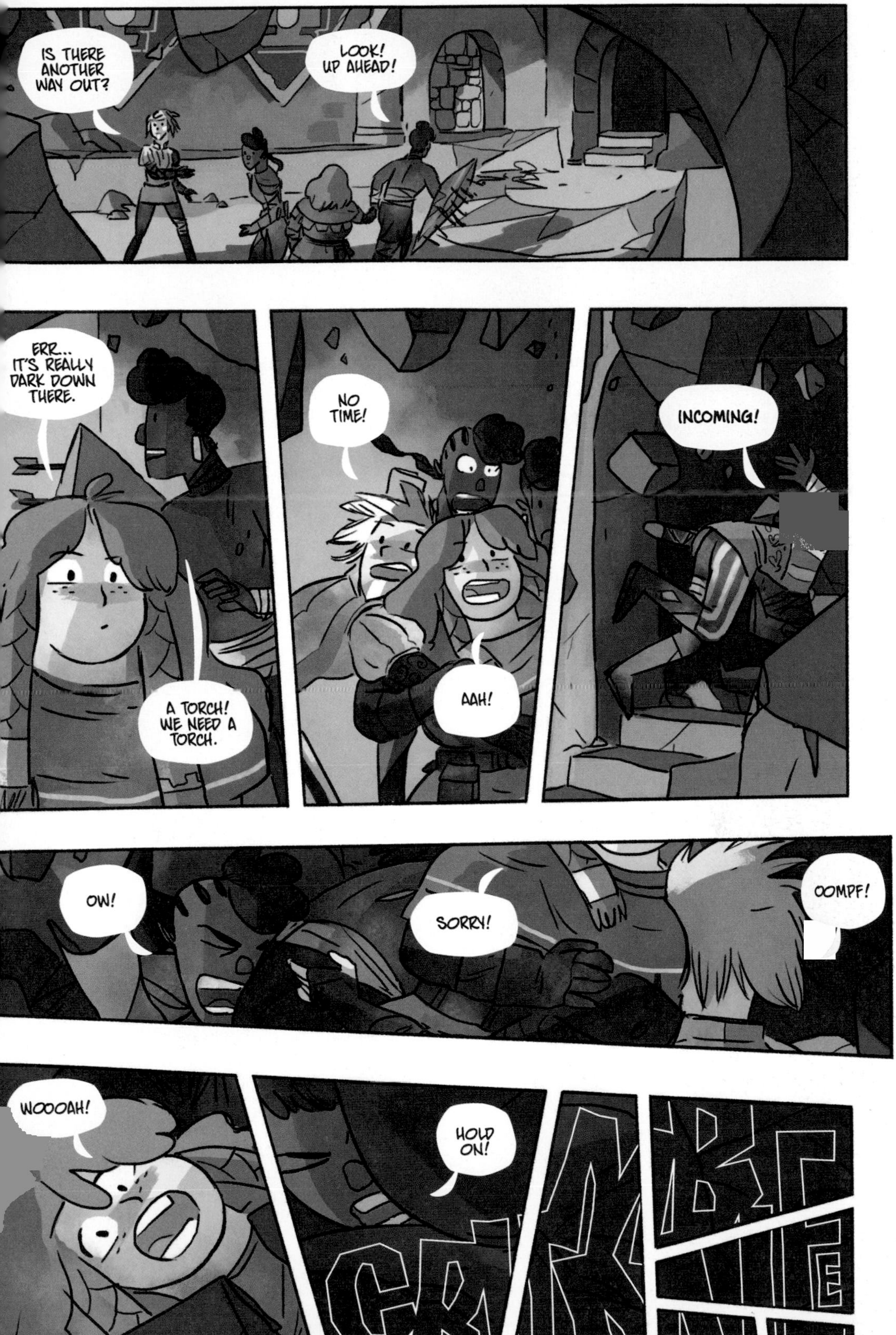
IS THERE ANOTHER WAY OUT?
LOOK! UP AHEAD!
ERR... IT'S REALLY DARK DOWN THERE.
A TORCH! WE NEED A TORCH.
NO TIME!
AAH!
INCOMING!
OW!
SORRY!
OOMPF!
WOOOAH!
HOLD ON!
CRUNK!

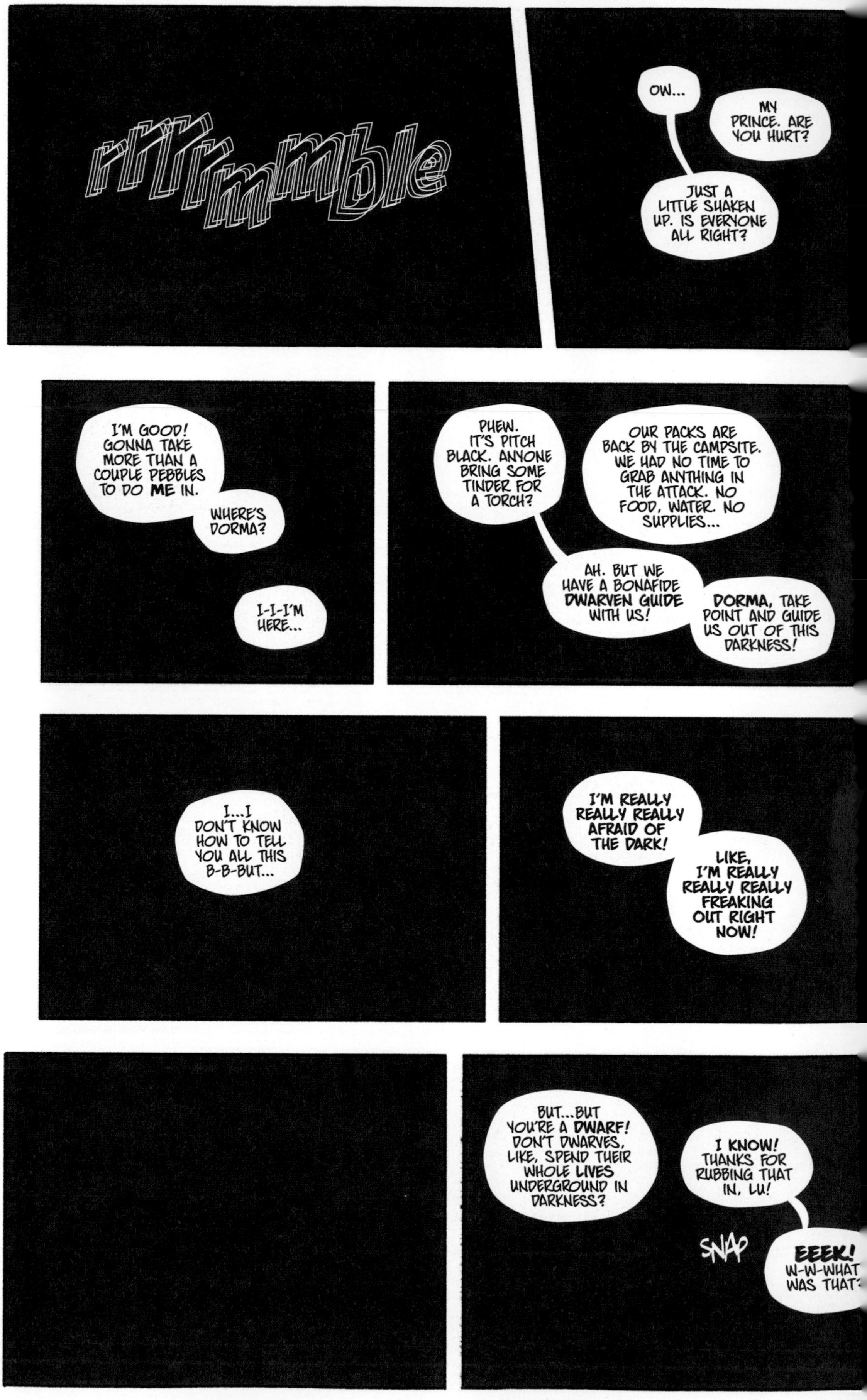
rrrrmmmble
OW...
MY PRINCE. ARE YOU HURT?
JUST A LITTLE SHAKEN UP. IS EVERYONE ALL RIGHT?
I'M GOOD! GONNA TAKE MORE THAN A COUPLE PEBBLES TO DO **ME** IN.
WHERE'S DORMA?
I-I-I'M HERE...
PHEW. IT'S PITCH BLACK. ANYONE BRING SOME TINDER FOR A TORCH?
OUR PACKS ARE BACK BY THE CAMPSITE. WE HAD NO TIME TO GRAB ANYTHING IN THE ATTACK. NO FOOD, WATER. NO SUPPLIES...
AH. BUT WE HAVE A BONAFIDE **DWARVEN GUIDE** WITH US!
DORMA, TAKE POINT AND GUIDE US OUT OF THIS DARKNESS!
I...I DON'T KNOW HOW TO TELL YOU ALL THIS B-B-BUT...
I'M REALLY REALLY REALLY AFRAID OF THE DARK!
LIKE, I'M REALLY REALLY REALLY FREAKING OUT RIGHT NOW!
BUT...BUT YOU'RE A **DWARF**! DON'T DWARVES, LIKE, SPEND THEIR WHOLE **LIVES** UNDERGROUND IN DARKNESS?
I KNOW! THANKS FOR RUBBING THAT IN, LU!
SNAP
EEEK! W-W-WHAT WAS THAT

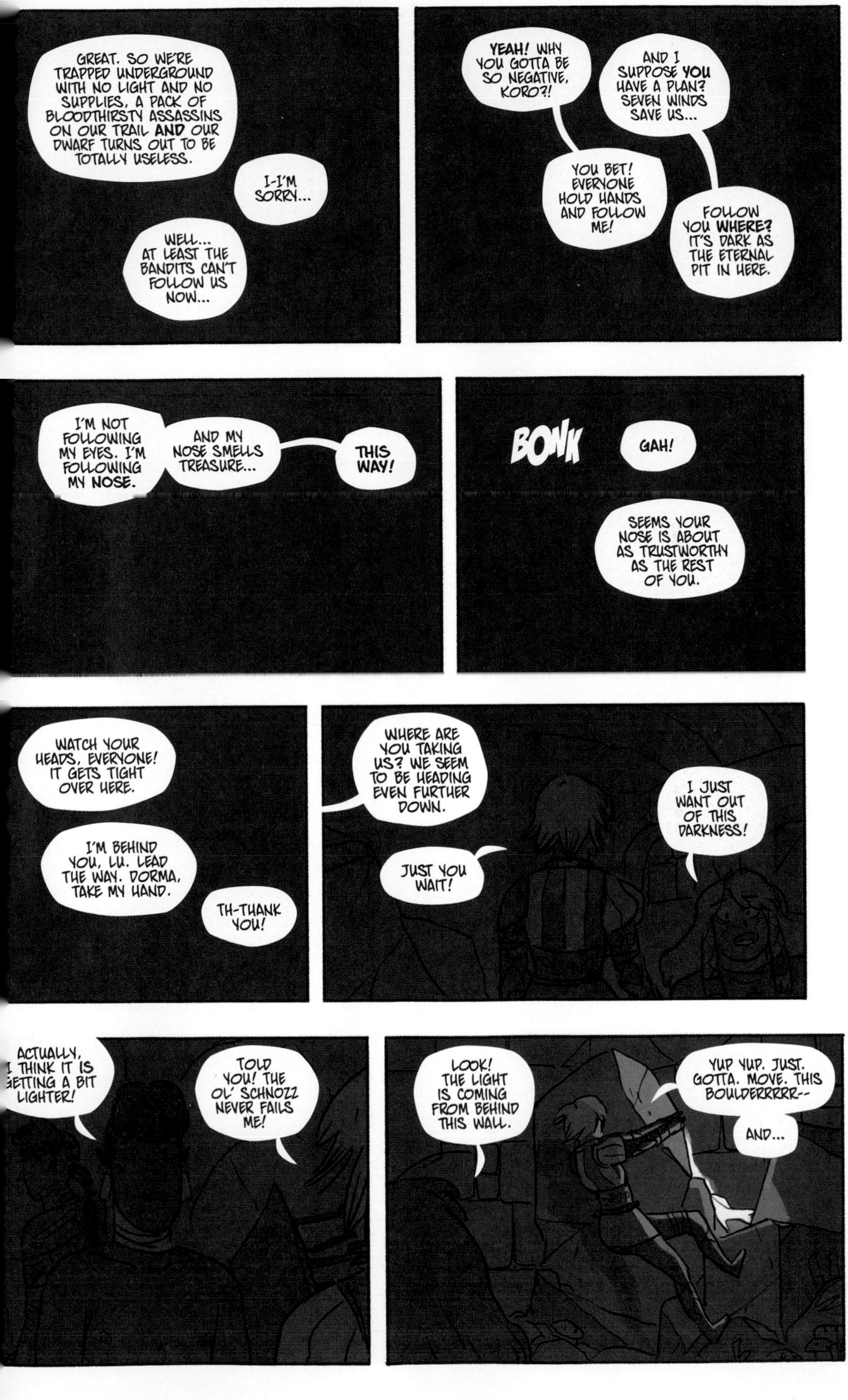
GREAT. SO WE'RE TRAPPED UNDERGROUND WITH NO LIGHT AND NO SUPPLIES, A PACK OF BLOODTHIRSTY ASSASSINS ON OUR TRAIL AND OUR DWARF TURNS OUT TO BE TOTALLY USELESS.
I-I'M SORRY...
WELL... AT LEAST THE BANDITS CAN'T FOLLOW US NOW...
YEAH! WHY YOU GOTTA BE SO NEGATIVE, KORO?!
YOU BET! EVERYONE HOLD HANDS AND FOLLOW ME!
AND I SUPPOSE YOU HAVE A PLAN? SEVEN WINDS SAVE US...
FOLLOW YOU WHERE? IT'S DARK AS THE ETERNAL PIT IN HERE.
I'M NOT FOLLOWING MY EYES. I'M FOLLOWING MY NOSE.
AND MY NOSE SMELLS TREASURE...
THIS WAY!
BONK
GAH!
SEEMS YOUR NOSE IS ABOUT AS TRUSTWORTHY AS THE REST OF YOU.
WATCH YOUR HEADS, EVERYONE! IT GETS TIGHT OVER HERE.
I'M BEHIND YOU, LU. LEAD THE WAY. DORMA, TAKE MY HAND.
TH-THANK YOU!
WHERE ARE YOU TAKING US? WE SEEM TO BE HEADING EVEN FURTHER DOWN.
JUST YOU WAIT!
I JUST WANT OUT OF THIS DARKNESS!
ACTUALLY, I THINK IT IS GETTING A BIT LIGHTER!
TOLD YOU! THE OL' SCHNOZZ NEVER FAILS ME!
LOOK! THE LIGHT IS COMING FROM BEHIND THIS WALL.
YUP YUP. JUST. GOTTA. MOVE. THIS BOULDERRRRR--
AND...

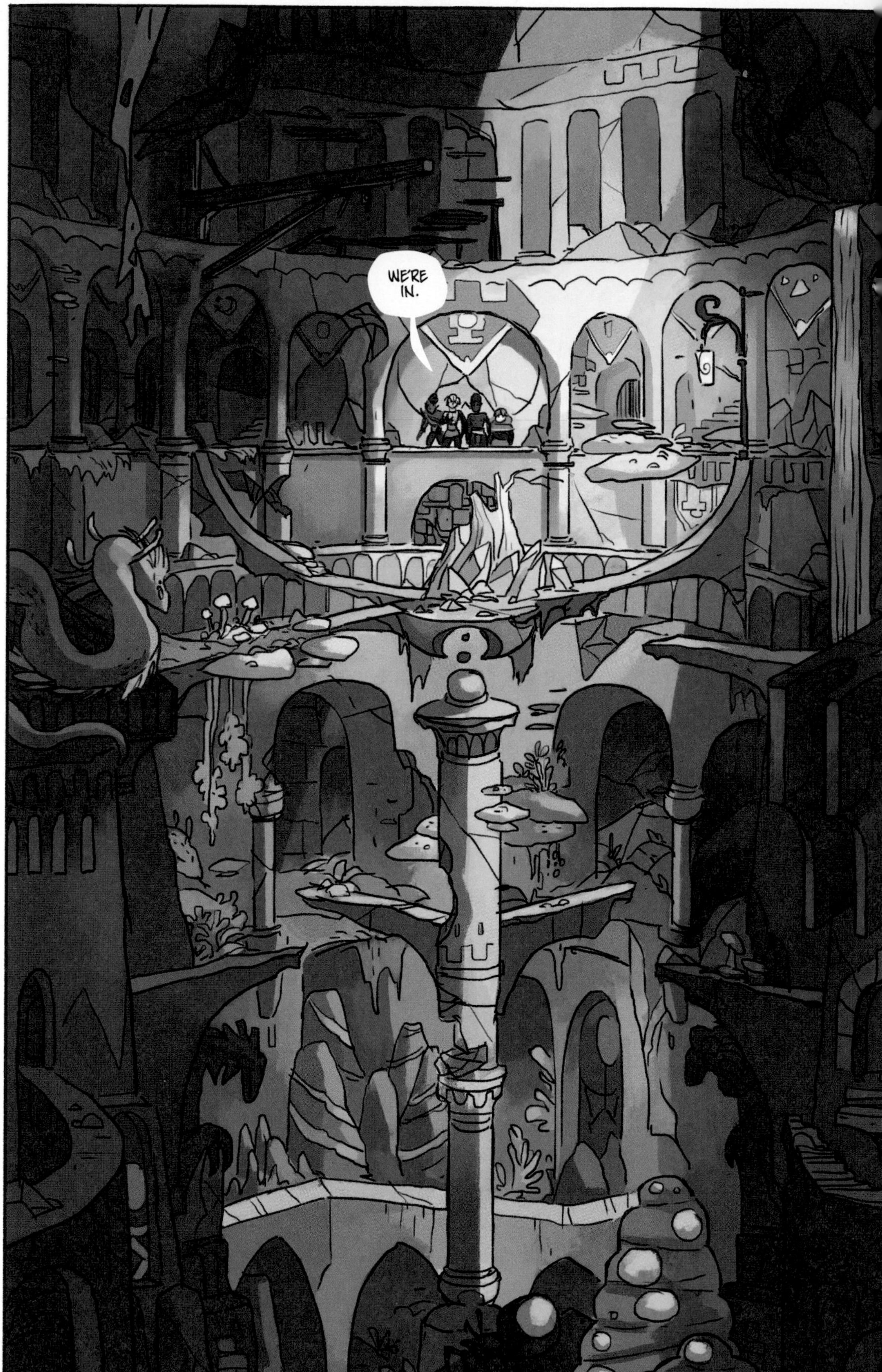
WE'RE IN.

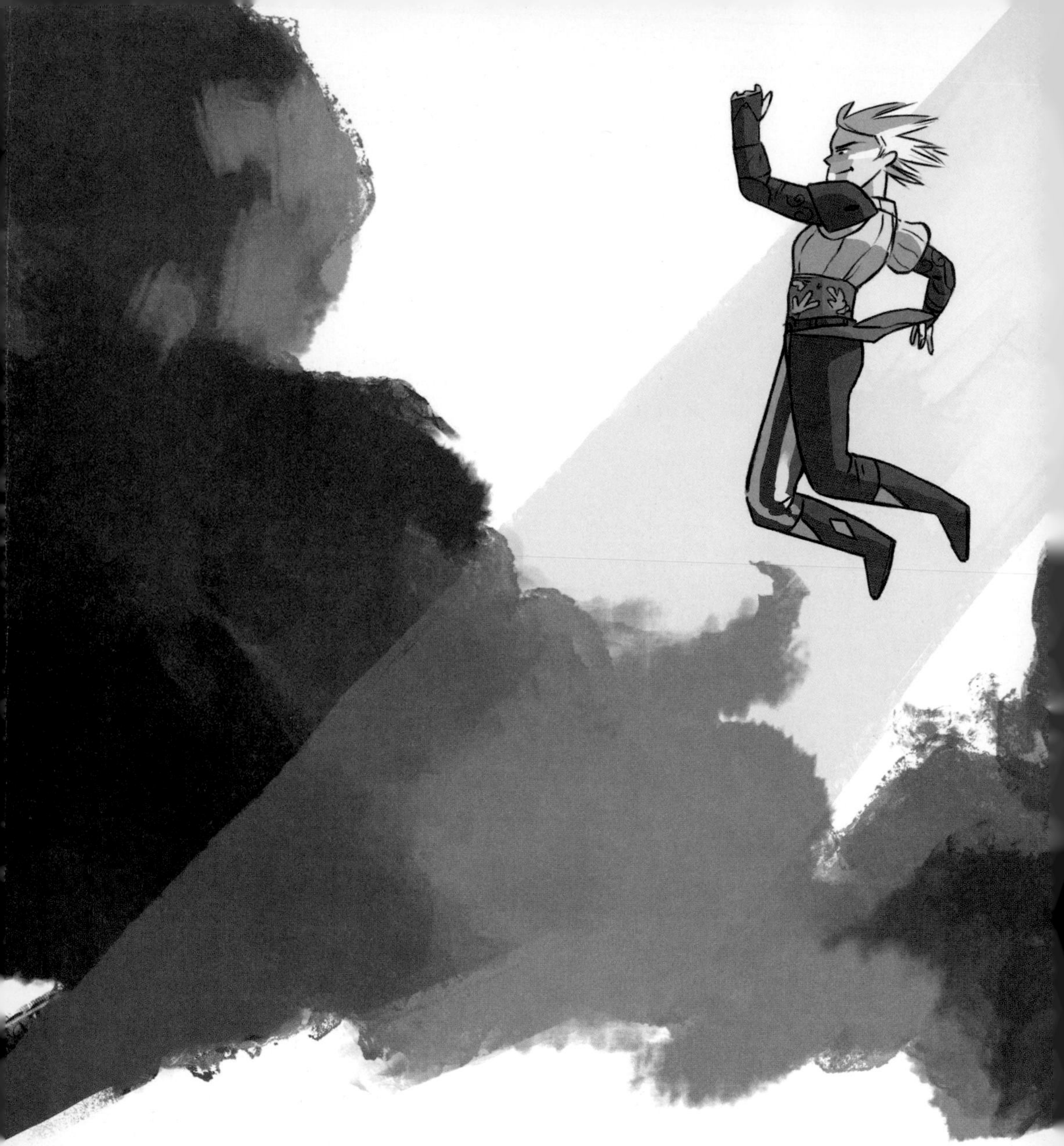

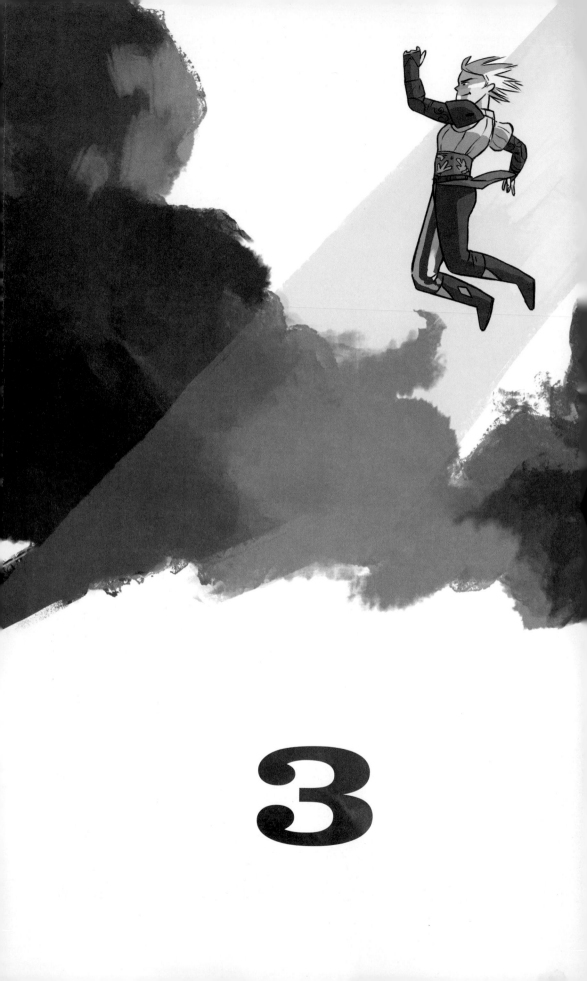

3

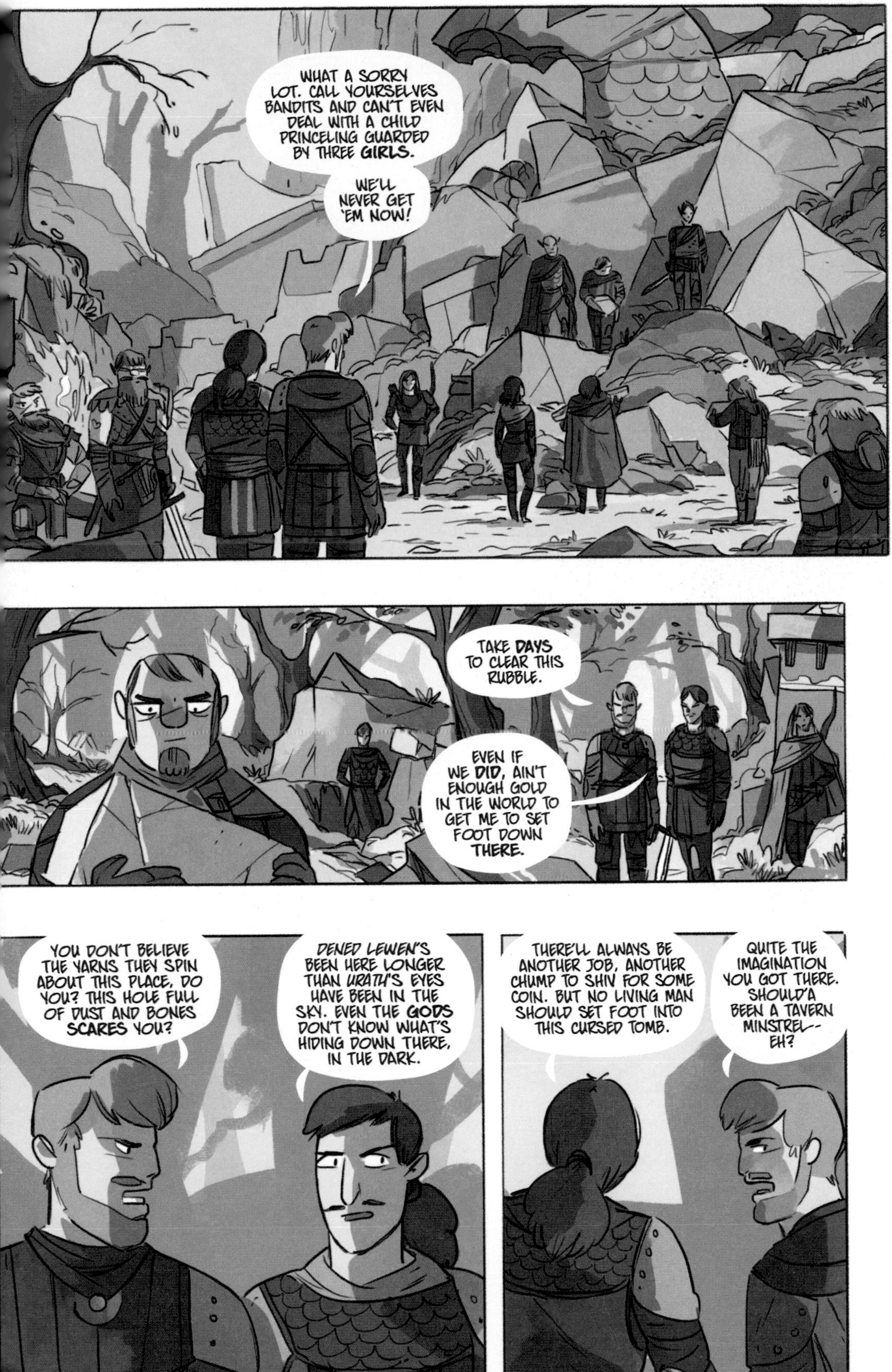
WHAT A SORRY LOT. CALL YOURSELVES BANDITS AND CAN'T EVEN DEAL WITH A CHILD PRINCELING GUARDED BY THREE GIRLS.
WE'LL NEVER GET 'EM NOW!
TAKE DAYS TO CLEAR THIS RUBBLE.
EVEN IF WE DID, AIN'T ENOUGH GOLD IN THE WORLD TO GET ME TO SET FOOT DOWN THERE.
YOU DON'T BELIEVE THE YARNS THEY SPIN ABOUT THIS PLACE, DO YOU? THIS HOLE FULL OF DUST AND BONES SCARES YOU?
DENED LEWEN'S BEEN HERE LONGER THAN URATH'S EYES HAVE BEEN IN THE SKY. EVEN THE GODS DON'T KNOW WHAT'S HIDING DOWN THERE, IN THE DARK.
THERE'LL ALWAYS BE ANOTHER JOB, ANOTHER CHUMP TO SHIV FOR SOME COIN. BUT NO LIVING MAN SHOULD SET FOOT INTO THIS CURSED TOMB.
QUITE THE IMAGINATION YOU GOT THERE. SHOULD'A BEEN A TAVERN MINSTREL--EH?

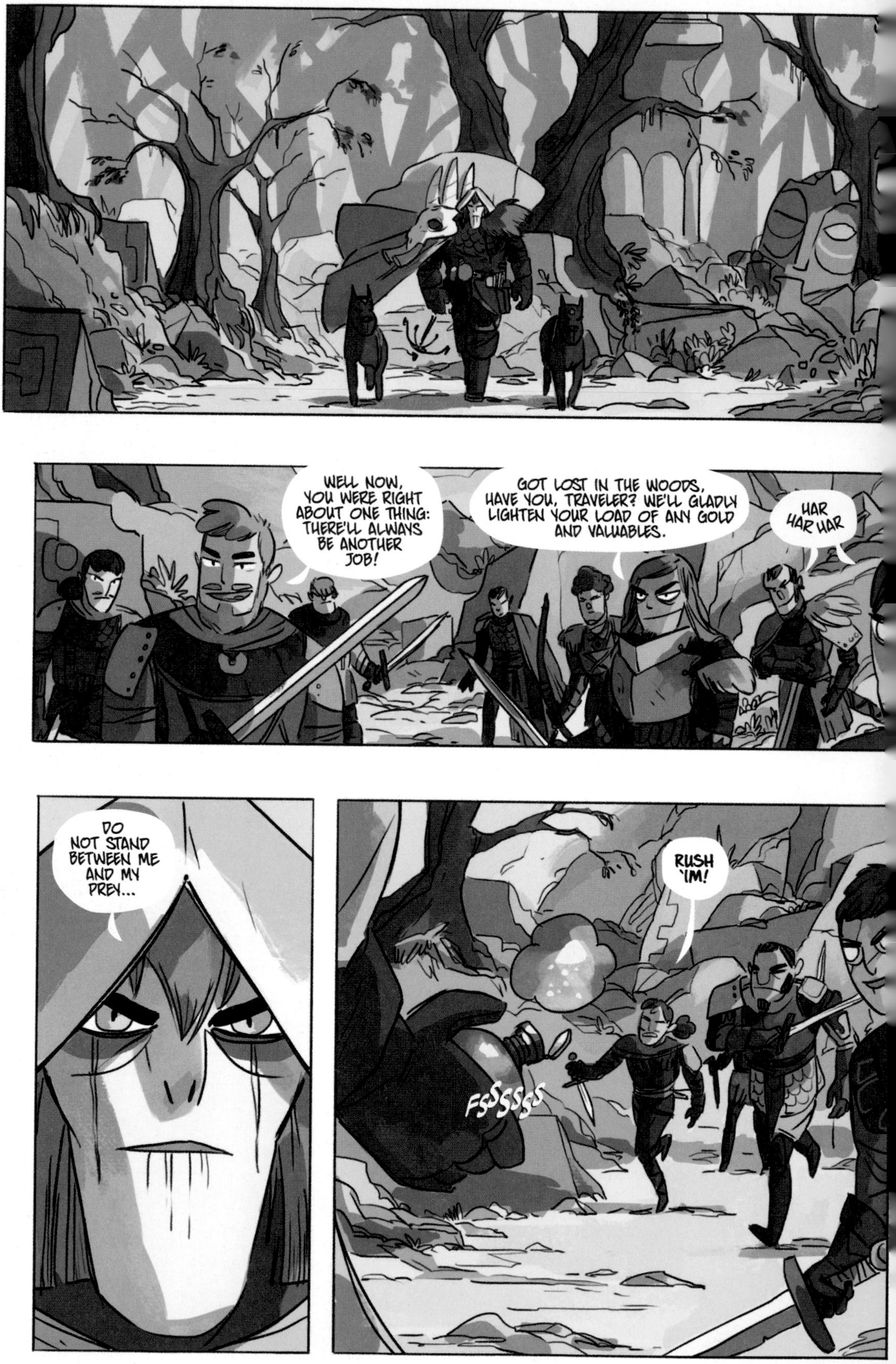
WELL NOW, YOU WERE RIGHT ABOUT ONE THING: THERE'LL ALWAYS BE ANOTHER JOB!
GOT LOST IN THE WOODS, HAVE YOU, TRAVELER? WE'LL GLADLY LIGHTEN YOUR LOAD OF ANY GOLD AND VALUABLES.
HAR HAR HAR
DO NOT STAND BETWEEN ME AND MY PREY...
RUSH 'IM!
FSSSSSS

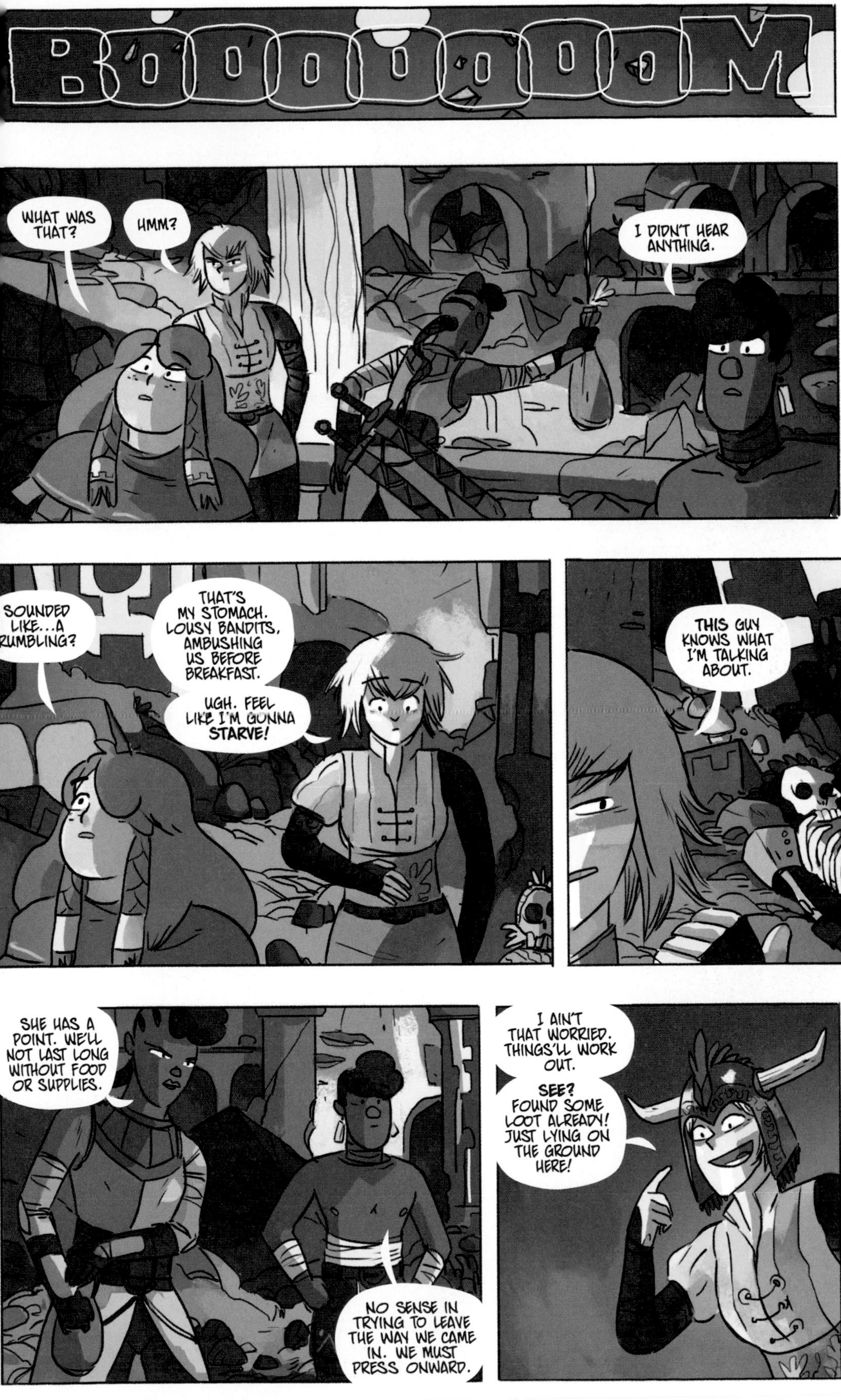
BOOOOOOOOM
WHAT WAS THAT?
HMM?
I DIDN'T HEAR ANYTHING.
SOUNDED LIKE...A RUMBLING?
THAT'S MY STOMACH. LOUSY BANDITS, AMBUSHING US BEFORE BREAKFAST.
UGH. FEEL LIKE I'M GONNA STARVE!
THIS GUY KNOWS WHAT I'M TALKING ABOUT.
SHE HAS A POINT. WE'LL NOT LAST LONG WITHOUT FOOD OR SUPPLIES.
NO SENSE IN TRYING TO LEAVE THE WAY WE CAME IN. WE MUST PRESS ONWARD.
I AIN'T THAT WORRIED. THINGS'LL WORK OUT.
SEE? FOUND SOME LOOT ALREADY! JUST LYING ON THE GROUND HERE!

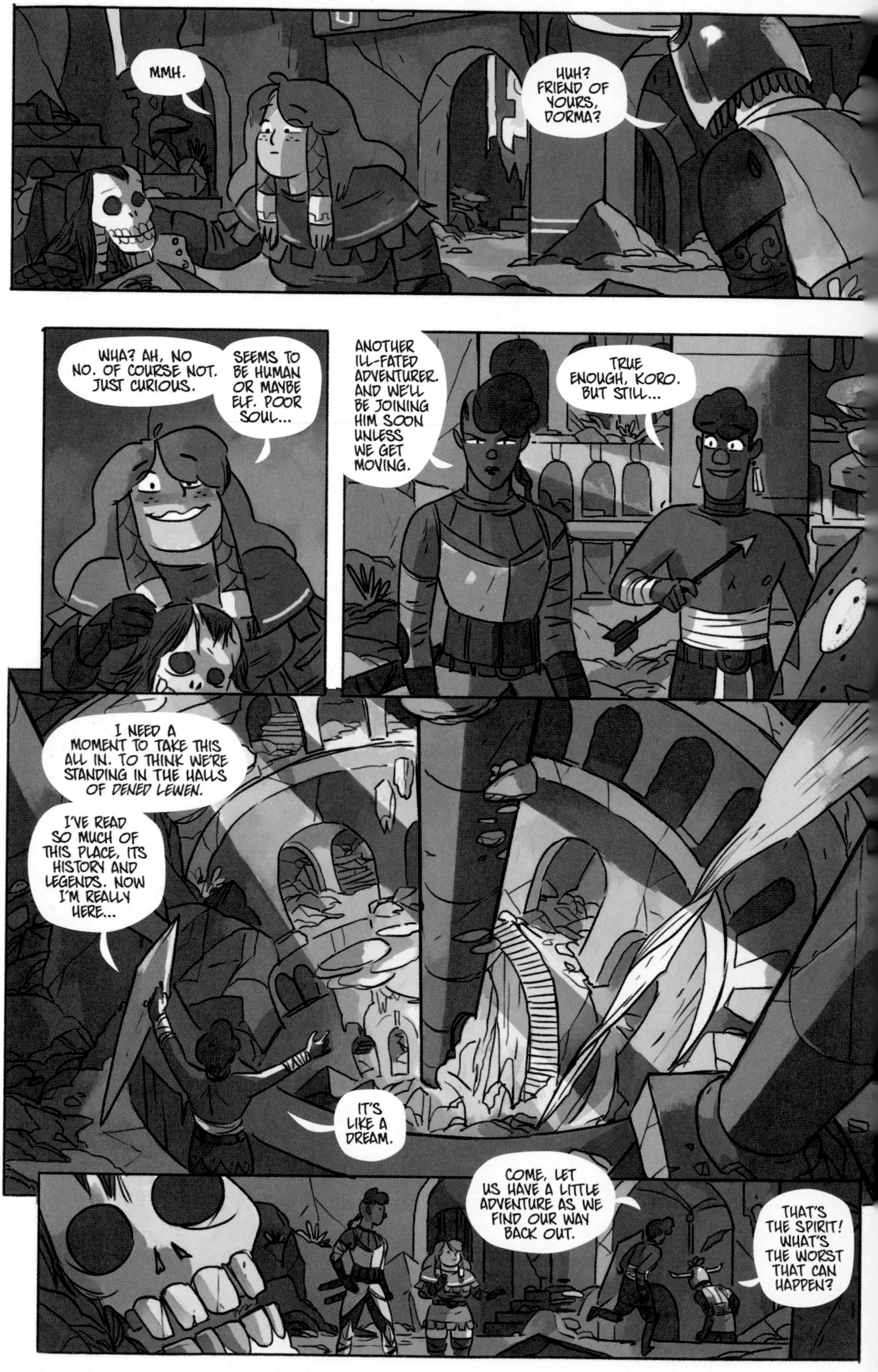
MMH.
HUH? FRIEND OF YOURS, DORMA?
WHA? AH, NO NO. OF COURSE NOT. JUST CURIOUS.
SEEMS TO BE HUMAN OR MAYBE ELF. POOR SOUL...
ANOTHER ILL-FATED ADVENTURER. AND WE'LL BE JOINING HIM SOON UNLESS WE GET MOVING.
TRUE ENOUGH, KORO. BUT STILL...
I NEED A MOMENT TO TAKE THIS ALL IN. TO THINK WE'RE STANDING IN THE HALLS OF DENED LEWEN.
I'VE READ SO MUCH OF THIS PLACE, ITS HISTORY AND LEGENDS. NOW I'M REALLY HERE...
IT'S LIKE A DREAM.
COME, LET US HAVE A LITTLE ADVENTURE AS WE FIND OUR WAY BACK OUT.
THAT'S THE SPIRIT! WHAT'S THE WORST THAT CAN HAPPEN?

DID YOUR STUDIES HAPPEN TO MENTION ANOTHER GATE THE INHABITANTS MAY HAVE USED, MY PRINCE?

YEAH, OR WHERE THEY KEPT ALL THEIR GOLD AND STUFF?

SADLY NOT. BUT UNLESS I'M MISTAKEN WE ARE IN ONE OF THE BURGS OF THE LATE BURROW LORDS.

THIRD OR FOURTH DYNASTY PERHAPS?

MY GRAN-GRAN TOLD ME STORIES ABOUT THE UNDER-KINGS. THE GREAT DWARVEN CITIES, CARVED FROM LIVING ROCK.

HERE, DORMA. MY DWARVISH IS WOEFULLY LACKING. CAN YOU READ THIS?

ONLY A BIT. IT'S A STRANGE DIALECT...

"WE DIG AND DIG UNTIL OUR PICKS RUST...BUT THE BOTTOM OF THE WORLD IS ONLY... THE BEGINNING."

GOTTA BE A WHOLE OCEAN OF TREASURE DOWN HERE THEN. KINGS ARE ALMOST AS GREEDY AS DRAGONS.

AND HERE, THIS PART IS STRANGE:

"IS...DALDEN LARIA REAL...OR JUST A TALE? AN URDEN CURSE PLACED ON US MORTALS TO KEEP US...DIGGING FOREVER...

...SEARCHING FOREVER."

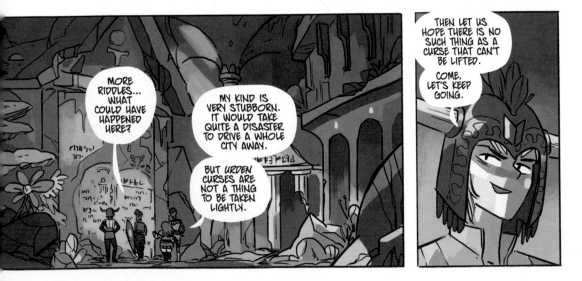

MORE RIDDLES... WHAT COULD HAVE HAPPENED HERE?

MY KIND IS VERY STUBBORN. IT WOULD TAKE QUITE A DISASTER TO DRIVE A WHOLE CITY AWAY.

BUT URDEN CURSES ARE NOT A THING TO BE TAKEN LIGHTLY.

THEN LET US HOPE THERE IS NO SUCH THING AS A CURSE THAT CAN'T BE LIFTED.

COME, LET'S KEEP GOING.

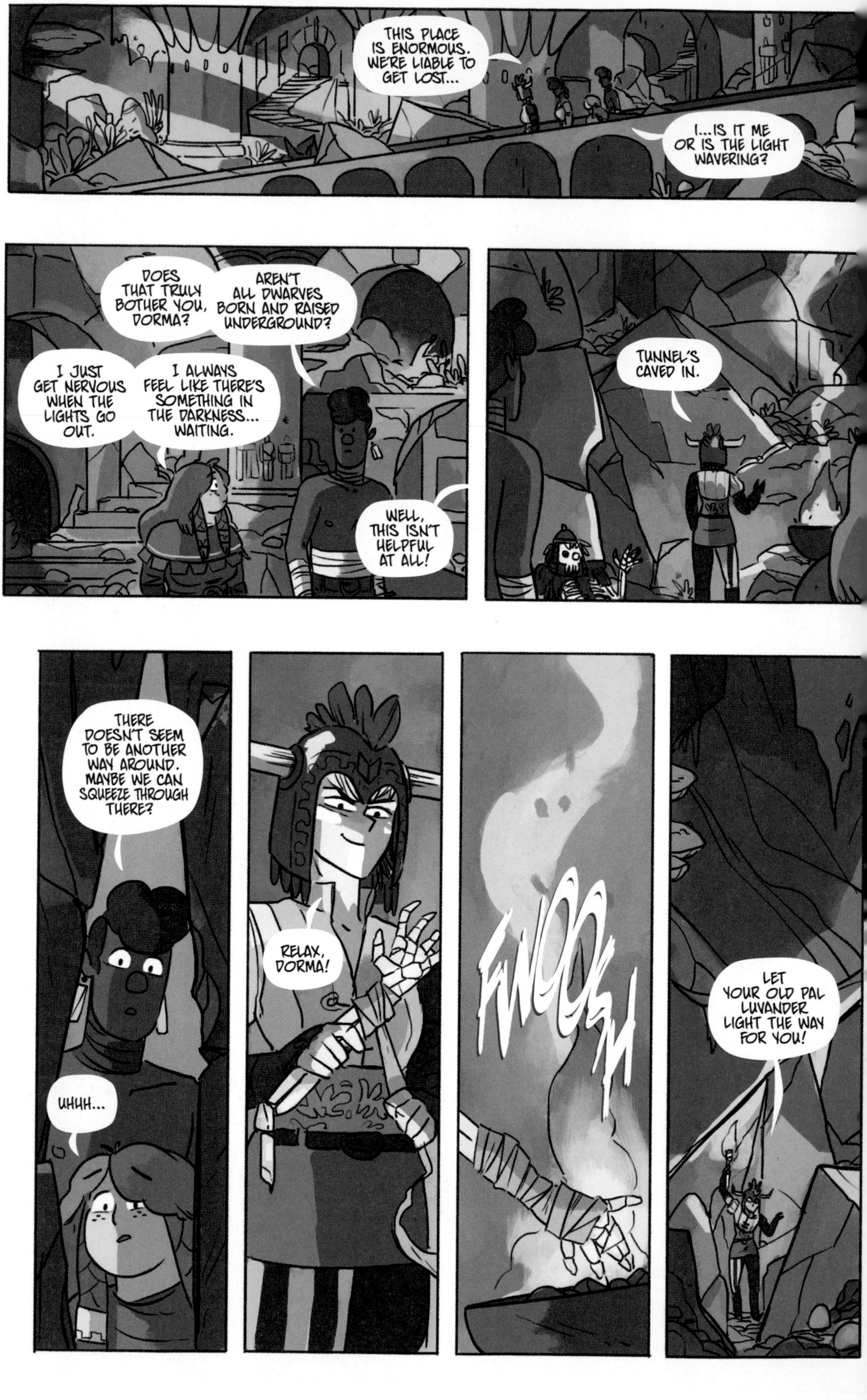
THIS PLACE IS ENORMOUS. WE'RE LIABLE TO GET LOST...
I...IS IT ME OR IS THE LIGHT WAVERING?
DOES THAT TRULY BOTHER YOU, DORMA?
AREN'T ALL DWARVES BORN AND RAISED UNDERGROUND?
I JUST GET NERVOUS WHEN THE LIGHTS GO OUT.
I ALWAYS FEEL LIKE THERE'S SOMETHING IN THE DARKNESS... WAITING.
WELL, THIS ISN'T HELPFUL AT ALL!
TUNNEL'S CAVED IN.
THERE DOESN'T SEEM TO BE ANOTHER WAY AROUND. MAYBE WE CAN SQUEEZE THROUGH THERE?
UHHH...
RELAX, DORMA!
FWOOOSH
LET YOUR OLD PAL LUVANDER LIGHT THE WAY FOR YOU!

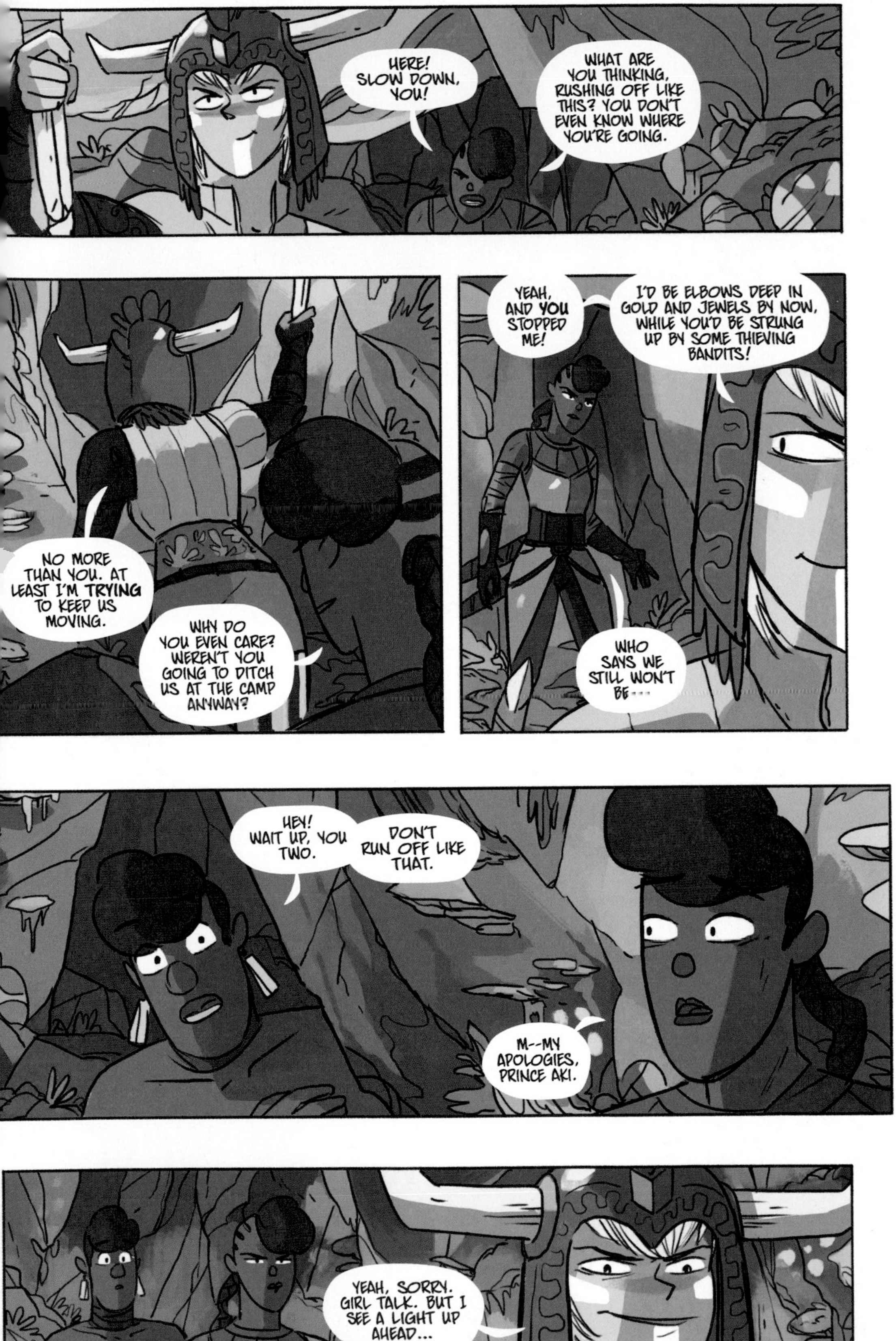
HERE! SLOW DOWN, YOU!
WHAT ARE YOU THINKING, RUSHING OFF LIKE THIS? YOU DON'T EVEN KNOW WHERE YOU'RE GOING.
NO MORE THAN YOU. AT LEAST I'M TRYING TO KEEP US MOVING.
WHY DO YOU EVEN CARE? WEREN'T YOU GOING TO DITCH US AT THE CAMP ANYWAY?
YEAH, AND YOU STOPPED ME!
I'D BE ELBOWS DEEP IN GOLD AND JEWELS BY NOW, WHILE YOU'D BE STRUNG UP BY SOME THIEVING BANDITS!
WHO SAYS WE STILL WON'T BE...
HEY! WAIT UP, YOU TWO.
DON'T RUN OFF LIKE THAT.
M--MY APOLOGIES, PRINCE AKI.
YEAH, SORRY. GIRL TALK. BUT I SEE A LIGHT UP AHEAD...

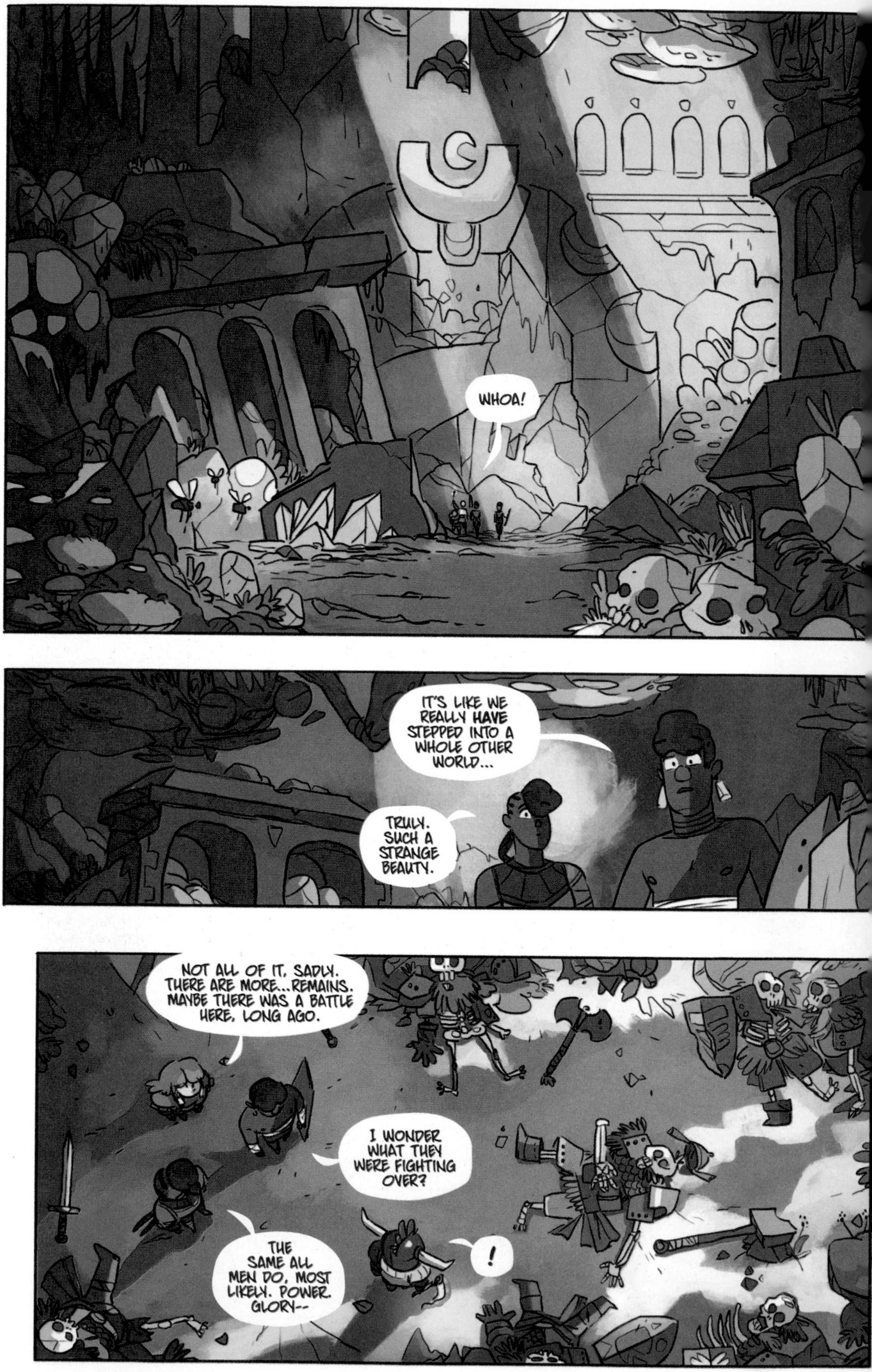
WHOA!
IT'S LIKE WE REALLY HAVE STEPPED INTO A WHOLE OTHER WORLD...
TRULY. SUCH A STRANGE BEAUTY.
NOT ALL OF IT, SADLY. THERE ARE MORE...REMAINS. MAYBE THERE WAS A BATTLE HERE, LONG AGO.
I WONDER WHAT THEY WERE FIGHTING OVER?
THE SAME ALL MEN DO, MOST LIKELY. POWER. GLORY--
!

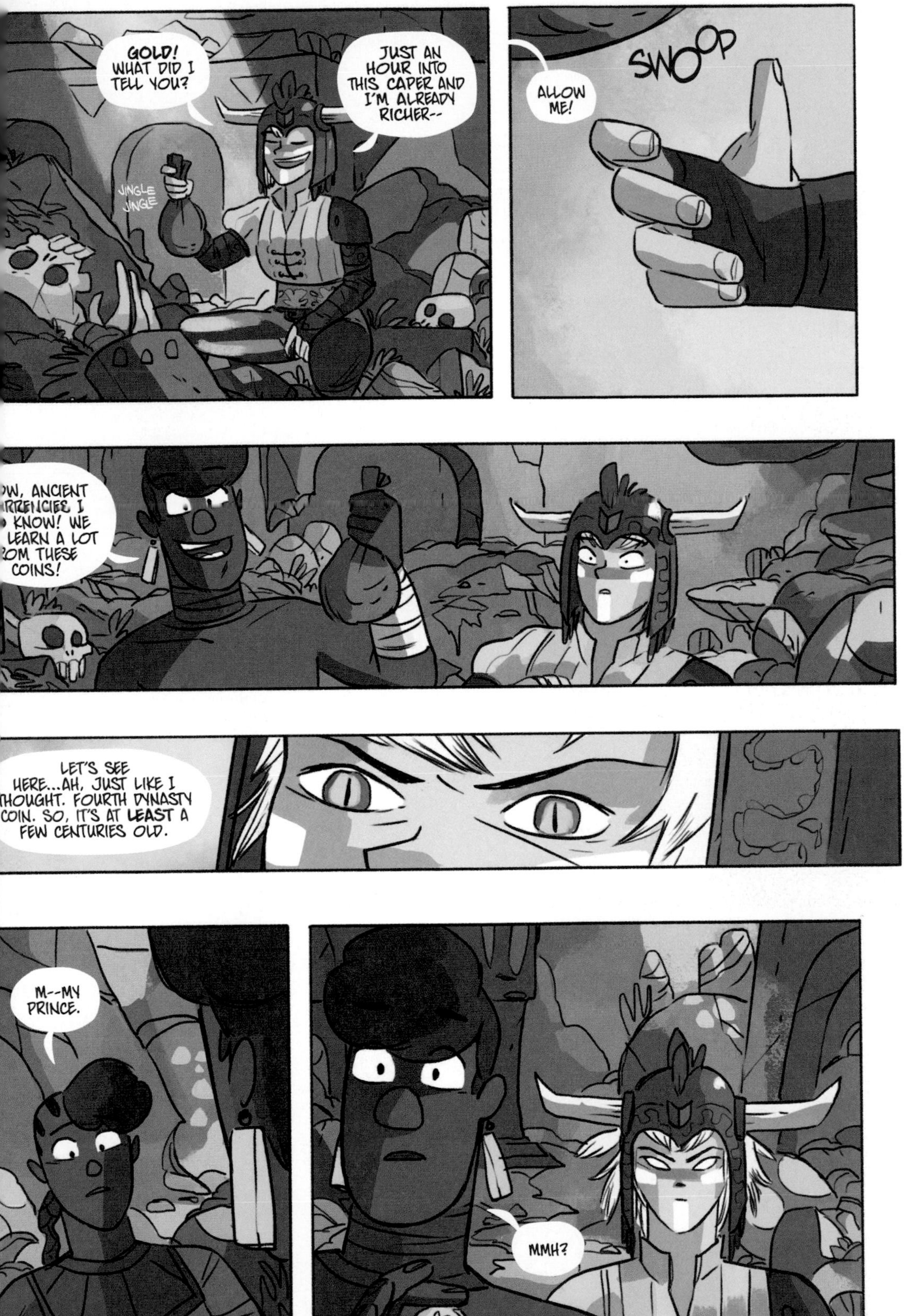
GOLD! WHAT DID I TELL YOU?
JINGLE JINGLE
JUST AN HOUR INTO THIS CAPER AND I'M ALREADY RICHER--
ALLOW ME!
SWOOP
OW, ANCIENT RRENCIES I KNOW! WE LEARN A LOT ROM THESE COINS!
LET'S SEE HERE...AH, JUST LIKE I THOUGHT. FOURTH DYNASTY COIN. SO, IT'S AT LEAST A FEW CENTURIES OLD.
M--MY PRINCE.
MMH?

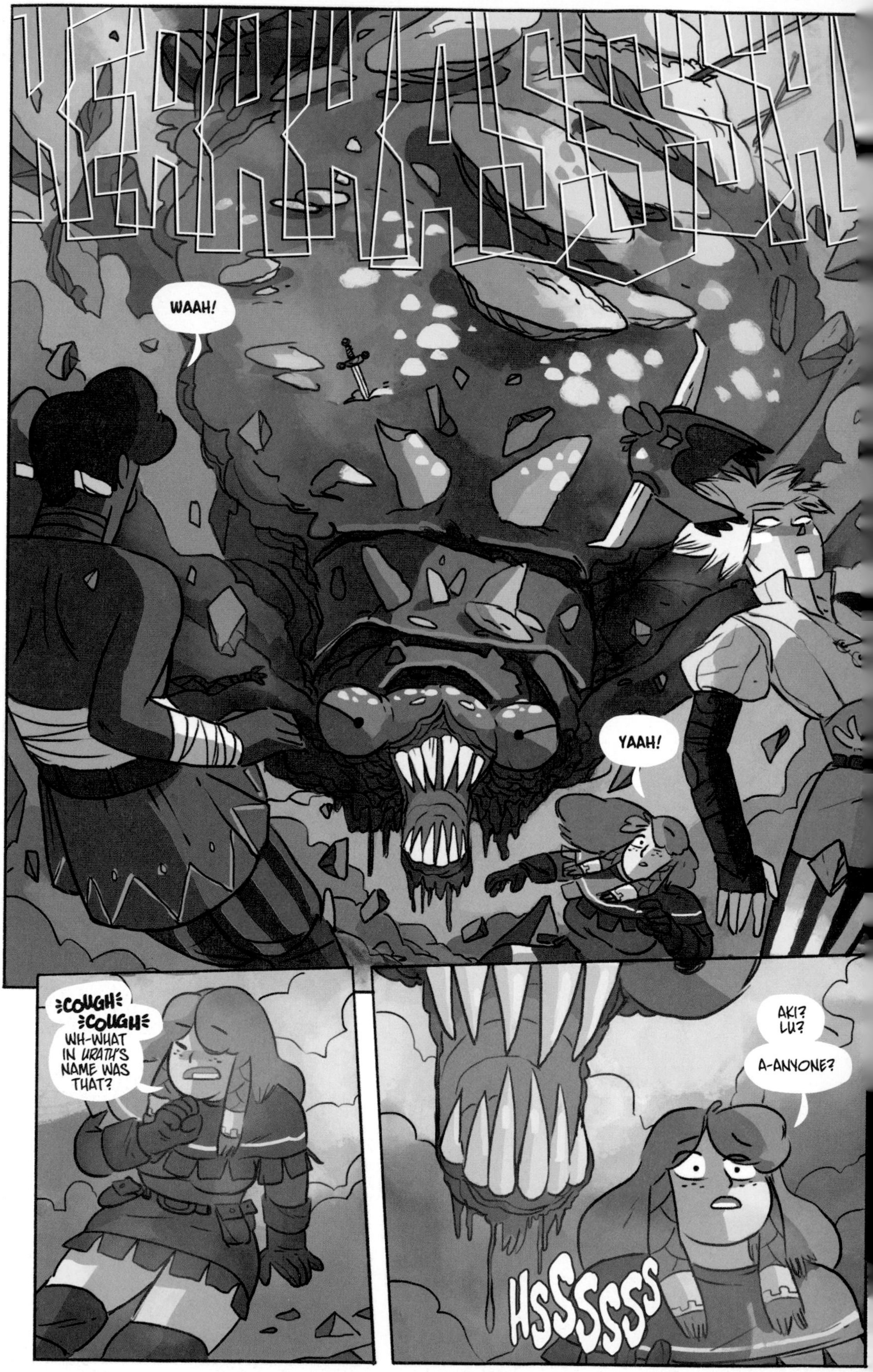
WAAH!
YAAH!
COUGH COUGH
WH-WHAT IN URATH'S NAME WAS THAT?
AKI? LU?
A-ANYONE?
HSSSSSS

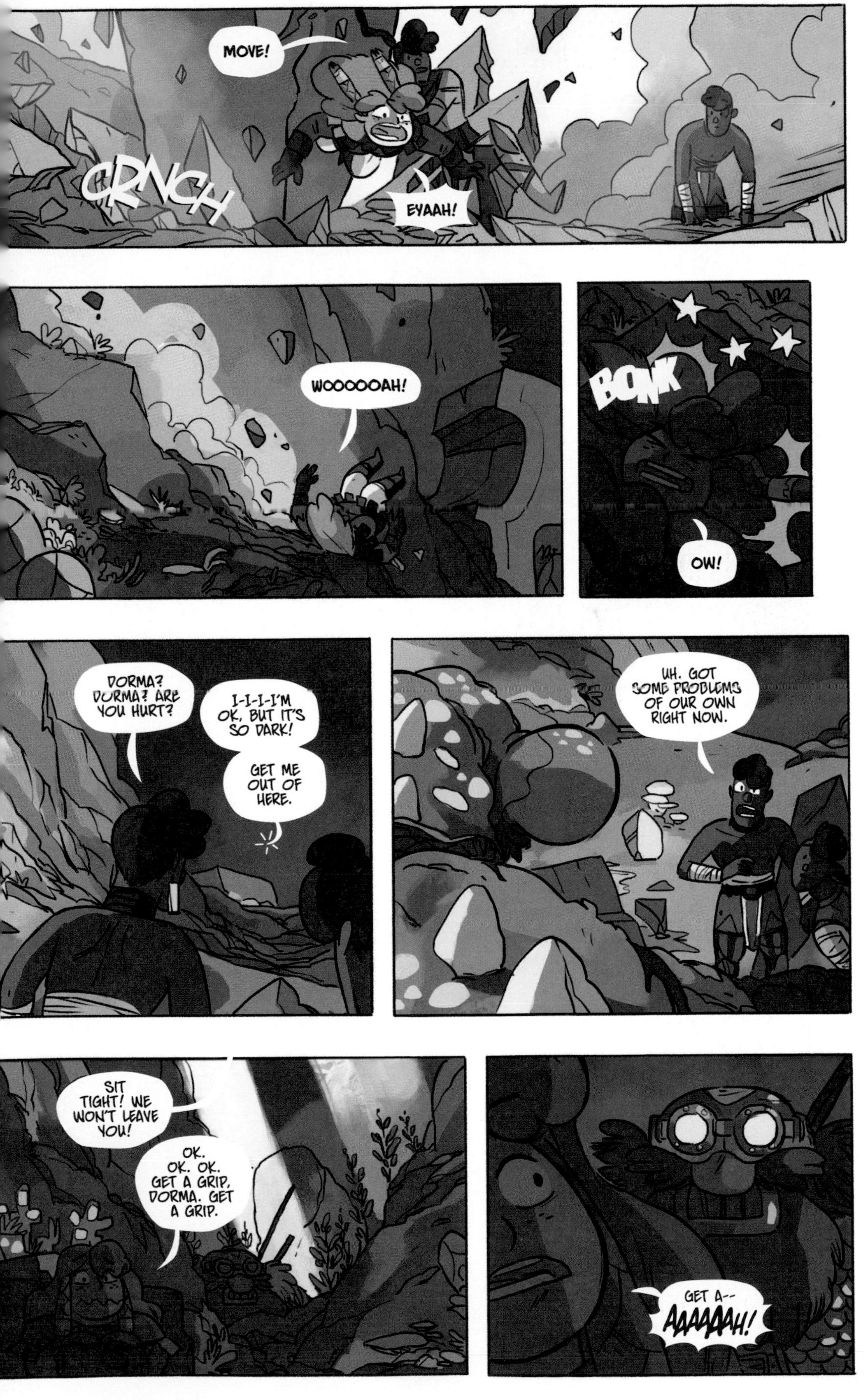
MOVE!
CRNCH
EYAAH!
WOOOOOAH!
BONK
OW!
DORMA? DORMA? ARE YOU HURT?
I-I-I-I'M OK, BUT IT'S SO DARK!
GET ME OUT OF HERE.
UH. GOT SOME PROBLEMS OF OUR OWN RIGHT NOW.
SIT TIGHT! WE WON'T LEAVE YOU!
OK. OK. OK. GET A GRIP, DORMA. GET A GRIP.
GET A--
AAAAAAH!

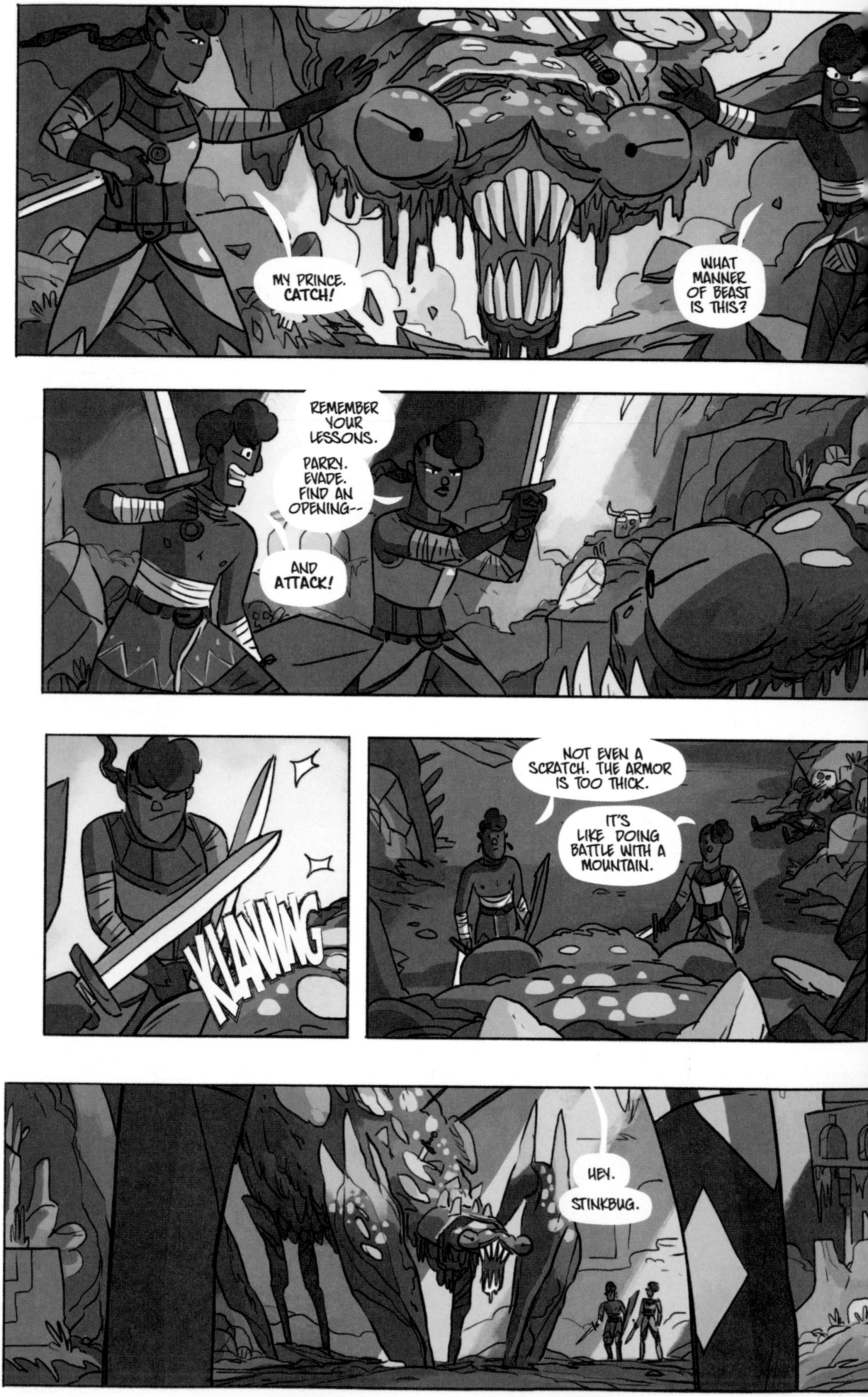
MY PRINCE. CATCH!
WHAT MANNER OF BEAST IS THIS?
REMEMBER YOUR LESSONS.
PARRY. EVADE. FIND AN OPENING--
AND ATTACK!
KLANNNG
NOT EVEN A SCRATCH. THE ARMOR IS TOO THICK.
IT'S LIKE DOING BATTLE WITH A MOUNTAIN.
HEY.
STINKBUG.

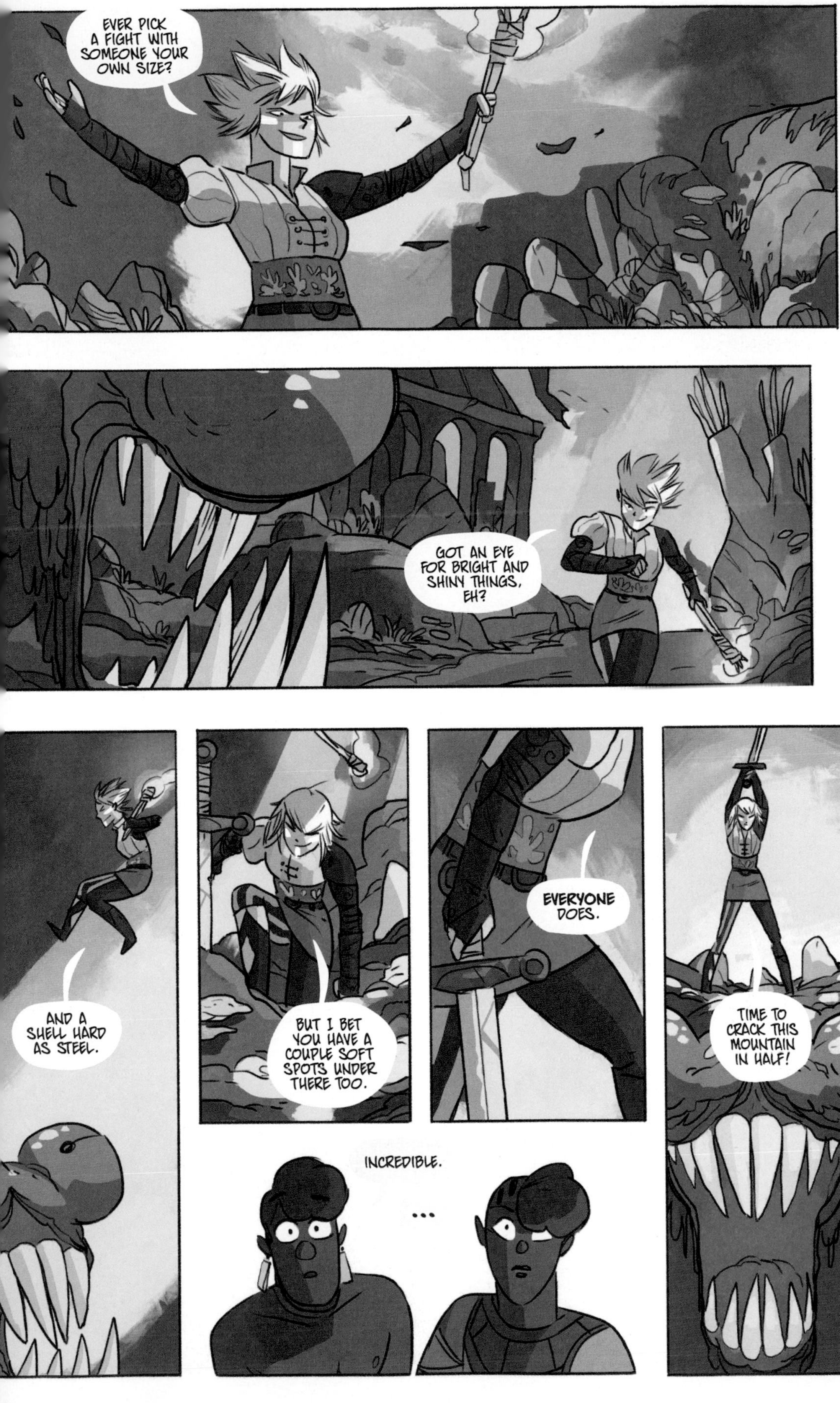
EVER PICK A FIGHT WITH SOMEONE YOUR OWN SIZE?
GOT AN EYE FOR BRIGHT AND SHINY THINGS, EH?
AND A SHELL HARD AS STEEL.
BUT I BET YOU HAVE A COUPLE SOFT SPOTS UNDER THERE TOO.
EVERYONE DOES.
TIME TO CRACK THIS MOUNTAIN IN HALF!
INCREDIBLE.
...

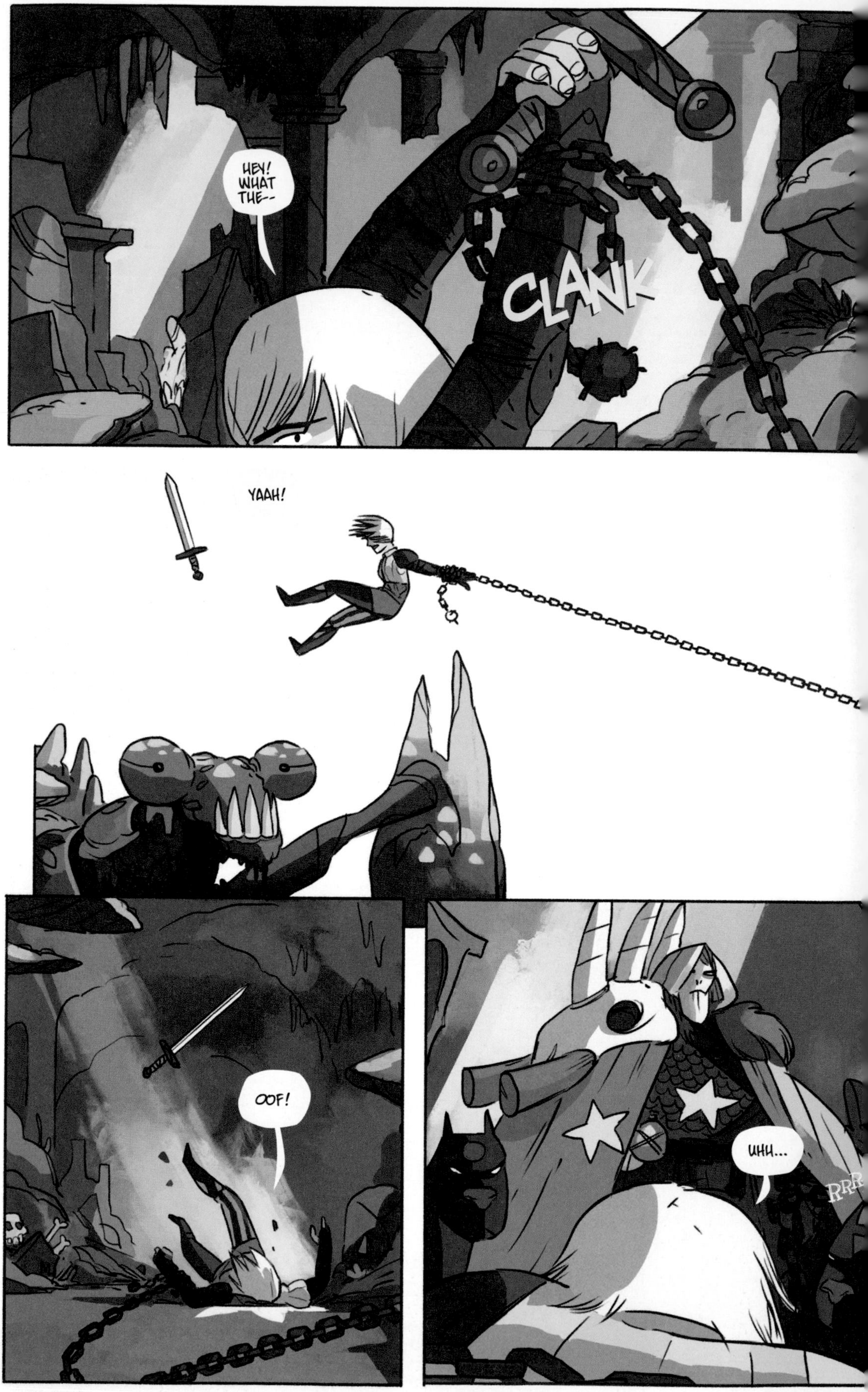
HEY! WHAT THE--
CLANK
YAAH!
OOF!
UHH...
RRR

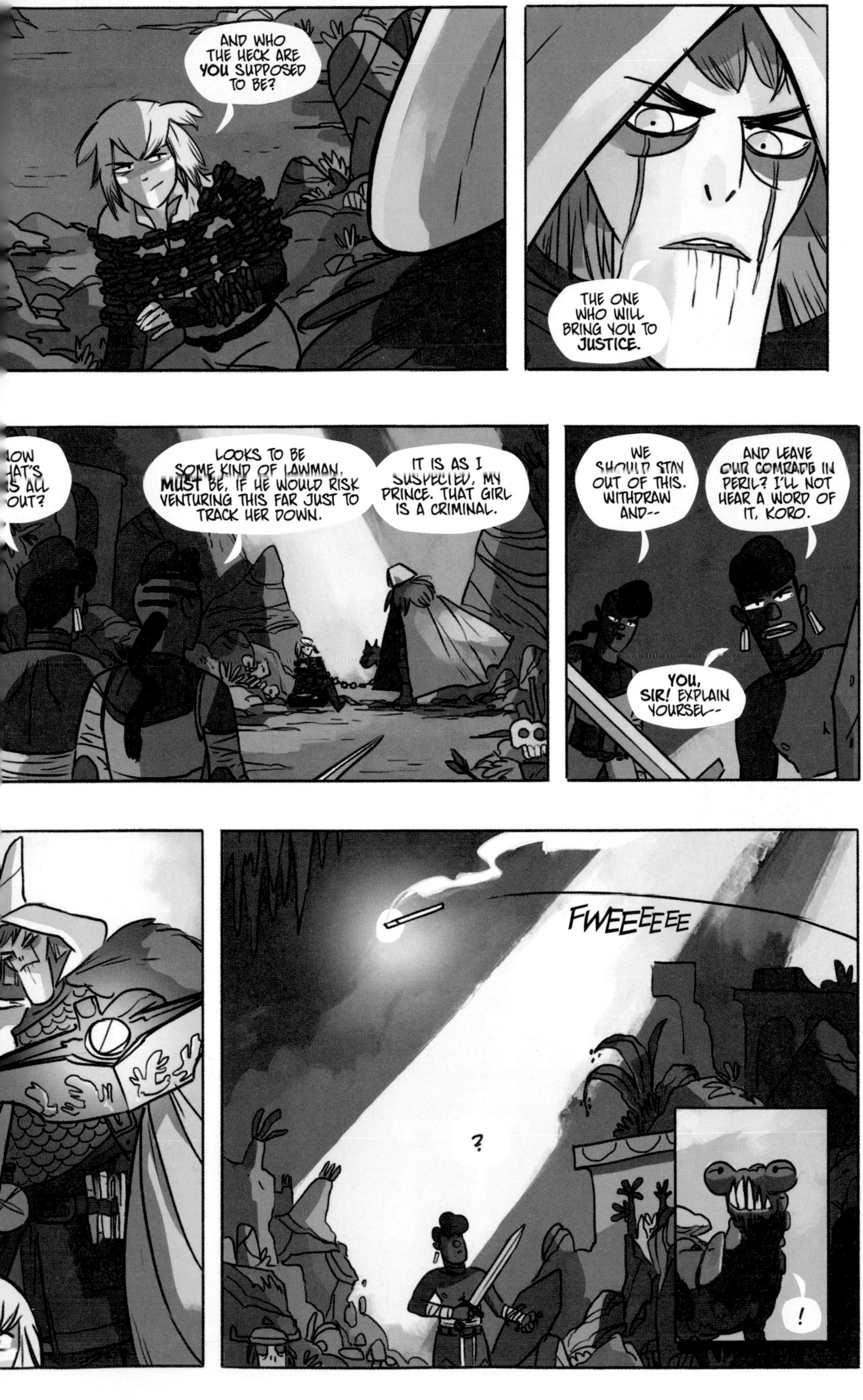
AND WHO THE HECK ARE YOU SUPPOSED TO BE?
THE ONE WHO WILL BRING YOU TO JUSTICE.
LOOKS TO BE SOME KIND OF LAWMAN. MUST BE, IF HE WOULD RISK VENTURING THIS FAR JUST TO TRACK HER DOWN.
IT IS AS I SUSPECTED, MY PRINCE. THAT GIRL IS A CRIMINAL.
WE SHOULD STAY OUT OF THIS. WITHDRAW AND--
AND LEAVE OUR COMRADE IN PERIL? I'LL NOT HEAR A WORD OF IT, KORO.
YOU, SIR! EXPLAIN YOURSEL--
FWEEEEEE
?
!

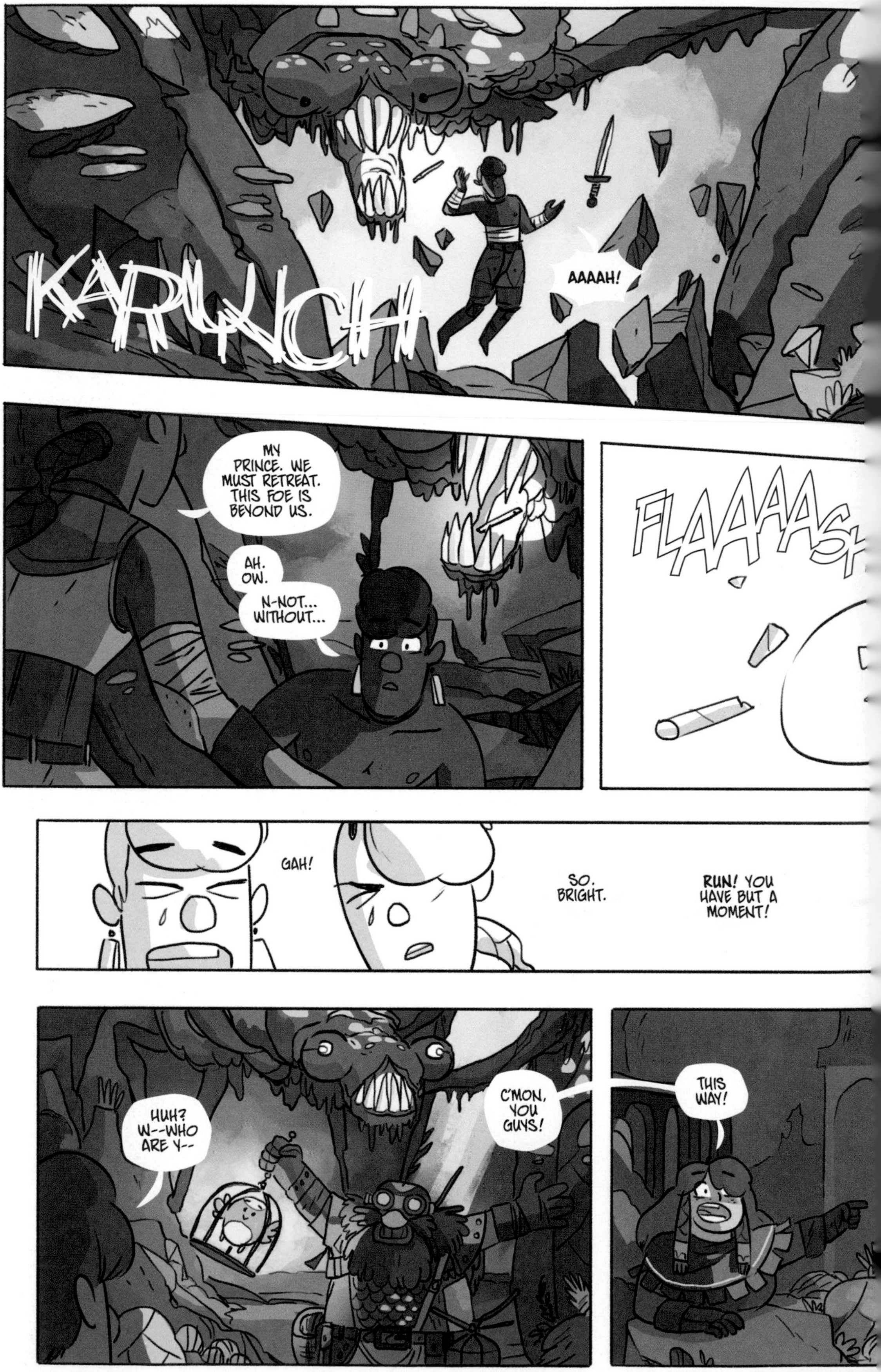

KARUNCH
AAAAH!
MY PRINCE. WE MUST RETREAT. THIS FOE IS BEYOND US.
AH. OW.
N-NOT... WITHOUT...
FLAAAASH
GAH!
SO. BRIGHT.
RUN! YOU HAVE BUT A MOMENT!
HUH? W--WHO ARE Y--
C'MON, YOU GUYS!
THIS WAY!

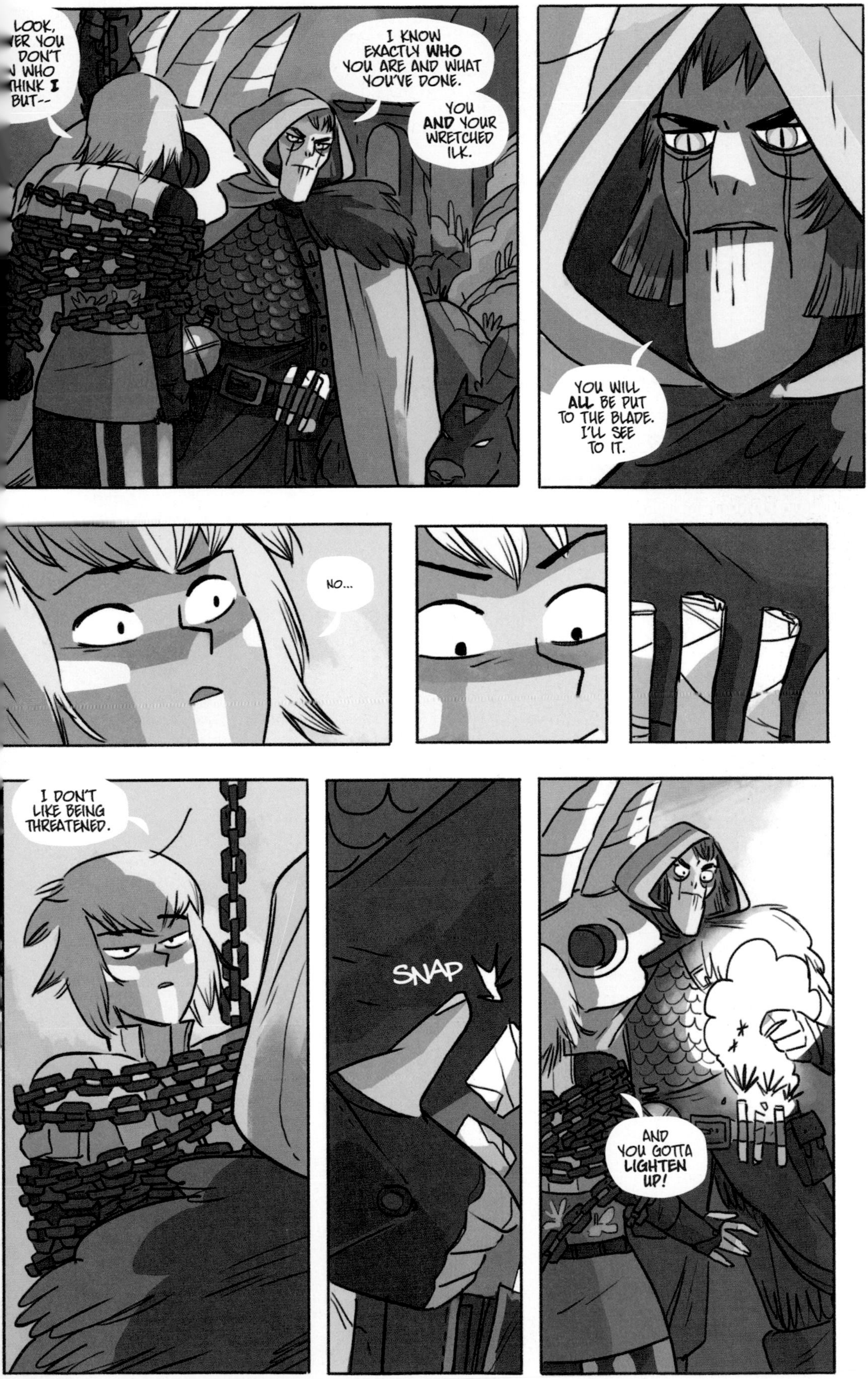

LOOK, ER YOU DON'T N WHO THINK I BUT--
I KNOW EXACTLY WHO YOU ARE AND WHAT YOU'VE DONE.
YOU AND YOUR WRETCHED ILK.
YOU WILL ALL BE PUT TO THE BLADE. I'LL SEE TO IT.
NO...
I DON'T LIKE BEING THREATENED.
SNAP
AND YOU GOTTA LIGHTEN UP!

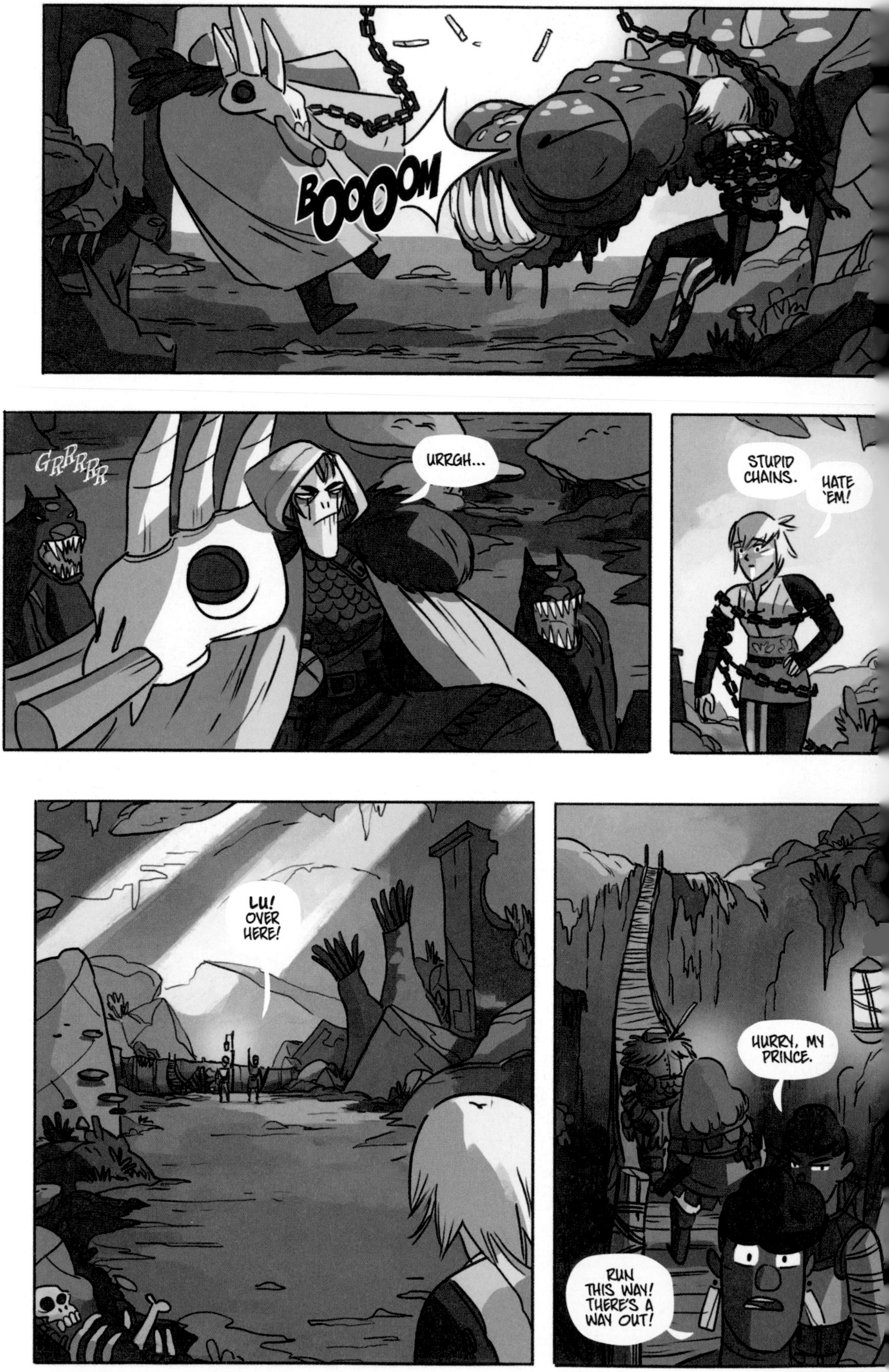
BOOOOM
GRRRRRR
URRGH...
STUPID CHAINS.
HATE 'EM!
LU! OVER HERE!
HURRY, MY PRINCE.
RUN THIS WAY! THERE'S A WAY OUT!

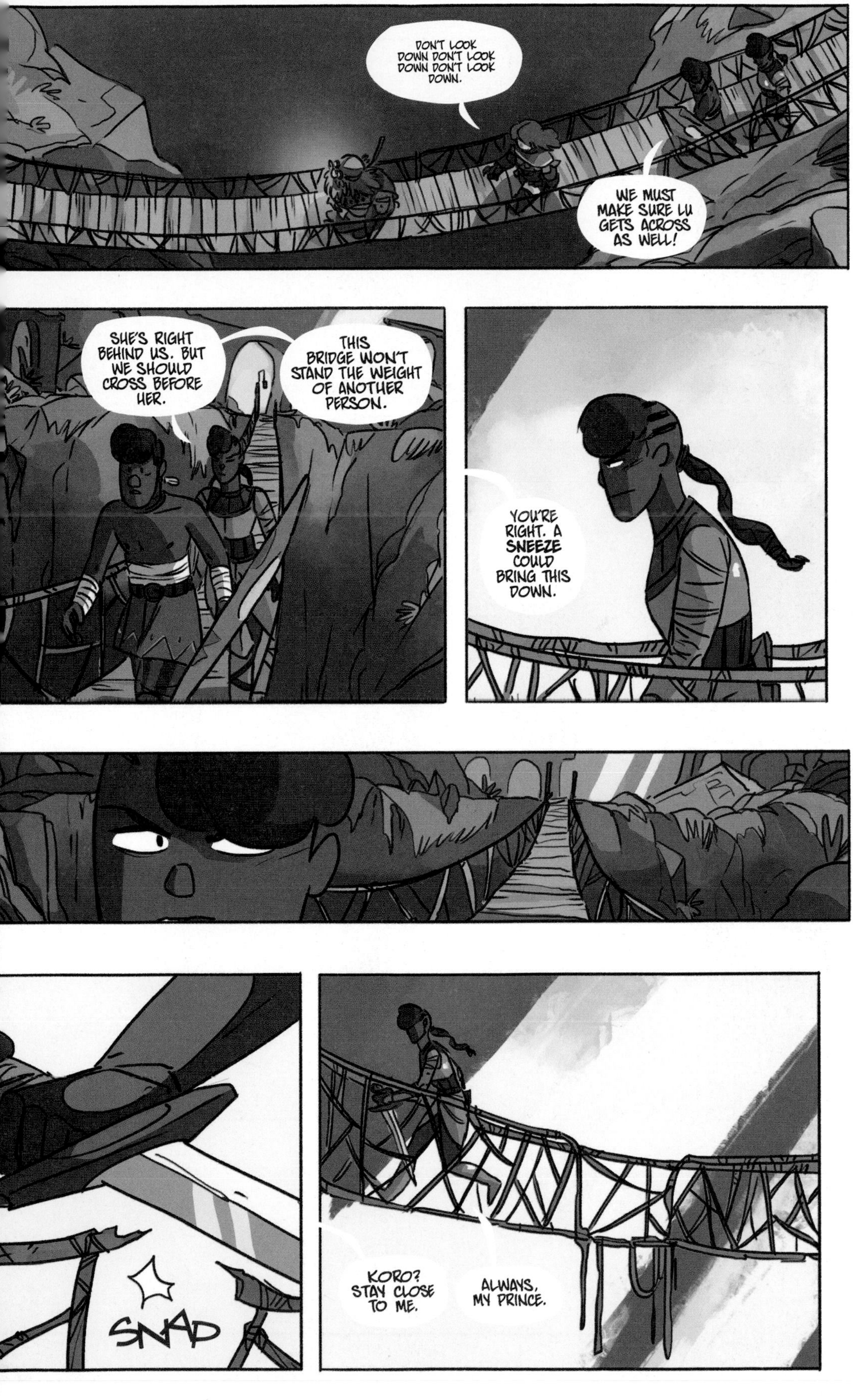
DON'T LOOK DOWN DON'T LOOK DOWN DON'T LOOK DOWN.
WE MUST MAKE SURE LU GETS ACROSS AS WELL!
SHE'S RIGHT BEHIND US. BUT WE SHOULD CROSS BEFORE HER.
THIS BRIDGE WON'T STAND THE WEIGHT OF ANOTHER PERSON.
YOU'RE RIGHT. A SNEEZE COULD BRING THIS DOWN.
SNAP
KORO? STAY CLOSE TO ME.
ALWAYS, MY PRINCE.

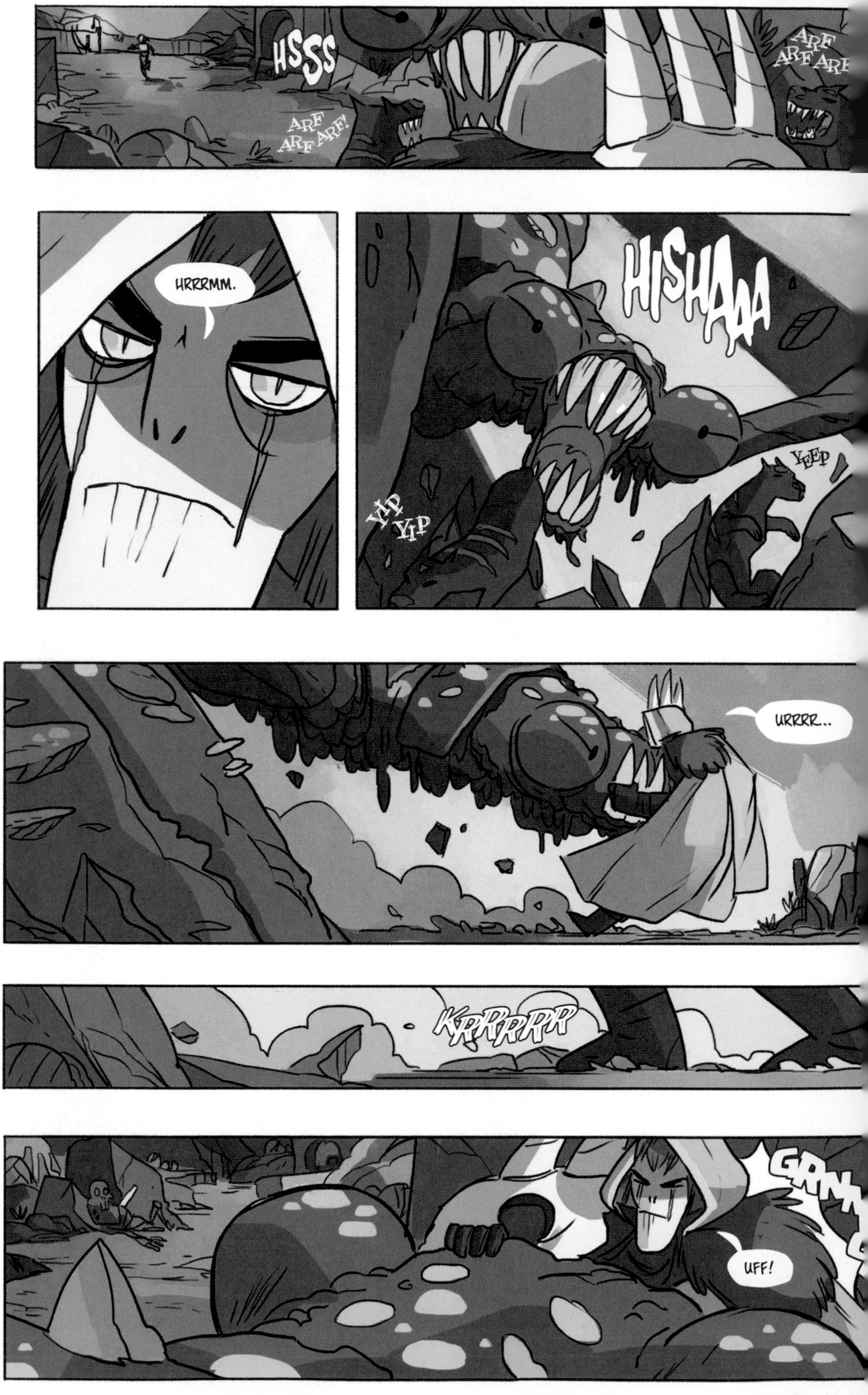
HSSS
ARF ARF ARF!
ARF ARF ARF
URRRMM.
HISHAAA
YIP YIP
YEEP
URRRR...
KRRRRRR
UFF!

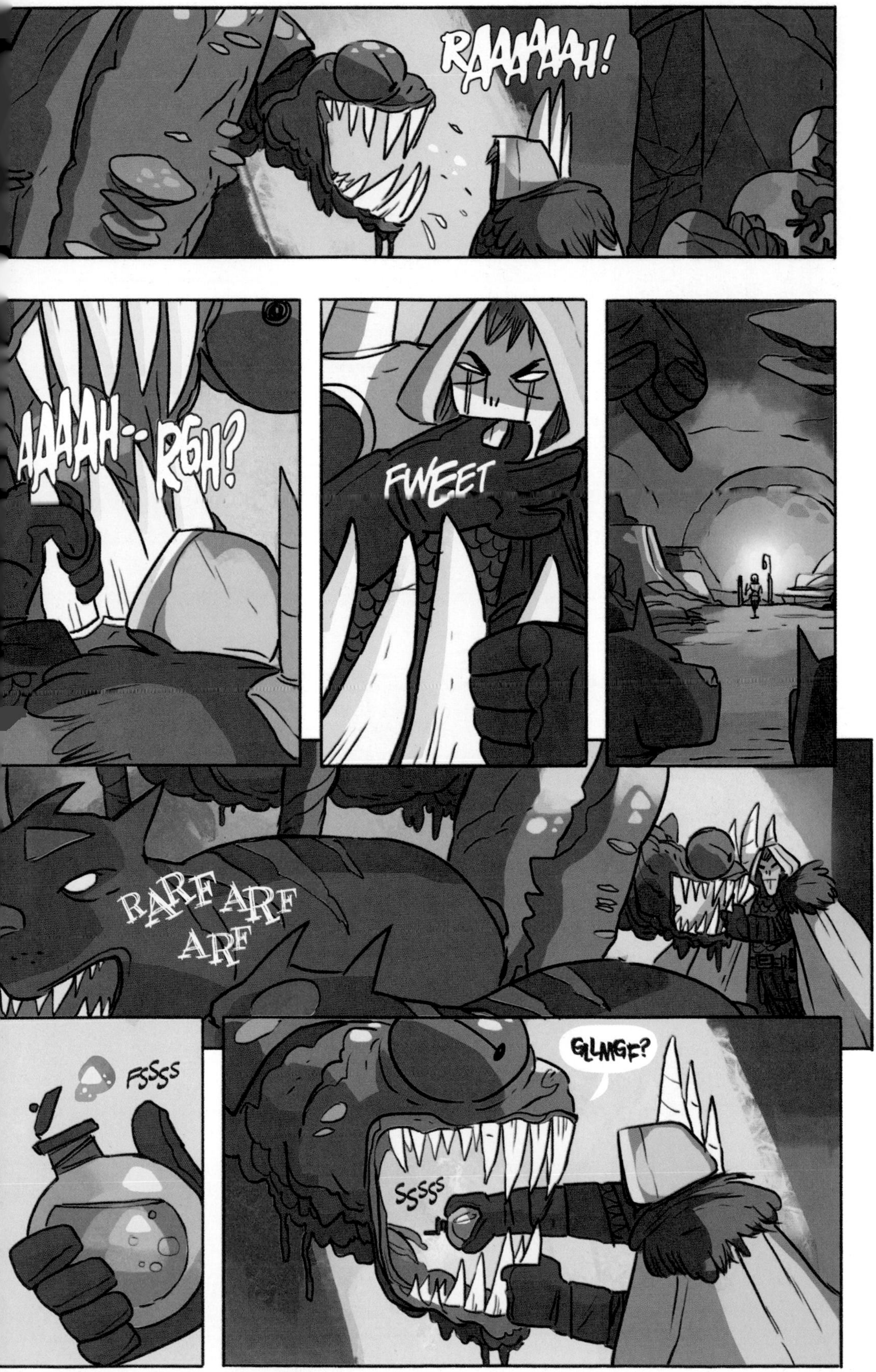
RAAAAAAH!
AAAAH-- RGH?
FWEET
RARF ARF
ARF
FSSSS
GLUGF?
SSSSS

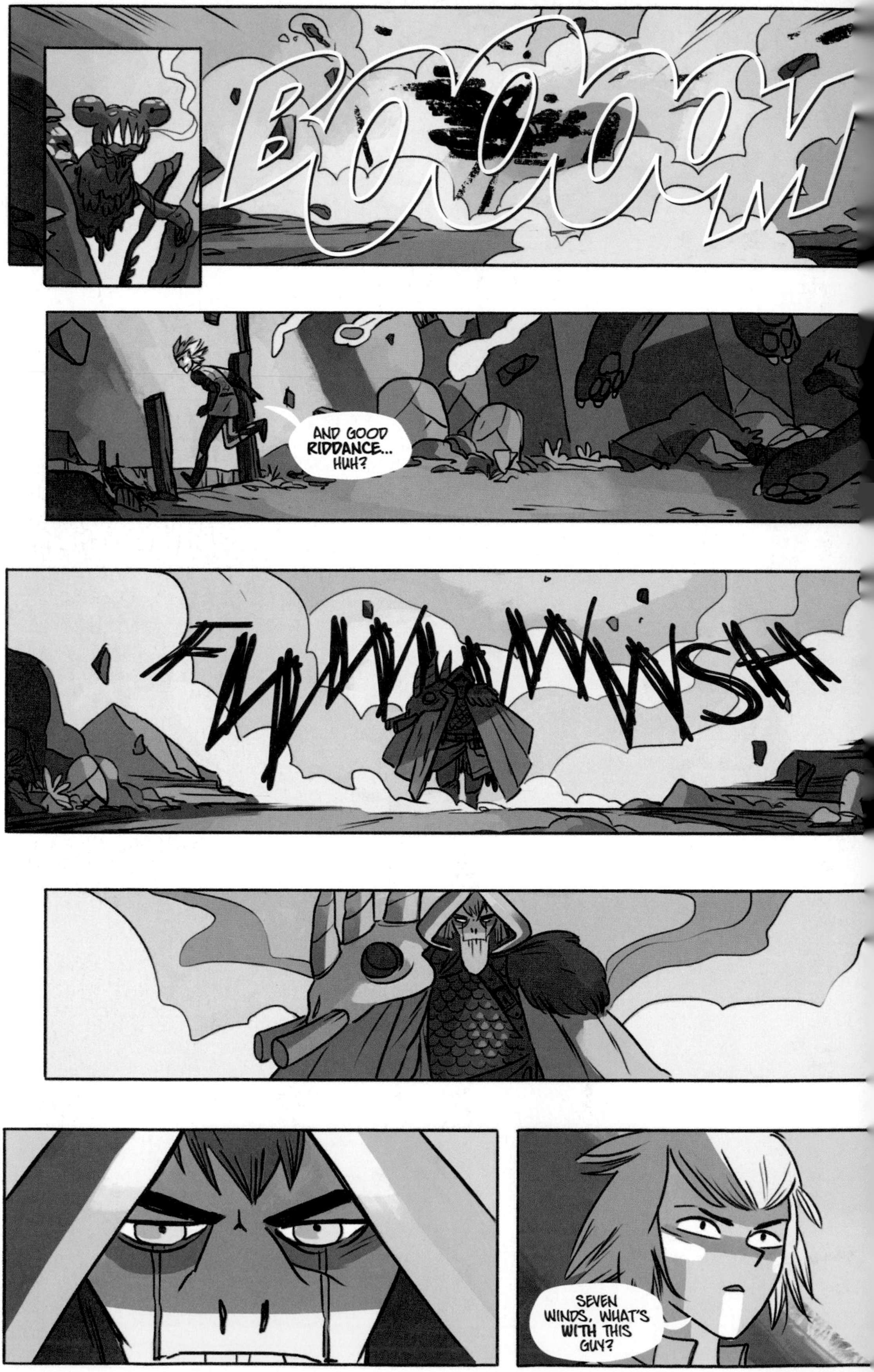
BOOOOOM
AND GOOD RIDDANCE... HUH?
FWWWWWSH
SEVEN WINDS, WHAT'S WITH THIS GUY?

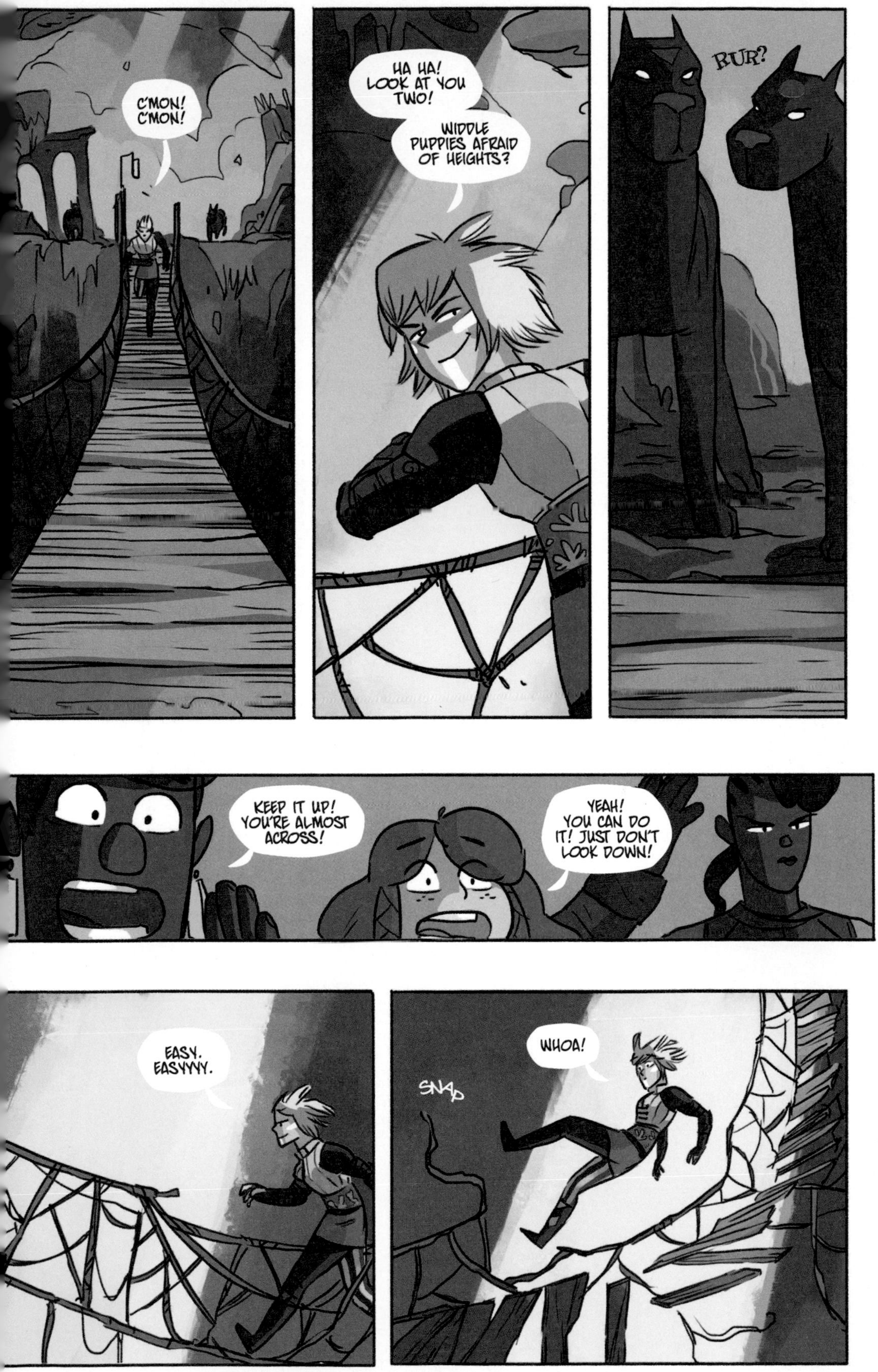

C'MON!
C'MON!
HA HA!
LOOK AT YOU
TWO!
WIDDLE
PUPPIES AFRAID
OF HEIGHTS?
BUR?
KEEP IT UP!
YOU'RE ALMOST
ACROSS!
YEAH!
YOU CAN DO
IT! JUST DON'T
LOOK DOWN!
EASY.
EASYYYY.
SNAP
WHOA!

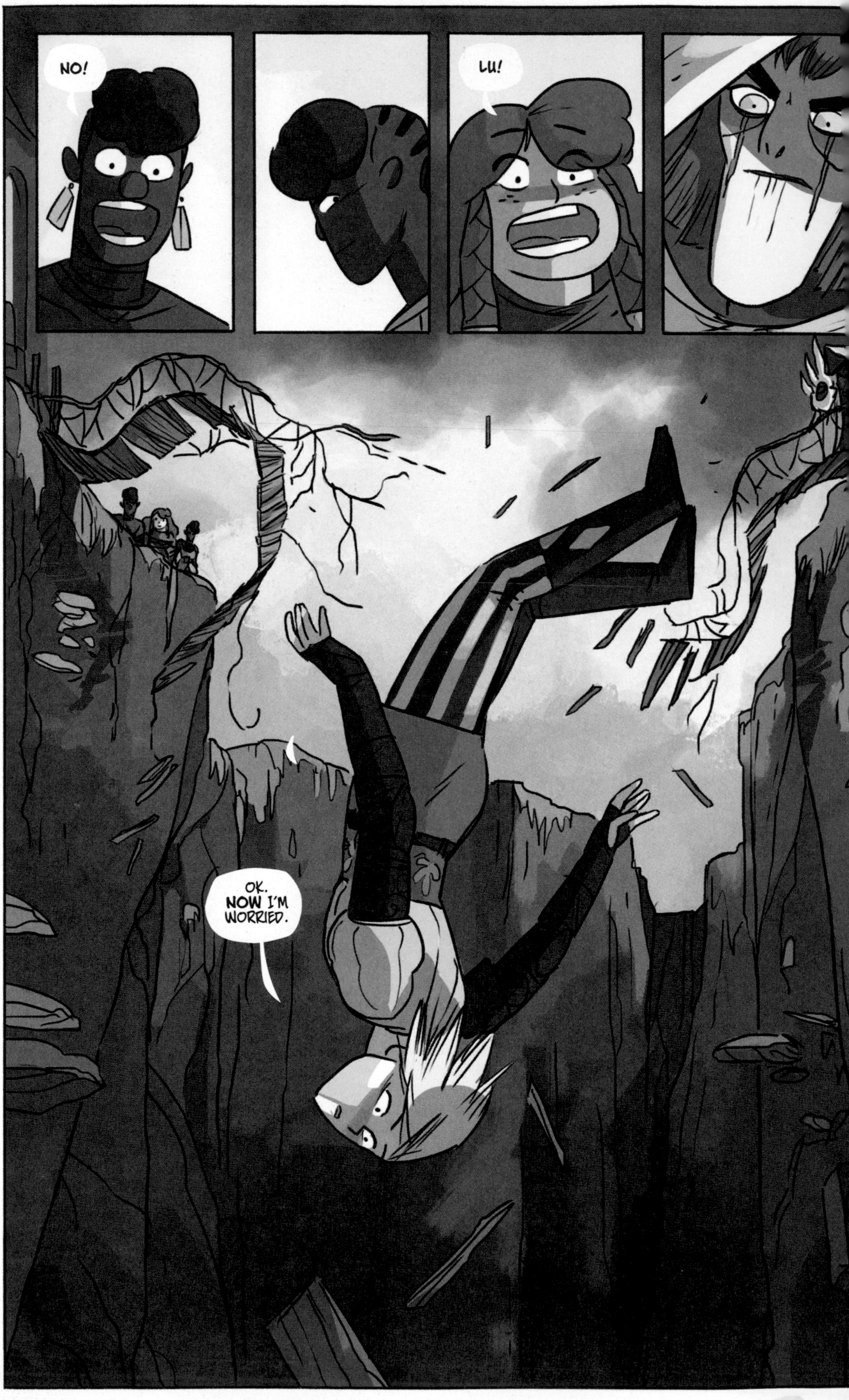
NO!
LU!
OK. NOW I'M WORRIED.

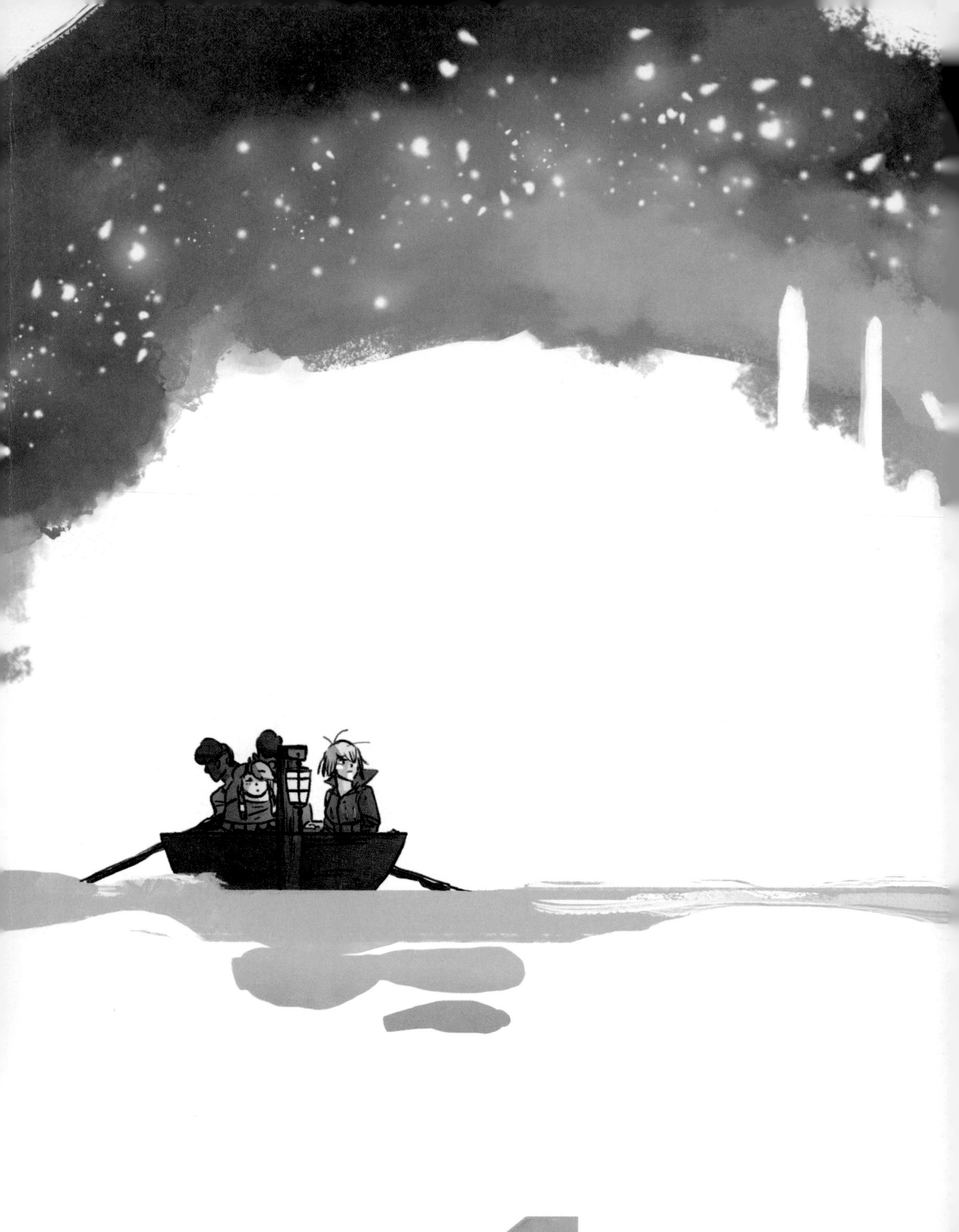

4

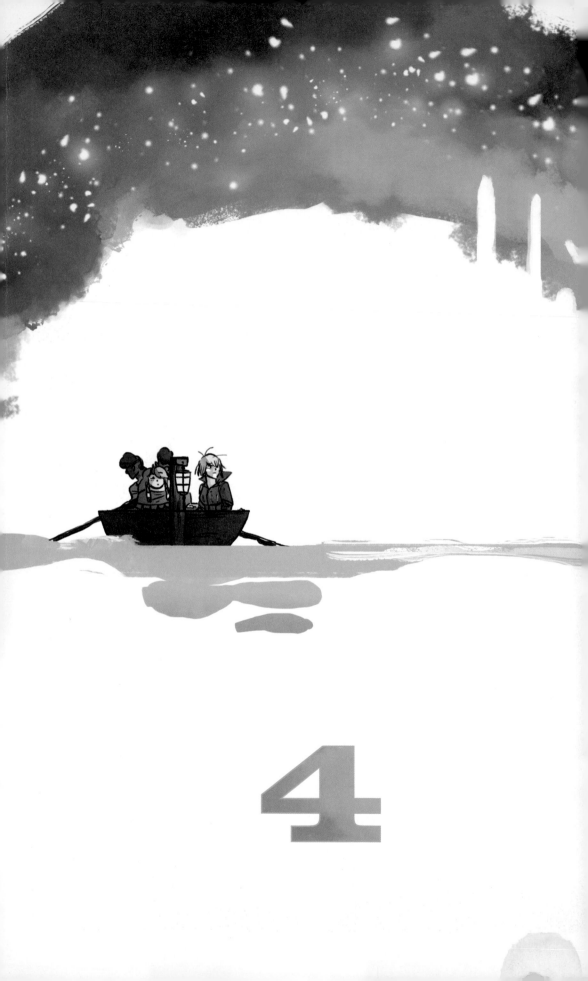

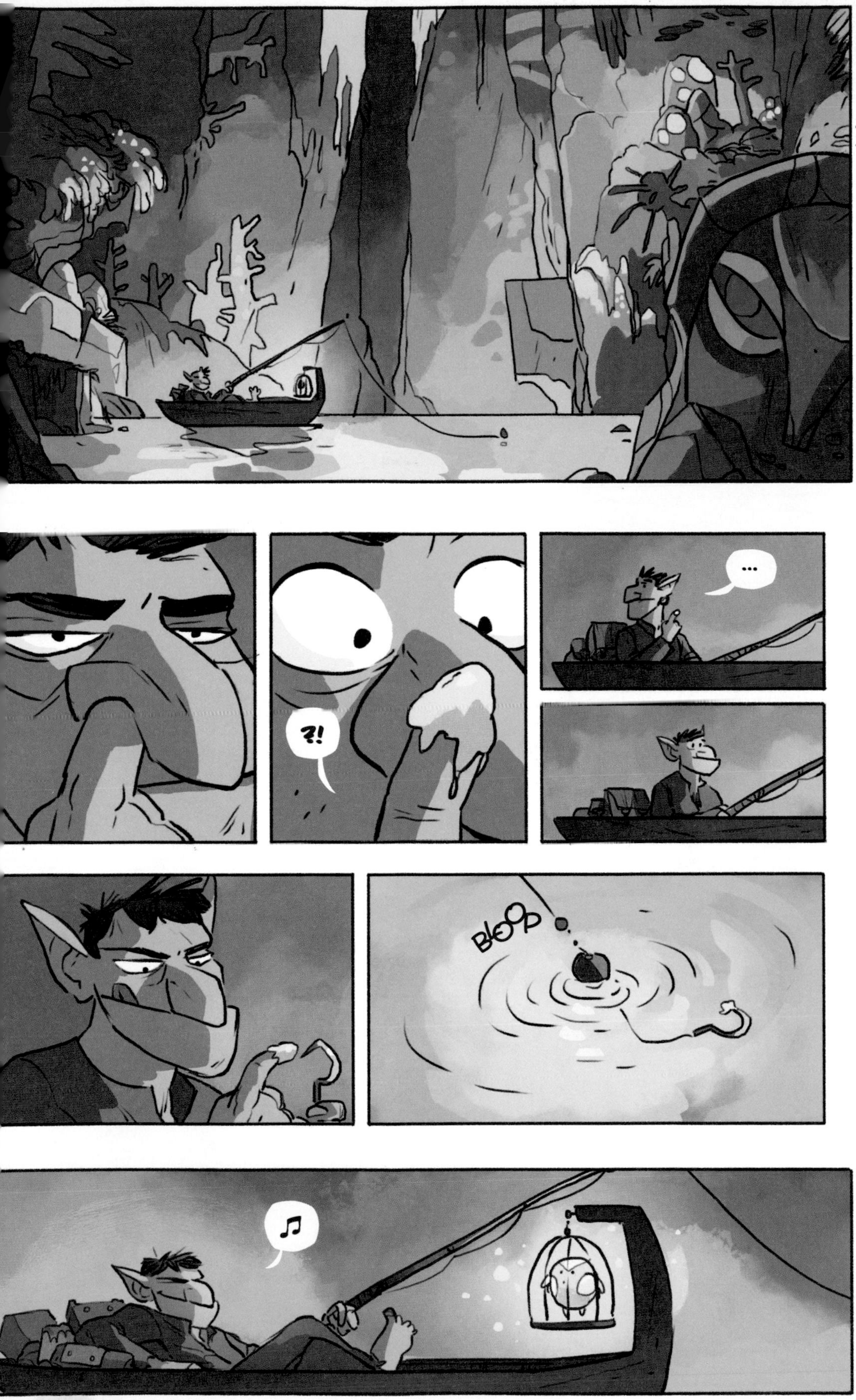

?!
...
BLOOP
♫

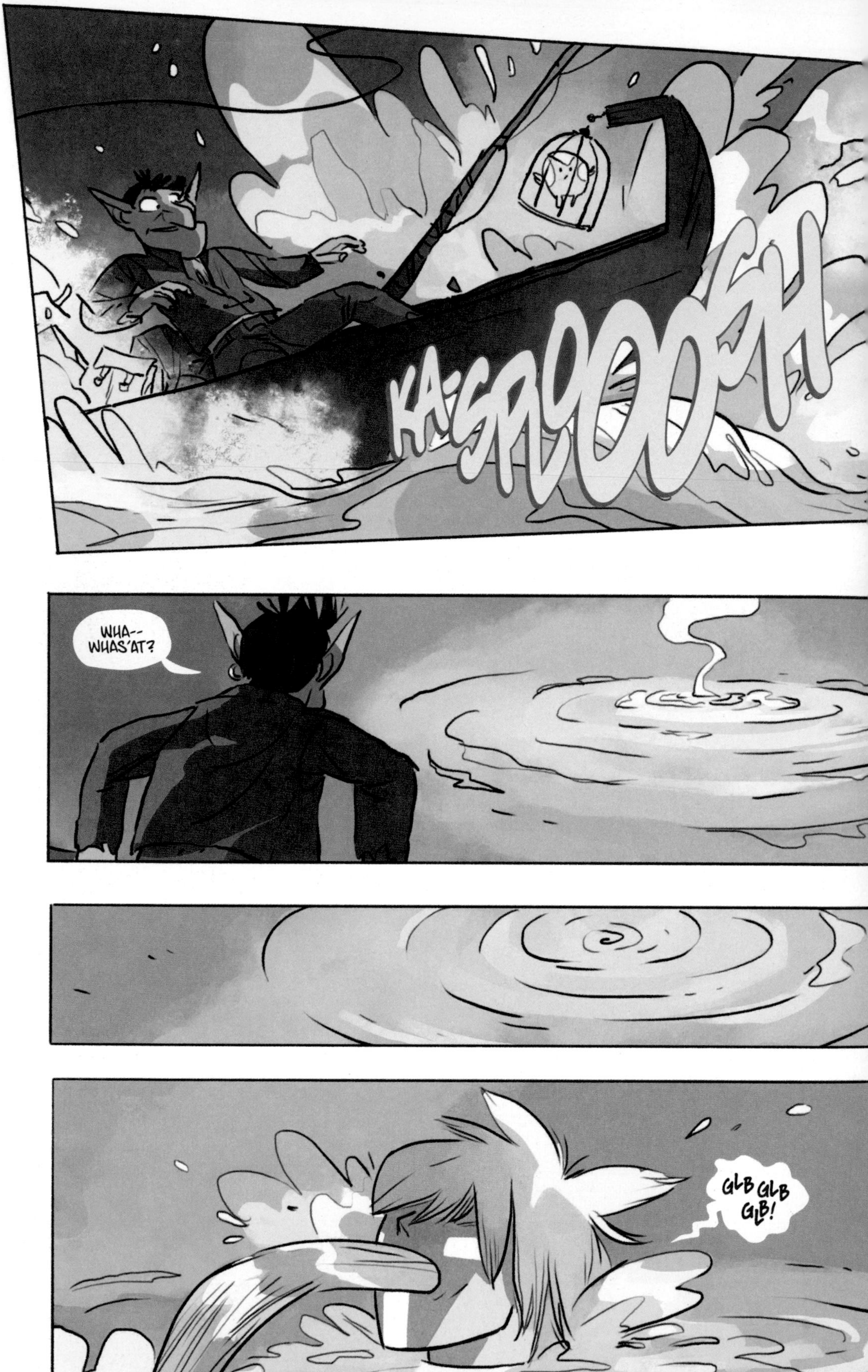
KA-SPLOOOSH
WHA-- WHAS'AT?
GLB GLB GLB!

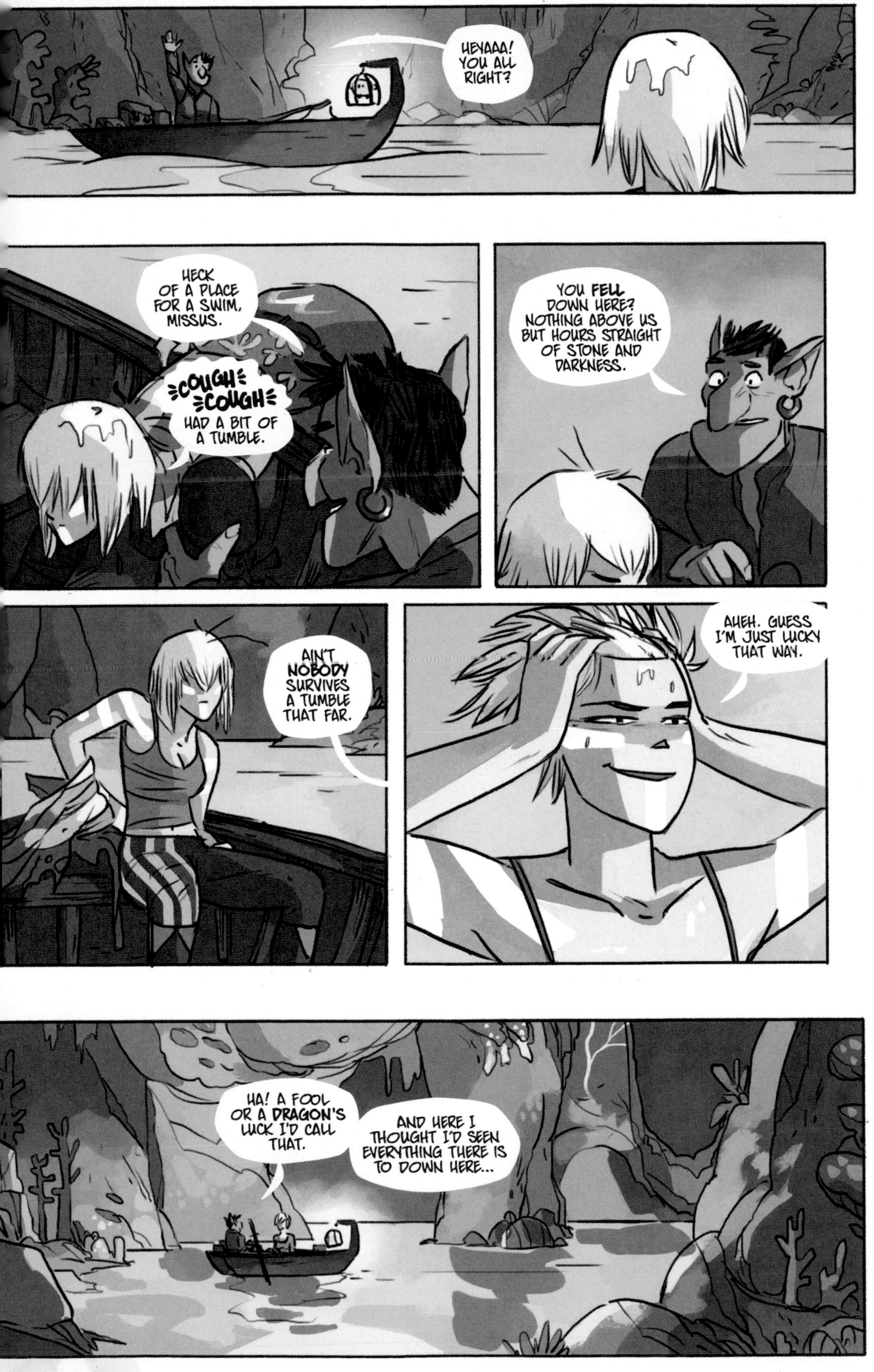
HEYAAA! YOU ALL RIGHT?
HECK OF A PLACE FOR A SWIM, MISSUS.
COUGH COUGH HAD A BIT OF A TUMBLE.
YOU FELL DOWN HERE? NOTHING ABOVE US BUT HOURS STRAIGHT OF STONE AND DARKNESS.
AIN'T NOBODY SURVIVES A TUMBLE THAT FAR.
AHEH. GUESS I'M JUST LUCKY THAT WAY.
HA! A FOOL OR A DRAGON'S LUCK I'D CALL THAT.
AND HERE I THOUGHT I'D SEEN EVERYTHING THERE IS TO DOWN HERE...

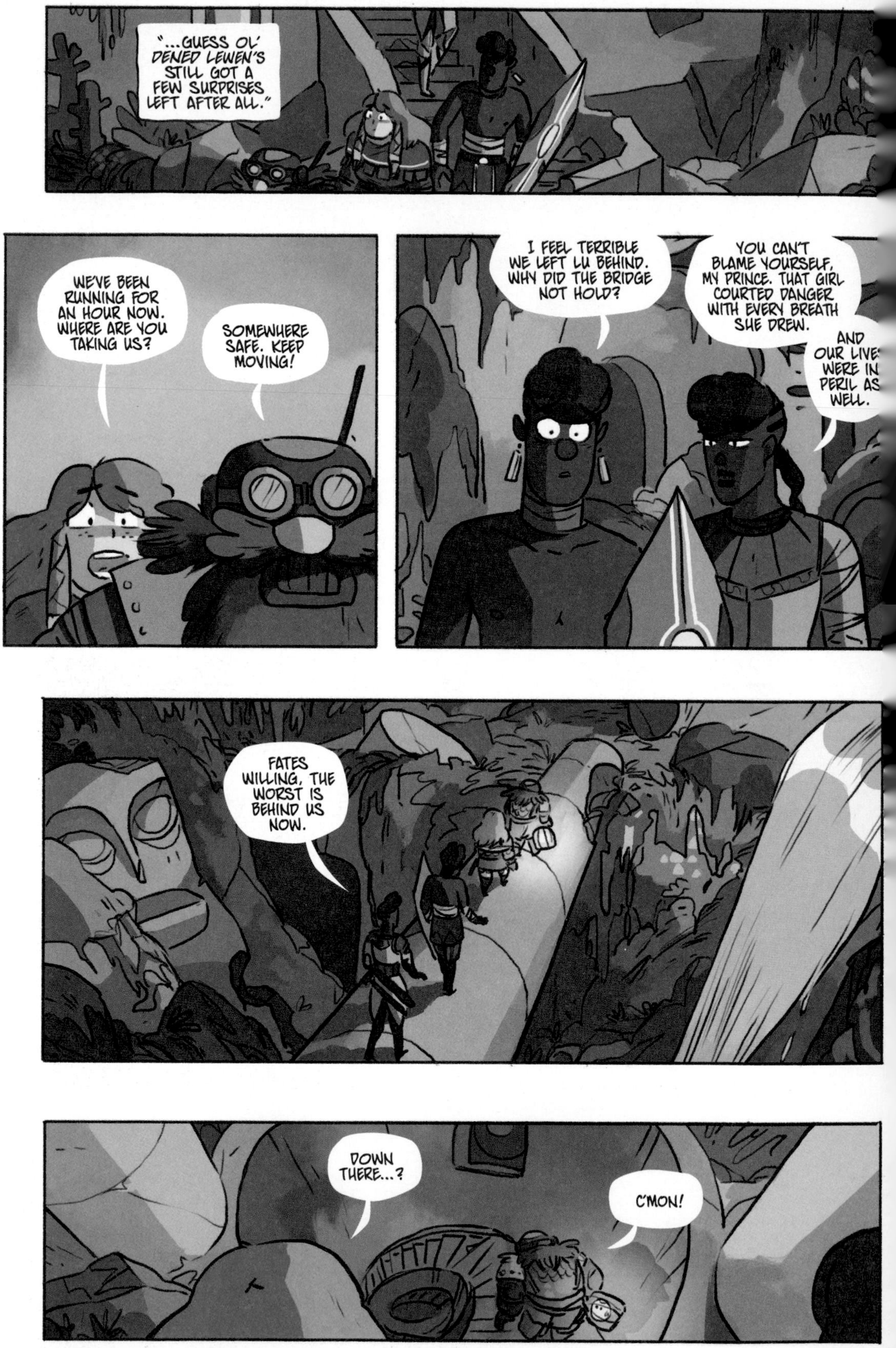
"...GUESS OL' DENED LEWEN'S STILL GOT A FEW SURPRISES LEFT AFTER ALL."
WE'VE BEEN RUNNING FOR AN HOUR NOW. WHERE ARE YOU TAKING US?
SOMEWHERE SAFE. KEEP MOVING!
I FEEL TERRIBLE WE LEFT LU BEHIND. WHY DID THE BRIDGE NOT HOLD?
YOU CAN'T BLAME YOURSELF, MY PRINCE. THAT GIRL COURTED DANGER WITH EVERY BREATH SHE DREW.
AND OUR LIVES WERE IN PERIL AS WELL.
FATES WILLING, THE WORST IS BEHIND US NOW.
DOWN THERE...?
C'MON!

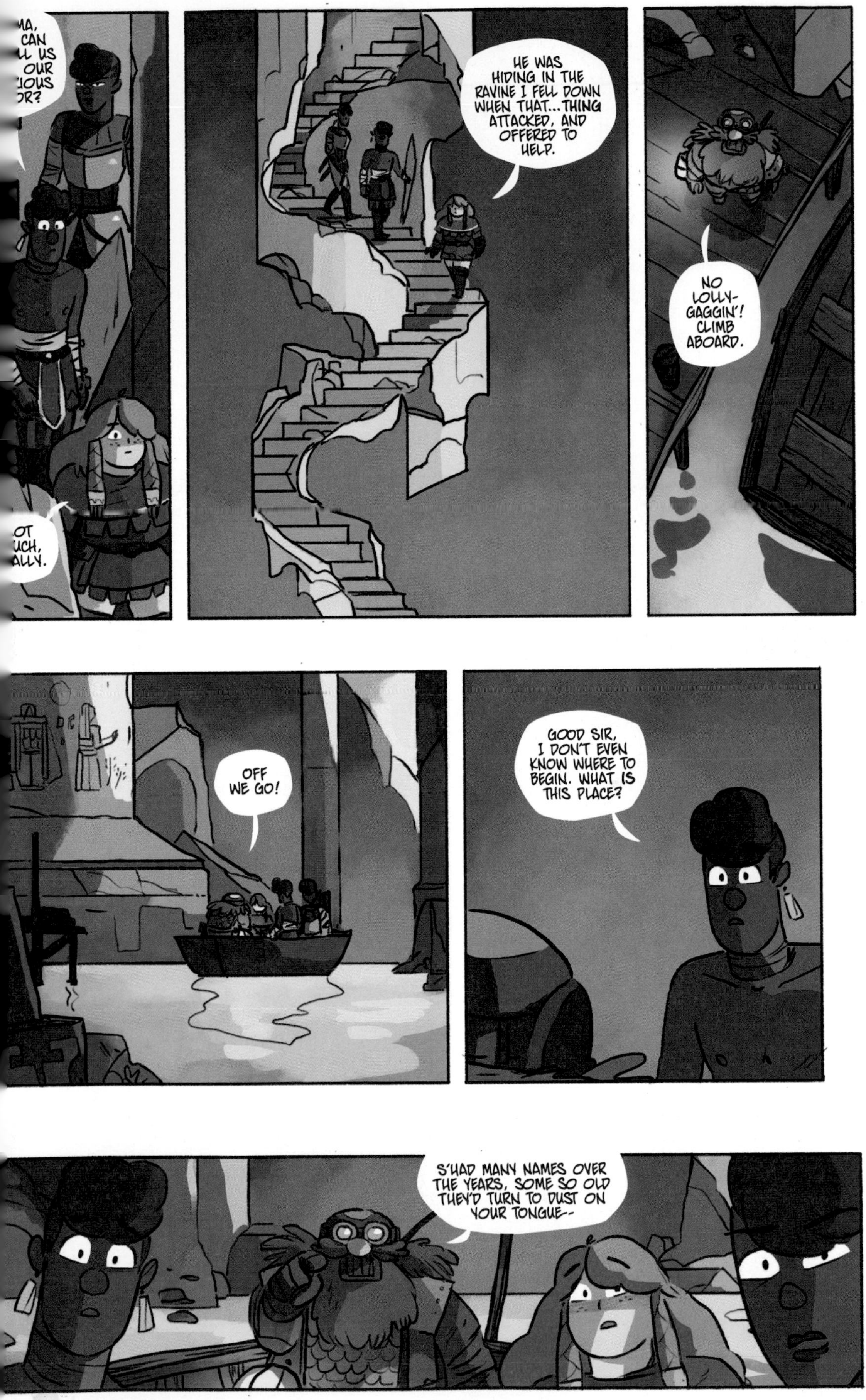

HE WAS HIDING IN THE RAVINE I FELL DOWN WHEN THAT...THING ATTACKED, AND OFFERED TO HELP.
NO LOLLY-GAGGIN'! CLIMB ABOARD.
OFF WE GO!
GOOD SIR, I DON'T EVEN KNOW WHERE TO BEGIN. WHAT IS THIS PLACE?
S'HAD MANY NAMES OVER THE YEARS, SOME SO OLD THEY'D TURN TO DUST ON YOUR TONGUE--

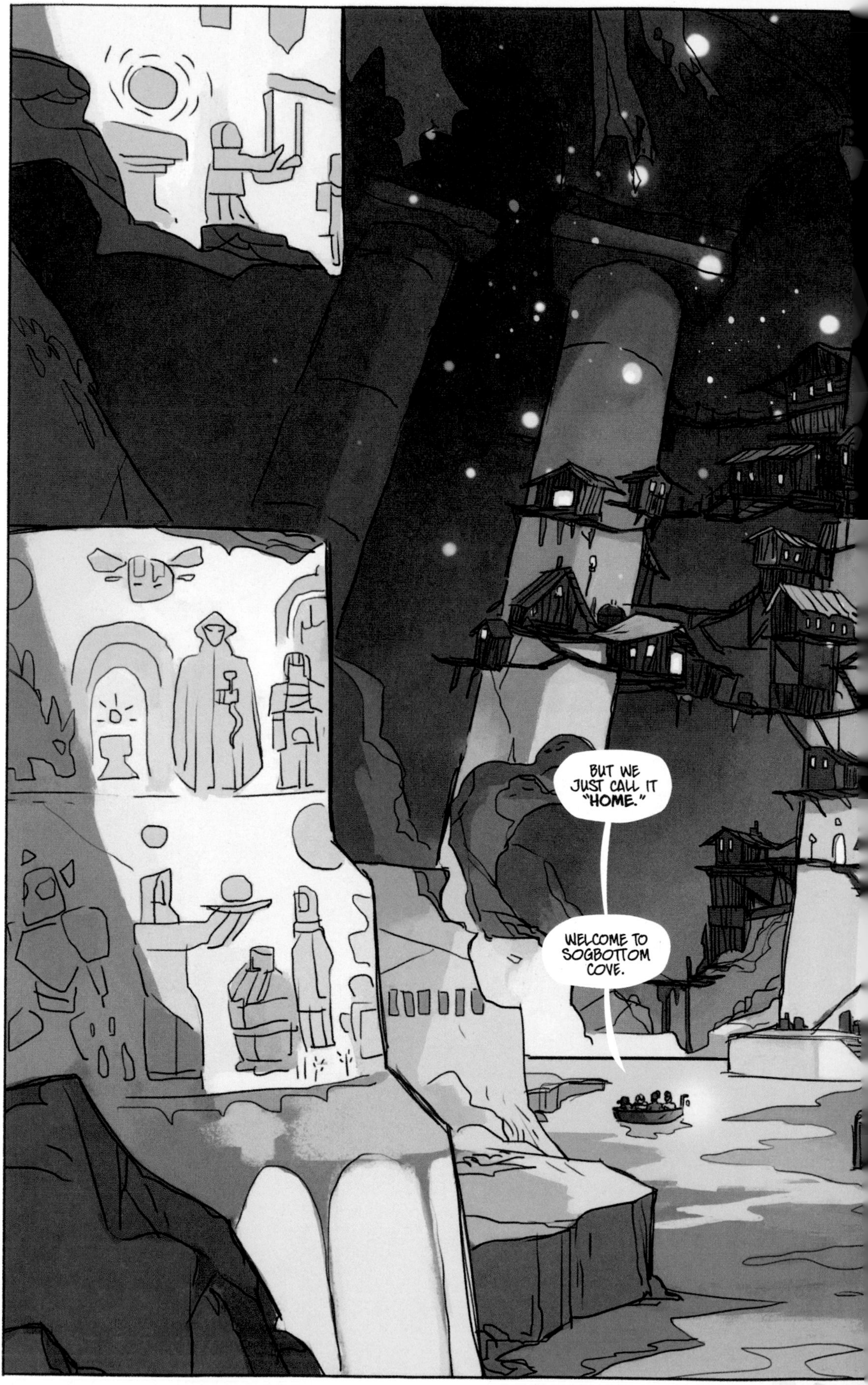
BUT WE JUST CALL IT "HOME."
WELCOME TO SOGBOTTOM COVE.

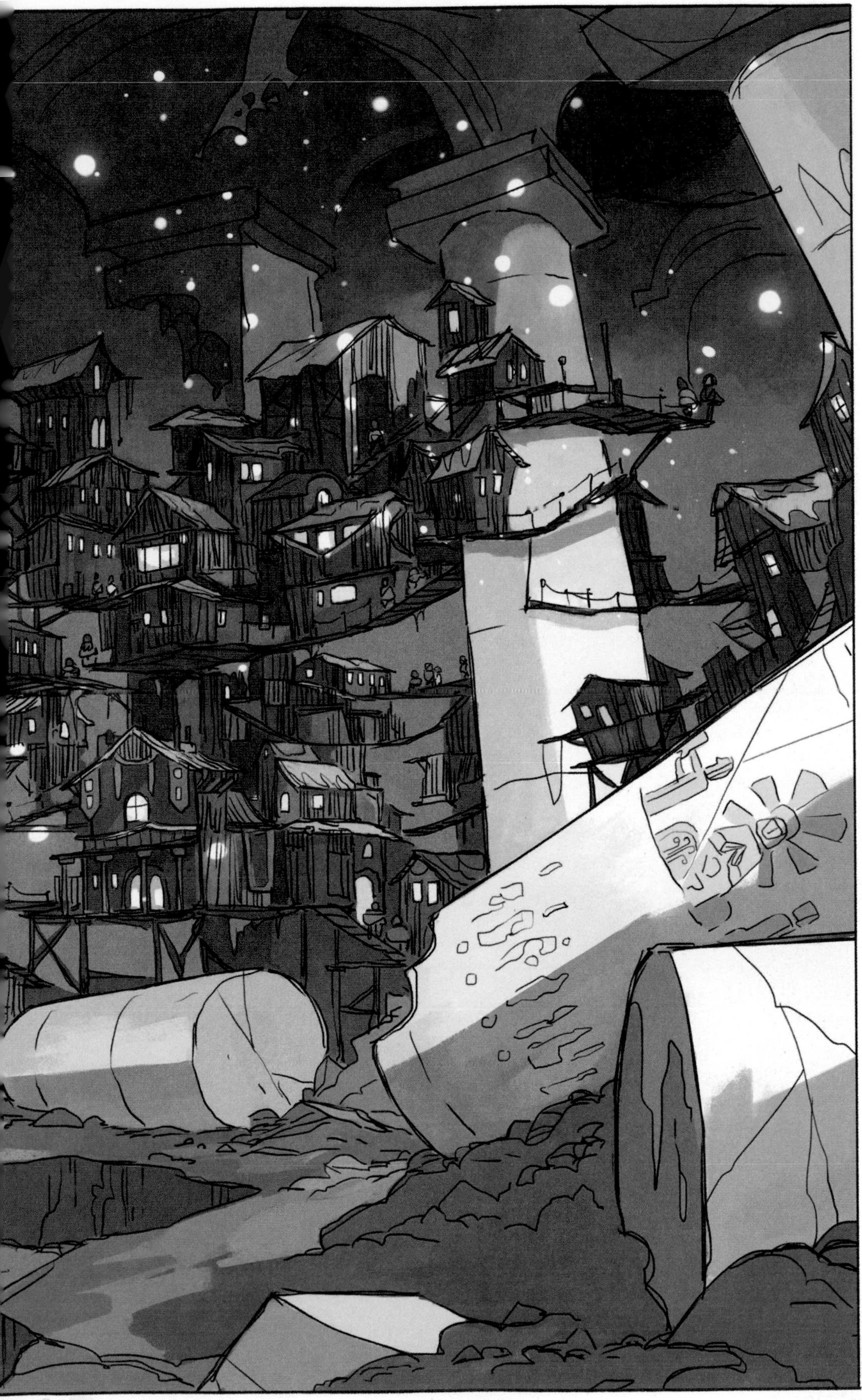

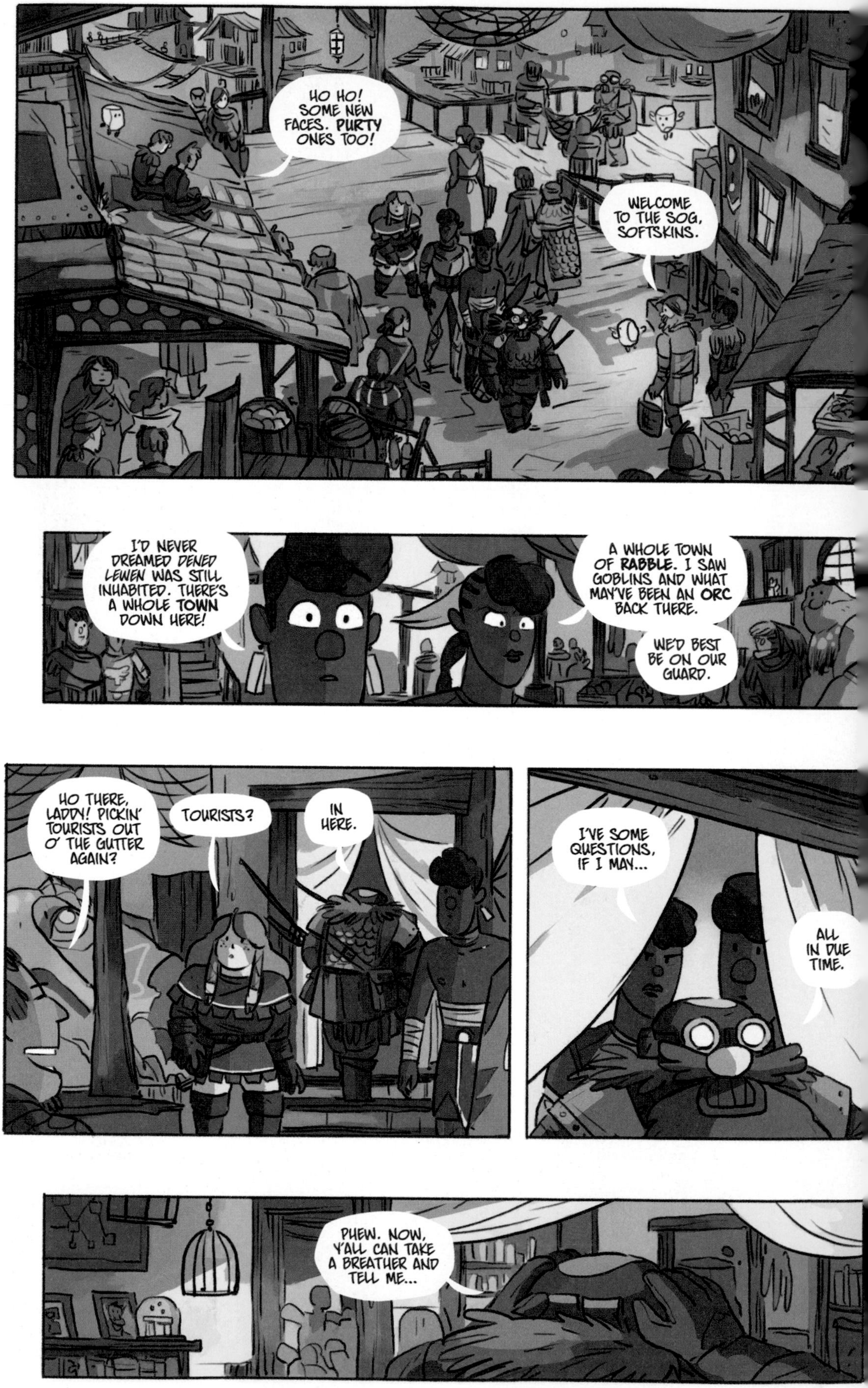
HO HO! SOME NEW FACES. PURTY ONES TOO!
WELCOME TO THE SOG, SOFTSKINS.
I'D NEVER DREAMED DENED LEWEN WAS STILL INHABITED. THERE'S A WHOLE TOWN DOWN HERE!
A WHOLE TOWN OF RABBLE. I SAW GOBLINS AND WHAT MAY'VE BEEN AN ORC BACK THERE.
WE'D BEST BE ON OUR GUARD.
HO THERE, LADDY! PICKIN' TOURISTS OUT O' THE GUTTER AGAIN?
TOURISTS?
IN HERE.
I'VE SOME QUESTIONS, IF I MAY...
ALL IN DUE TIME.
PHEW. NOW, Y'ALL CAN TAKE A BREATHER AND TELL ME...

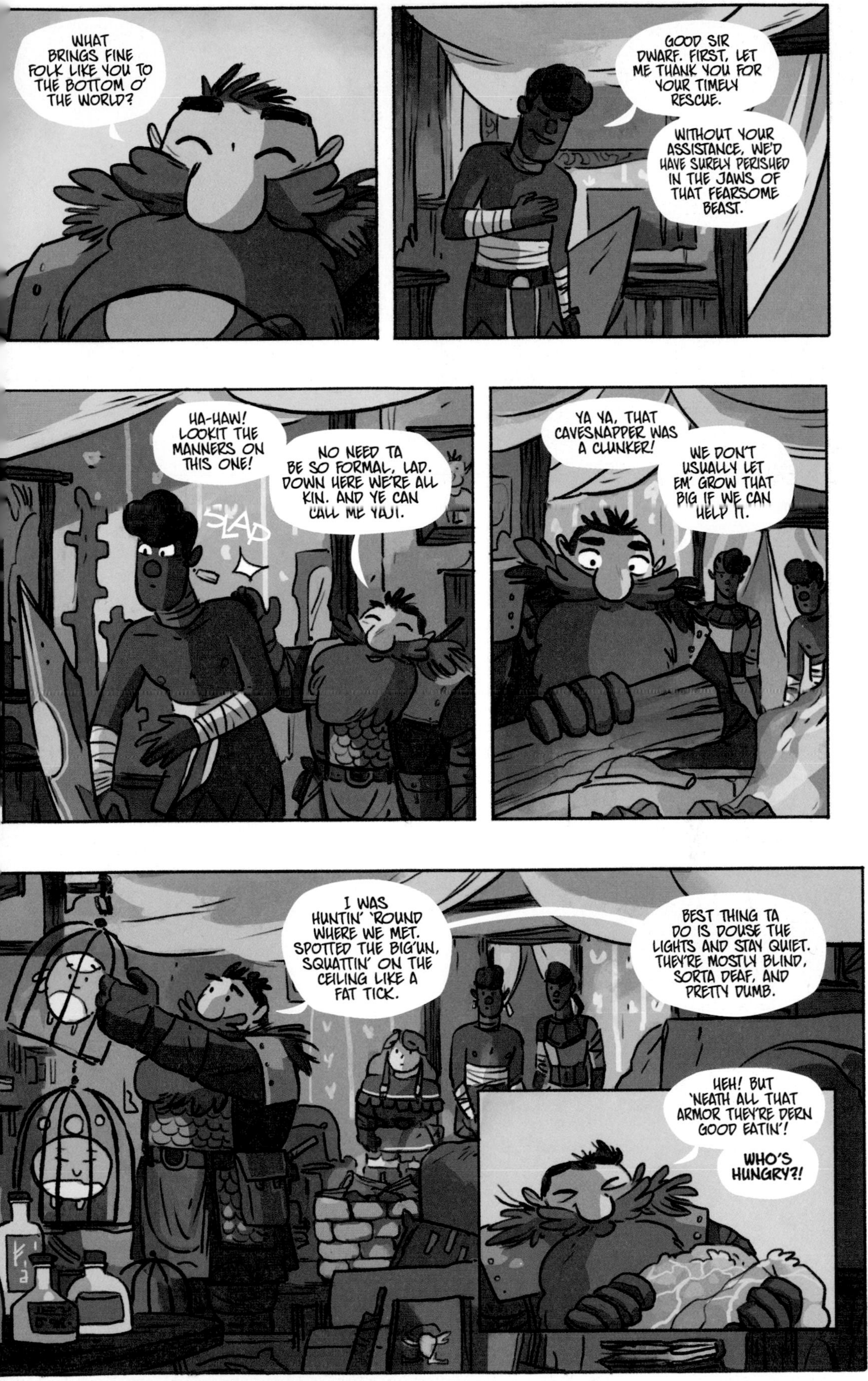
WHAT BRINGS FINE FOLK LIKE YOU TO THE BOTTOM O' THE WORLD?
GOOD SIR DWARF. FIRST, LET ME THANK YOU FOR YOUR TIMELY RESCUE.
WITHOUT YOUR ASSISTANCE, WE'D HAVE SURELY PERISHED IN THE JAWS OF THAT FEARSOME BEAST.
HA-HAW! LOOKIT THE MANNERS ON THIS ONE!
SLAP
NO NEED TA BE SO FORMAL, LAD. DOWN HERE WE'RE ALL KIN. AND YE CAN CALL ME YAJI.
YA YA, THAT CAVESNAPPER WAS A CLUNKER!
WE DON'T USUALLY LET EM' GROW THAT BIG IF WE CAN HELP IT.
I WAS HUNTIN' 'ROUND WHERE WE MET. SPOTTED THE BIG'UN, SQUATTIN' ON THE CEILING LIKE A FAT TICK.
BEST THING TA DO IS DOUSE THE LIGHTS AND STAY QUIET. THEY'RE MOSTLY BLIND, SORTA DEAF, AND PRETTY DUMB.
HEH! BUT 'NEATH ALL THAT ARMOR THEY'RE DERN GOOD EATIN'!
WHO'S HUNGRY?!

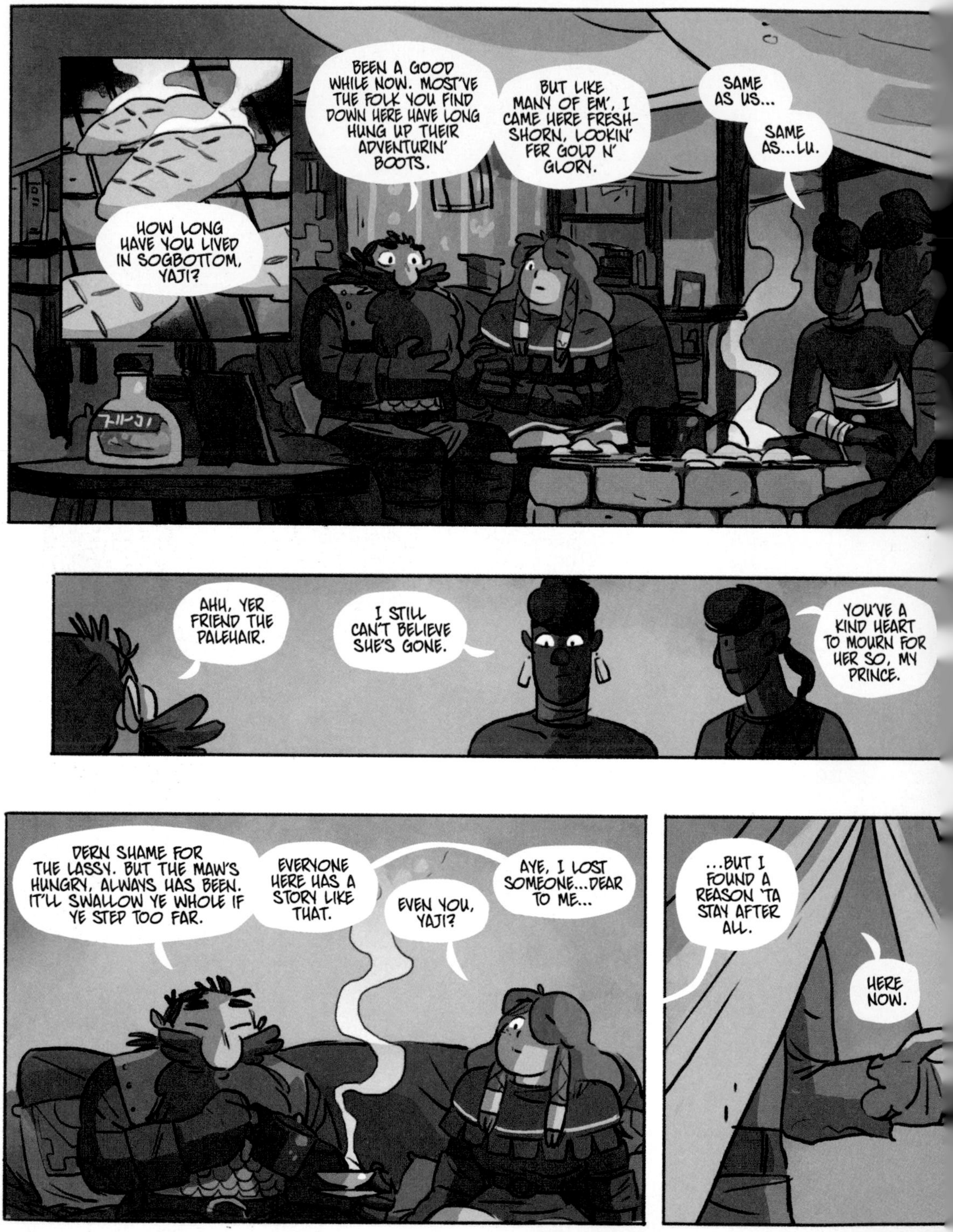
HOW LONG HAVE YOU LIVED IN SOGBOTTOM, YAJI?
BEEN A GOOD WHILE NOW. MOST'VE THE FOLK YOU FIND DOWN HERE HAVE LONG HUNG UP THEIR ADVENTURIN' BOOTS.
BUT LIKE MANY OF EM', I CAME HERE FRESH-SHORN, LOOKIN' FER GOLD N' GLORY.
SAME AS US...
SAME AS...LU.
AHU, YER FRIEND THE PALEHAIR.
I STILL CAN'T BELIEVE SHE'S GONE.
YOU'VE A KIND HEART TO MOURN FOR HER SO, MY PRINCE.
DERN SHAME FOR THE LASSY. BUT THE MAW'S HUNGRY, ALWAYS HAS BEEN. IT'LL SWALLOW YE WHOLE IF YE STEP TOO FAR.
EVERYONE HERE HAS A STORY LIKE THAT.
EVEN YOU, YAJI?
AYE, I LOST SOMEONE...DEAR TO ME...
...BUT I FOUND A REASON 'TA STAY AFTER ALL.
HERE NOW.
YOU'LL NEVER GUESS WHAT I CAUGHT-- HUH?
!!
?!

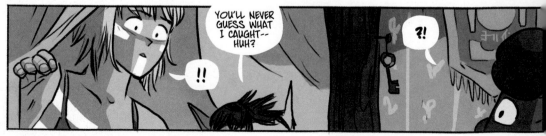

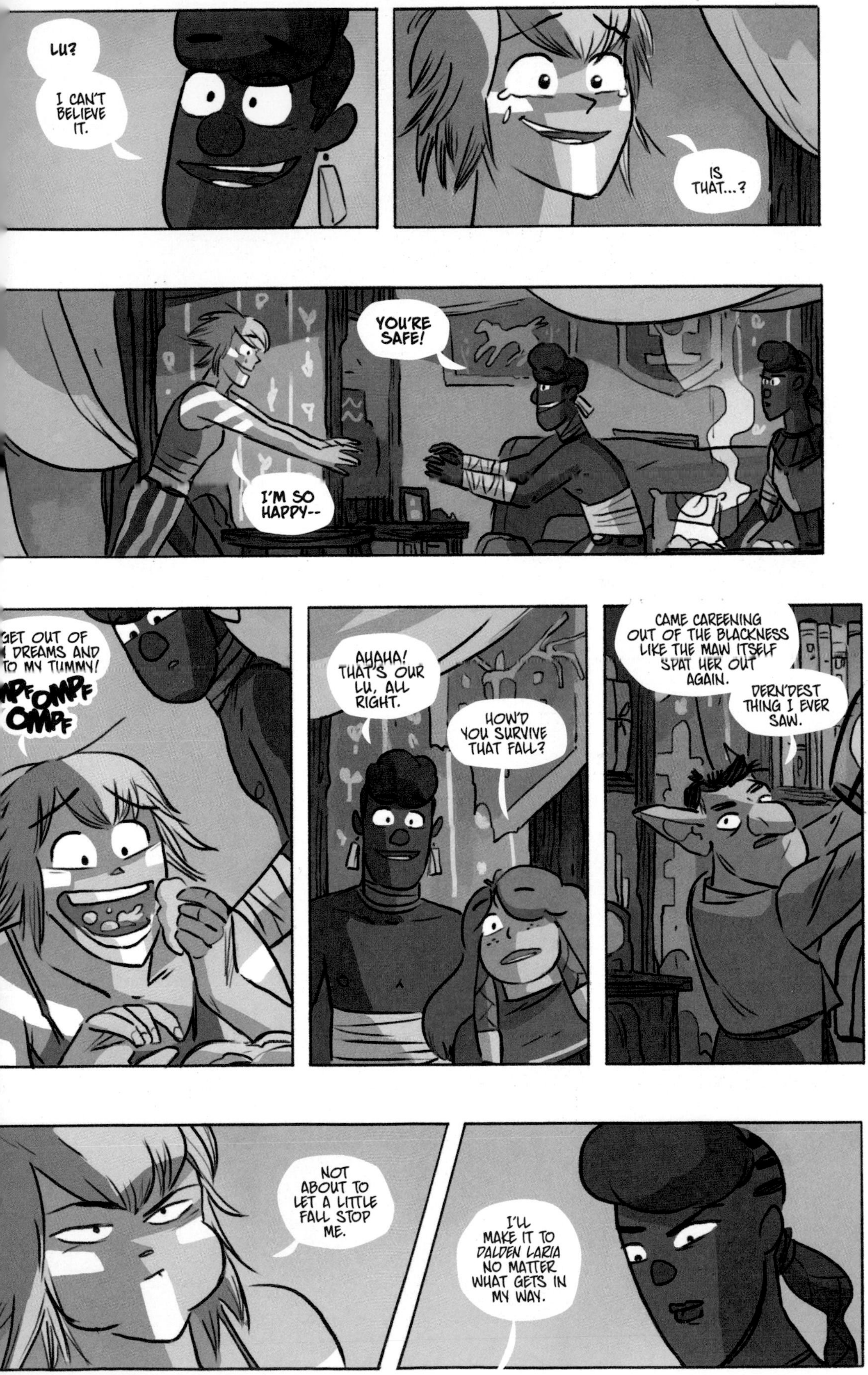

LU?
I CAN'T BELIEVE IT.
IS THAT...?
YOU'RE SAFE!
I'M SO HAPPY--
GET OUT OF
DREAMS AND
TO MY TUMMY!
OMPF OMPF
AHAHA! THAT'S OUR LU, ALL RIGHT.
HOW'D YOU SURVIVE THAT FALL?
CAME CAREENING OUT OF THE BLACKNESS LIKE THE MAW ITSELF SPAT HER OUT AGAIN.
DERN'DEST THING I EVER SAW.
NOT ABOUT TO LET A LITTLE FALL STOP ME.
I'LL MAKE IT TO DALDEN LARIA NO MATTER WHAT GETS IN MY WAY.

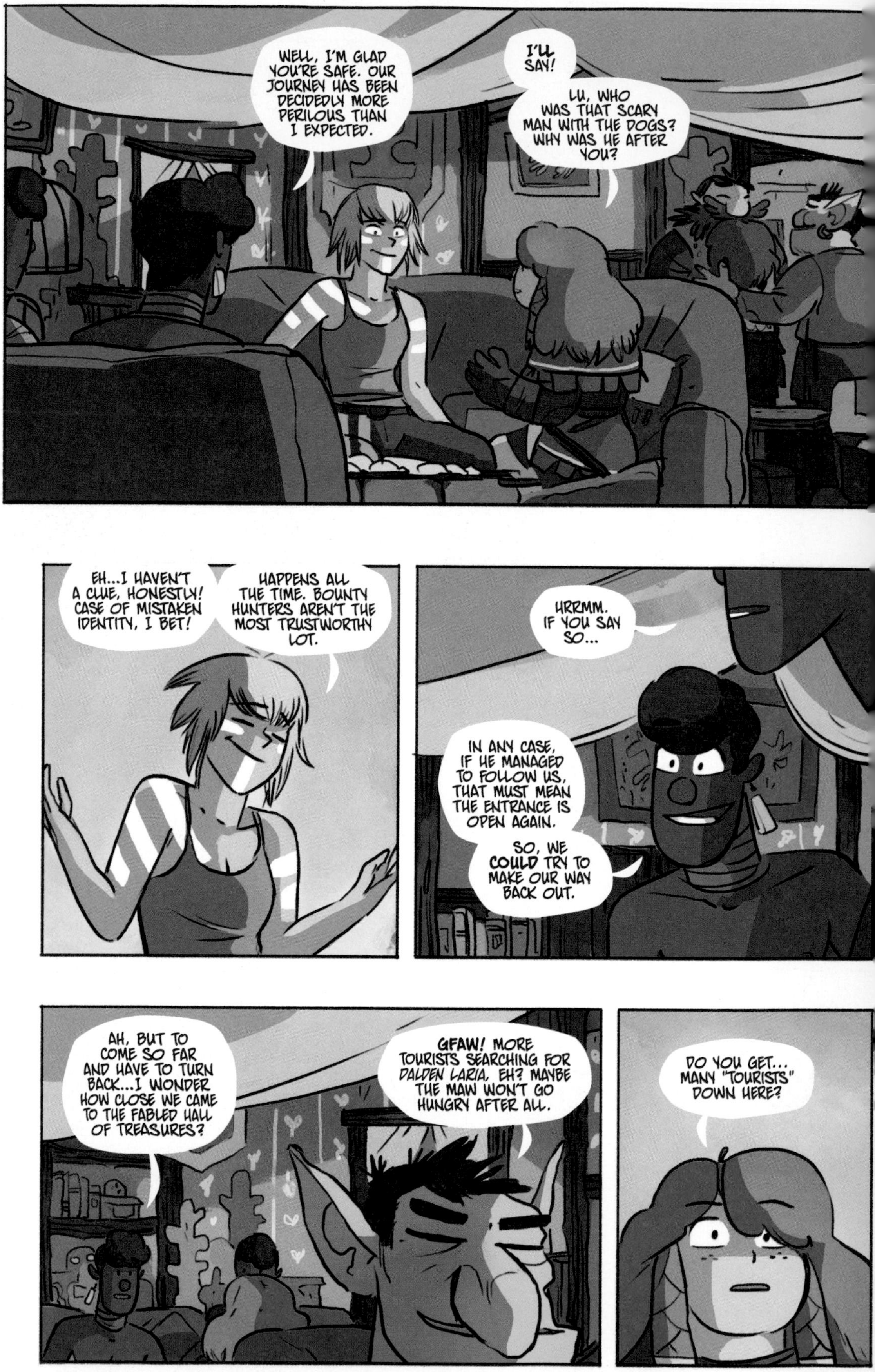

WELL, I'M GLAD YOU'RE SAFE. OUR JOURNEY HAS BEEN DECIDEDLY MORE PERILOUS THAN I EXPECTED.
I'LL SAY!
LU, WHO WAS THAT SCARY MAN WITH THE DOGS? WHY WAS HE AFTER YOU?
EH...I HAVEN'T A CLUE, HONESTLY! CASE OF MISTAKEN IDENTITY, I BET!
HAPPENS ALL THE TIME. BOUNTY HUNTERS AREN'T THE MOST TRUSTWORTHY LOT.
HRRMM. IF YOU SAY SO...
IN ANY CASE, IF HE MANAGED TO FOLLOW US, THAT MUST MEAN THE ENTRANCE IS OPEN AGAIN.
SO, WE COULD TRY TO MAKE OUR WAY BACK OUT.
AH, BUT TO COME SO FAR AND HAVE TO TURN BACK...I WONDER HOW CLOSE WE CAME TO THE FABLED HALL OF TREASURES?
GFAW! MORE TOURISTS SEARCHING FOR DALDEN LARIA, EH? MAYBE THE MAW WON'T GO HUNGRY AFTER ALL.
DO YOU GET... MANY "TOURISTS" DOWN HERE?

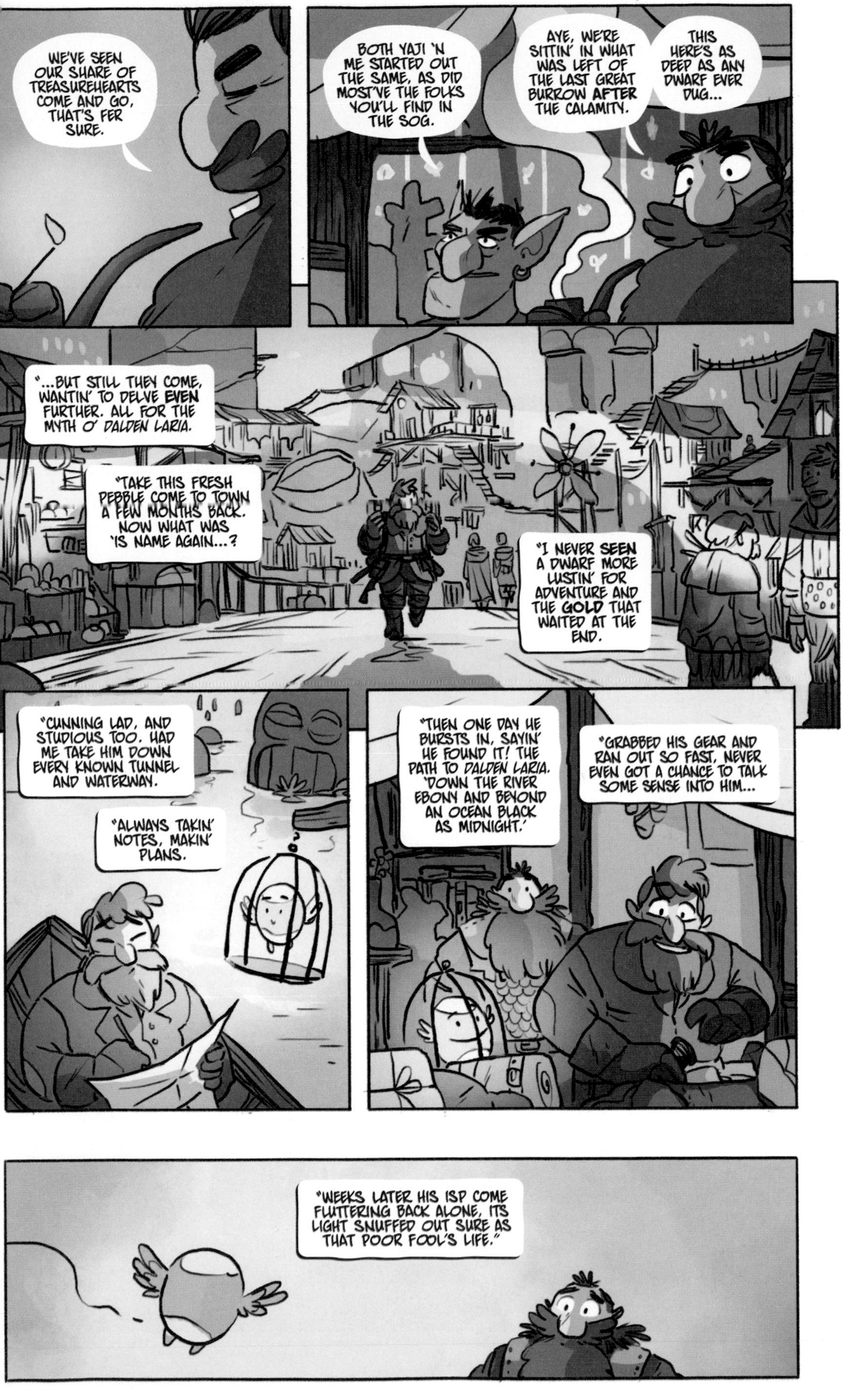
WE'VE SEEN OUR SHARE OF TREASUREHEARTS COME AND GO, THAT'S FER SURE.
BOTH YAJI 'N ME STARTED OUT THE SAME, AS DID MOST'VE THE FOLKS YOU'LL FIND IN THE SOG.
AYE, WE'RE SITTIN' IN WHAT WAS LEFT OF THE LAST GREAT BURROW AFTER THE CALAMITY.
THIS HERE'S AS DEEP AS ANY DWARF EVER DUG...
"...BUT STILL THEY COME, WANTIN' TO DELVE EVEN FURTHER. ALL FOR THE MYTH O' DALDEN LARIA.
"TAKE THIS FRESH PEBBLE COME TO TOWN A FEW MONTHS BACK. NOW WHAT WAS 'IS NAME AGAIN...?
"I NEVER SEEN A DWARF MORE LUSTIN' FOR ADVENTURE AND THE GOLD THAT WAITED AT THE END.
"CUNNING LAD, AND STUDIOUS TOO. HAD ME TAKE HIM DOWN EVERY KNOWN TUNNEL AND WATERWAY.
"ALWAYS TAKIN' NOTES, MAKIN' PLANS.
"THEN ONE DAY HE BURSTS IN, SAYIN' HE FOUND IT! THE PATH TO DALDEN LARIA. 'DOWN THE RIVER EBONY AND BEYOND AN OCEAN BLACK AS MIDNIGHT.'
"GRABBED HIS GEAR AND RAN OUT SO FAST, NEVER EVEN GOT A CHANCE TO TALK SOME SENSE INTO HIM...
"WEEKS LATER HIS ISP COME FLUTTERING BACK ALONE, ITS LIGHT SNUFFED OUT SURE AS THAT POOR FOOL'S LIFE."

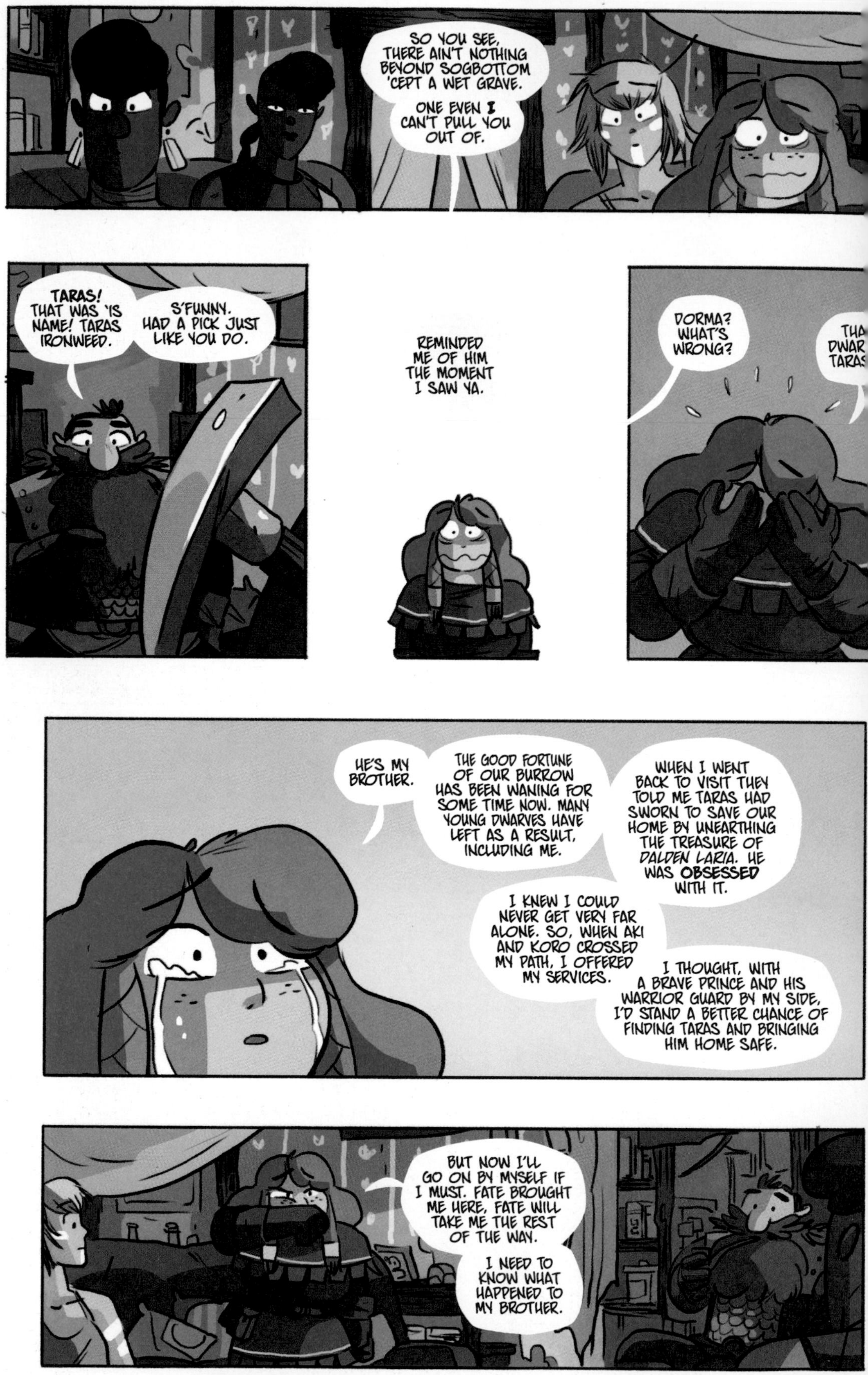
SO YOU SEE, THERE AIN'T NOTHING BEYOND SOGBOTTOM 'CEPT A WET GRAVE.
ONE EVEN I CAN'T PULL YOU OUT OF.
TARAS! THAT WAS 'IS NAME! TARAS IRONWEED.
S'FUNNY. HAD A PICK JUST LIKE YOU DO.
REMINDED ME OF HIM THE MOMENT I SAW YA.
DORMA? WHAT'S WRONG?
HE'S MY BROTHER.
THE GOOD FORTUNE OF OUR BURROW HAS BEEN WANING FOR SOME TIME NOW. MANY YOUNG DWARVES HAVE LEFT AS A RESULT, INCLUDING ME.
WHEN I WENT BACK TO VISIT THEY TOLD ME TARAS HAD SWORN TO SAVE OUR HOME BY UNEARTHING THE TREASURE OF DALDEN LARIA. HE WAS OBSESSED WITH IT.
I KNEW I COULD NEVER GET VERY FAR ALONE. SO, WHEN AKI AND KORO CROSSED MY PATH, I OFFERED MY SERVICES.
I THOUGHT, WITH A BRAVE PRINCE AND HIS WARRIOR GUARD BY MY SIDE, I'D STAND A BETTER CHANCE OF FINDING TARAS AND BRINGING HIM HOME SAFE.
BUT NOW I'LL GO ON BY MYSELF IF I MUST. FATE BROUGHT ME HERE, FATE WILL TAKE ME THE REST OF THE WAY.
I NEED TO KNOW WHAT HAPPENED TO MY BROTHER.

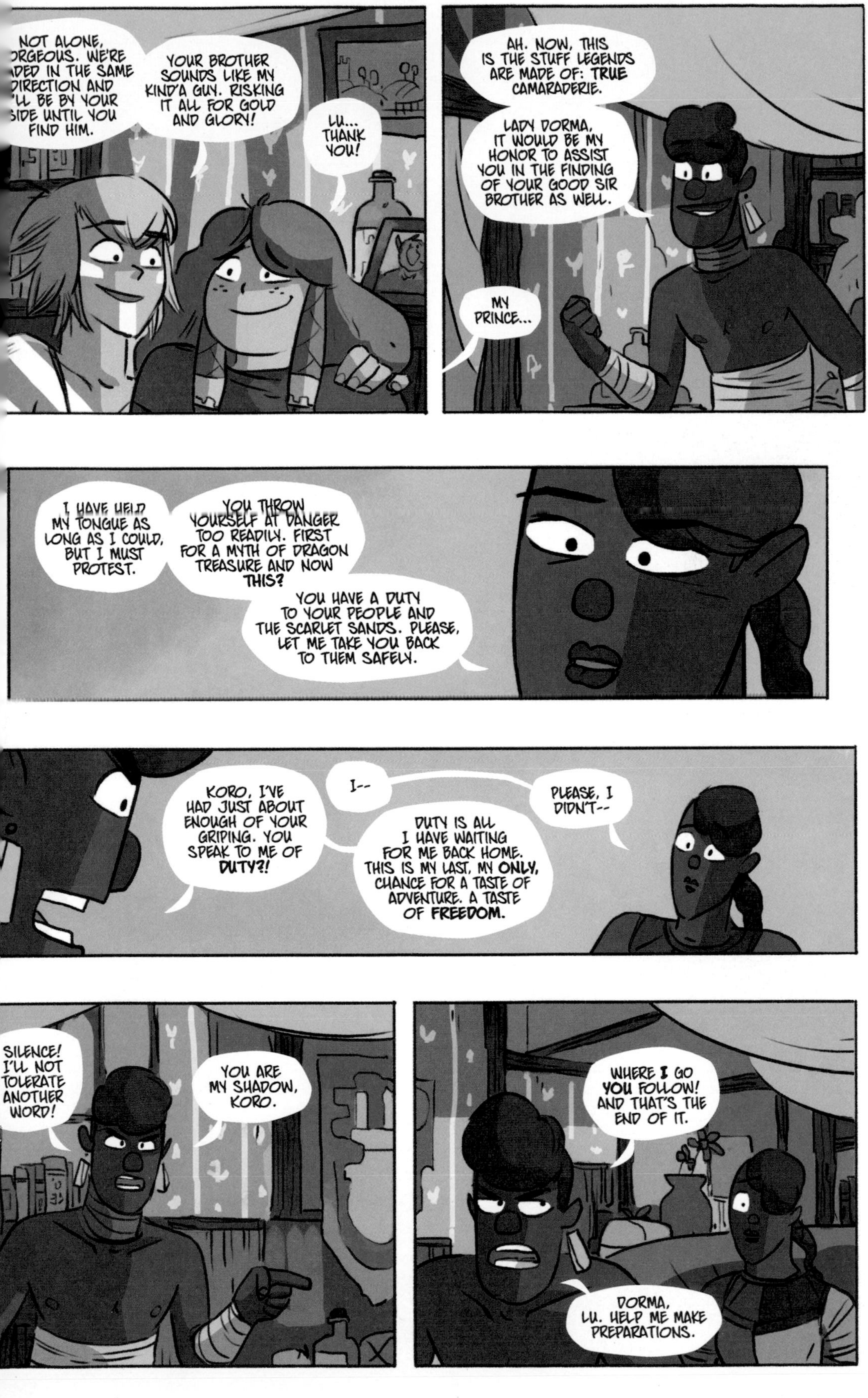
NOT ALONE, ORGEOUS. WE'RE ADED IN THE SAME DIRECTION AND 'LL BE BY YOUR SIDE UNTIL YOU FIND HIM.
YOUR BROTHER SOUNDS LIKE MY KIND'A GUY. RISKING IT ALL FOR GOLD AND GLORY!
LU... THANK YOU!
AH. NOW, THIS IS THE STUFF LEGENDS ARE MADE OF: TRUE CAMARADERIE.
LADY DORMA, IT WOULD BE MY HONOR TO ASSIST YOU IN THE FINDING OF YOUR GOOD SIR BROTHER AS WELL.
MY PRINCE...
I HAVE HELD MY TONGUE AS LONG AS I COULD, BUT I MUST PROTEST.
YOU THROW YOURSELF AT DANGER TOO READILY. FIRST FOR A MYTH OF DRAGON TREASURE AND NOW THIS?
YOU HAVE A DUTY TO YOUR PEOPLE AND THE SCARLET SANDS. PLEASE, LET ME TAKE YOU BACK TO THEM SAFELY.
KORO, I'VE HAD JUST ABOUT ENOUGH OF YOUR GRIPING. YOU SPEAK TO ME OF DUTY?!
I--
PLEASE, I DIDN'T--
DUTY IS ALL I HAVE WAITING FOR ME BACK HOME. THIS IS MY LAST, MY ONLY, CHANCE FOR A TASTE OF ADVENTURE. A TASTE OF FREEDOM.
SILENCE! I'LL NOT TOLERATE ANOTHER WORD!
YOU ARE MY SHADOW, KORO.
WHERE I GO YOU FOLLOW! AND THAT'S THE END OF IT.
DORMA, LU. HELP ME MAKE PREPARATIONS.

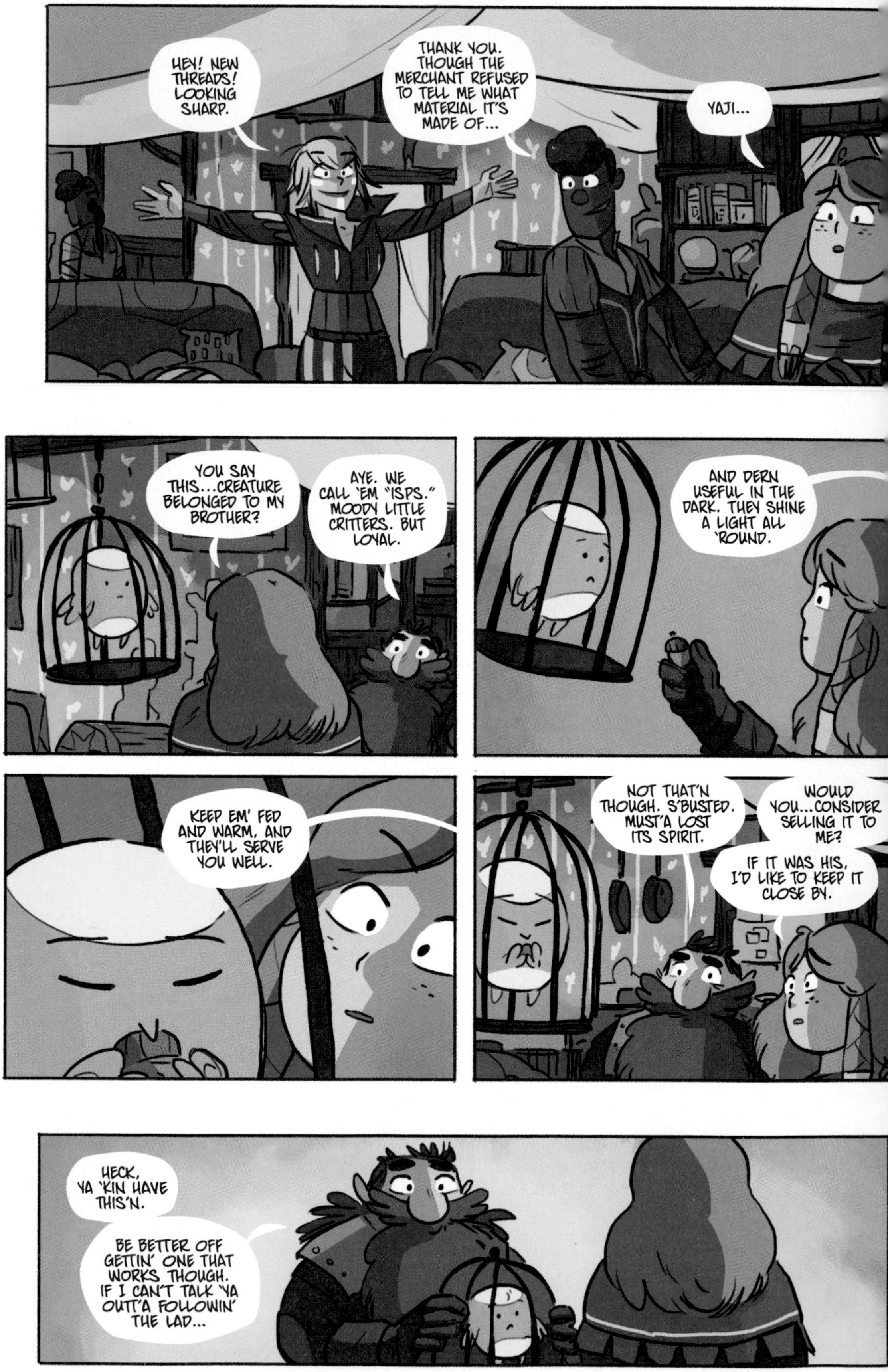
HEY! NEW THREADS! LOOKING SHARP.
THANK YOU. THOUGH THE MERCHANT REFUSED TO TELL ME WHAT MATERIAL IT'S MADE OF...
YAJI...
YOU SAY THIS...CREATURE BELONGED TO MY BROTHER?
AYE. WE CALL 'EM "ISPS." MOODY LITTLE CRITTERS. BUT LOYAL.
AND DERN USEFUL IN THE DARK. THEY SHINE A LIGHT ALL 'ROUND.
KEEP EM' FED AND WARM, AND THEY'LL SERVE YOU WELL.
NOT THAT'N THOUGH. S'BUSTED. MUST'A LOST ITS SPIRIT.
WOULD YOU...CONSIDER SELLING IT TO ME?
IF IT WAS HIS, I'D LIKE TO KEEP IT CLOSE BY.
HECK, YA 'KIN HAVE THIS'N.
BE BETTER OFF GETTIN' ONE THAT WORKS THOUGH. IF I CAN'T TALK 'YA OUTT'A FOLLOWIN' THE LAD...

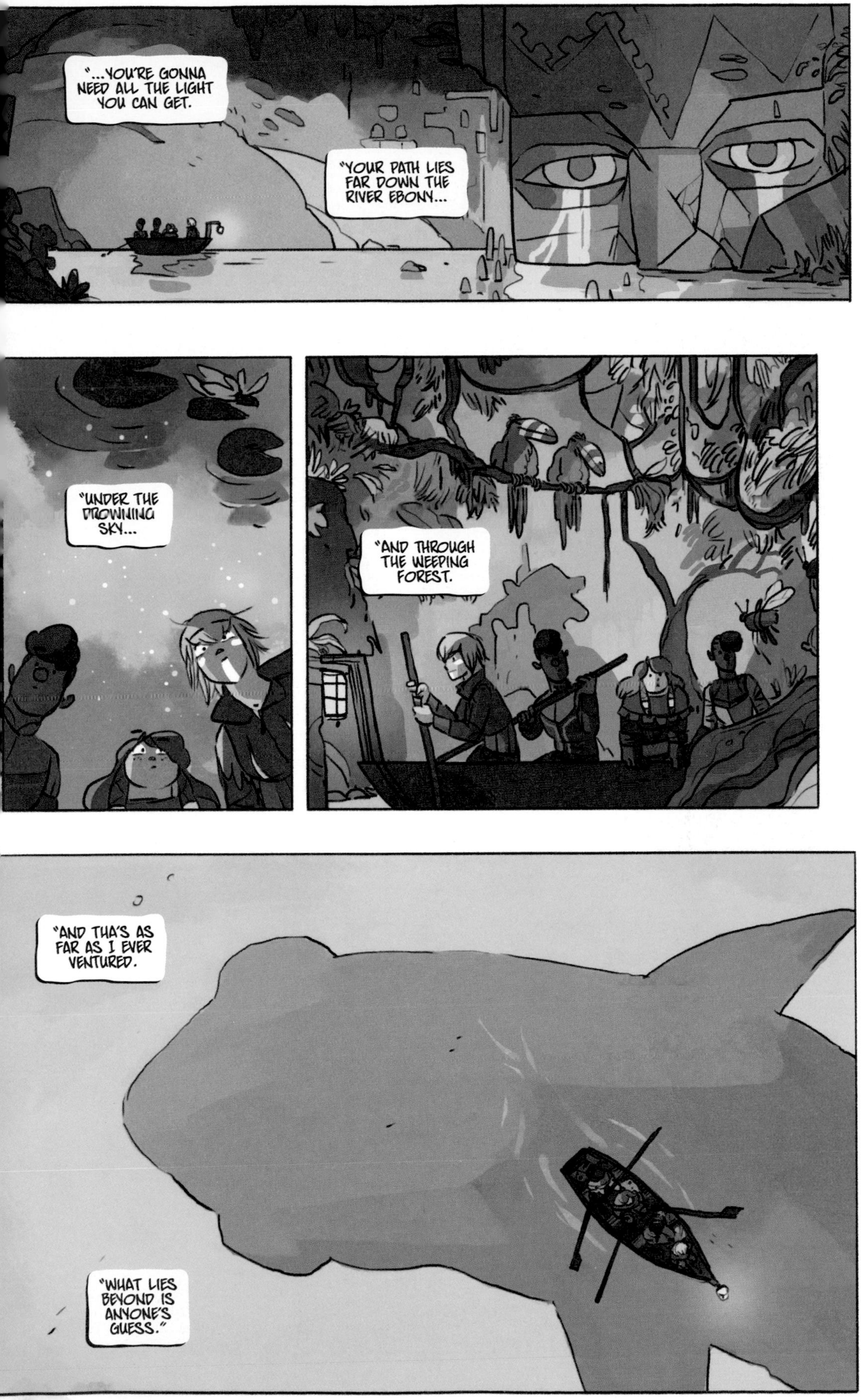
"...YOU'RE GONNA NEED ALL THE LIGHT YOU CAN GET.
"YOUR PATH LIES FAR DOWN THE RIVER EBONY...
"UNDER THE DROWNING SKY...
"AND THROUGH THE WEEPING FOREST.
"AND THA'S AS FAR AS I EVER VENTURED.
"WHAT LIES BEYOND IS ANYONE'S GUESS."

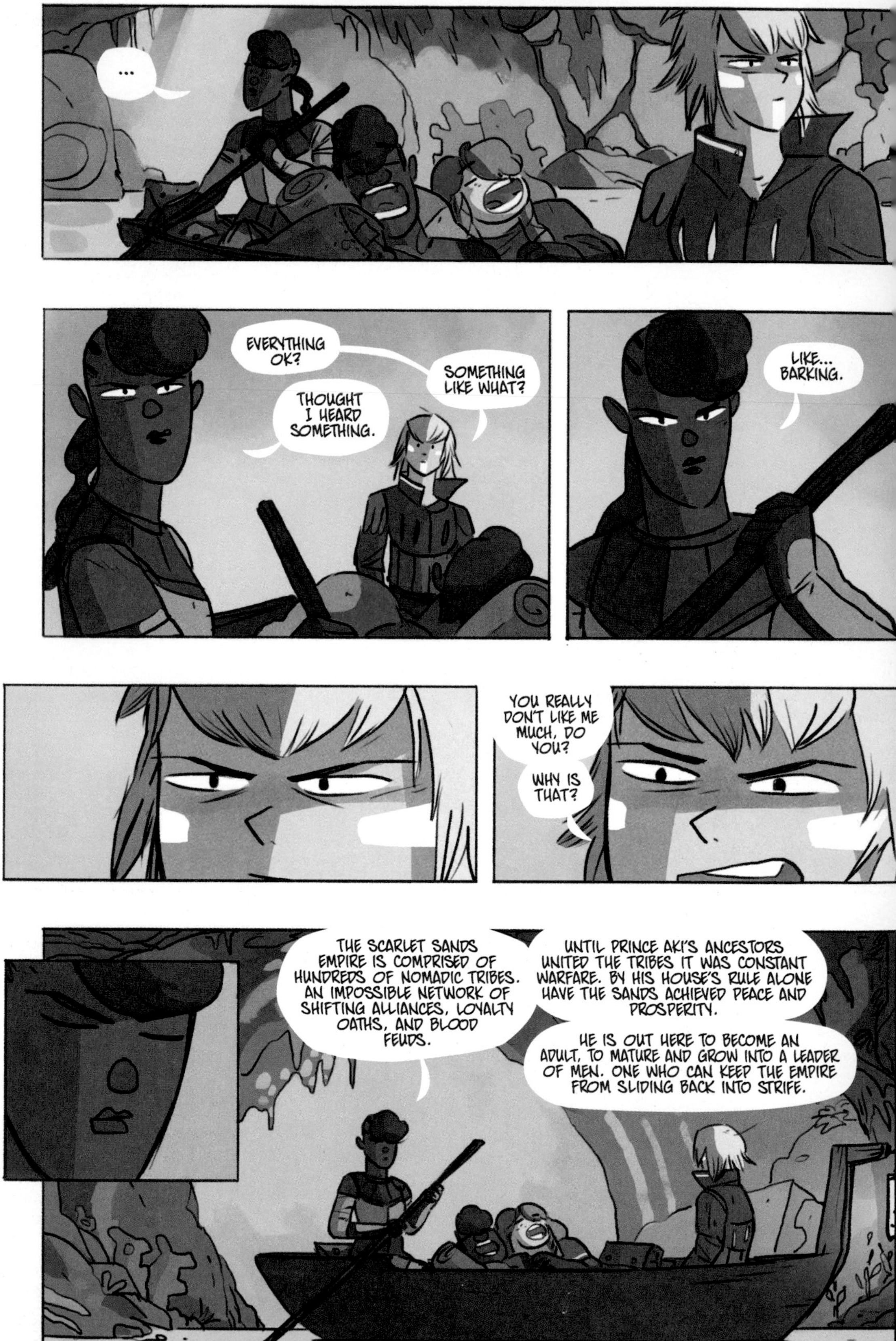

...
EVERYTHING OK?
THOUGHT I HEARD SOMETHING.
SOMETHING LIKE WHAT?
LIKE... BARKING.
YOU REALLY DON'T LIKE ME MUCH, DO YOU?
WHY IS THAT?
THE SCARLET SANDS EMPIRE IS COMPRISED OF HUNDREDS OF NOMADIC TRIBES. AN IMPOSSIBLE NETWORK OF SHIFTING ALLIANCES, LOYALTY OATHS, AND BLOOD FEUDS.
UNTIL PRINCE AKI'S ANCESTORS UNITED THE TRIBES IT WAS CONSTANT WARFARE. BY HIS HOUSE'S RULE ALONE HAVE THE SANDS ACHIEVED PEACE AND PROSPERITY.
HE IS OUT HERE TO BECOME AN ADULT, TO MATURE AND GROW INTO A LEADER OF MEN. ONE WHO CAN KEEP THE EMPIRE FROM SLIDING BACK INTO STRIFE.

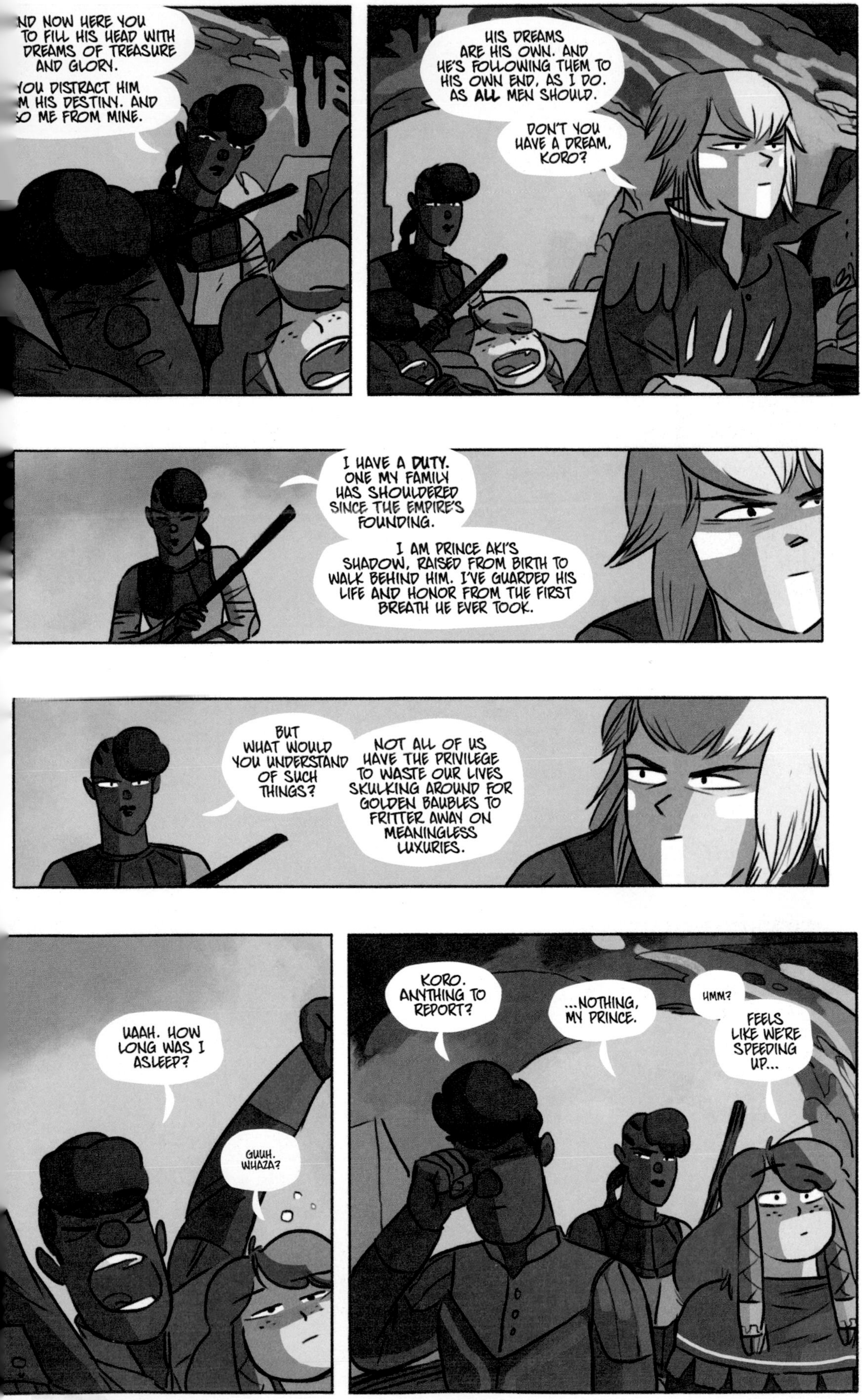
ND NOW HERE YOU TO FILL HIS HEAD WITH DREAMS OF TREASURE AND GLORY.
YOU DISTRACT HIM M HIS DESTINY. AND SO ME FROM MINE.
HIS DREAMS ARE HIS OWN. AND HE'S FOLLOWING THEM TO HIS OWN END, AS I DO. AS ALL MEN SHOULD.
DON'T YOU HAVE A DREAM, KORO?
I HAVE A DUTY. ONE MY FAMILY HAS SHOULDERED SINCE THE EMPIRE'S FOUNDING.
I AM PRINCE AKI'S SHADOW, RAISED FROM BIRTH TO WALK BEHIND HIM. I'VE GUARDED HIS LIFE AND HONOR FROM THE FIRST BREATH HE EVER TOOK.
BUT WHAT WOULD YOU UNDERSTAND OF SUCH THINGS?
NOT ALL OF US HAVE THE PRIVILEGE TO WASTE OUR LIVES SKULKING AROUND FOR GOLDEN BAUBLES TO FRITTER AWAY ON MEANINGLESS LUXURIES.
UAAH. HOW LONG WAS I ASLEEP?
GUUH. WHAZA?
KORO. ANYTHING TO REPORT?
...NOTHING, MY PRINCE.
HMM?
FEELS LIKE WE'RE SPEEDING UP...

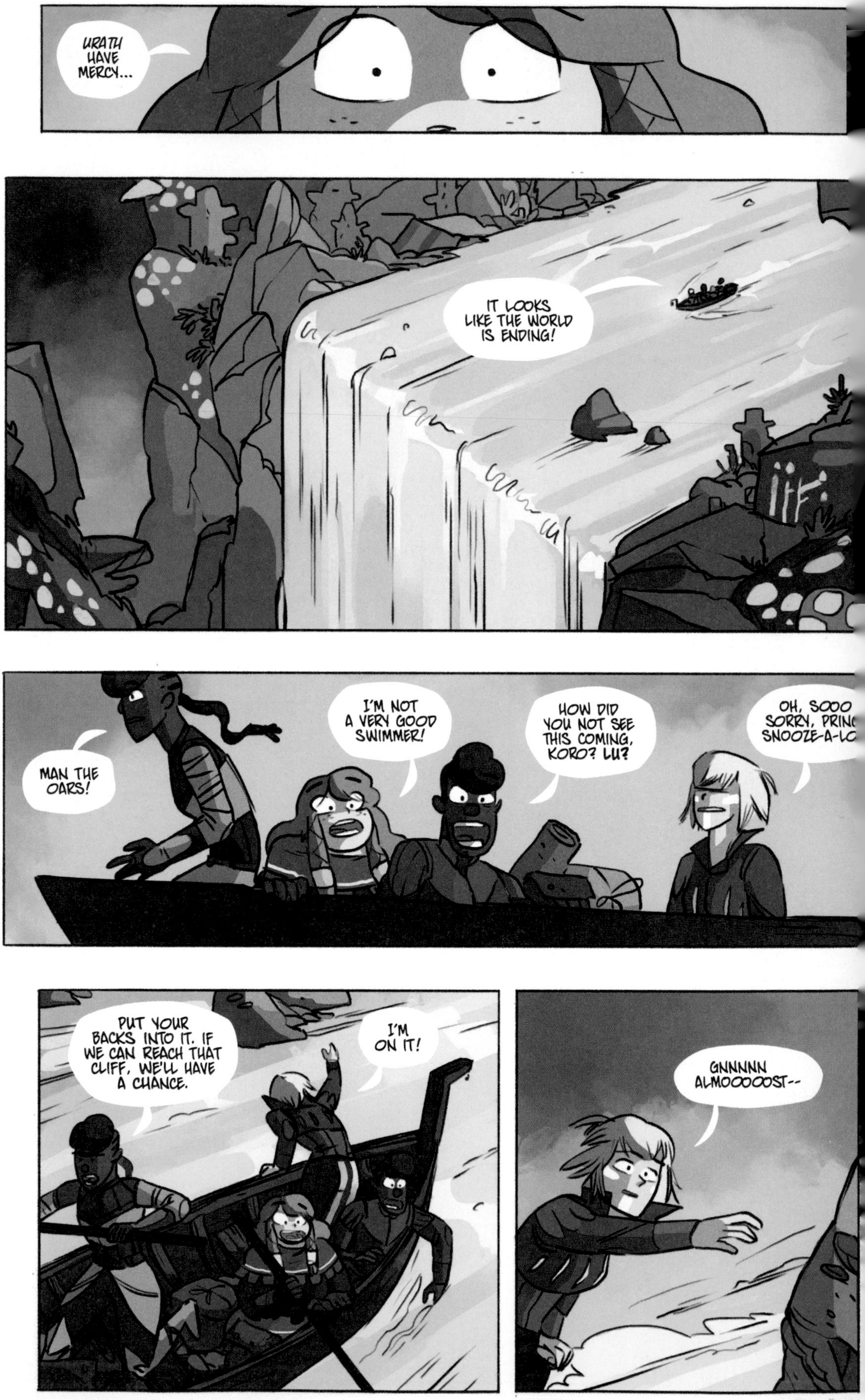
URATH HAVE MERCY...
IT LOOKS LIKE THE WORLD IS ENDING!
MAN THE OARS!
I'M NOT A VERY GOOD SWIMMER!
HOW DID YOU NOT SEE THIS COMING, KORO? LU?
OH, SOOO SORRY, PRIN
SNOOZE-A-LO
PUT YOUR BACKS INTO IT. IF WE CAN REACH THAT CLIFF, WE'LL HAVE A CHANCE.
I'M ON IT!
GNNNNN ALMOOOOOST--

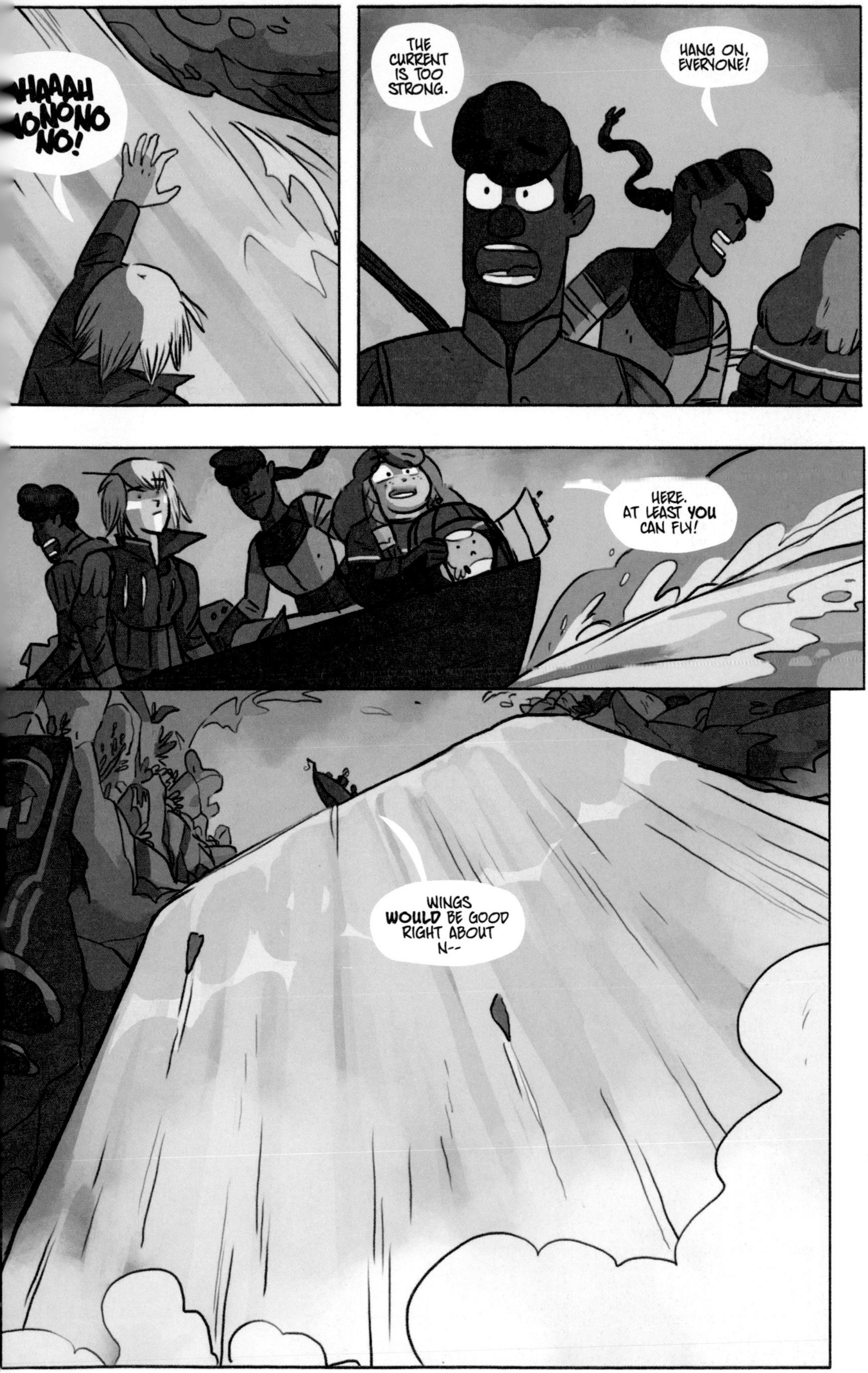
WHAAAH NONONO NO!
THE CURRENT IS TOO STRONG.
HANG ON, EVERYONE!
HERE. AT LEAST **YOU** CAN FLY!
WINGS **WOULD** BE GOOD RIGHT ABOUT N--

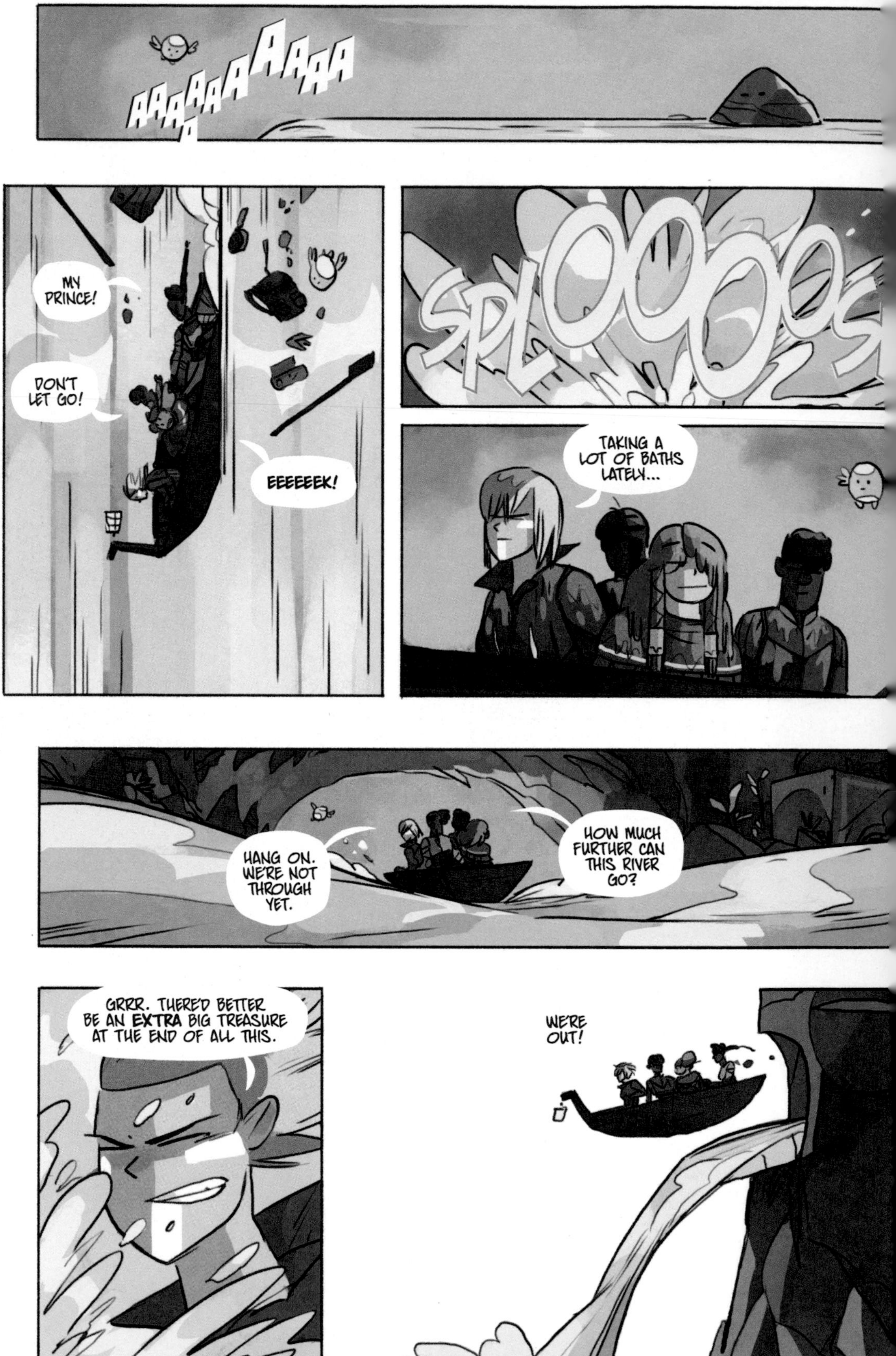
AAAAAAAAAAAA
MY PRINCE!
DON'T LET GO!
EEEEEEK!
SPLOOOOOS
TAKING A LOT OF BATHS LATELY...
HANG ON. WE'RE NOT THROUGH YET.
HOW MUCH FURTHER CAN THIS RIVER GO?
GRRR. THERE'D BETTER BE AN EXTRA BIG TREASURE AT THE END OF ALL THIS.
WE'RE OUT!

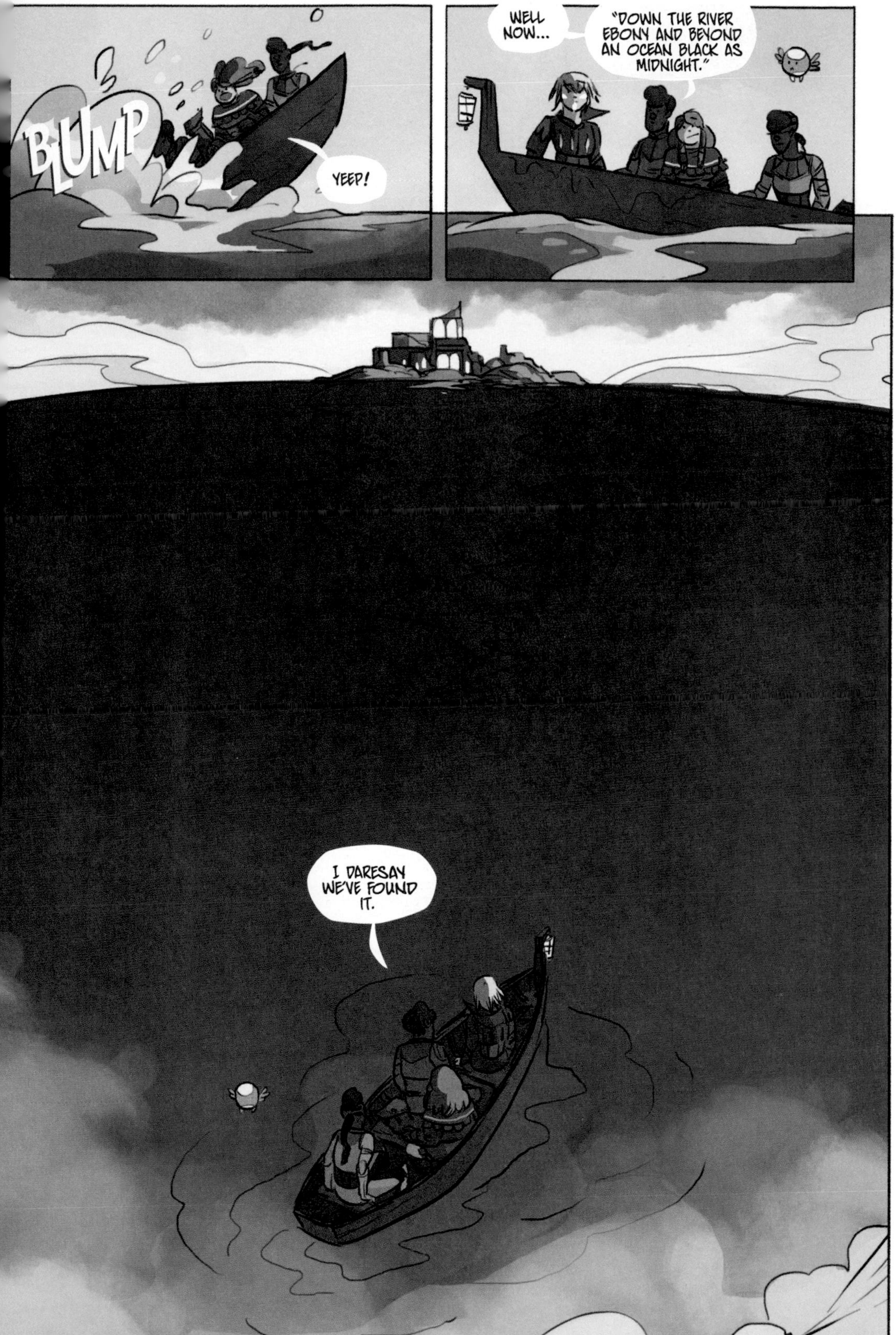
BLUMP
YEEP!
WELL NOW...
"DOWN THE RIVER EBONY AND BEYOND AN OCEAN BLACK AS MIDNIGHT."
I DARESAY WE'VE FOUND IT.

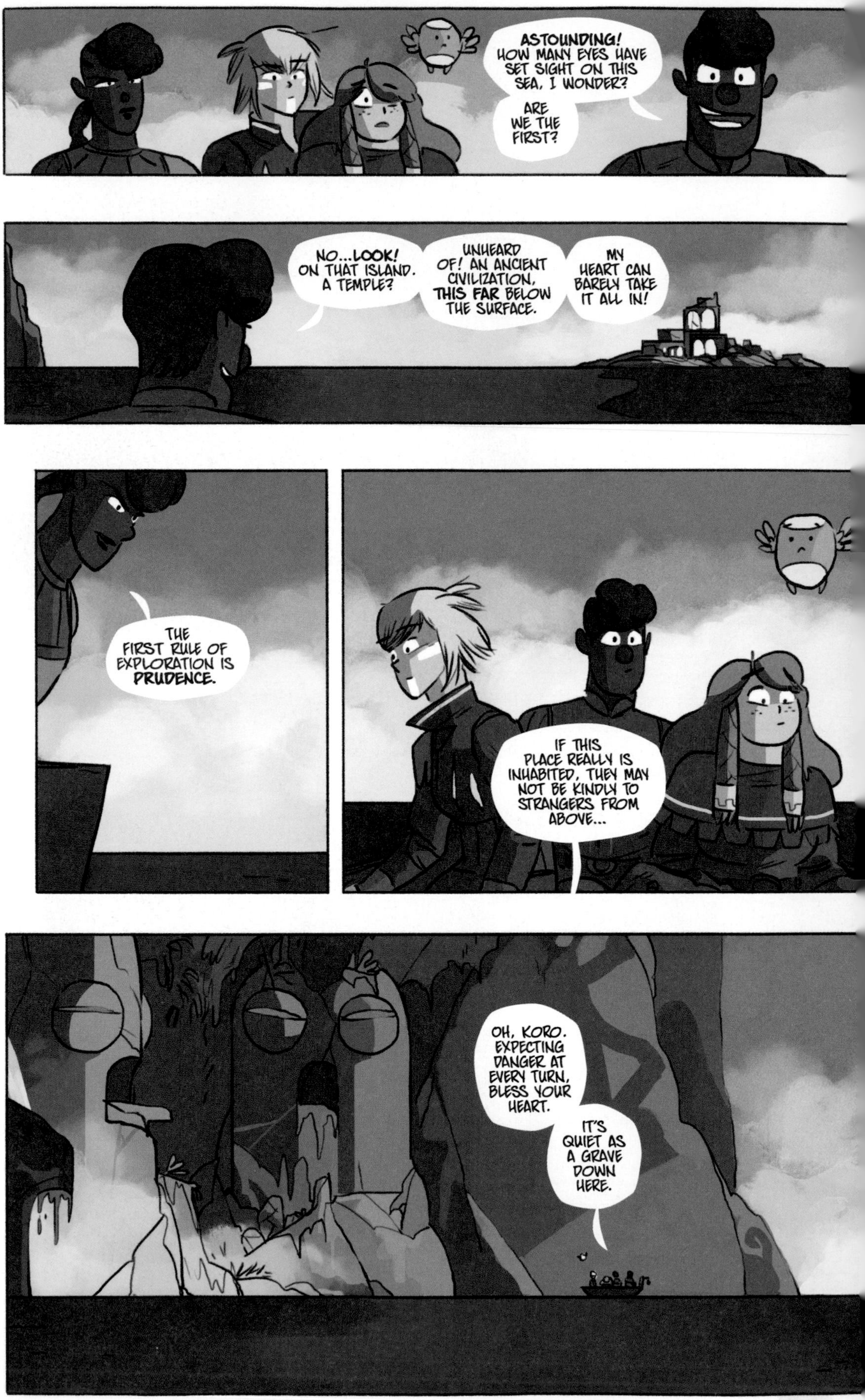
ASTOUNDING! HOW MANY EYES HAVE SET SIGHT ON THIS SEA, I WONDER?
ARE WE THE FIRST?
NO...LOOK! ON THAT ISLAND. A TEMPLE?
UNHEARD OF! AN ANCIENT CIVILIZATION, THIS FAR BELOW THE SURFACE.
MY HEART CAN BARELY TAKE IT ALL IN!
THE FIRST RULE OF EXPLORATION IS PRUDENCE.
IF THIS PLACE REALLY IS INHABITED, THEY MAY NOT BE KINDLY TO STRANGERS FROM ABOVE...
OH, KORO. EXPECTING DANGER AT EVERY TURN, BLESS YOUR HEART.
IT'S QUIET AS A GRAVE DOWN HERE.

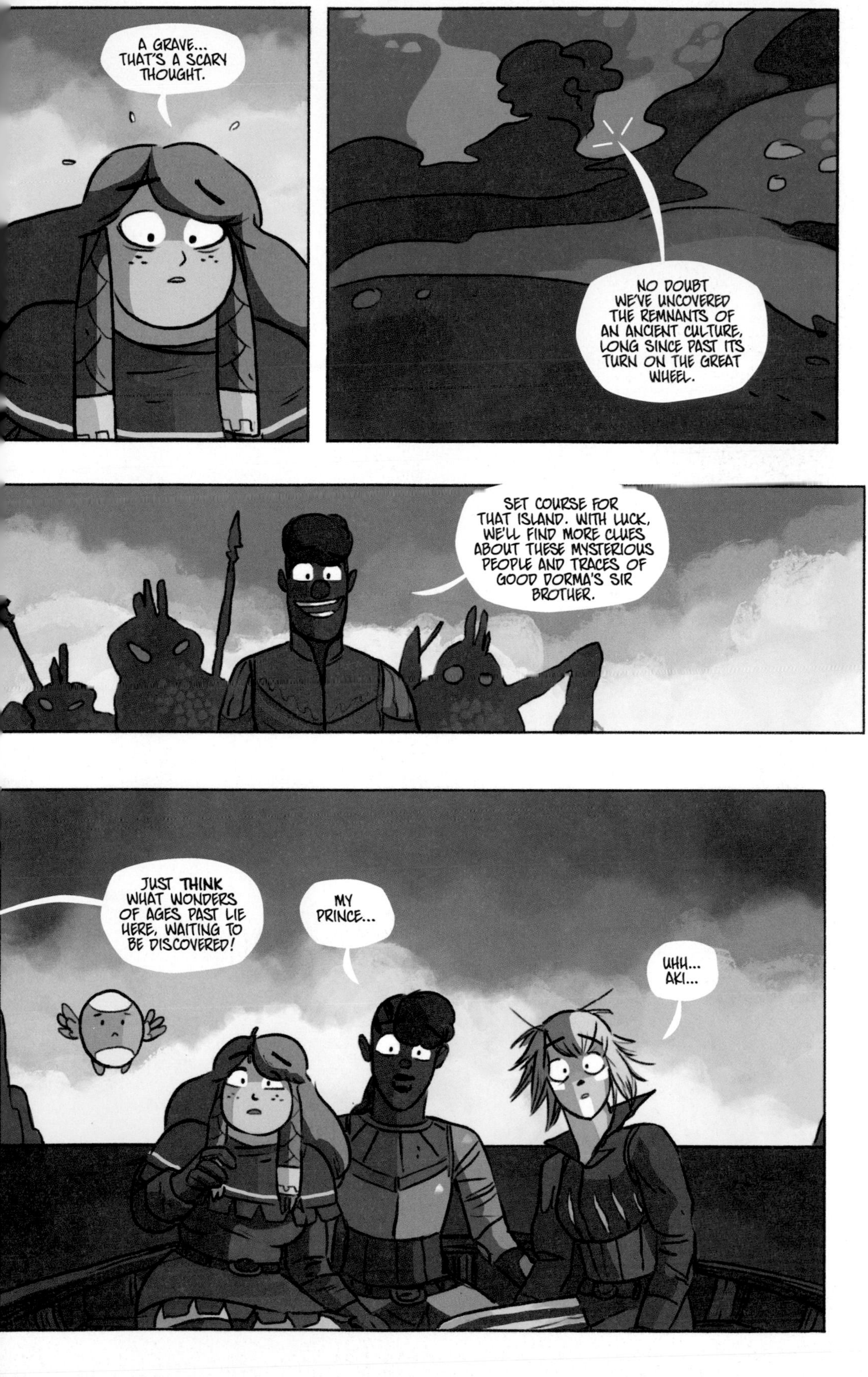
A GRAVE... THAT'S A SCARY THOUGHT.
NO DOUBT WE'VE UNCOVERED THE REMNANTS OF AN ANCIENT CULTURE, LONG SINCE PAST ITS TURN ON THE GREAT WHEEL.
SET COURSE FOR THAT ISLAND. WITH LUCK, WE'LL FIND MORE CLUES ABOUT THESE MYSTERIOUS PEOPLE AND TRACES OF GOOD DORMA'S SIR BROTHER.
JUST THINK WHAT WONDERS OF AGES PAST LIE HERE, WAITING TO BE DISCOVERED!
MY PRINCE...
UHH... AKI...

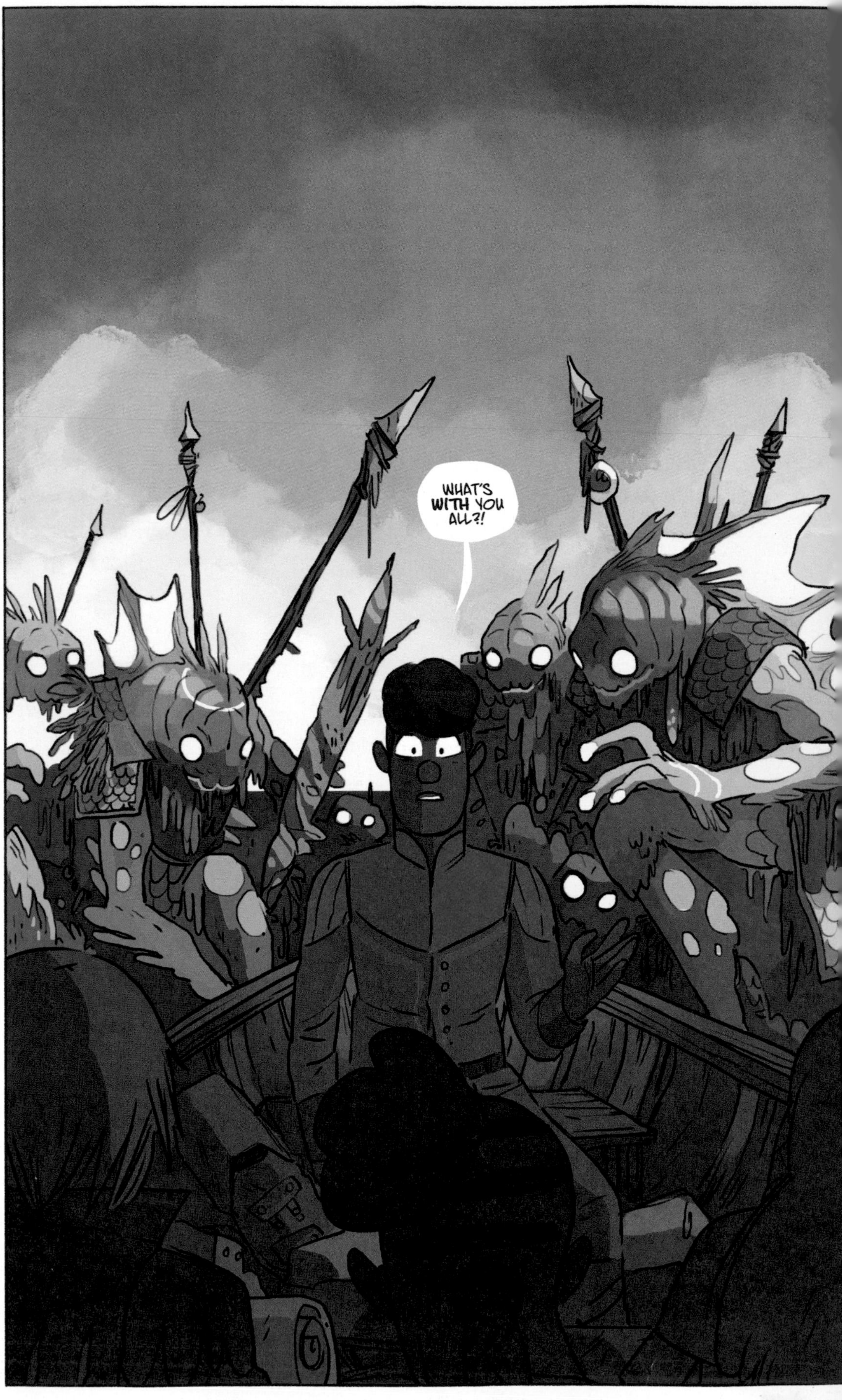
WHAT'S WITH YOU ALL?!

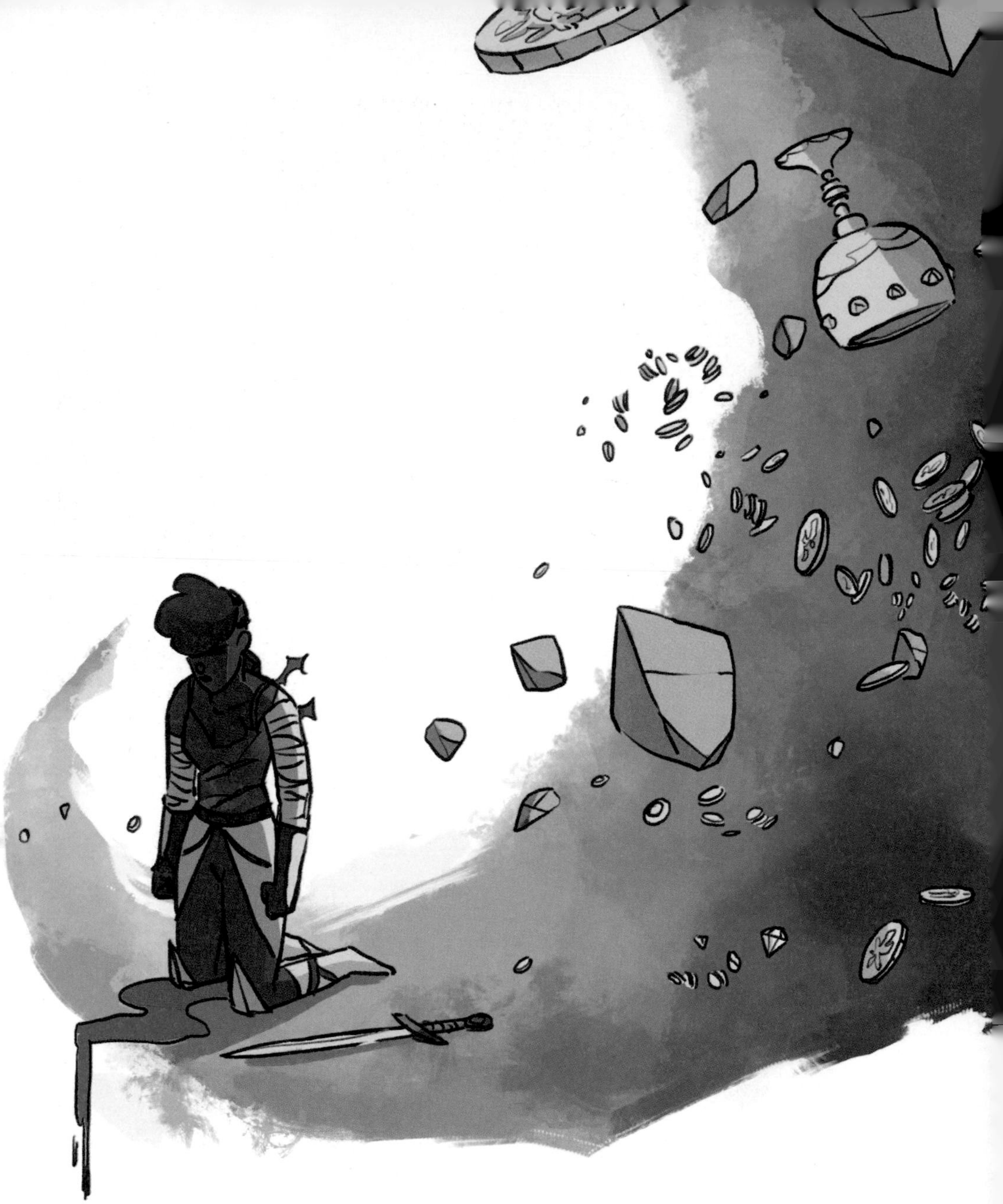

5

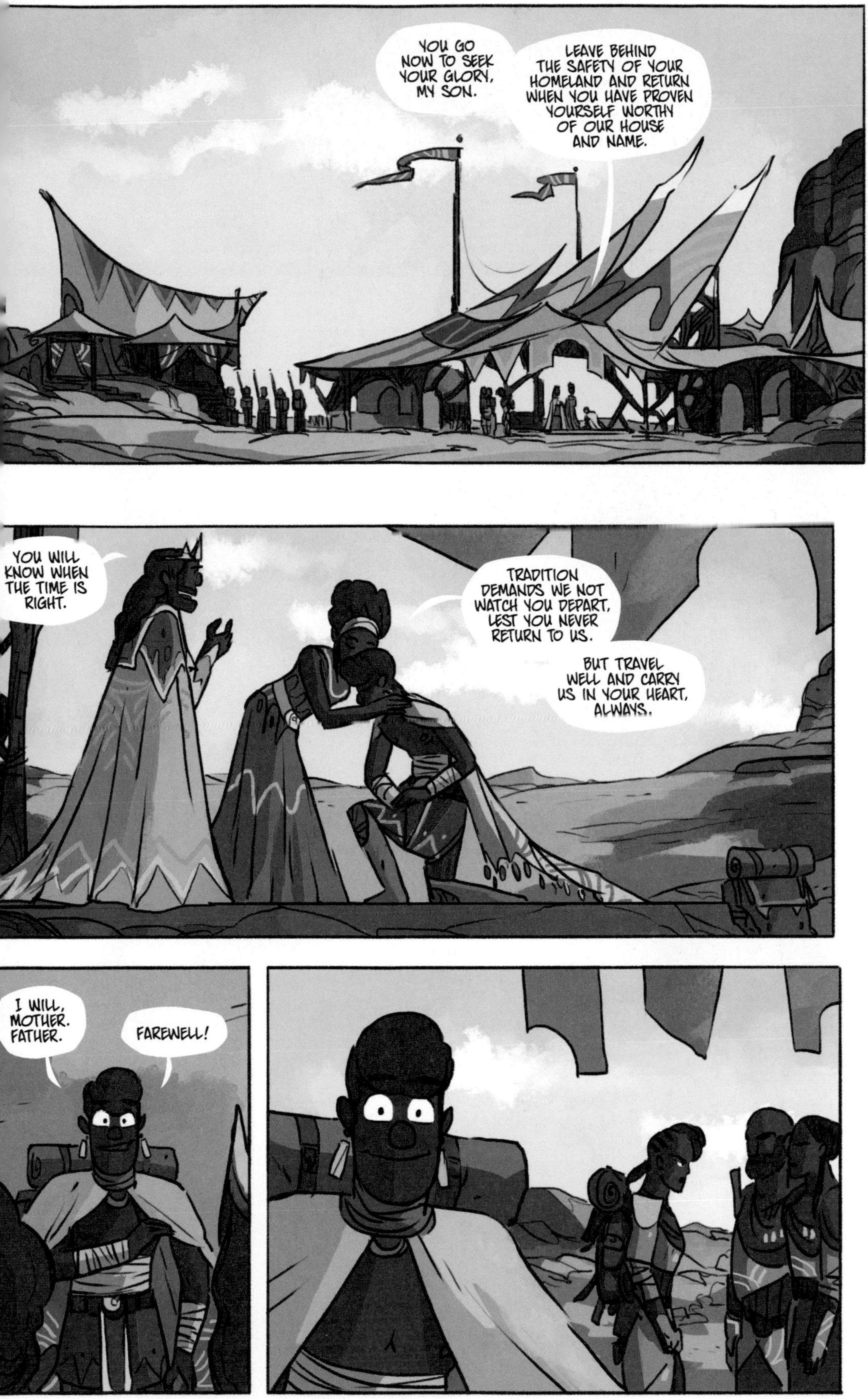
YOU GO NOW TO SEEK YOUR GLORY, MY SON.
LEAVE BEHIND THE SAFETY OF YOUR HOMELAND AND RETURN WHEN YOU HAVE PROVEN YOURSELF WORTHY OF OUR HOUSE AND NAME.
YOU WILL KNOW WHEN THE TIME IS RIGHT.
TRADITION DEMANDS WE NOT WATCH YOU DEPART, LEST YOU NEVER RETURN TO US.
BUT TRAVEL WELL AND CARRY US IN YOUR HEART, ALWAYS.
I WILL, MOTHER. FATHER.
FAREWELL!

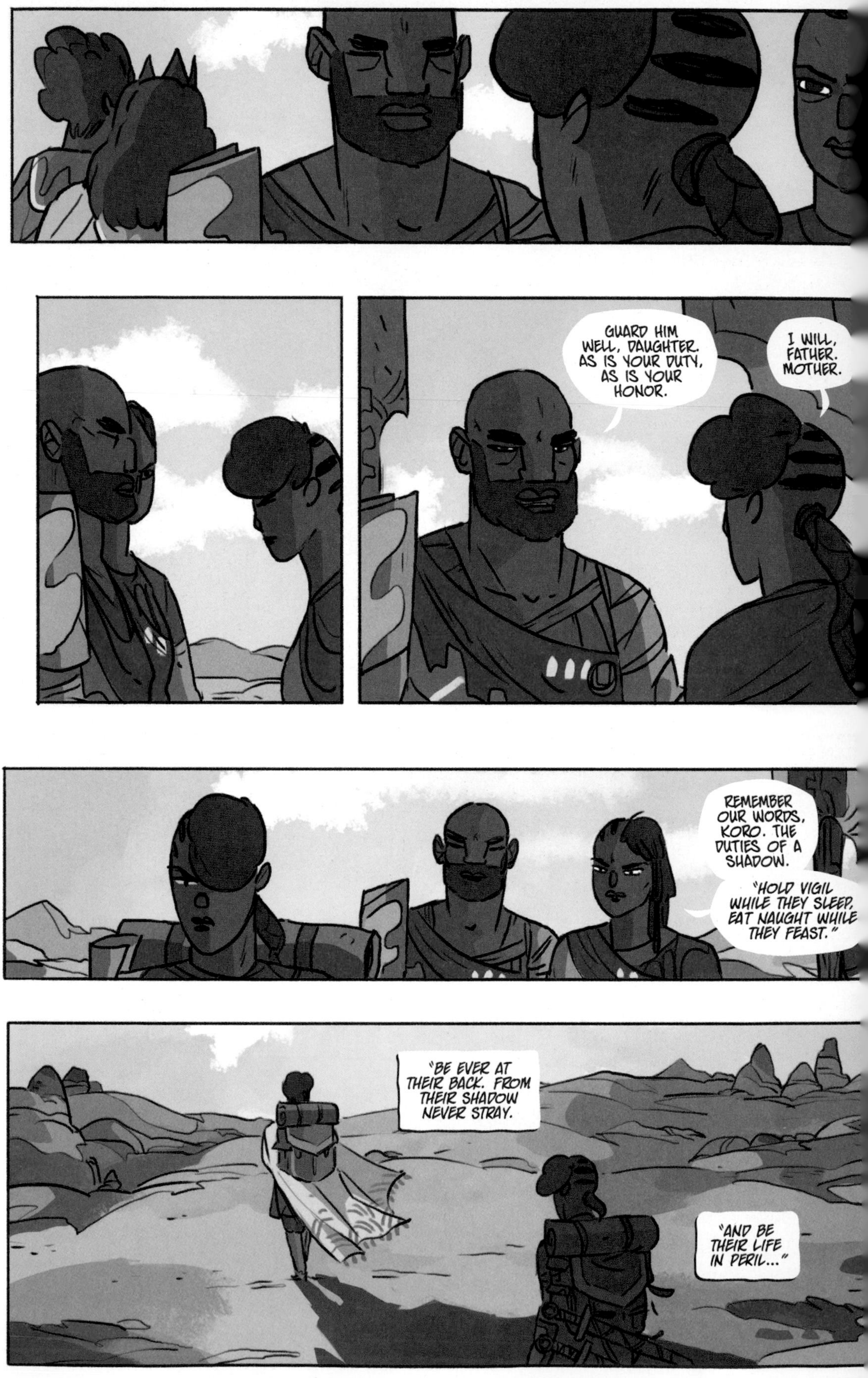
GUARD HIM WELL, DAUGHTER. AS IS YOUR DUTY, AS IS YOUR HONOR.
I WILL, FATHER. MOTHER.
REMEMBER OUR WORDS, KORO. THE DUTIES OF A SHADOW.
"HOLD VIGIL WHILE THEY SLEEP, EAT NAUGHT WHILE THEY FEAST."
"BE EVER AT THEIR BACK. FROM THEIR SHADOW NEVER STRAY.
"AND BE THEIR LIFE IN PERIL..."

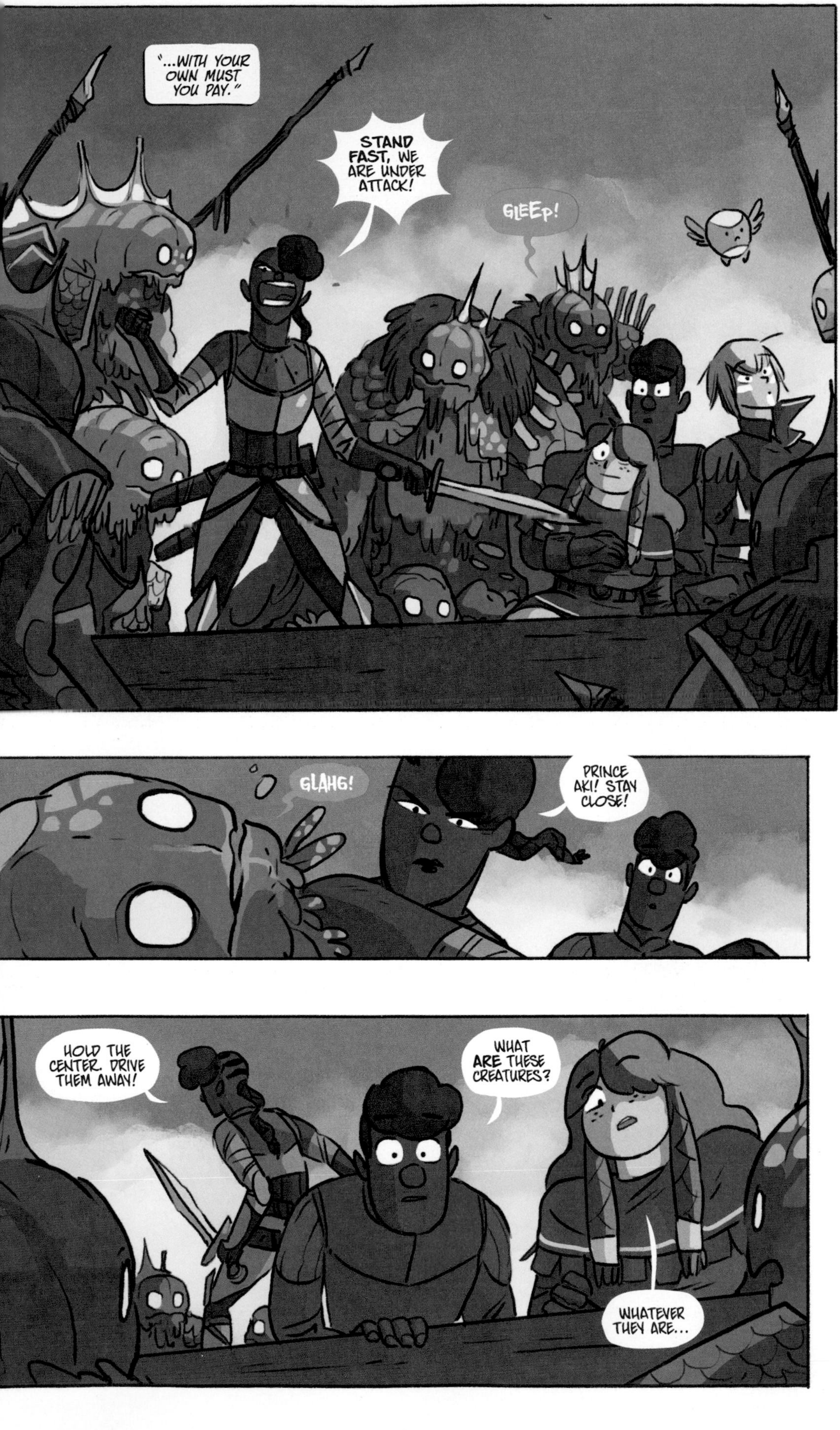
"...WITH YOUR OWN MUST YOU PAY."
STAND FAST, WE ARE UNDER ATTACK!
GLEEP!
GLAHG!
PRINCE AKI! STAY CLOSE!
HOLD THE CENTER. DRIVE THEM AWAY!
WHAT ARE THESE CREATURES?
WHATEVER THEY ARE...

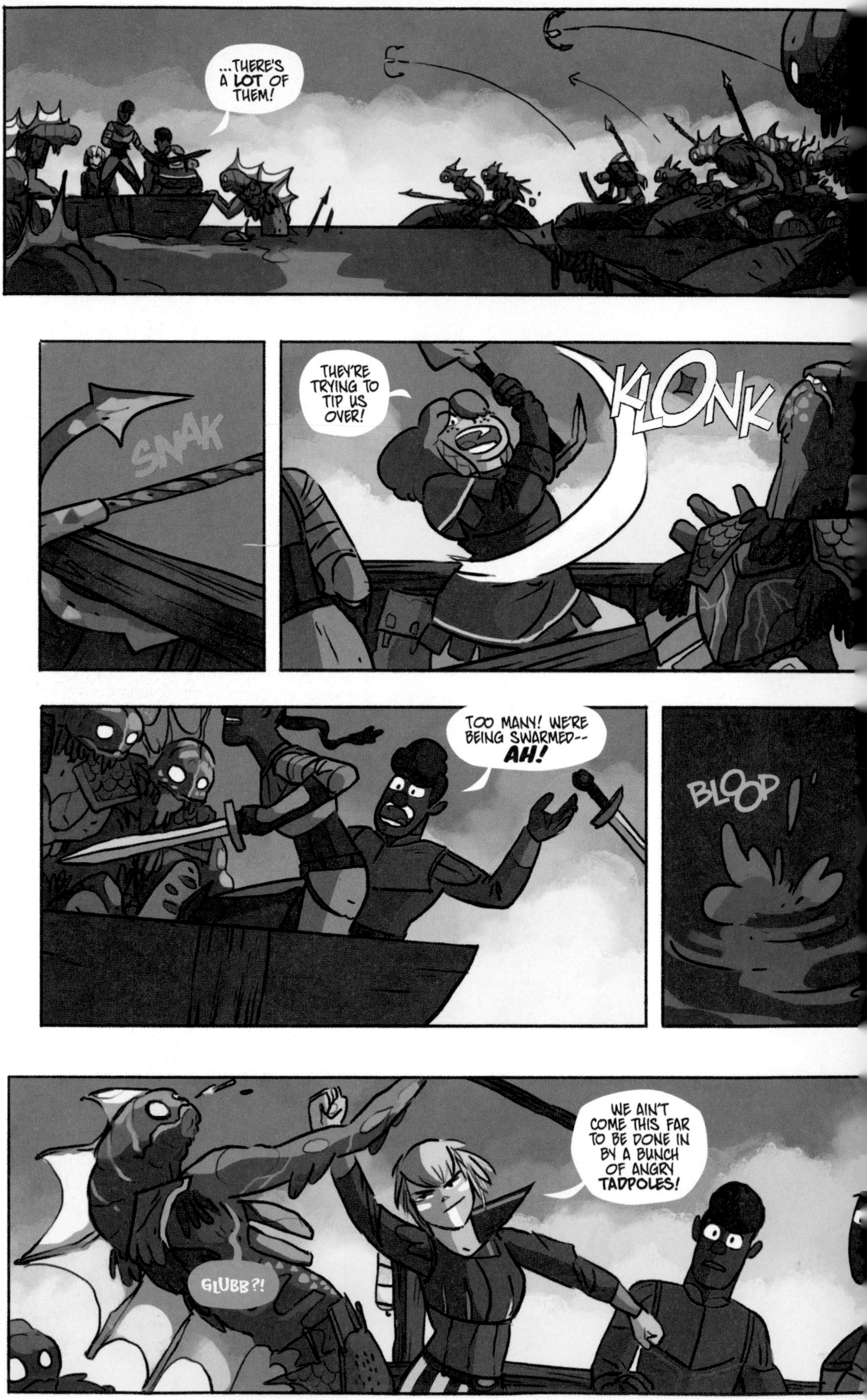

...THERE'S A LOT OF THEM!
SNAK
THEY'RE TRYING TO TIP US OVER!
KLONK
TOO MANY! WE'RE BEING SWARMED-- AH!
BLOOP
WE AIN'T COME THIS FAR TO BE DONE IN BY A BUNCH OF ANGRY TADPOLES!
GLUBB?!

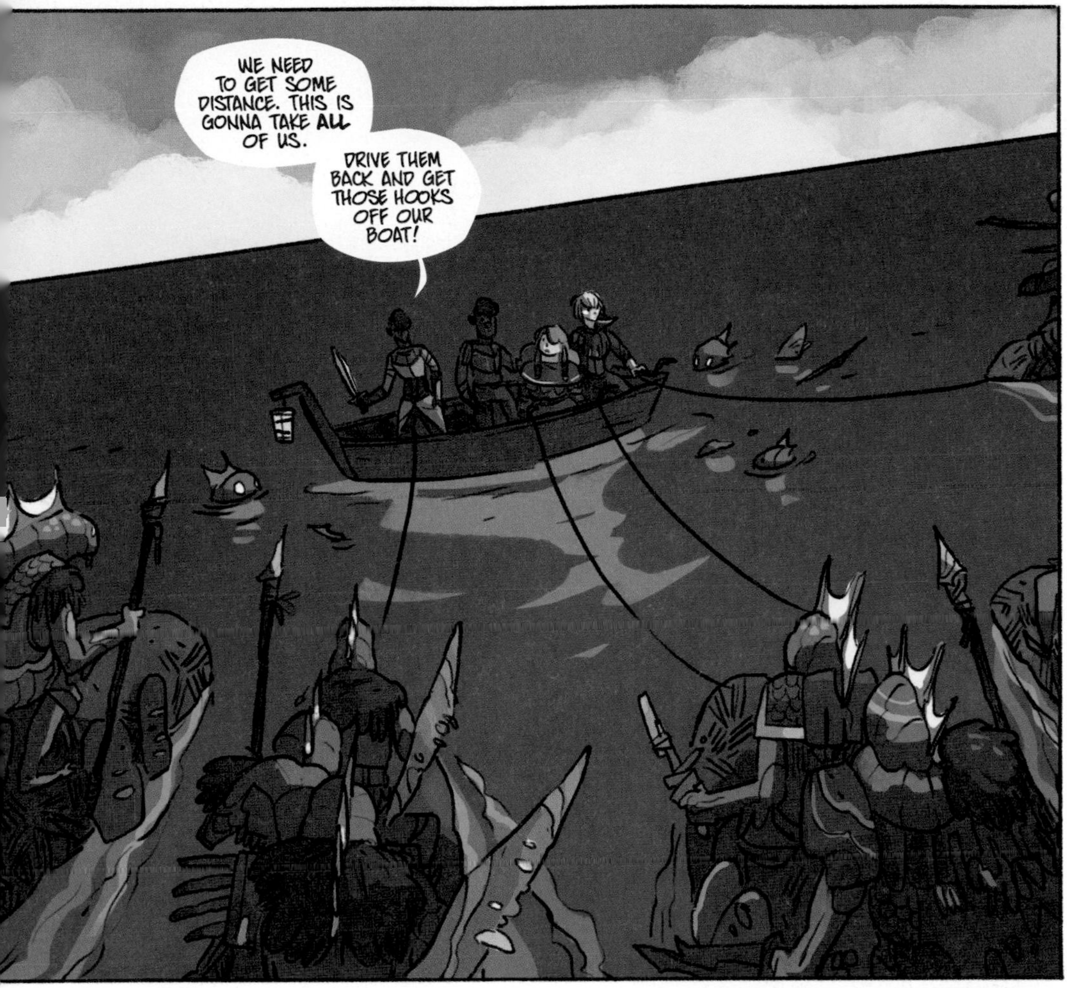
WE NEED TO GET SOME DISTANCE. THIS IS GONNA TAKE ALL OF US.
DRIVE THEM BACK AND GET THOSE HOOKS OFF OUR BOAT!

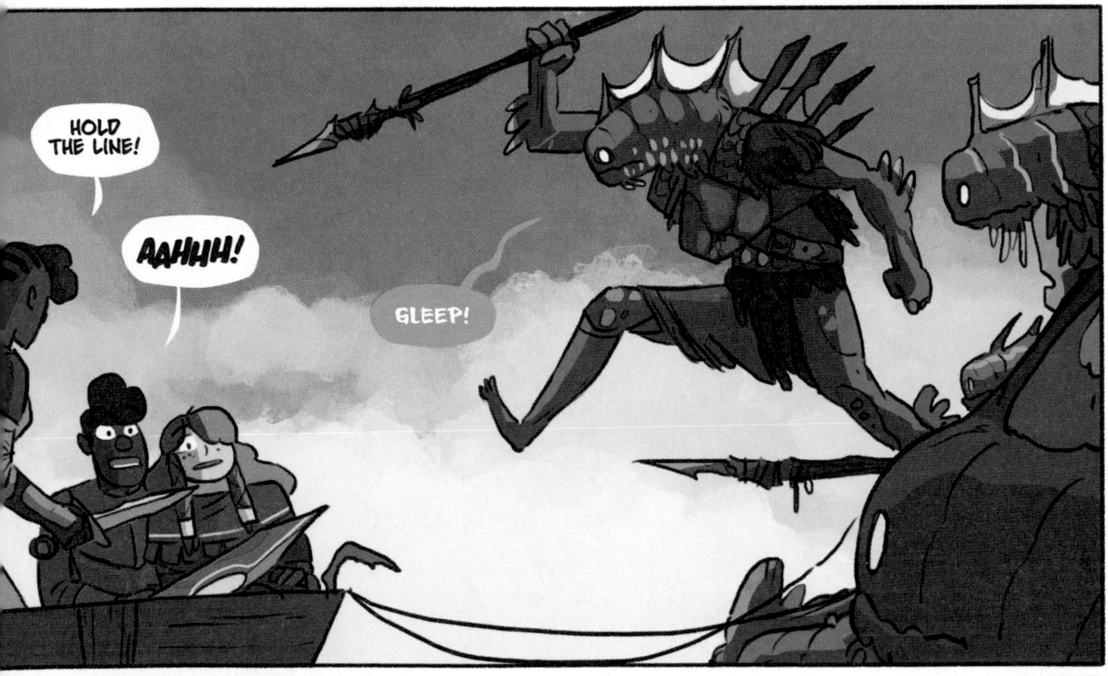
HOLD THE LINE!
AAHHH!
GLEEP!

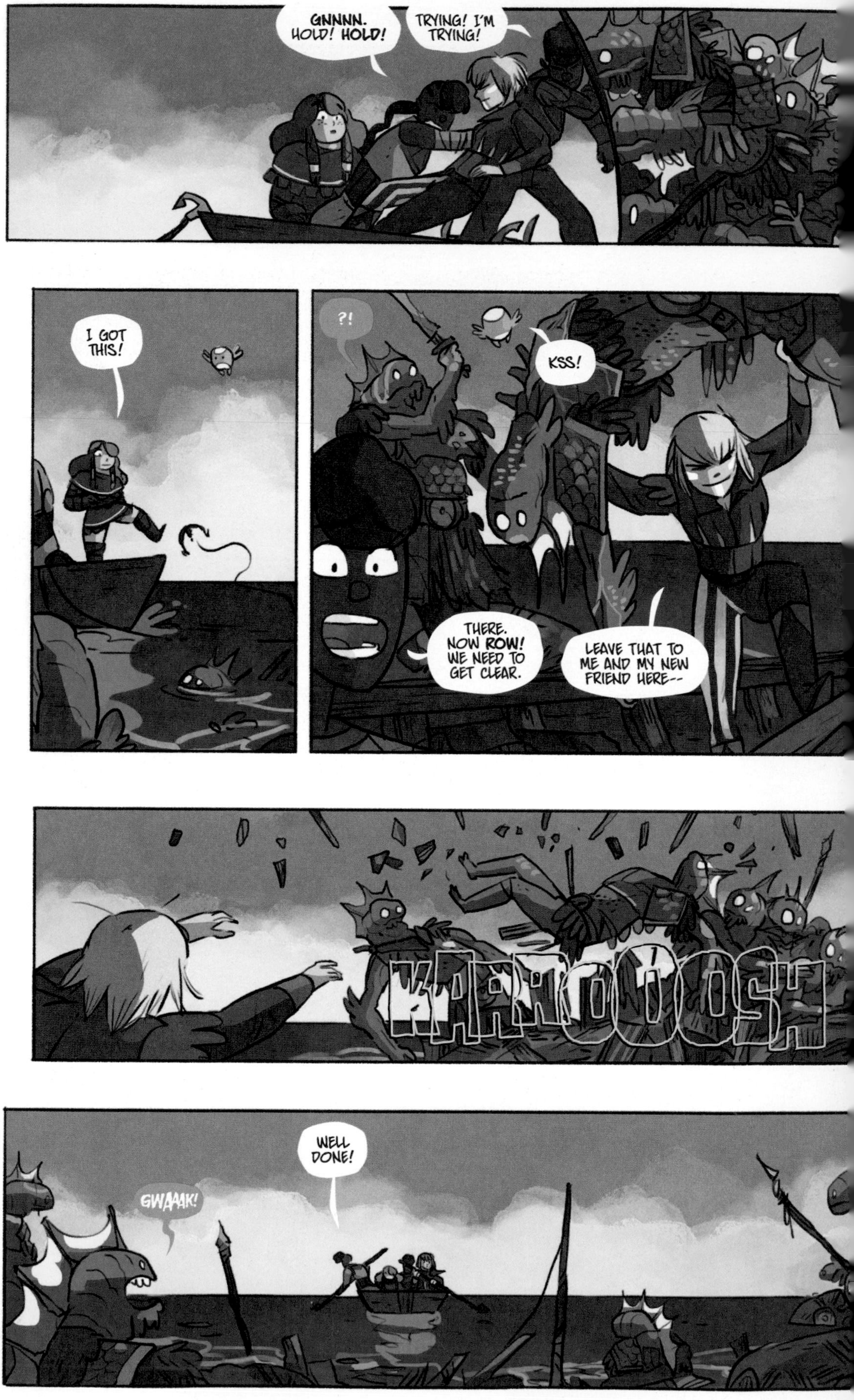
GNNNN. HOLD! HOLD!
TRYING! I'M TRYING!
I GOT THIS!
?!
KSS!
THERE. NOW ROW! WE NEED TO GET CLEAR.
LEAVE THAT TO ME AND MY NEW FRIEND HERE--
KARROOOOSH
WELL DONE!
GWAAAK!

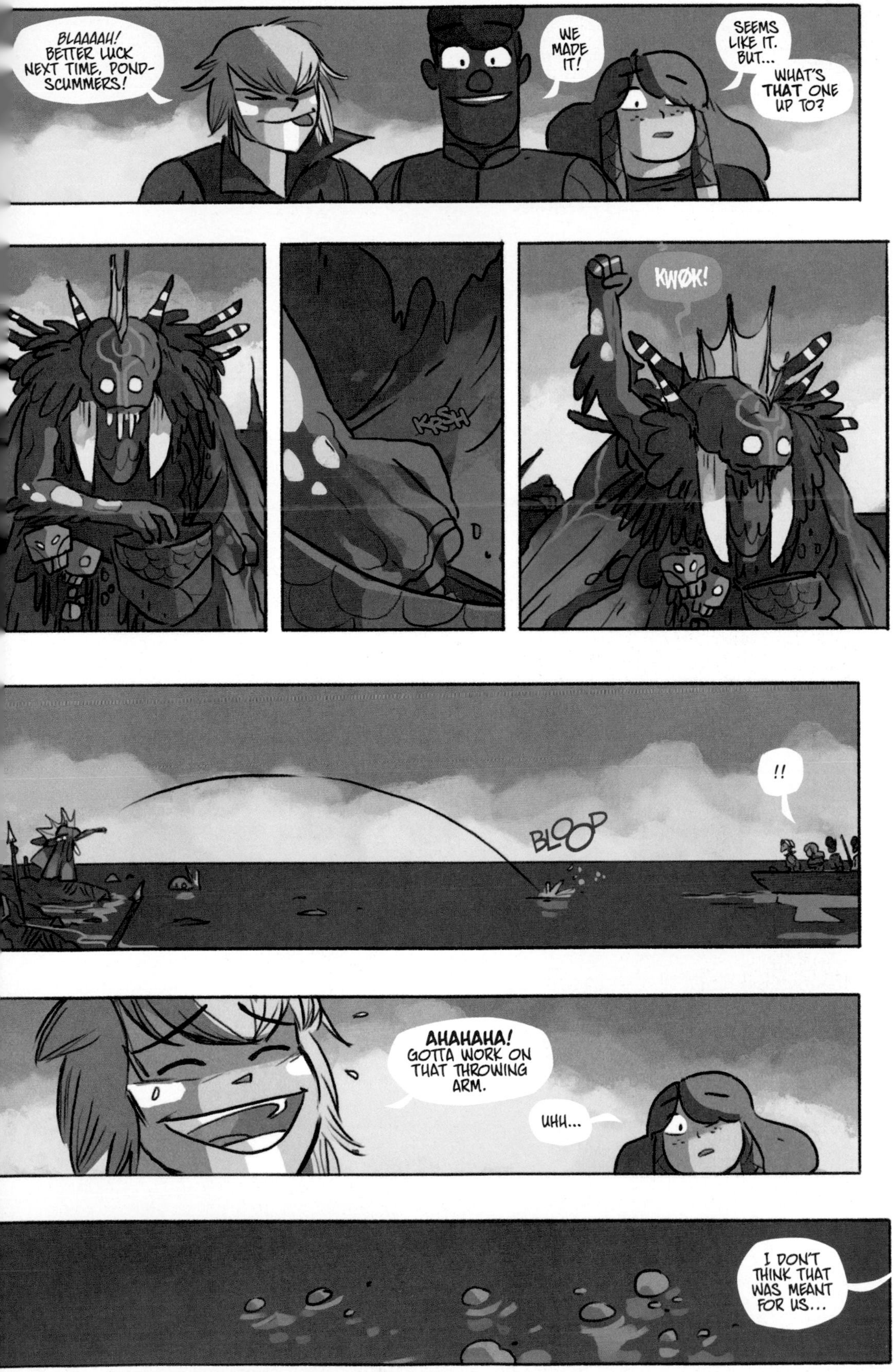
BLAAAAH! BETTER LUCK NEXT TIME, POND-SCUMMERS!
WE MADE IT!
SEEMS LIKE IT. BUT...
WHAT'S THAT ONE UP TO?
KRSH
KWØK!
BLOOP
!!
AHAHAHA! GOTTA WORK ON THAT THROWING ARM.
UHH...
I DON'T THINK THAT WAS MEANT FOR US...

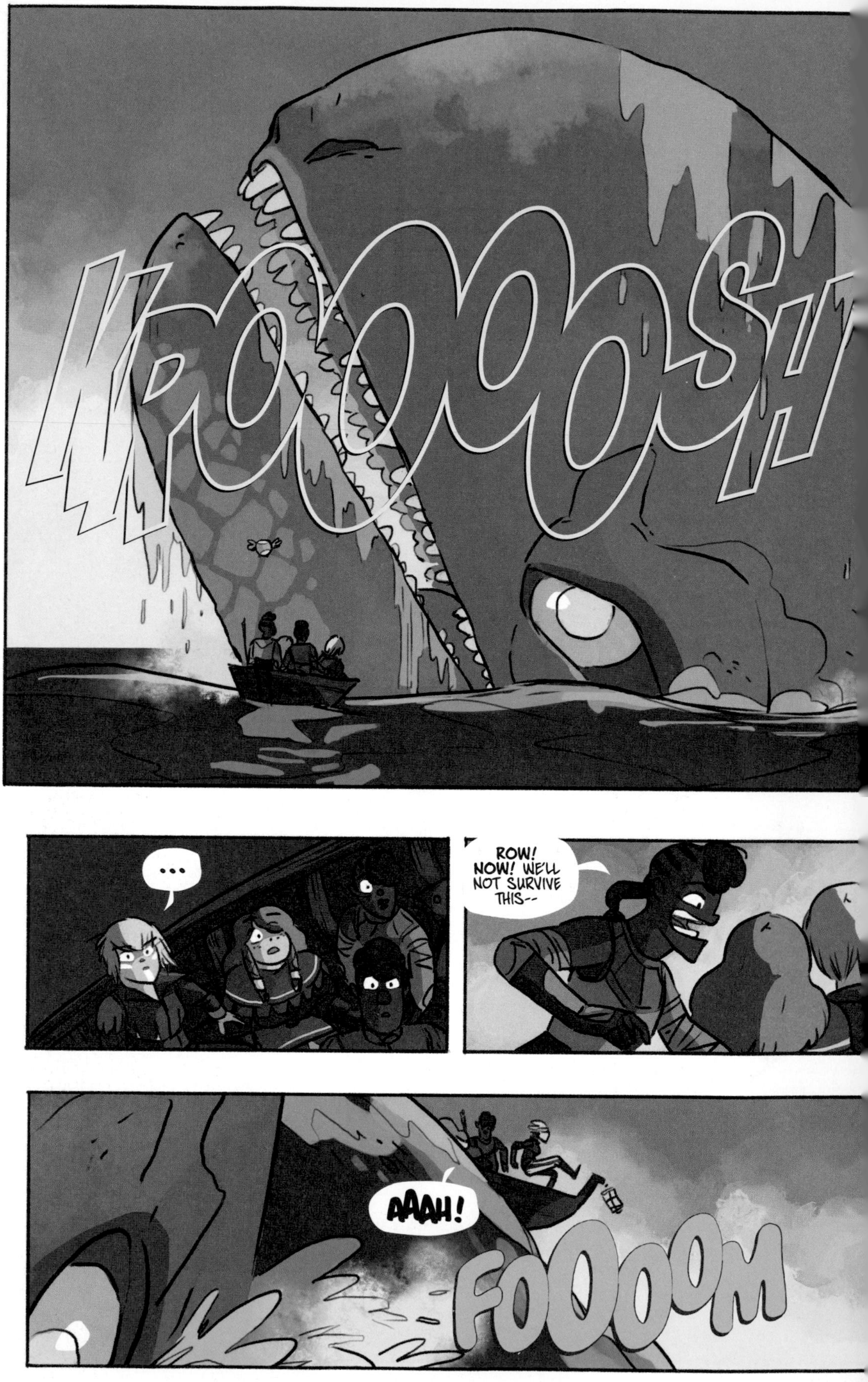
KROOOOSH
...
ROW! NOW! WE'LL NOT SURVIVE THIS--
AAAH!
FOOOOM

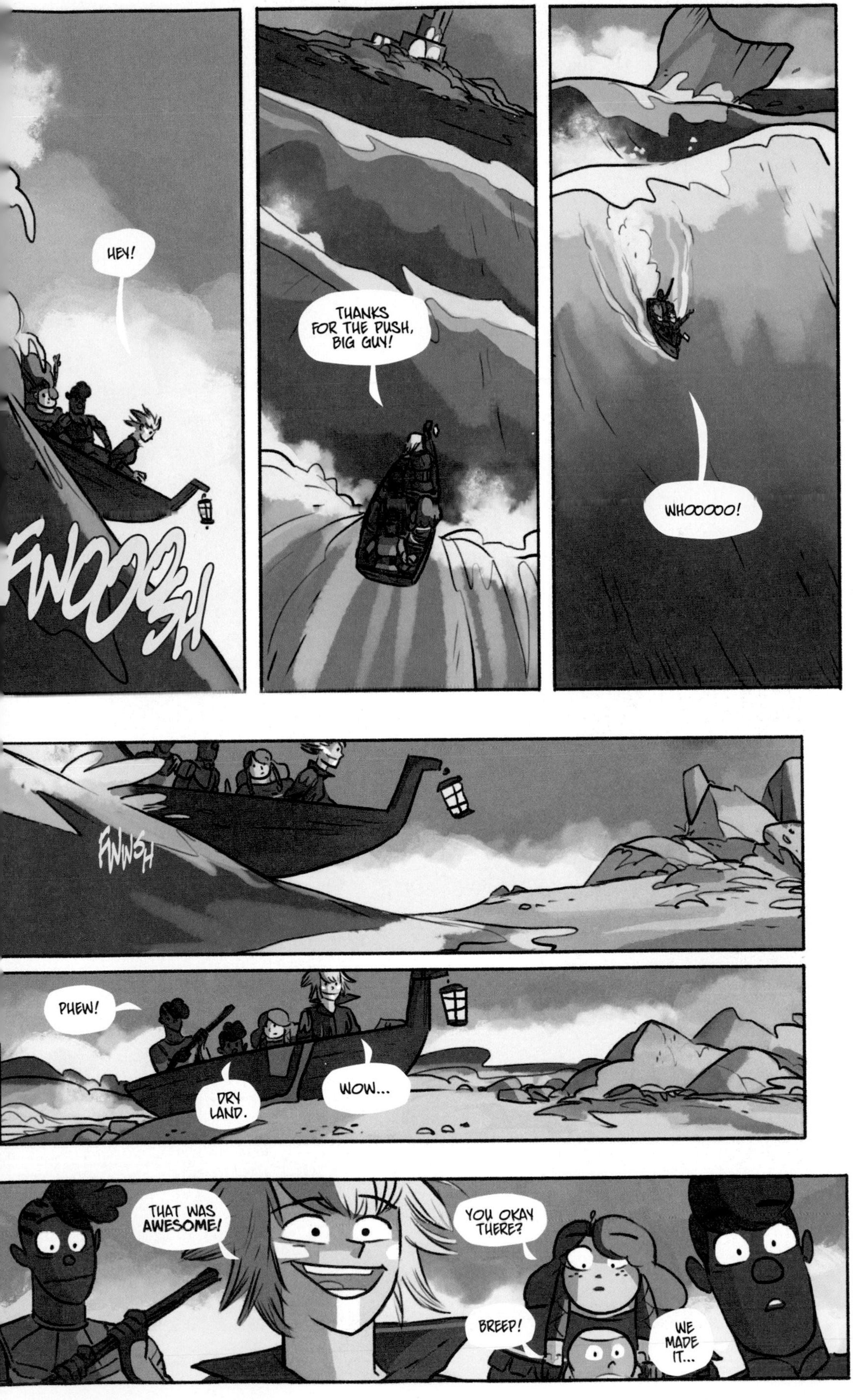
HEY!
FWOOOSH
THANKS FOR THE PUSH, BIG GUY!
WHOOOOO!
FWWSH
PHEW!
DRY LAND.
WOW...
THAT WAS AWESOME!
YOU OKAY THERE?
BREEP!
WE MADE IT...

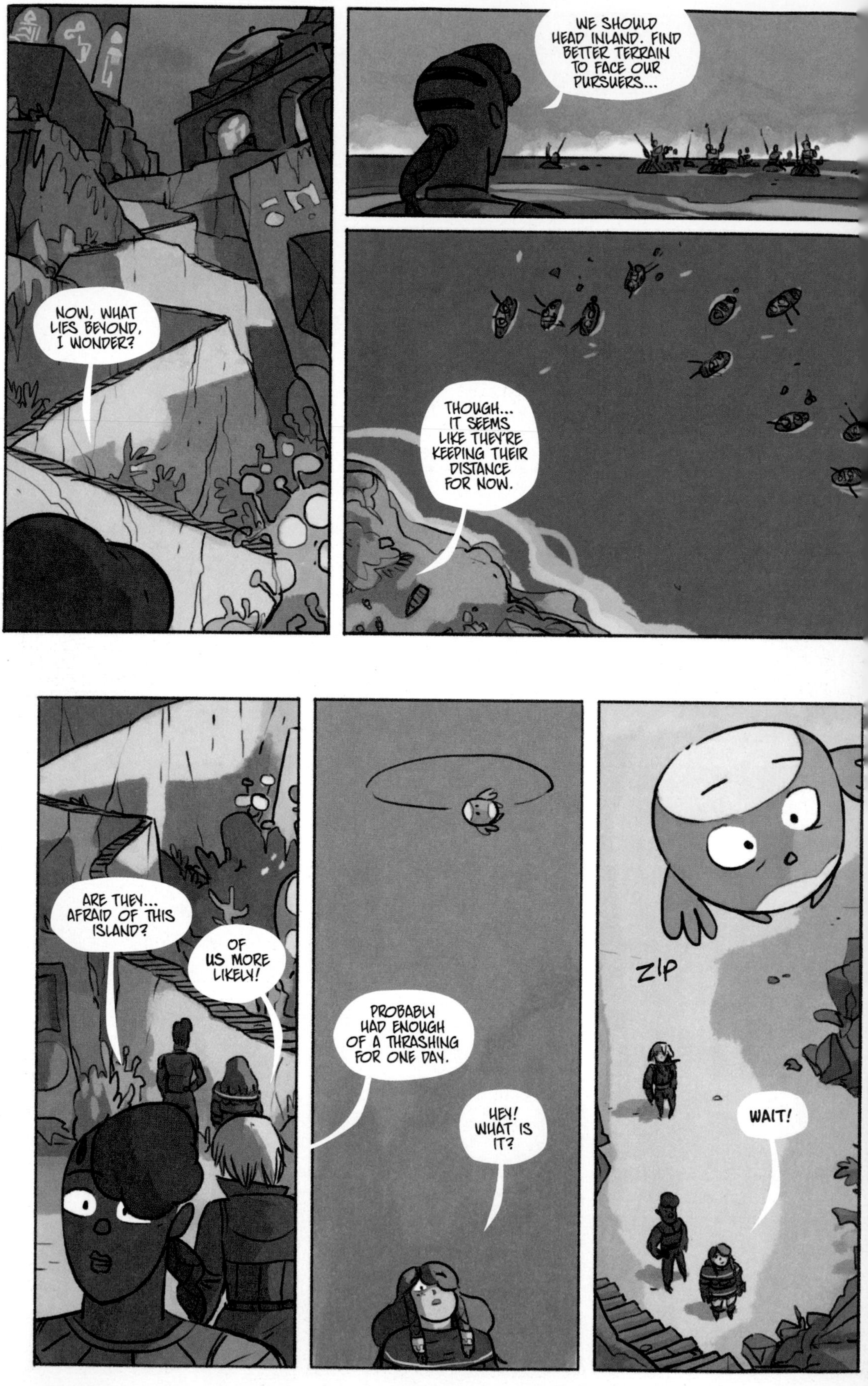
NOW, WHAT LIES BEYOND, I WONDER?
WE SHOULD HEAD INLAND. FIND BETTER TERRAIN TO FACE OUR PURSUERS...
THOUGH... IT SEEMS LIKE THEY'RE KEEPING THEIR DISTANCE FOR NOW.
ARE THEY... AFRAID OF THIS ISLAND?
OF US MORE LIKELY!
PROBABLY HAD ENOUGH OF A THRASHING FOR ONE DAY.
HEY! WHAT IS IT?
ZIP
WAIT!

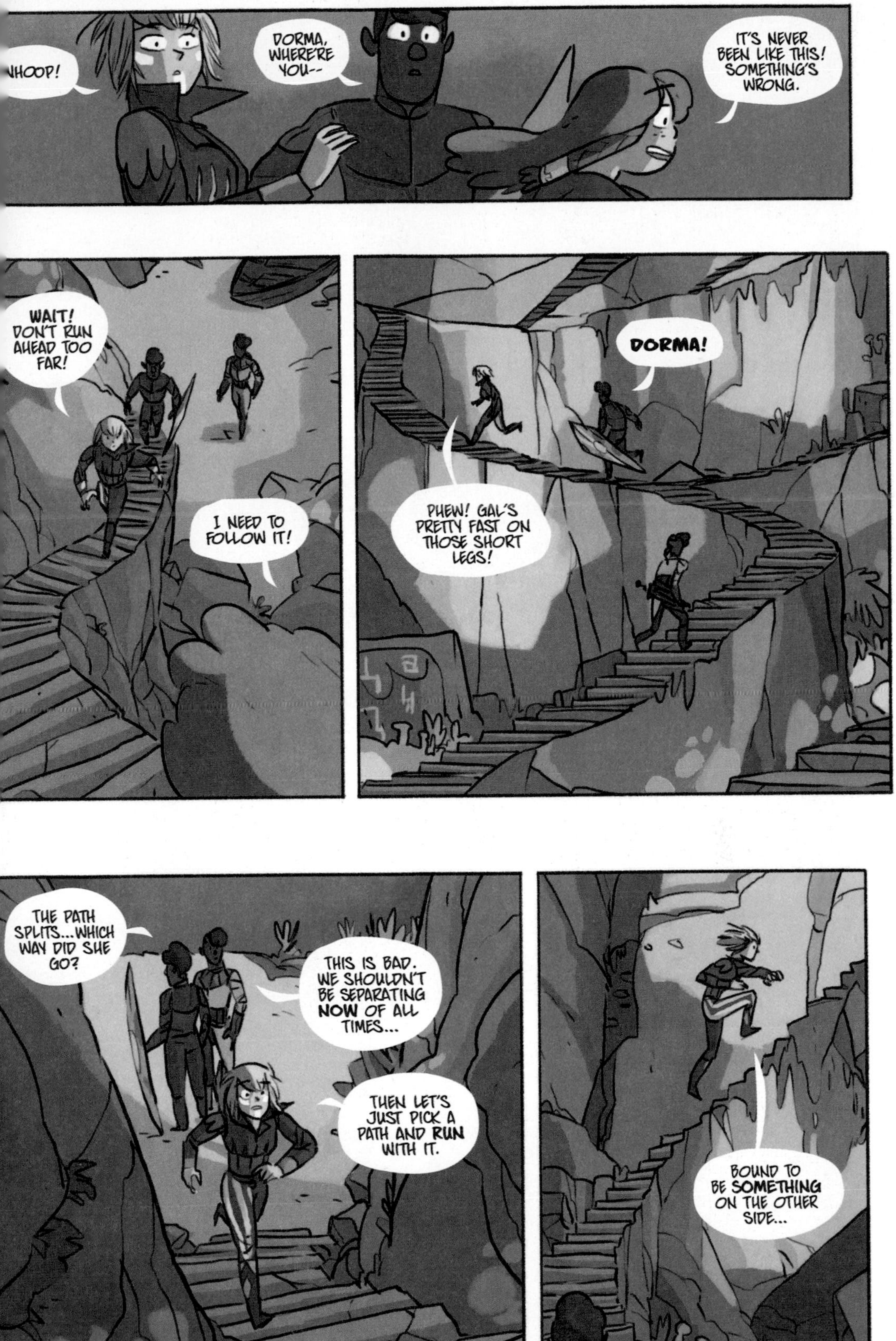
WHOOP!
DORMA, WHERE'RE YOU--
IT'S NEVER BEEN LIKE THIS! SOMETHING'S WRONG.
WAIT! DON'T RUN AHEAD TOO FAR!
I NEED TO FOLLOW IT!
DORMA!
PHEW! GAL'S PRETTY FAST ON THOSE SHORT LEGS!
THE PATH SPLITS...WHICH WAY DID SHE GO?
THIS IS BAD. WE SHOULDN'T BE SEPARATING NOW OF ALL TIMES...
THEN LET'S JUST PICK A PATH AND RUN WITH IT.
BOUND TO BE SOMETHING ON THE OTHER SIDE...

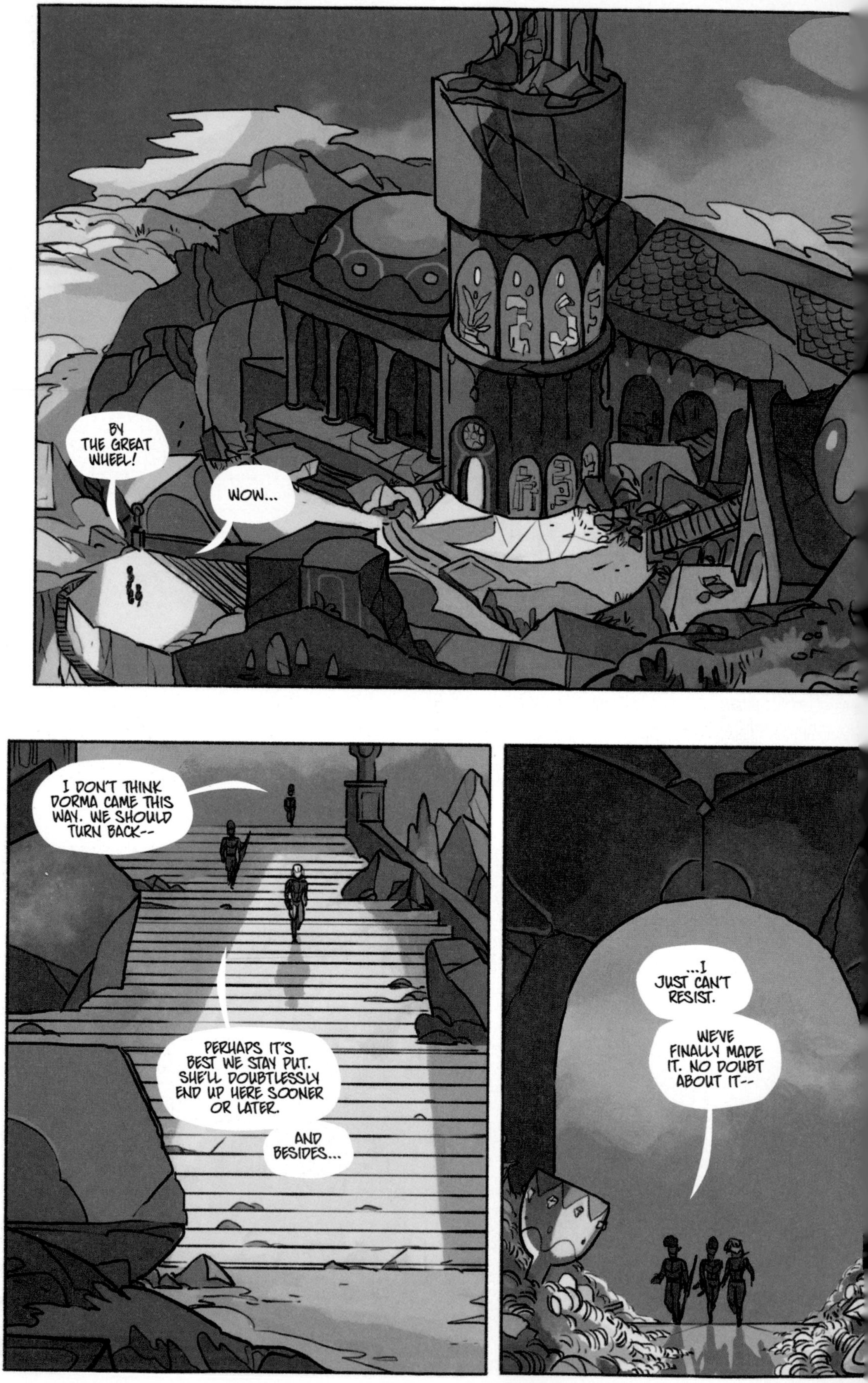
BY THE GREAT WHEEL!
WOW...
I DON'T THINK DORMA CAME THIS WAY. WE SHOULD TURN BACK--
PERHAPS IT'S BEST WE STAY PUT. SHE'LL DOUBTLESSLY END UP HERE SOONER OR LATER.
AND BESIDES...
...I JUST CAN'T RESIST.
WE'VE FINALLY MADE IT. NO DOUBT ABOUT IT--

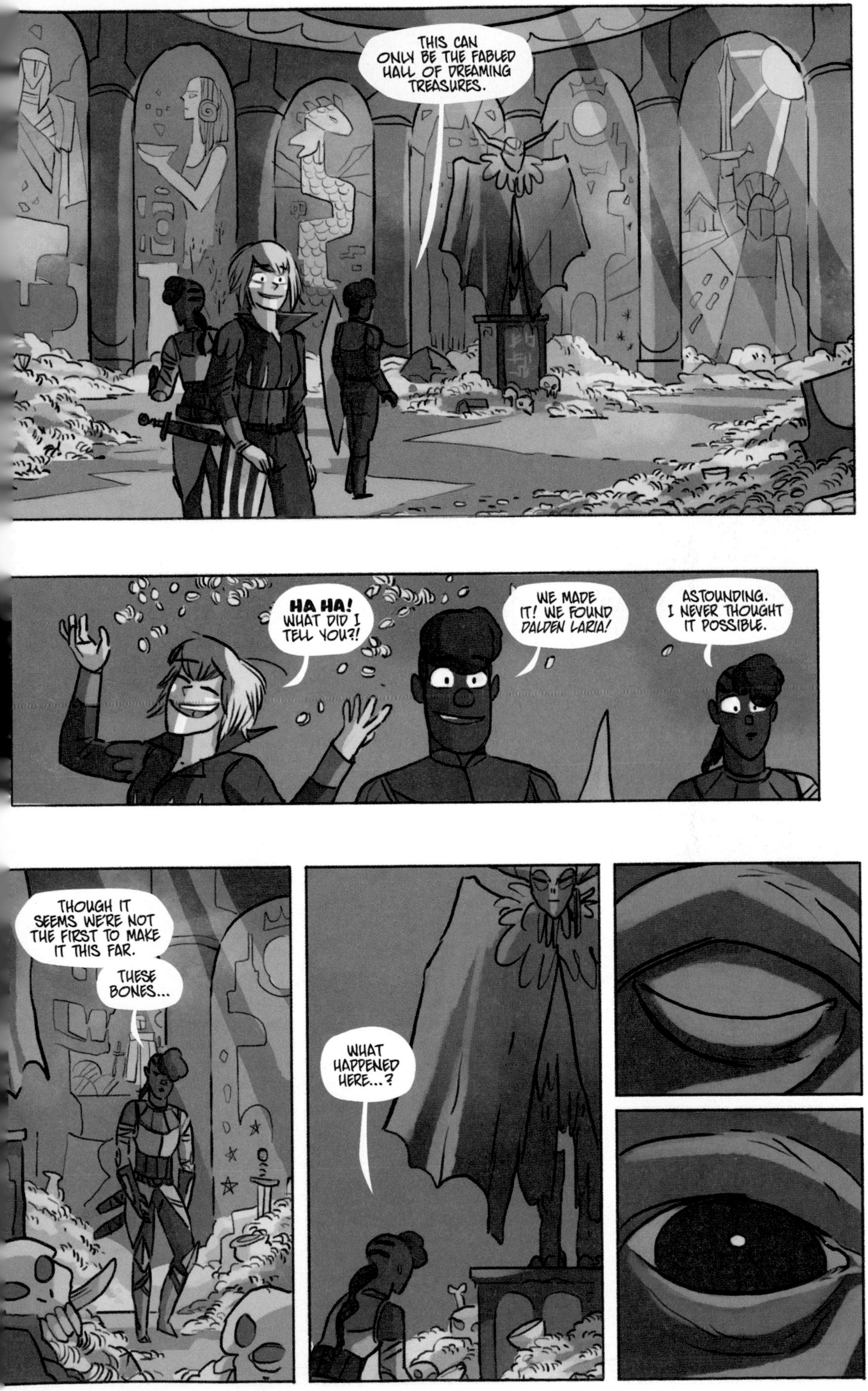
THIS CAN ONLY BE THE FABLED HALL OF DREAMING TREASURES.
HA HA! WHAT DID I TELL YOU?!
WE MADE IT! WE FOUND DALDEN LARIA!
ASTOUNDING. I NEVER THOUGHT IT POSSIBLE.
THOUGH IT SEEMS WE'RE NOT THE FIRST TO MAKE IT THIS FAR.
THESE BONES...
WHAT HAPPENED HERE...?

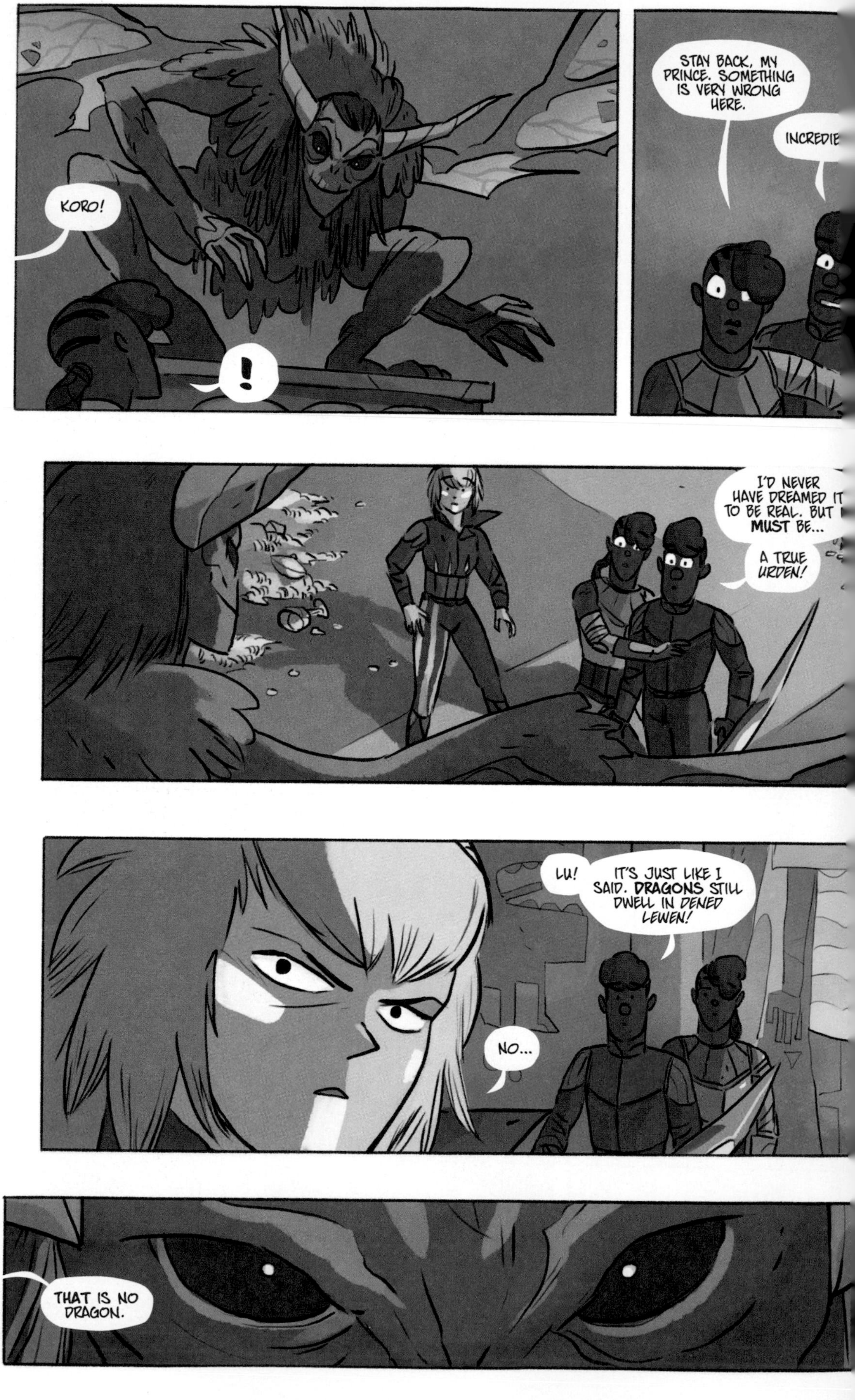
KORO!
!
STAY BACK, MY PRINCE. SOMETHING IS VERY WRONG HERE.
INCREDIE
I'D NEVER HAVE DREAMED IT TO BE REAL. BUT MUST BE...
A TRUE URDEN!
LU!
IT'S JUST LIKE I SAID. DRAGONS STILL DWELL IN DENED LEWEN!
NO...
THAT IS NO DRAGON.

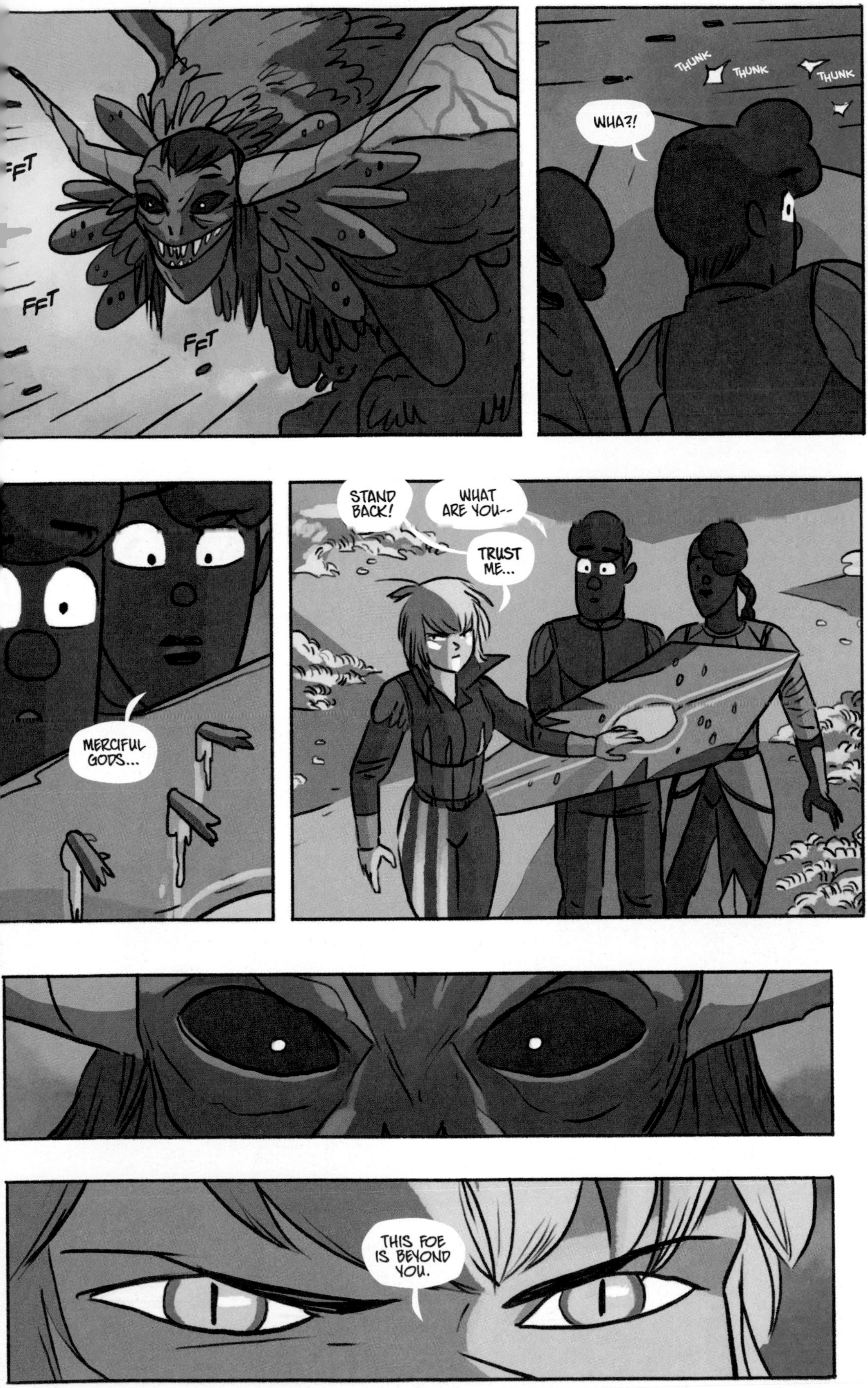
FFT
FFT
FFT
THUNK
THUNK
THUNK
WHA?!
MERCIFUL GODS...
STAND BACK!
WHAT ARE YOU--
TRUST ME...
THIS FOE IS BEYOND YOU.

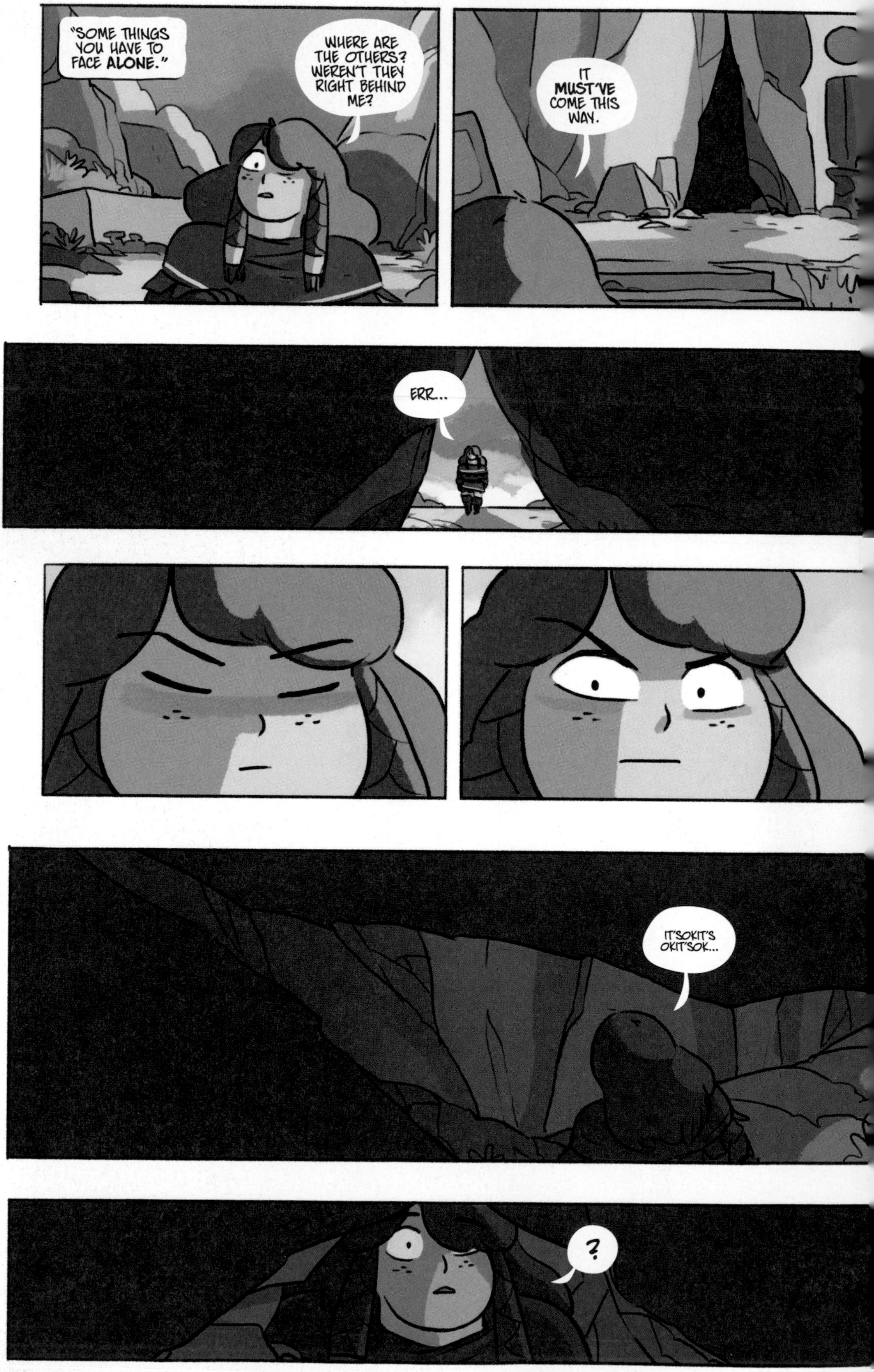
"SOME THINGS YOU HAVE TO FACE ALONE."
WHERE ARE THE OTHERS? WEREN'T THEY RIGHT BEHIND ME?
IT MUST'VE COME THIS WAY.
ERR...
IT'SOKIT'S OKIT'SOK...
?

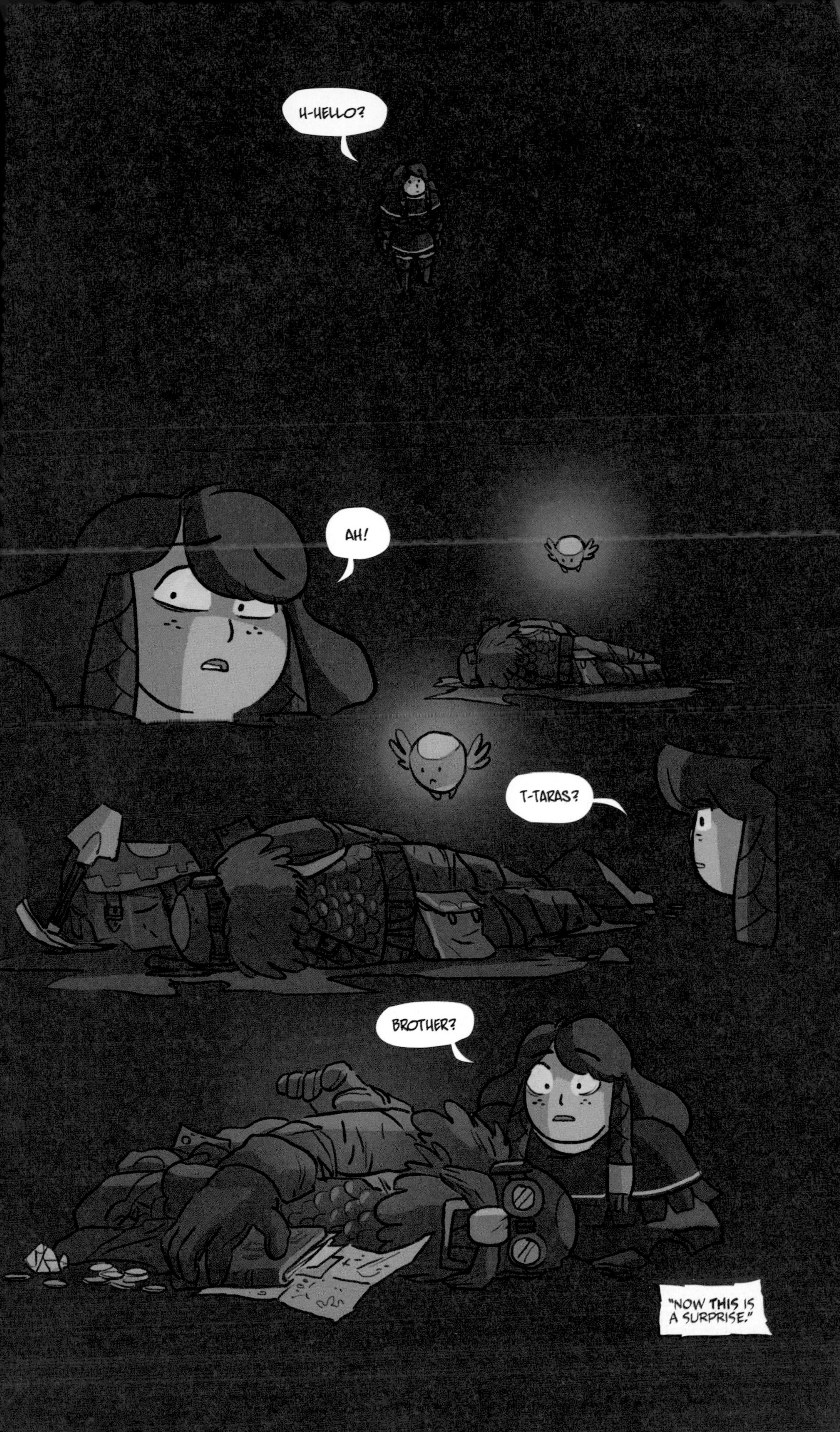
H-HELLO?
AH!
T-TARAS?
BROTHER?
"NOW THIS IS A SURPRISE."

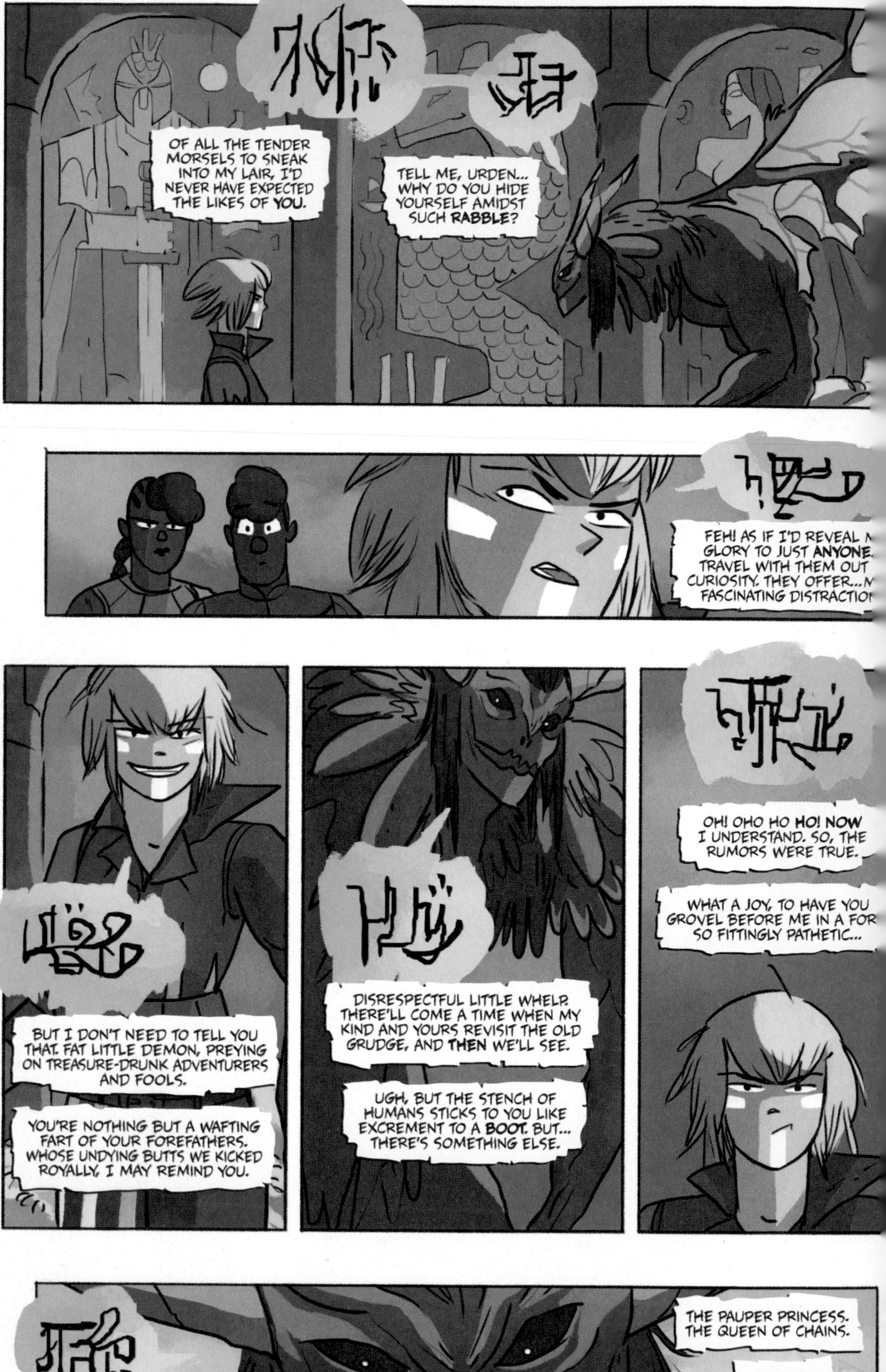

OF ALL THE TENDER MORSELS TO SNEAK INTO MY LAIR, I'D NEVER HAVE EXPECTED THE LIKES OF **YOU**.
TELL ME, URDEN... WHY DO YOU HIDE YOURSELF AMIDST SUCH **RABBLE**?
FEH! AS IF I'D REVEAL M GLORY TO JUST **ANYONE**. TRAVEL WITH THEM OUT CURIOSITY. THEY OFFER... M FASCINATING DISTRACTIO
BUT I DON'T NEED TO TELL YOU THAT. FAT LITTLE DEMON, PREYING ON TREASURE-DRUNK ADVENTURERS AND FOOLS.
YOU'RE NOTHING BUT A WAFTING FART OF YOUR FOREFATHERS. WHOSE UNDYING BUTTS WE KICKED ROYALLY, I MAY REMIND YOU.
DISRESPECTFUL LITTLE WHELP. THERE'LL COME A TIME WHEN MY KIND AND YOURS REVISIT THE OLD GRUDGE, AND **THEN** WE'LL SEE.
UGH, BUT THE STENCH OF HUMANS STICKS TO YOU LIKE EXCREMENT TO A **BOOT**. BUT... THERE'S SOMETHING ELSE.
OH! OHO HO **HO**! **NOW** I UNDERSTAND. SO, THE RUMORS WERE TRUE.
WHAT A JOY, TO HAVE YOU GROVEL BEFORE ME IN A FOR SO FITTINGLY PATHETIC...
THE PAUPER PRINCESS. THE QUEEN OF CHAINS.
THE **LADY LUVANDER**.

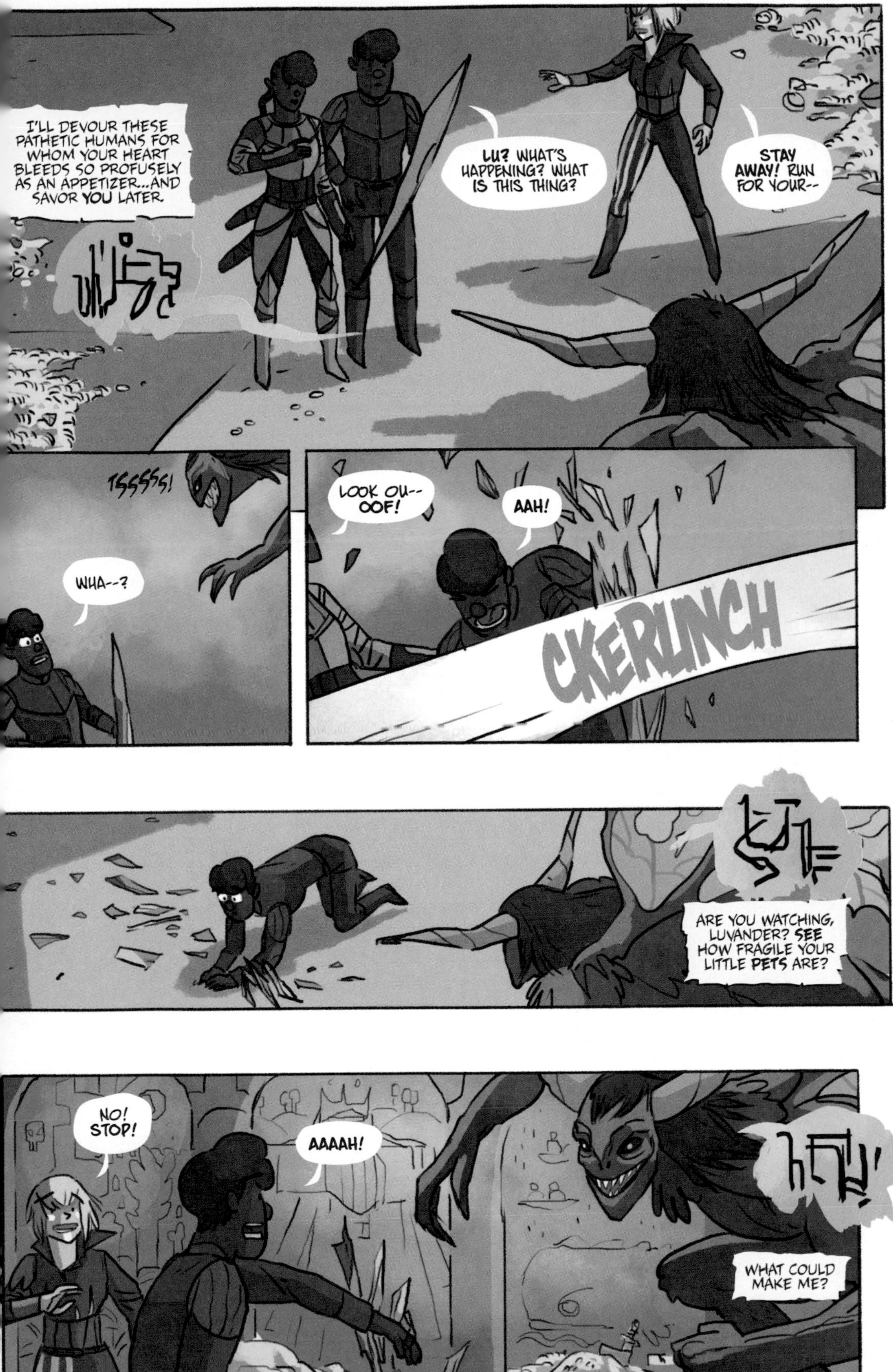
I'LL DEVOUR THESE PATHETIC HUMANS FOR WHOM YOUR HEART BLEEDS SO PROFUSELY AS AN APPETIZER...AND SAVOR YOU LATER.
LU? WHAT'S HAPPENING? WHAT IS THIS THING?
STAY AWAY! RUN FOR YOUR--
TSSSSS!
WHA--?
LOOK OU-- OOF!
AAH!
CKERUNCH
ARE YOU WATCHING, LUVANDER? SEE HOW FRAGILE YOUR LITTLE PETS ARE?
NO! STOP!
AAAAH!
WHAT COULD MAKE ME?

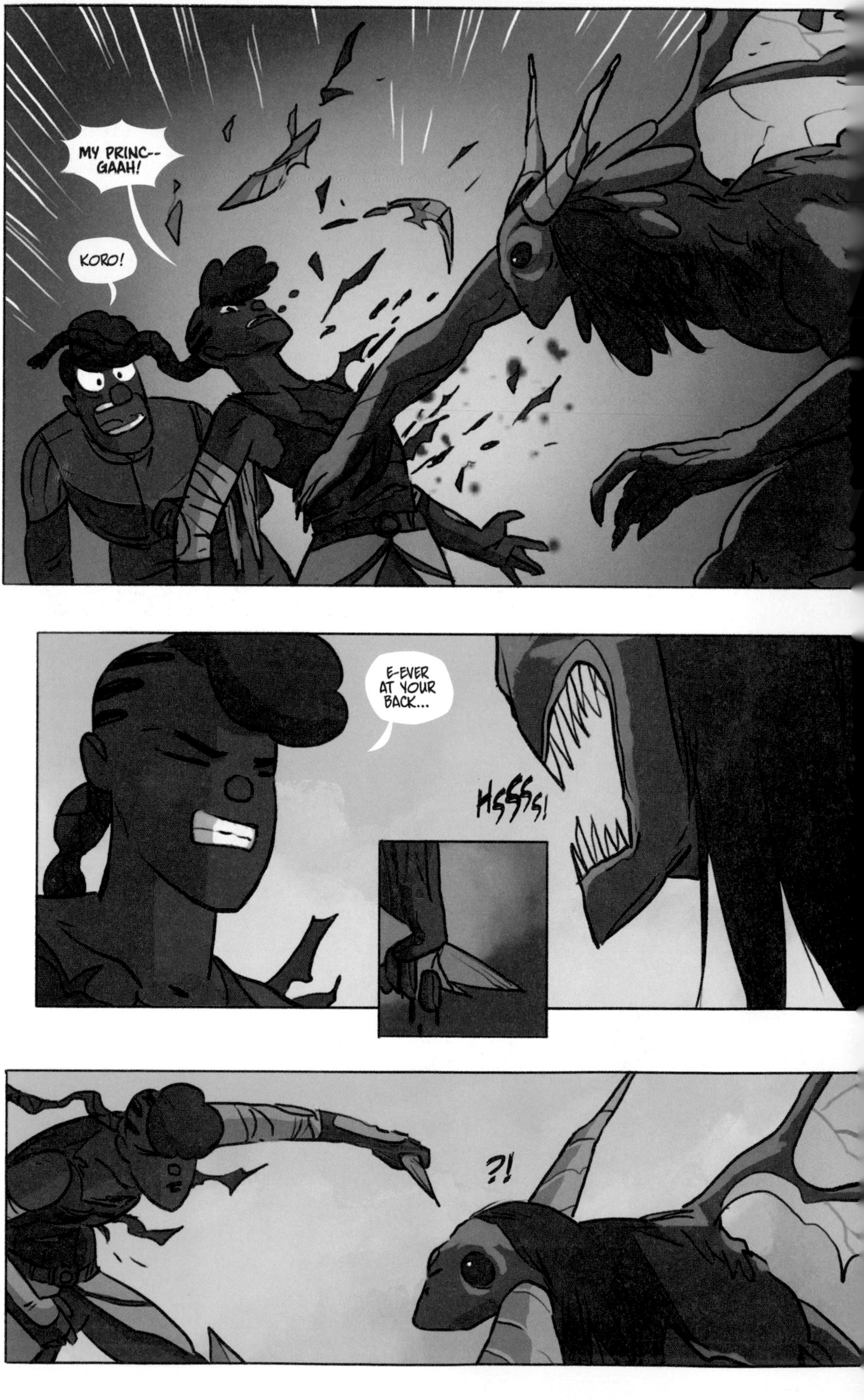
KORO!
MY PRINC-- GAAH!
E-EVER AT YOUR BACK...
HSSSS!
?!

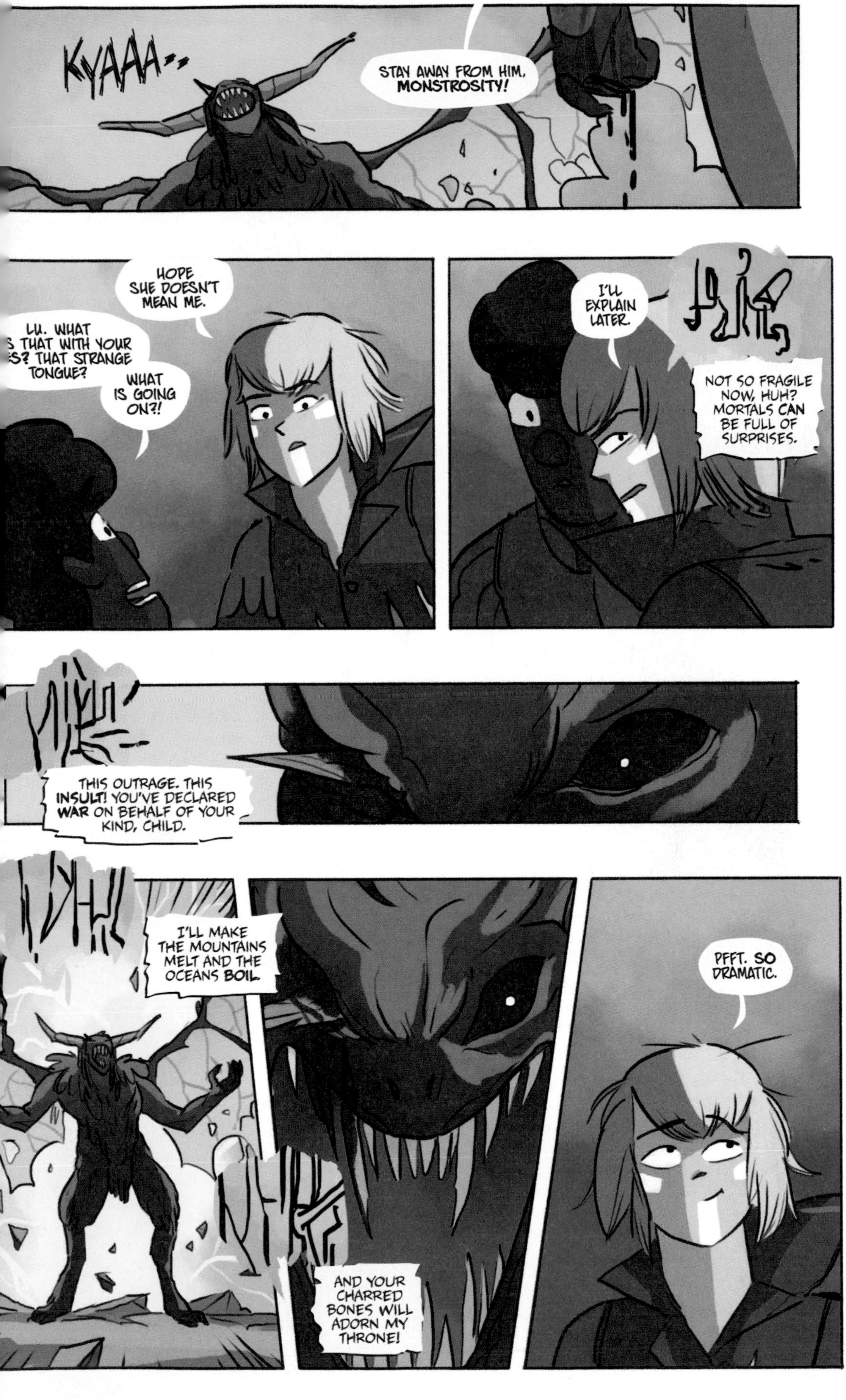
KYAAA
STAY AWAY FROM HIM, MONSTROSITY!
HOPE SHE DOESN'T MEAN ME.
LU. WHAT S THAT WITH YOUR ES? THAT STRANGE TONGUE?
WHAT IS GOING ON?!
I'LL EXPLAIN LATER.
NOT SO FRAGILE NOW, HUH? MORTALS CAN BE FULL OF SURPRISES.
THIS OUTRAGE. THIS INSULT! YOU'VE DECLARED WAR ON BEHALF OF YOUR KIND, CHILD.
I'LL MAKE THE MOUNTAINS MELT AND THE OCEANS BOIL.
AND YOUR CHARRED BONES WILL ADORN MY THRONE!
PFFT. SO DRAMATIC.

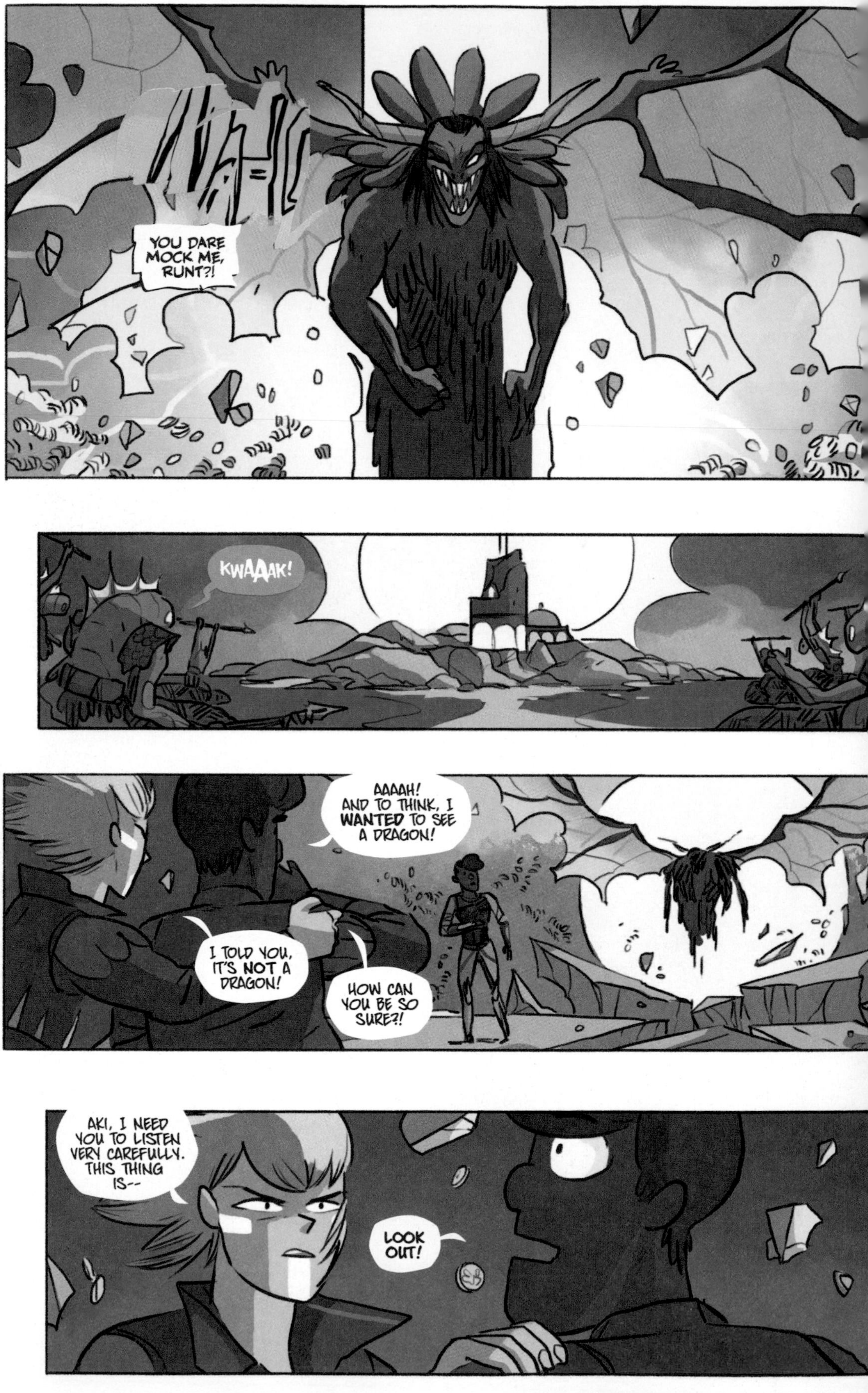
YOU DARE MOCK ME, RUNT?!
KWAAAK!
AAAAH! AND TO THINK, I WANTED TO SEE A DRAGON!
I TOLD YOU, IT'S NOT A DRAGON!
HOW CAN YOU BE SO SURE?!
AKI, I NEED YOU TO LISTEN VERY CAREFULLY. THIS THING IS--
LOOK OUT!

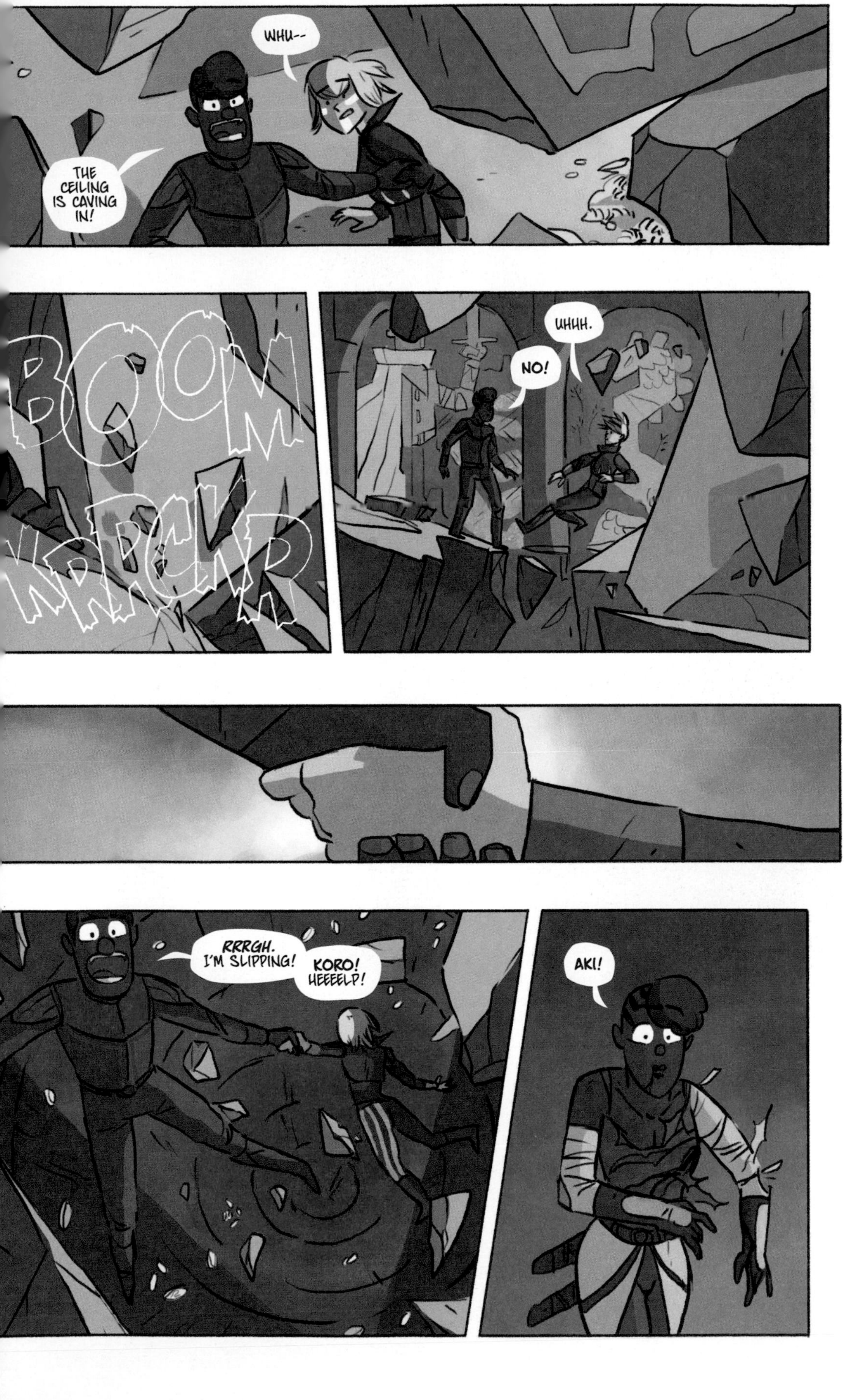
WHU--
THE CEILING IS CAVING IN!
BOOM
KRRCKR
UHHH.
NO!
RRRGH. I'M SLIPPING!
KORO! HEEEELP!
AKI!

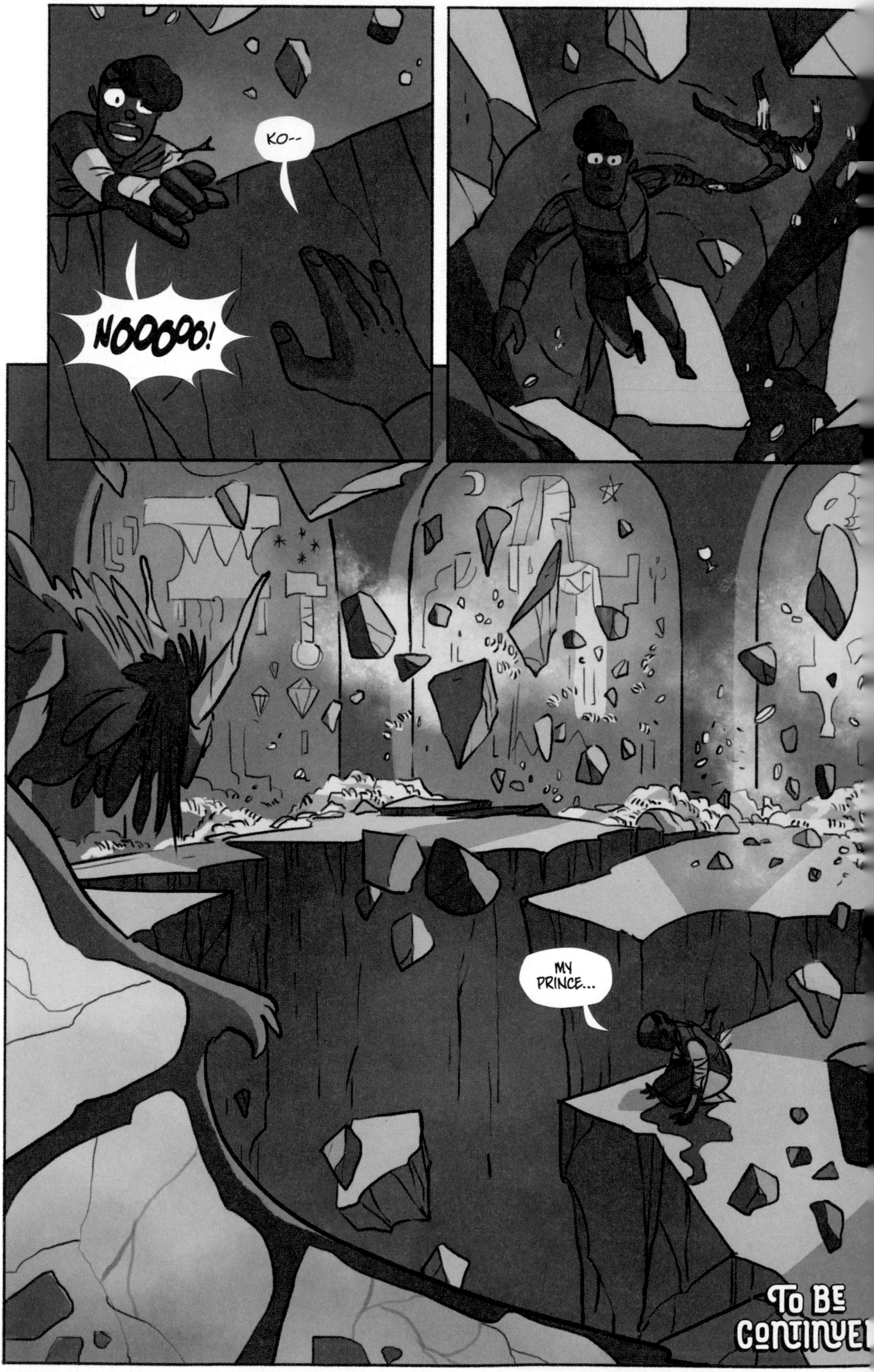
KO--
NOOOOO!
MY PRINCE...
TO BE CONTINUE

CHARACTER DESIGNS

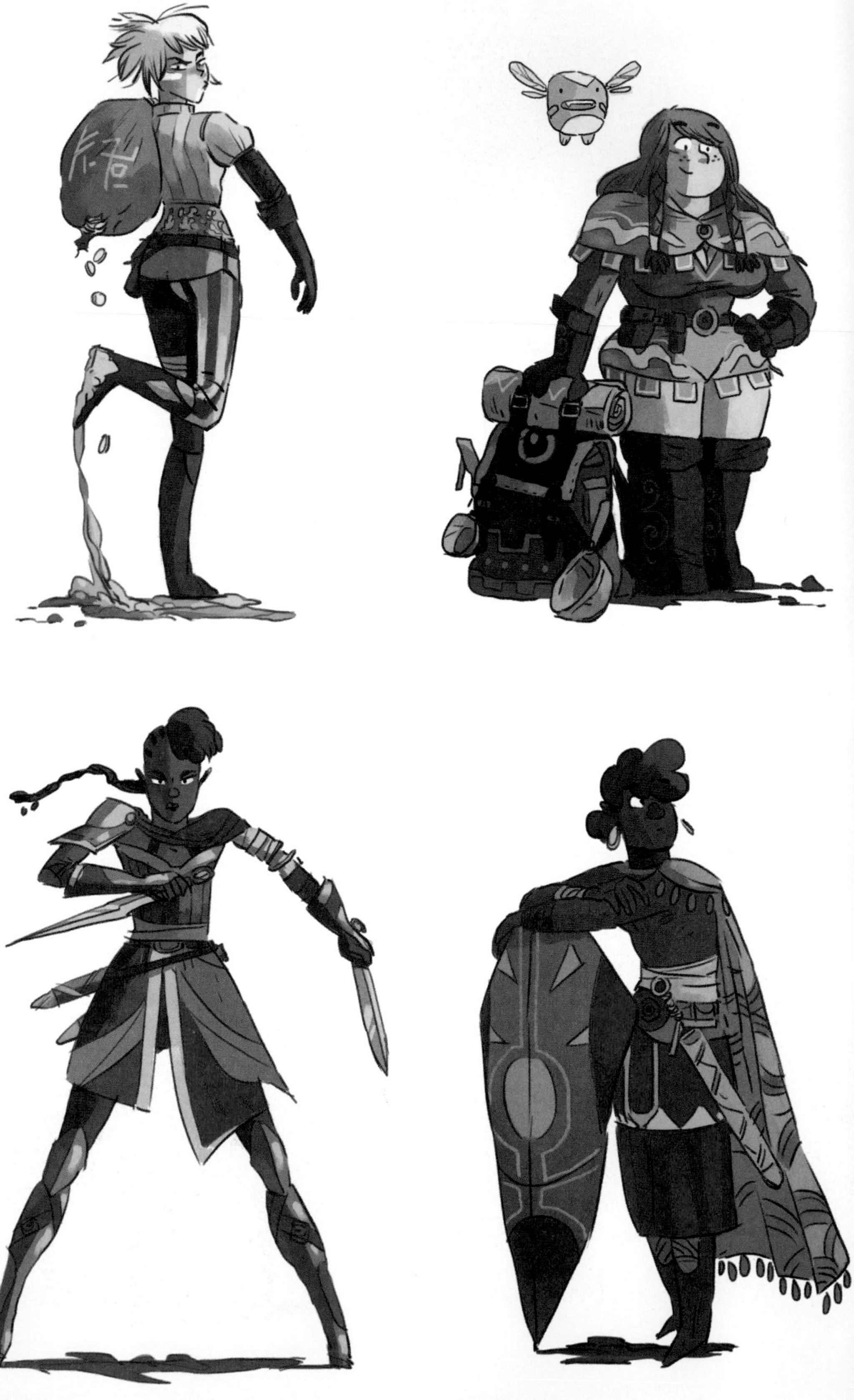

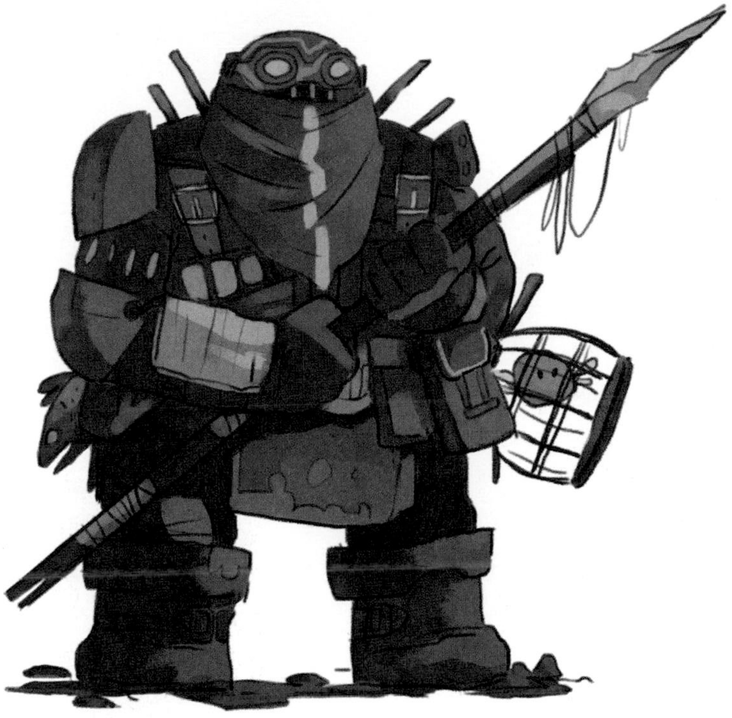

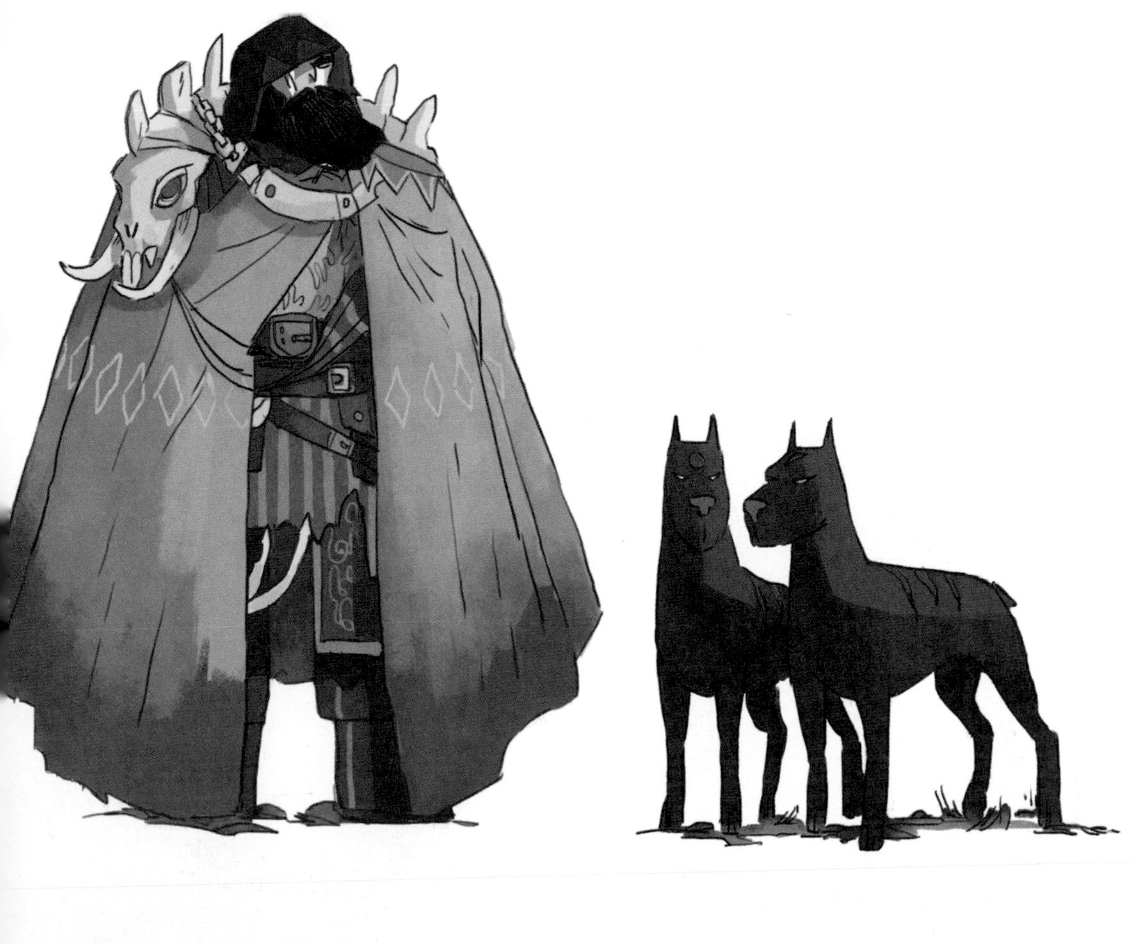

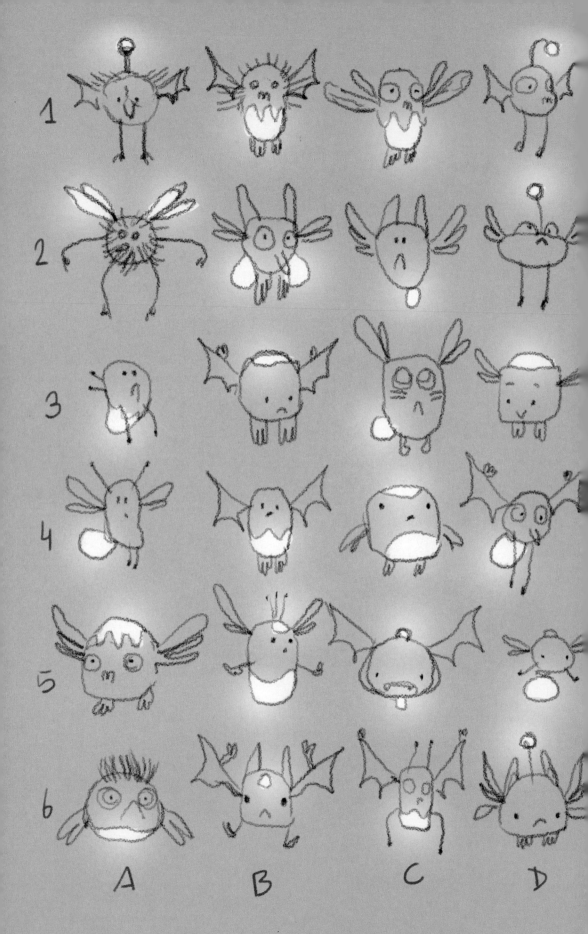

1

2

3

4

5

6

A   B   C   D

ISP DESIGNS

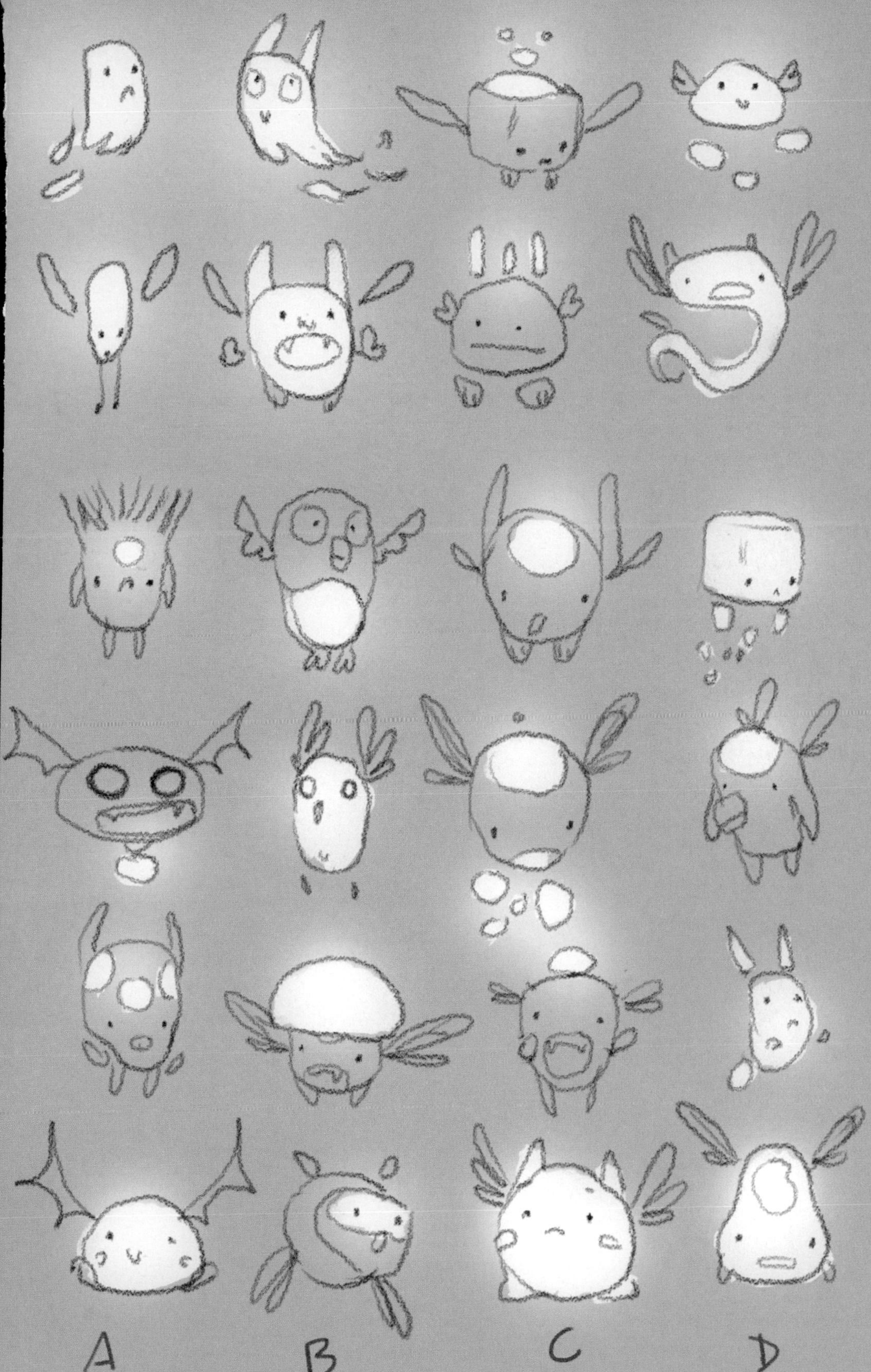
A
B
C
D

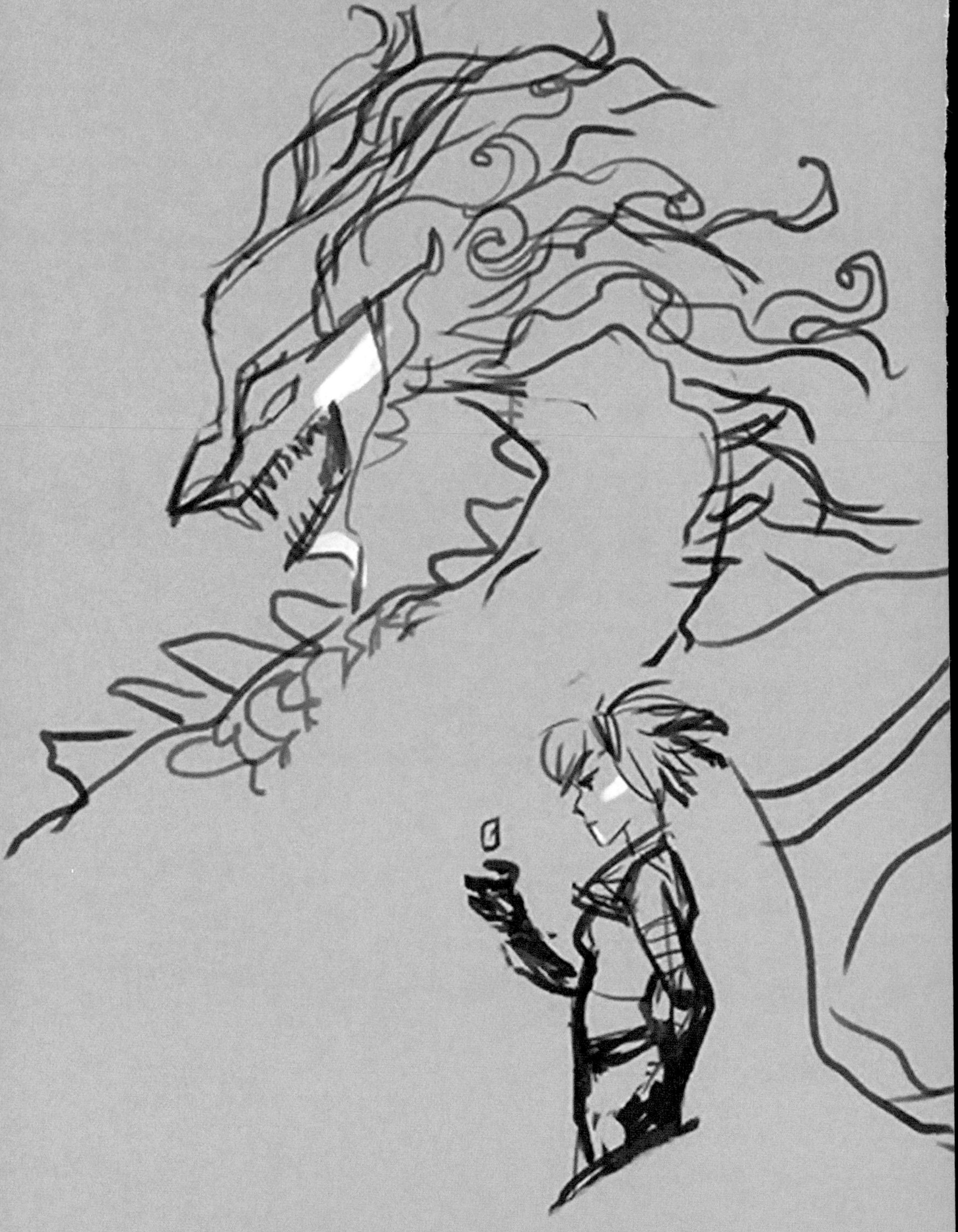

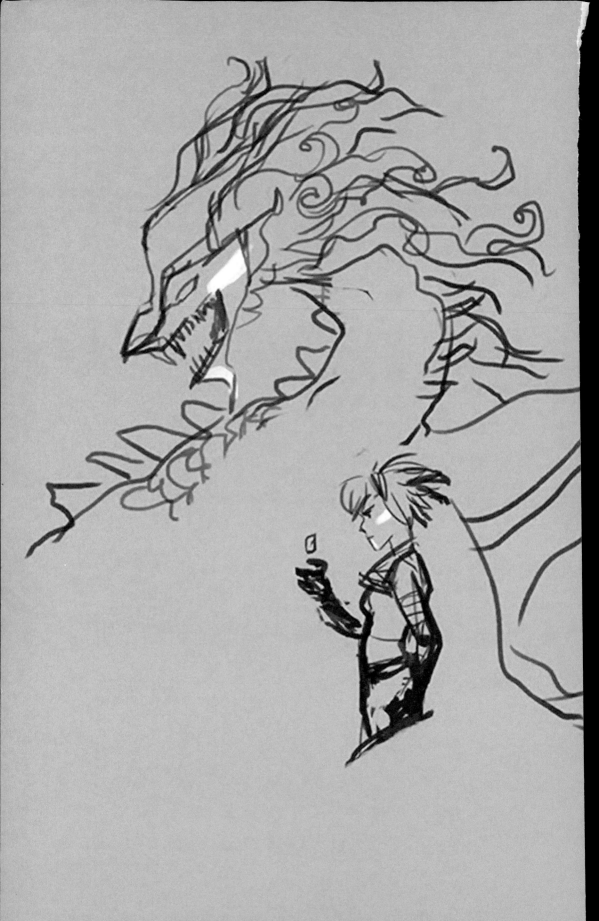

SKETCH FOR #1 COVER

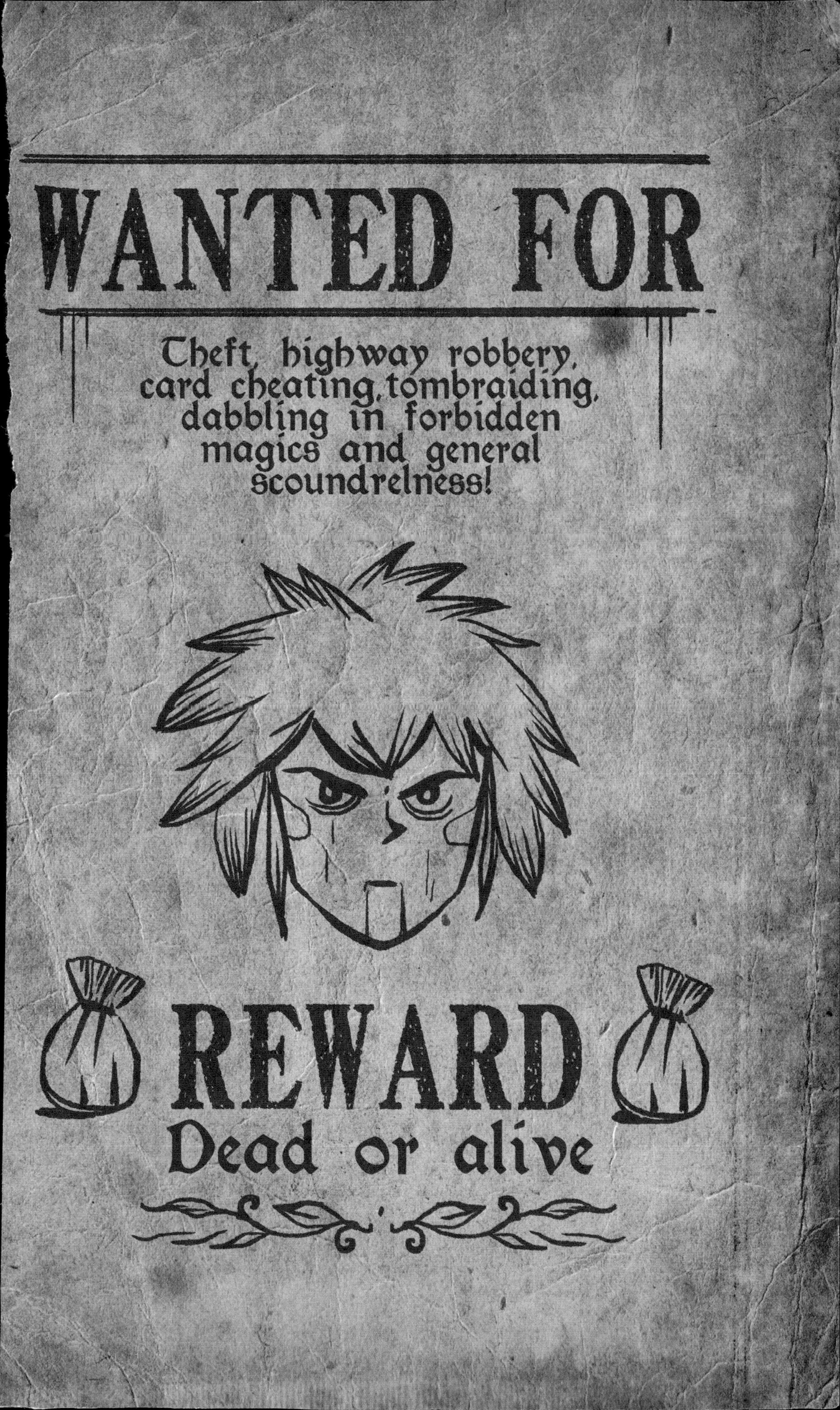
WANTED FOR
Theft, highway robbery, card cheating, tombraiding, dabbling in forbidden magics and general scoundrelness!
REWARD
Dead or alive

MEET THE SCOUNDRELS

SEBASTIAN GIRNER

is a German-born, American-raised comic writer and editor. Beginning his career at Marvel Entertainment, Sebastian has gone on to edit a number of critically acclaimed creator-owned Image Comics series including *Deadly Class*, *Drifter* and the Harvey and Eisner Award-winning *Southern Bastards*. In 2017 he released two comic writing debuts: *Scales & Scoundrels* and *Shirtless Bear-Fighter!* from Image Comics.

GALAAD

is a French freelance illustrator, animator, concept artist and storyboard artist working for videogame companies such as Ubisoft and Goodgame Studios, as well as European animation studios. A child of the 80s, his art style was heavily influenced by the Japanese animation of this era, among them *The Secret of Blue Water*, *Nausicaa of the Valley of the Wind*, and *Princess Mononoke*. *Scales & Scoundrels* is his debut work as a comic book creator.

JEFF POWELL

has been working as a letterer in the comic book industry for nearly two decades. He has worked on a variety of titles including *Teenage Mutant Ninja Turtles*, *Sonic the Hedgehog*, and *The Punisher* and currently letter the Eisner-nominated *Atomic Robo*. Jeff has designed books, logo and trade dress for Marvel, Archie, IDW, Image Comics and other He is neither German nor French.